DO NOT REMOVE
CARDS FROM POCKET

FICTION   **2216365**

LOST SOULS

JUN 1 1990

Lost Souls

"The Voice in the Night" by D. W. Miller
Courtesy of *The Twilight Zone*

LOST SOULS

A COLLECTION

OF ENGLISH GHOST STORIES

EDITED BY JACK SULLIVAN

Ohio University Press
Athens, Ohio

Notes and Introduction © copyright 1983 by Jack Sullivan
Printed in the United States of America
All rights reserved

Library of Congress Cataloging in Publication Data

Main entry under title:

Lost souls.

    Bibliography: p.
    1. Ghost stories, English.   I. Sullivan, Jack, 1946–
PR1309.G5L67   1983   823'.0872'08   82–14420
ISBN 0-8214-0652-3
ISBN 0-8214-0653-1 (pbk.)

2216366

For My Parents

ACKNOWLEDGMENTS

I would like to thank Hugh Lamb, E. F. Bleiler, T. E. D. Klein, Gary Crawford, and Kirby McCauley for their generous professional advice—the finest advice in the business. I am also grateful to George Chastain, David Bell, and R. J. Hadji, all erudite enthusiasts of the genre who alerted me to numerous rare gems. Finally, a special thanks goes to Robin Bromley, on whom I tested all of these stories, insisting dogmatically that they be read only at night, at whatever cost to sleep.

" 'He Cometh and He Passeth By!' " by H. R. Wakefield, from *They Return at Evening*. Reprinted by permission of Curtis Brown Limited.

"The Silver Mask" by Sir Hugh Walpole, from *All Souls' Night*. Reprinted by permission of Sir Rupert Hart-Davis.

"The Troll" by T. H. White, from *The Maharajah and Other Stories*. Reprinted by permission of G. P. Putnam's Sons. Copyright © 1935, 1937, 1950, 1953, 1954, 1981 by Lloyds Bank Trust Company (Channel Islands) Limited.

"The Mine" by L. T. C. Rolt, from *Sleep No More*. Reprinted by permission of Mrs. L. T. C. Rolt.

"Hand in Glove" by Elizabeth Bowen, from *A Day in the Dark*. Reprinted by permission of Random House Inc., Alfred A. Knopf, Inc., and Pantheon Books.

"Men Without Bones" by Gerald Kersh, from *Esquire* (August, 1954). Copyright © by Esquire Publishing Inc.

"Harry" by Rosemary Timperley, from *The Third Ghost Book*. Reprinted by permission of the author's agent, Harvey Unna and Stephen Durbridge Limited.

"Bad Company" by Walter de la Mare, from *A Beginning*. Reprinted by permission of the Society of Authors.

"The Same Dog" by Robert Aickman, from *Cold Hand in Mine*. Reprinted by permission of the author's agent, Kirby McCauley.

"The Scar" and "The Invocation" by Ramsey Campbell, from *The Height of the Scream* and *Dark Companions*, respectively. Reprinted by permission of the author's agent, Kirby McCauley.

CONTENTS

PREFACE

This collection of English ghost stories can be treated as a companion volume to my earlier book, *Elegant Nightmares: The English Ghost Story from Le Fanu to Blackwood,* or as a volume to be enjoyed and studied entirely on its own. The organization of the collection and the selection of authors do parallel *Elegant Nightmares* in such a way as to offer, in the two books, a thorough introduction to the English ghostly tale.

In addition to an overall introduction, I have provided a brief introduction to each story. These are designed for general readers, for fans of the genre, and for students. They touch not only on the qualities of the story but also on each author's distinctive contribution to the development of the genre.

That this collection is devoted to English stories is in no way a judgment on the American tradition of ghostly fiction. The contributions of Poe, Bierce, Hawthorne, Chambers, Wharton, Henry James, Lovecraft, Bradbury, Etchison, Jackson, Oates, and others offer sinister delights quite distinctly their own. The English tradition, like the American, is so large that a separate volume, at the very least, is needed to do it justice.

I. INTRODUCTION

The first modern short stories in English were ghost stories. I mean this statement to be as blunt as it sounds. It is generally recognized that among American writers, Poe was the first to pay strict attention to the unity of mood and economy of means, which are crucial to the modern short story. These characteristics were present to a startling degree in the grim and spellbinding "Ms. Found in a Bottle" published in 1833, Poe's first horror tale and one of his few unabashedly supernatural ones. What is not generally recognized is that a similar phenomenon occurred in English fiction. Sheridan Le Fanu, the first English writer to orchestrate an aesthetic of otherworldly terror, was also writing stories in the 1830s and was also manipulating atmosphere, plot, and imagery with the kind of dexterity and compression that we associate with modern fiction. To be sure, earlier writers for magazines like the *Tatler*, *Blackwood's*, and the *London Magazine* turned out short pieces; but these character sketches, satirical jibes, retold legends, and "little histories" had a basically didactic rather than aesthetic thrust.[1] The creation of mood for its own sake was not their purpose.

Le Fanu inaugurated a long tradition. His "Fortunes of Sir Robert Ardagh" (1838), a tale of demonic possession narrated from two different points of view, and "Schalken the Painter" (1839), the story of a woman seduced and raped by a zombie, are perhaps the first self-contained, tightly unified stories in English fiction. Later nineteenth-century English writers who established the short story as a major form—Hardy, Dickens, Kipling, James—also had a penchant for the occult and the horrific. Dickens may not have devoted his best prose to ghost stories like "The Signal Man," but Kipling and James produced some of their most distinguished work within the genre. A surprising number of their contemporaries—Conrad, Forster, Lawrence, de la Mare, Stevenson—did as well.

If we think about the intent of this fiction, it should not be difficult to understand why the birth of the modern ghostly tale and the modern short story are virtually synonymous. There are more ghost stories with unity of tone than other kinds of early stories precisely because mood is

1

so basic to the genre. According to H. P. Lovecraft, "Atmosphere is the all-important thing," even more important than plot.[2] It is especially important in the many stories that move from a staid ordinary reality to a frightening alternate reality. "Atmosphere" is not just a vague sense of doom and scariness but a precise sense of emotional gradation and nuance; the master of atmosphere is the writer who has a sense of the every-day as well as a sense of the fantastic.

Le Fanu seemed to know this instinctively. In orchestrating the crescendo of terror that suspends disbelief and sends a shiver up the spine, Le Fanu was probably not out to invent a new form; he was simply doing what he intuitively knew to be the most persuasive way to deliver a burst of wonder and horror. Understatement, irony, credibility in point of view, narrative distance, and other devices of modern fiction were always part of Le Fanu's craft because he knew as a very pragmatic matter that without them his living corpses, crawling hands, lesbian vampires, and satanic monkeys would become as ludicrous as they seem.

Indeed, one reason the tales of Le Fanu and his better disciples work is that the authors are sophisticated enough to be conscious of the element of absurdity in the genre and to blend that absurdity into their tone. This awareness converts a liability into a strength. As Ambrose Bierce puts it in "The Damned Thing," "A jest in the death chamber conquers by surprise";[3] black humor makes horror more horrific. But grim humor is more than just a technique or a mode of surprise. It is also thematic: the horror in stories like Le Fanu's "Green Tea" and Munby's "The Tudor Chimney" is the realization that something silly or trivial (a tenacious monkey, a smelly fireplace) can haunt us or drive us mad.

Closely related to black humor in ghostly fiction, and equally modern, is black enigma. Beginning with Le Fanu, the climactic shudder is the sudden awareness that the world is a chaotic and threatening place, that no moral or empirical framework advanced by priests or scientists can explain away the erupting horror. (If it can, the story does not belong in this genre: the pseudo-supernatural tale with the rational explanation in the denouement is not only a disappointment but a species of cheating.) The manner in which the protagonist comes to perceive the deadly unknowableness of the world constitutes the basic tension in the story. The realization itself—sometimes a ghostly vision or apparition, sometimes a revelatory dream, sometimes a powerful insight generated from a seemingly small incident—is the "moment" or "epiphany" that typically constitutes the climax of the modern short story. As developed by Le

Fanu, the ghost story was thus a remarkably sophisticated and forward-looking form that anticipated twentieth-century themes and techniques.

By the turn of the century—with the fiction of Machen, Kipling, Stevenson, and Henry James paving the way and the fiction of Blackwood and M. R. James soon to come—the supernatural thriller had reached an apex. In sheer numbers of tales as well as literary quality, the early-modern period was an incredibly fertile one, a period when Victorian and Neo-Gothic chain rattlers were banished to their graves to be replaced by more formidable spooks—menacing, lethal, unrepentently supernatural spooks who meant business. Earlier Gothic novels had considerable vividness and vitality, but their best scenes were not their ghost scenes; indeed Mrs. Radcliffe and others were so uneasy with their ghosts that they often explained them away. In the eighteenth century (and in much of the nineteenth, as E. F. Bleiler has pointed out),[4] it was often enough for a ghost simply to appear on a staircase to inspire the requisite chills. But by the twentieth century there had been far too many ghosts in English literature for readers to be awed by their mere appearance. Something more was required. The ante of terror needed to be raised. The distinctive achievement of early modern writers was their ability to make their apparitions do far more unpleasant things than appear on staircases but without resorting to the indiscriminate mayhem and violence (a decidedly unghostly tactic) that has disfigured much contemporary work. There was horror aplenty but also refinement of perception and a sense of wonder.

For the more established writers, those with mainstream reputations, the role of ghost-story writer represented an underground persona and a means of developing their major themes at the most direct, intense pitch. This surrogate self in a double career can be seen in Kipling, E. F. Benson, Elizabeth Bowen, de la Mare, and many others. For M. R. James and his antiquarian followers, whose major careers were in disciplines other than fiction, the role was even more removed from their established reputations and sometimes at odds with them; James's 1936 obituary in the *Proceedings of the British Academy* makes only the scantiest mention of his ghost stories and does so in a manner that barely conceals the writer's embarrassment and chagrin.

The sense of darkness and chaos these writers saw in the world could be projected in the most uninhibited way in the ghostly tale. It could also reach a double, perhaps triple audience: the highbrow audience already following the writer's work; the loyal enthusiasts of the genre; and, as in the case of Lady Cynthia Asquith's popular *Ghost Book* series, a more general popular audience. Conditions were propitious: novels like Stoker's *Dracula* and Wilde's *Picture of Dorian Gray* were long-standing sensations, such magazines as *Blackwood's* and the *London Mercury* frequently printed ghost stories, and the new respectability of occult societies created a favorable atmosphere.[5] By being willing, as Henry James put it, to "toss off a spook or two,"[6] the "respectable" writer could project his most personal and apocalyptic fears into a piece of short fiction and reach a wider audience in the bargain.

That writers no longer need to concoct an underground role, that important figures such as Jorge Luis Borges and Gabriel Garcia Marquez can experiment with the weird and the horrific as their major mode, testifies to the new respectability of the genre. The tale of terror has emerged from the underground to invade both popular and highbrow culture, sometimes with enough force (as was once the case with Gothic novels) to blur the distinction between the two. This blurring is perhaps most dramatic in recent films. Is Stanley Kubrick's *The Shining* a commercial genre film or a work of art? And why did Kubrick choose to direct the film instead of leaving it to the kind of *B* movie director usually associated with horror? One could ask the same question of Werner Herzog (*Nosferatu*), Peter Weir (*The Last Wave*), Philip Kaufman (*The Invasion of the Body Snatchers*), Nicholas Roeg (*Don't Look Now*), and numerous others.

On a purely commercial level, the current appetite for the genre ("current" meaning at least since the mid-1970s) is more voracious and more interesting than is commonly suspected. Probably no form of commercial fiction is more popular today than supernatural horror. Much more significant than the popularity of horror novels (since *Dracula*, numerous blockbuster horror novels have been bestsellers) is the less-expected, sweeping success of Stephen King's collection of stories, *Night Shift* (1978), at a time when publishers had prematurely pronounced the short story to be a dead form. Since supernatural horror was largely responsible for the germination of the modern short story, it is fitting that it should also be responsible for its revival.

The reasons why the genre is currently so popular probably have a great deal to do with why it was popular at the turn of the century. In important ways, the period beginning with the late sixties and stretching into the eighties is similar to the period beginning with the Edwardians and stretching through World War I. Both periods were characterized by wrenching social change, heavy repercussions of an unpopular war, economic instability, a fundamental cynicism about government and the established order, and an interest in countercultures and occultist movements. This is the neurotic climate in which the tale of terror flourishes, probably because it gives us a safe, slightly ludicrous context for fantasizing the worst, for going beyond our most sour predictions. Grim and unpredictable events make the reading of this fiction a perversely pleasant luxury, a harmless form of masochism, a way, as M. R. James put it, of feeling "pleasantly uncomfortable."[7] The ghostly tale strikes a unique balance; even if the plots seem delightfully unreal, the feelings evoked by the careful use of language are certainly real enough. Ghost stories are deftly in touch with our most exaggerated feelings of powerlessness in a chaotic world. Because they are supernatural, they allow us to project this powerlessness onto a spectacularly wide canvas of paranoia. They are a splendid form of self-indulgence.

The question of choice undoubtedly has a great deal to do with the pleasure of these stories; there is the fun of making an actual decision to keep oneself awake at night instead of being kept awake by the anxieties of the day. As Elizabeth Bowen puts it: "Ghosts draw us together: one might leave it at that. Can there be something tonic about pure, active fear in these times of passive, confused oppression? It is nice to *choose* to be frightened, when one need not be."[8]

The significance of ghost stories is currently being recognized not only as a social symptom of the apocalyptic texture of our times but also as a subject worthy of serious study in its own right. Numerous new scholarly journals, bibliographies, and books devoted to Gothic horror have appeared; and scholarly activity in the genre is expected to pick up even more. For the first time it is possible to look up someone like R. H. Benson or Arthur Machen in several easily obtainable reference sources and find detailed bibliographic and critical information.

Yet for all the outpouring of scholarship, the genre still retains a bit of its offbeat, underground status—as it must if it is also to retain its seductiveness and its antiquarian charm. Those who are contemptuous of supernatural thrillers—or are temperamentally incapable of being moved by them—are not going to be won over no matter how many impressive names associated with the genre (V. S. Pritchett, T. S. Eliot, Jacques Barzun) are trotted out by enthusiasts. Perhaps this genre will never entirely lose its aura of the "grotesque and arabesque," and that is just as well.

In any case, scholarship still centers on Gothic novels rather than on the modern supernatural tale. Many of the masterworks in the genre remain not only ignored by critics but unavailable to general readers as well. That is the situation this book addresses. Hundreds of enticing stories from the late Victorian period through the First World War exist—not to mention tales by Hartley, Wakefield, and others who contributed ghost stories on a more erratic basis after the war—stories that have dropped out of sight or have vanished after brief reprints. In *Elegant Nightmares* I attempted to describe and evaluate these undeservedly obscure pieces because they represent an important genre and because many of them are first-rate stories that can be appreciated by anyone interested in short fiction. Unfortunately, many readers have told me that the stories are every bit as obscure and hard to find as *Elegant Nightmares* presented them as being. The purpose of *Lost Souls* is to reprint a representative sampling so that readers can discover the magic of these tales for themselves.

One of the most surprising things the reader will discover in encountering these stories is their emotional variety. Fear is no simple emotion, and numerous commentators—Edmund Burke, Ann Radcliffe, Samuel Taylor Coleridge, Sir Walter Scott, and H. P. Lovecraft, to name the most notable—have attempted over the centuries to sort out distinctions between emotions like terror and horror, not to mention genres like the Gothic tale, the fantasy tale, the horror story, and the ghost story.[9] If we add the subgenres of the structuralists (the "uncanny," the "marvelous," the "fantastic-uncanny," the "fantastic-marvelous" the "meta-uncanny"), we find ourselves in a tangled morass of definitions and permutations that grows as relentlessly as the fungus in the House of Usher.[10] (Further attempts to distinguish between the "expansion" of terror and the "contraction" of horror seem especially finicky and foolish, particularly since Mrs. Radcliffe did the job so eloquently more than a century ago.) The genre-labeling game has become a tiresome one.

The basic definitions offered by the writers themselves are still the most sensible. H. G. Wells, for example, labels the most inclusive category "the fantastic." All fantastic literature, says Wells, including science fiction and supernatural fiction, has as its basic dynamic a single (or at least carefully limited) disruption of everyday reality: "Anyone can invent human beings turned inside out or worlds like dumbbells or gravitation that repels. The thing that makes such imaginations interesting is their translation into commonplace terms and a rigid exclusion of other marvels from the story. Then it becomes human. . . . Nothing remains interesting when anything can happen."[11]

The writer of ghost stories, who represents a significant aspect of the fantastic, uses this limited departure from the factual to create fear, which usually encompasses both the subtlety of terror and the physicality of horror. Lovecraft, who fuses the ghost story and the horror story into a single term, "supernatural horror," states that the best stories excite "a profound sense of dread . . . a subtle attitude of awed listening, as if for the beating of black wings or the scratching of outside shapes and entities on the known universe's outmost rim."[12]

Lovecraft, as usual, is marvelously hyperbolic, but the key word is "subtle": the apparition may be as extravagantly outrageous (i.e., Lovecraftian) as the writer desires—with black wings and cosmic scratchings—as long as it is evoked with the care and control necessary to produce and sustain what Coleridge calls the "willing suspension of disbelief."

It was not always done this way, of course, and the issues of subtlety and verisimilitude really establish the line of separation between the stories in this book and the Gothic thrillers of the past. No matter how torturously recent critics have struggled to make early Gothic novels appear artful, sophisticated, and profound, the reality is that Gothic novels are overwhelmingly defined by their delightfully ludicrous and melodramatic paraphernalia—their clanking chains, bleeding statues, unctuous maidens, evil noblemen, and chivalric heroes. It is especially disingenuous for Gothic specialists to quote Lovecraft as a promoter of the Gothic romance when he specifically attacked the archetypal *Castle of Otranto* as "tedious, artificial and melodramatic," generalized that it "nowhere permits the creation of a truly weird atmosphere," and declared that the "line of actual artists" begins with Poe.[13]

As Lovecraft points out, the modern supernatural tale often retains Gothic elements, but in the better stories these always exist in "less naive" forms.[14] In a Ramsey Campbell story, for example, the oppressive haunted castle of the Gothic period becomes the oppressive modern office building. Nevertheless, Campbell's attention to understatement and to the details of everyday reality is so pronounced that despite mechanical resemblances his fiction is really not Gothic—nor is the fiction of Bowen, de la Mare, Timperley, or the other modern masters. Thus, in a strictly historical sense Le Fanu was more revolutionary than Poe, for he began the process of dismantling the Gothic props and placing the supernatural tale within everyday settings.

Although the introductions to individual tales in this collection use "horror story" and "ghost story" interchangeably in the many instances when the two overlap, I am still convinced (following the lead of Le Fanu, M. R. James, Wakefield, and many others) that the latter is the more graceful and accurate general term, despite protests from readers of *Elegant Nightmares* that these are actually "horror stories." Many of these pieces ("Men Without Bones," "The Scar," "Count Magnus," "The Voice in the Night") are indeed horrific, sometimes vividly so, but the fundamental criterion, as Bowen points out, is an apparition that inspires a sense of the ghostly: "That austere other world, the world of the ghost, should inspire, when it impacts on our own, not so much shock or revulsion as a sort of awe." Ann Radcliffe calls this emotion "terror"; Lovecraft calls it "supernatural horror"; Robert Aickman calls it "poetry."[15] Whatever one calls it, it surely has little to do with the mutilation and sadism (especially the sadism directed at women) perpetrated by a nauseatingly large number of contemporary "horror" writers and film-makers. This tendency has developed into a movement so aggressive that one anthology editor, Leonard Wolf (in *Wolf's Complete Book of Terror* [1979]), went as far as to cut, without warning, the ominous and evocative ending of Le Fanu's vampire tale "Carmilla" so that the story would end with a gruesome staking scene. (Wolf also reprints such "tales of terror" as an extended sexual torture episode from de Sade's *Justine*).

Another, more delightful complaint about the term "ghost stories" comes from readers who object that many stories are about demons, vampires, and various other kinds of monsters instead of "ghosts." But the writers themselves have always understood the term within a broad context. Le Fanu and M. R. James rarely wrote a story in which the apparition was not animalistic, hairy, demonic, or, in James's case, inexplicably froglike, but both writers referred to their contributions as "ghost stories." What they were striving to create was a brief, shuddery encounter with an intractable, mysterious "other" who could appear in a dazzling variety of ghostly forms.

This encounter leads us to our title. "Lost Souls" has a double meaning; it refers not only to the supernatural invader, a lost soul in the most literal sense, but also to the victim, who is often in the process of becoming one himself. The sense of lostness, of sudden helplessness in a malign universe, is the dominant theme in this fiction and one that every notable writer, from Le Fanu to Campbell, has addressed.

In choosing stories for this collection, I have tried to strike a balance between works that are genuinely rare and works that are beginning to emerge as classics in the genre. I have designed what I hope is a truly representative selection, one that will appeal both to the enthusiast and to the general reader. Many of the stories reprinted here—especially antiquarian ghost stories by E. G. Swain, Sir Arthur Gray, E. F. Benson, and R. H. Malden—are unknown to the point of virtual oblivion; some have never appeared in America before. I can only hope that readers will experience the same delightful sense of discovery with them that I did. Another category of rare stories in this volume comprises those that are perhaps familiar to specialists but can be obtained only in hard-to-find British editions or defunct anthologies. These include tales by Walter de la Mare, Sir Hugh Walpole, R. H. Benson, L. T. C. Rolt, and Algernon Blackwood.

I see no reason for reprinting yet again items such as W. W. Jacobs's "The Monkey's Paw," Saki's "Sredni Vashtar," and others that are not only available elsewhere but endlessly recycled. At the same time, landmark classics like Le Fanu's "Green Tea" and Machen's "White People," though obtainable (with difficulty) elsewhere, have an essential place in a representative anthology. In reports from readers and in discussions with students, I have learned that these masterworks are still largely unknown even among horror and mystery fans. I hope to make it clear in the individual story introductions what constitutes a "classic": the general criteria are that the stories have helped inaugurate a new tendency and that they themselves are beautifully wrought specimens of it.

Most of the work here comes from the late-Victorian and early-modern eras for the simple reason that more fine stories appeared during those periods than any other. The collection is organized according to the chapter scheme of *Elegant Nightmares*, with an additional section of contemporary stories. The latter should demonstrate conclusively that the tradition is still very much alive; indeed some of the most powerful and finely crafted stories appear in this section.

There are obviously many conceivable ways to classify ghost stories. Some editors have played with creature categories (vampire stories, zombie stories, witch stories); others have tried plot categories (revenge stories, *femme fatale* stories); E. F. Bleiler, in his excellent *Checklist of Science Fiction and Supernatural Fiction*, a bibliographic aid, has come up with a hair-raisingly complex scheme that incorporates themes, motifs, plots, and settings. (Sax Rohmer's *Brood of the Witch Queen*, for example, is classified as NPY2, which translates as Magic and Witchcraft, Reincarnation, Egypt!) My own preference continues to be to divide the stories according to two basic emotional and stylistic impulses: the antiquarian stories of the M. R. James persuasion, with their wit, subtlety, conciseness, and unexpected nastiness lurking under a veneer of scholarly reticence; and the visionary stories of the Algernon Blackwood persuasion, with their mysticism, intensity, otherworldliness, and flight from the grayness of the modern world. These are imaginative tendencies, not rigid categories; some writers, such as E. F. Benson and Walter de la Mare, have a fluidity of temperament and imagination that puts them sometimes in one camp, sometimes in the other. Other writers are more reliable: Blackwood, for example, evinces such a thoroughgoing mysticism in his language, plot, and atmosphere that it is hard to imagine him writing a story in the bookish antiquarian mode.

I have attempted to make this anthology representative not only in its diversity of authors but also its range of emotion and complexity. Most British writers of ghostly fiction tend toward the Le Fanu model of understatement and suggestion rather than toward the more explicit ghastliness of Poe and Lovecraft. Nevertheless, some stories are considerably more overt than others, and one reader's disappointment in a given tale may be another's most exquisite jolt. The reader who is puzzled by the sly reticence of Sir Arthur Gray's "Everlasting Club" (a story likely to bedazzle mystery fans) will probably be delighted by the almost palpable dread that permeates Blackwood's "Haunted Island" or Kersh's "Men Without Bones"; the reader who finds the bracing, cynical dialogue of Hartley's "Travelling Grave" inimical to the proper mood of a horror tale will relish the somber atmosphere of Campbell's "Invocation." On the other hand, the reader who approaches this collection with a minimum of preconceptions may well find that each story offers a unique and memorable shudder.

Certain distinctive paradoxes are present in all these stories. The most striking, and the most distinctively English, is their seductive charm and pleasantness in the face of material that is thoroughly uncharming and unpleasant. This contradiction between form and content is most exaggerated in the antiquarian works, but it gives all the stories a special tension and richness. The world is chaotic and dangerous, these stories seem to say, but the art of storytelling can make it a bit easier to face.

Equally paradoxical is the sound of these stories; instead of the percussive Gothic effects of earlier writers, there is a haunting silence in the modern ghost story that exists in spite of the emotional intensities and extremities it explores. Timbres are muted and attenuated; orchestrations are spare and precise. This silence is partly a function of the anti-

Gothic aesthetic of this fiction, but it is also part of the isolation and *ennui* experienced by the characters. These stories are part of a modern experience depicted in literature in which absence is stronger, more powerfully infused with expectation, than anything present. "Absence is the highest form of presence," as Joyce phrased it in "A Painful Case," is an eloquent subtext in these stories, especially "Harry," "The Bath-Chair," and "The Same Dog." Here, ghosts represent loss, the loss of someone who, in his or her very absence, is pregnantly "present." The most tenacious specter that haunts these stories is loneliness.

The unique way the ghost story has of speaking to our feelings of loss and powerlessness makes it a form that is very likely to endure. Nevertheless, Phillip Van Doren Stern bewailed the decline and collapse of the genre forty years ago,[16] and to this day critics issue absurdly premature obituaries. Julia Briggs, for example, recently claimed that the ghost story "no longer has any capacity for growth or adaptation."[17] Anyone who believes this nonsense should sample the stories of Aickman, Timperley, and Campbell offered here, and then try tales by Americans such as Jonothan Carroll, Dennis Etchison, T. E. D. Klein, A. A. Attanasio, Russell Kirk, Isaac Bashevis Singer, Joyce Carol Oates, and others who are doing excellent work in the field. With the exception of a few period pieces, these stories feature completely contemporary characters who inhabit such settings as condominiums, twenty-four-hour stores, highway rest stops, and impersonal office buildings.

Indeed, as Elizabeth Bowen once said, "The universal battiness of our century" is actually quite congenial to ghosts.[18] They are probably more at home with us than they were in their earlier rigid confinement to depressing Gothic houses.

Since ghost stories are fundamentally about death, it is no accident that they have prospered and attained a new pungency in the twentieth century. Ours is an age that believes in death (or at least purports to), and this belief goes a long way toward explaining the transformation of the ghost story from allegory and melodrama to awe and terror. Paradoxically, the gradual decay of belief in an afterlife has been an enormous boon to ghosts, who are able to terrify us precisely to the extent that their existence is denied. If, as in an earlier age, it is assumed that death is merely another life, one which is charted in inspirational books and for which we fastidiously prepare ourselves, the supernatural ceases to be terribly mysterious or menacing. Ghosts become prosaic rectifiers of injustice or chatty tour guides for an impending journey. But if death is absolute, or at least unknowable, ghosts become mysterious and terrible, just as the life and sanity they threaten—the only life and sanity we have—become more vulnerable and precious; the stakes become higher, the shudders more authentic.

Jack Sullivan
New York City

NOTES

1. For more information on early short fiction, see Wendell V. Harris, *British Short Fiction in the Nineteenth Century* (New York: Wayne State University Press, 1979), and Robert D. Mayo, *The English Novel in the Magazines* (London: Oxford University Press, 1962).

2. H. P. Lovecraft, *Supernatural Horror in Literature* (1927; rpt. New York: Dover, 1973), p. 16.

3. Ambrose Bierce, *Ghost and Horror Stories of Ambrose Bierce* (New York: Dover, 1964), p. 34.

4. E. F. Bleiler, Introduction, *The Collected Ghost Stories of Mrs. J. H. Riddell* (New York: Dover, 1977), p. xvii.

5. See Samuel Hynes, *The Edwardian Turn of Mind* (1968; rpt. Princeton, N.J.: Princeton University Press, 1971).

6. Henry James, letter to W. D. Howells, in Robert Kimbrough, Backgrounds and Sources, *The Turn of the Screw* (New York: Norton, 1966), p. 116.

7. M. R. James, Preface, *Ghost Stories of an Antiquary* (1904; rpt. New York: Dover, 1971), p. 8.

8. Elizabeth Bowen, Introduction, *The Second Ghost Book*, ed. Cynthia Asquith (1952; rpt. New York: Beagle, 1970), p. viii.

9. Edmunde Burke, *A Philosophical Enquiry into the Origin of our Ideas of the Sublime and Beautiful* (1756; rpt. London: Routledge and Kegan Paul, 1958); Ann Radcliffe, "On the Supernatural in Poetry," *New Monthly Magazine and Literary Journal* 16 (1826):145-150; Samuel Taylor Coleridge, *General Character of the Gothic Literature and Art* in *Complete Works* (New York: Harper, 1853); Sir Walter Scott, "On the Supernatural in Fictitious Composition," *Foreign Quarterly Review* 1 (July and November 1827):60-98.

10. See Tzetvan Todorov, *The Fantastic* (Ithaca, N.Y.: Cornell University Press, 1970).

11. H. G. Wells, Preface, *Seven Novels*, in *Great Ghost Stories*, ed. Philip Van Doren Stern (New York: Washington Square Press, 1947), p. xx.

12. Lovecraft, p. 16.

13. Ibid., pp. 24-25.

14. Ibid., p. 26.

15. Robert Aickman, Introduction, *The Fontana Book of Great Ghost Stories* (New York: Beagle, 1966), p. 7.

16. Stern, p. xvii.

17. Julia Briggs, *Night Visitors: The Rise and Fall of the English Ghost Story* (London: Faber, 1977), p. 14.

18. Bowen, p. vii.

II. BEGINNINGS

SHERIDAN LE FANU

Schalken the Painter (1839)

Green Tea (1869)

Although "Schalken the Painter" is an early work in the Le Fanu canon, its bold originality and technical adroitness are thoroughly typical of his best work. Already present in this 1839 story is Le Fanu's obsessive theme of innocence persecuted by supernatural evil, of helplessness in a hostile universe. The Faustian motif so prevalent in Gothic fiction is here turned on its head: it is not the victim who makes a deal with the devil but her greedy guardian, who prospers while she suffers the fate he himself clearly merits. The terrible sexual underground implied in the story is merely an extension of the jungle above; Rose's uncle is hardly less rapacious than her demon lover.

Stylistically, the story is remarkably advanced. Le Fanu was the first writer to reject Gothic hyperbole for modern understatement, and he manipulates the sordid and terrifying theme of lust beyond the grave with a paradoxical grace and restraint. Especially sophisticated is the elaborate dream vision of a coffin being transformed into a bed, a scene which serves as a climactic coda instead of an overture. In "Schalken the Painter," as in real life, a dream is not a melodramatic "premonition" but a clue to what is already happening; the plot is a premonition of the dream.

Le Fanu's own nightmares served as the basis of his ghostly tales, imparting an unmistakably dreamlike texture and logic. "Schalken the Painter" is chillingly in tune with the world of nightmare, especially in its tiny, ominous motifs that nonchronologically weave their way in and out of the story and are connected in the young victim's mind, in some horribly inexplicable way, with her demonic suitor. A good example is the terrible wooden figure in the old Rotterdam church, the kind of enigmatic talisman that later appears in the work of M. R. James and Arthur

14

Machen. As is always the case in Le Fanu, there is a larger otherworldly conspiracy at work than is revealed in the story. For this reason, he is often even more deliciously frightening in the second reading than in the first.

The later "Green Tea" is even more intricate and ambiguous. It is also curiously humorous, and its dark humor contributes a good deal to its problematic theme. *Why* does this ludicrous and lethal persecution occur, and why is poor Reverend Jennings singled out? Has he really been swilling too much green tea? Has he read too many unorthodox, un-Christian books? Or at the other, Freudian, extreme, has he led an overly pious, sexless life? Or could it be that the whole point of the diabolical persecution—after all the contradictory theological and psychological theories are exhausted by characters in the story and critics outside it—is its pointlessness, its utter randomness and absurdity? Like the luckless Reverend Jennings, we never really know the reason why he is so cruelly monkeyed with by this striking, yet somehow ridiculous ghost—or indeed if there is a reason. The moral void from which Le Fanu's apparitions materialize, a void consistent with his bleakly monochromatic imagery, makes him a peculiarly modern writer, closer to Henry James, Kafka, and Conrad than to his contemporaries.

Also revolutionary is the complex narrative structure that presents the tale from four different points of view, creating an icy distance and forcing us to draw our own conclusions about the horror. Le Fanu was not only the premier nineteenth-century ghost-story writer but also an important innovator in the history of modern fiction. Long before Joyce, Conrad, or James, Le Fanu had grown tired of the omniscient narrator; he knew how to keep himself out of his stories.

One of the narrators in "Green Tea" is Dr. Martin Hesselius, a "doctor of metaphysical medicine" who is really a Victorian psychiatrist. Le Fanu's subtle, unflattering portrait of Dr. Hesselius (who appears in other Le Fanu tales as well) is an example of his deft use of dramatic irony. Despite Dr. Hesselius's self-serving "metaphysical" jargon, he is about as useful to the victims in these despairing stories as Le Fanu's priests and physicians, who perform incompetent exorcisms and prescribe stomachache pills. Once the forces of chaos project themselves at Le Fanu's characters, the forces of order offer only the feeblest protection.

∽ SCHALKEN THE PAINTER ∽

"For he is not a man as I am that we should come together; neither is there any that might lay his hand upon us both. Let him, therefore, take his rod away from me, and let not his fear terrify me."

There exists, at this moment, in good preservation a remarkable work of Schalken's. The curious management of its lights constitutes, as usual in his pieces, the chief apparent merit of the picture. I say *apparent*, for in its subject, and not in its handling, however exquisite, consists its real value. The picture represents the interior of what might be a chamber in some antique religious building; and its foreground is occupied by a female figure, in a species of white robe, part of which is arranged so as to form a veil. The dress, however, is not that of any religious order. In her hand the figure bears a lamp, by which alone her figure and face are illuminated; and her features wear such an arch smile, as well becomes a pretty woman when practising some prankish roguery; in the background, and, excepting where the dim red light of an expiring fire serves to define the form, in total shadow, stands the figure of a man dressed in the old Flemish fashion, in an attitude of alarm, his hand being placed upon the hilt of his sword, which he appears to be in the act of drawing.

There are some pictures, which impress one, I know not how, with a conviction that they represent not the mere ideal shapes and combinations which have floated through the imagination of the artist, but scenes, faces, and situations which have actually existed. There is in that strange picture, something that stamps it as the representation of a reality.

And such in truth it is, for it faithfully records a remarkable and mysterious occurrence, and perpetuates, in the face of the female figure, which occupies the most prominent place in the design, an accurate portrait of Rose Velderkaust, the niece of Gerard Douw, the first, and I believe, the only love of Godfrey Schalken. My great grandfather knew the painter well; and from Schalken himself he learned the fearful story of the painting, and from him too he ultimately received the picture itself as a bequest. The story and the picture have become heir-looms in my family, and having described the latter, I shall, if you please, attempt to relate the tradition which has descended with the canvas.

16

There are few forms on which the mantle of romance hangs more ungracefully than upon that of the uncouth Schalken—the boorish but most cunning worker in oils, whose pieces delight the critics of our day almost as much as his manners disgusted the refined of his own; and yet this man, so rude, so dogged, so slovenly, in the midst of his celebrity, had in his obscure, but happier days, played the hero in a wild romance of mystery and passion.

When Schalken studied under the immortal Gerard Douw, he was a very young man; and in spite of his phlegmatic temperament, he at once fell over head and ears in love with the beautiful niece of his wealthy master. Rose Velderkaust was still younger than he, having not yet attained her seventeenth year, and, if tradition speaks truth, possessed all the soft and dimpling charms of the fair, light-haired Flemish maidens. The young painter loved honestly and fervently. His frank adoration was rewarded. He declared his love, and extracted a faltering confession in return. He was the happiest and proudest painter in all Christendom. But there was somewhat to dash his elation; he was poor and undistinguished. He dared not ask old Gerard for the hand of his sweet ward. He must first win a reputation and a competence.

There were, therefore, many dread uncertainties and cold days before him; he had to fight his way against sore odds. But he had won the heart of dear Rose Velderkaust, and that was half the battle. It is needless to say his exertions were redoubled, and his lasting celebrity proves that his industry was not unrewarded by success.

These ardent labours, and worse still, the hopes that elevated and beguiled them, were however, destined to experience a sudden interruption —of a character so strange and mysterious as to baffle all inquiry and to throw over the events themselves a shadow of preternatural horror.

Schalken had one evening outstayed all his fellow-pupils, and still pursued his work in the deserted room. As the daylight was fast falling, he laid aside his colours, and applied himself to the completion of a sketch on which he had expressed extraordinary pains. It was a religious composition, and represented the temptations of a pot-bellied Saint Anthony. The young artist, however destitute of elevation, had, nevertheless, discernment enough to be dissatisfied with his own work, and many were the patient erasures and improvements which saint and devil underwent, yet all in vain. The large, old-fashioned room was silent, and, with the exception of himself, quite emptied of its usual inmates. An hour had thus passed away, nearly two, without any improved result. Daylight had already declined, and twilight was deepening into the darkness of night. The patience of the young painter was exhausted, and he stood before his unfinished production, angry and mortified, one hand buried in the folds of his long hair, and the other holding the piece of charcoal which had so ill-performed its office, and which he now rubbed, without much regard to the sable streaks it produced, with irritable pressure upon his ample Flemish inexpressibles. "Curse the subject!" said the young man aloud; "curse the picture, the devils, the saint—"

At this moment a short, sudden sniff uttered close behind him made the artist turn sharply round, and he now, for the first time, became aware that his labours had been overlooked by a stranger. Within about a yard and half, and rather behind him, there stood the figure of an elderly man in a cloak and broad-brimmed, conical hat; in his hand, which was protected with a heavy gauntlet-shaped glove, he carried a long ebony walking-stick, surmounted with what appeared, as it glittered dimly in the twilight, to be a massive head of gold, and upon his breast, through the folds of the cloak, there shone the links of a rich chain of the same metal. The room was so obscure that nothing further of the appearance of the figure could be ascertained, and his hat threw his features into profound shadow. It would not have been easy to conjecture the age of the intruder; but a quantity of dark hair escaping from beneath his sombre hat, as well as his firm and upright carriage served to indicate that his years could not yet exceed threescore, or thereabouts. There was an air of gravity and importance about the garb of the person, and something indescribably odd, I might say awful, in the perfect, stone-like stillness of the figure, that effectually checked the testy comment which had at once risen to the lips of the irritated artist. He, therefore, as soon as he had sufficiently recovered his surprise, asked the stranger, civilly, to be seated, and desired to know if he had any message to leave for his master.

"Tell Gerard Douw," said the unknown, without altering his attitude in the smallest degree, "that Minheer Vanderhausen, of Rotterdam, desires to speak with him on tomorrow evening at this hour, and if he please, in this room, upon matters of weight; that is all."

The stranger, having finished this message, turned abruptly, and, with a quick, but silent step quitted the room, before Schalken had time to say a word in reply. The young man felt a curiosity to see in what direction the burgher of Rotterdam would turn, on quitting the *studio*, and for that purpose he went directly to the window which commanded the door. A lobby of considerable extent intervened between the inner door of the

painter's room and the street entrance, so that Schalken occupied the
post of observation before the old man could possibly have reached the
street. He watched in vain, however. There was no other mode of exit.
Had the queer old man vanished, or was he lurking about the recesses of
the lobby for some sinister purpose? This last suggestion filled the mind
of Schalken with a vague uneasiness, which was so unaccountably intense as to make him alike afraid to remain in the room alone, and reluctant to pass through the lobby. However, with an effort which appeared
very disproportioned to the occasion, he summoned resolution to leave
the room, and, having locked the door and thrust the key in his pocket,
without looking to the right or left, he traversed the passage which had so
recently, perhaps still, contained the person of his mysterious visitant,
scarcely venturing to breathe till he had arrived in the open street.

"Minheer Vanderhausen!" said Gerard Douw within himself, as the
appointed hour approached, "Minheer Vanderhausen, of Rotterdam! I
never heard of the man till yesterday. What can he want of me? A portrait, perhaps, to be painted; or a poor relation to be apprenticed; or a
collection to be valued; or—pshaw! there's no one in Rotterdam to leave
me a legacy. Well, whatever the business may be, we shall soon know it
all."

It was now the close of day, and again every easel, except that of Schalken, was deserted. Gerard Douw was pacing the apartment with the restless step of impatient expectation, sometimes pausing to glance over the
work of one of his absent pupils, but more frequently placing himself at
the window, from whence he might observe the passengers who threaded
the obscure by-street in which his studio was placed.

"Said you not, Godfrey," exclaimed Douw, after a long and fruitful
gaze from his post of observation, and turning to Schalken, "that the
hour he appointed was about seven by the clock of the Stadhouse?"

"It had just told seven when I first saw him, sir," answered the
student.

"The hour is close at hand, then," said the master, consulting a
horologe as large and as round as an orange. "Minheer Vanderhausen
from Rotterdam—is it not so?

"Such was the name."

"And an elderly man, richly clad?" pursued Douw, musingly.

"As well as I might see," replied his pupil; "he could not be young,
nor yet very old, neither; and his dress was rich and grave, as might become a citizen of wealth and consideration."

At this moment the sonorous boom of the Stadhouse clock told, stroke after stroke, the hour of seven; the eyes of both master and student were directed to the door; and it was not until the last peal of the bell had ceased to vibrate, that Douw exclaimed—

"So, so; we shall have his worship presently, that is, if he means to keep his hour; if not, you may wait for him, Godfrey, if you court his acquaintance. But what, after all, if it should prove but a mummery got up by Vankarp, or some such wag? I wish you had run all risks, and cudgelled the old burgomaster soundly. I'd wager a dozen of Rhenish, his worship would have unmasked, and pleaded old acquaintance in a trice."

"Here he comes, sir," said Schalken, in a low monitory tone; and instantly, upon turning towards the door, Gerard Douw observed the same figure which had, on the day before, so unexpectedly greeted his pupil Schalken.

There was something in the air of the figure which at once satisfied the painter that there was no masquerading in the case, and that he really stood in the presence of a man of worship; and so, without hesitation, he doffed his cap, and courteously saluting the stranger, requested him to be seated. The visitor waved his hand slightly, as if in acknowledgment of the courtesy, but remained standing.

"I have the honour to see Minheer Vanderhausen of Rotterdam?" said Gerard Douw.

"The same," was the laconic reply of his visitor.

"I understand your worship desires to speak with me," continued Douw, "and I am here by appointment to wait your commands."

"Is that a man of trust?" said Vanderhausen, turning towards Schalken, who stood at a little distance behind his master.

"Certainly," replied Gerard.

"Then let him take this box, and get the nearest jeweller or goldsmith to value its contents, and let him return hither with a certificate of the valuation."

At the same time, he placed a small case about nine inches square in the hands of Gerard Douw, who was as much amazed at its weight as at the strange abruptness with which it was handed to him. In accordance with the wishes of the stranger, he delivered it into the hands of Schalken, and repeating his direction, despatched him upon the mission.

Schalken disposed his precious charge securely beneath the folds of his cloak, and rapidly traversing two or three narrow streets, he stopped at a corner house, the lower part of which was then occupied by the shop of a

Jewish goldsmith. He entered the shop, and calling the little Hebrew into the obscurity of its back recesses, he proceeded to lay before him Vanderhausen's casket. On being examined by the light of a lamp, it appeared entirely cased with lead, the outer surface of which was much scraped and soiled, and nearly white with age. This having been partially removed, there appeared beneath a box of some hard wood; which also they forced open and after the removal of two or three folds of linen, they discovered its contents to be a mass of golden ingots, closely packed, and, as the Jew declared, of the most perfect quality. Every ingot underwent the scrutiny of the little Jew, who seemed to feel an epicurean delight in touching and testing these morsels of the glorious metal; and each one of them was replaced in its berth with the exclamation: *"Mein Gott*, how very perfect! not one grain of alloy—beautiful, beautiful!" The task was at length finished, and the Jew certified under his hand the value of the ingots submitted to his examination, to amount to many thousand rix-dollars. With the desired document in his pocket, and the rich box of gold carefully pressed under his arm, and concealed by his cloak, he retraced his way, and entering the studio, found his master and the stranger in close conference. Schalken had no sooner left the room, in order to execute the commission he had taken in charge, than Vanderhausen addressed Gerard Douw in the following terms:—

"I cannot tarry with you to-night more than a few minutes, and so I shall shortly tell you the matter upon which I come. You visited the town of Rotterdam some four months ago, and then I saw in the church of St. Lawrence your niece, Rose Velderkaust. I desire to marry her; and if I satisfy you that I am wealthier than any husband you can dream of for her, I expect that you will forward my suit with your authority. If you approve my proposal, you must close with it here and now, for I cannot wait for calculations and delays."

Gerard Douw was hugely astonished by the nature of Minheer Vanderhausen's communication, but he did not venture to express surprise; for besides the motives supplied by prudence and politeness, the painter experienced a kind of chill and oppression like that which is said to intervene when one is placed in unconscious proximity with the object of a natural antipathy—an undefined but overpowering sensation, while standing in the presence of the eccentric stranger, which made him very unwilling to say anything which might reasonably offend him.

"I have no doubt," said Gerard, after two or three prefatory hems, "that the alliance which you propose would prove alike advantageous and honourable to my niece; but you must be aware that she has a will of her own, and may not acquiesce in what *we* may design for her advantage."

"Do not seek to deceive me, sir painter," said Vanderhausen; "you are her guardian—she is your ward—she is mine if *you* like to make her so."

The man of Rotterdam moved forward a little as he spoke, and Gerard Douw, he scarce knew why, inwardly prayed for the speedy return of Schalken.

"I desire," said the mysterious gentleman, "to place in your hands at once an evidence of my wealth, and a security for my liberal dealing with your niece. The lad will return in a minute or two with a sum in value five times the fortune which she has a right to expect from her husband. This shall lie in your hands, together with her dowry, and you may apply the united sum as suits her interest best; it shall be all exclusively hers while she lives: is that liberal?"

Douw assented, and inwardly acknowledged that fortune had been extraordinarily kind to his niece; the stranger, he thought, must be both wealthy and generous, and such an offer was not to be despised, though made by a humourist, and one of no very prepossessing presence. Rose had no very high pretensions for she had but a modest dowry, which she owed entirely to the generosity of her uncle; neither had she any right to raise exceptions on the score of birth, for her own origin was far from splendid, and as the other objections, Gerald resolved, and indeed, by the usages of the time, was warranted in resolving, not to listen to them for a moment.

"Sir" said he, addressing the stranger, "your offer is liberal, and whatever hesitation I may feel in closing with it immediately, arises solely from my not having the honour of knowing anything of your family or station. Upon these points you can, of course, satisfy me without difficulty?"

"As to my respectability," said the stranger, drily, "you must take that for granted at present; pester me with no inquiries; you can discover nothing more about me than I choose to make known. You shall have sufficient security for my respectability—my word, if you are honourable: if you are sordid, my gold."

"A testy old gentleman," thought Douw, "he must have his own way; but, all things considered, I am not justified to declining his offer. I will not pledge myself unnecessarily, however."

"You will not pledge yourself unnecessarily," said Vanderhausen, strangely uttering the very words which had just floated through the mind of his companion; "but you will do so if it *is* necessary, I presume;

and I will show you that I consider it indispensable. If the gold I mean to leave in your hands satisfy you, and if you don't wish my proposal to be at once withdrawn, you must, before I leave this room, write your name to this engagement."

Having thus spoken, he placed a paper in the hands of the master, the contents of which expressed an engagement entered into by Gerard Douw, to give to Wilken Vanderhausen of Rotterdam, in marriage, Rose Velderkaust, and so forth, within one week of the date thereof. While the painter was employed in reading this covenant, by the light of a twinkling oil lamp in the far wall of the room, Schalken, as we have stated, entered the studio, and having delivered the box and the valuation of the Jew, into the hands of the stranger, he was about to retire, when Vanderhausen called to him to wait; and, presenting the case and the certificate to Gerard Douw, he paused in silence until he had satisfied himself, by an inspection of both, respecting the value of the pledge left in his hands. At length he said—

"Are you content?"

The painter said he would fain have another day to consider.

"Not an hour," said the suitor, apathetically.

"Well then," said Douw, with a sore effort, "I *am* content, it is a bargain."

"Then sign at once," said Vanderhausen, "for I am weary."

At the same time he produced a small case of writing materials, and Gerard signed the important document.

"Let this youth witness the covenant," said the old man; and Godfrey Schalken unconsciously attested the instrument which for ever bereft him of his dear Rose Velderkaust.

The compact being thus completed, the strange visitor folded up the paper, and stowed it safely in an inner pocket.

"I will visit you to-morrow night at nine o'clock, at your own house, Gerard Douw, and will see the object of our contract;" and so saying Wilken Vanderhausen moved stiffly, but rapidly, out of the room.

Schalken, eager to resolve his doubts, had placed himself by the window, in order to watch the street entrance; but the experiment served only to support his suspicions, for the old man did not issue from the door. This was *very* strange, odd, nay fearful. He and his master returned together, and talked but little on the way, for each had his own subjects of reflection, of anxiety, and of hope. Schalken, however, did not know the ruin which menaced his dearest projects.

Gerard Douw knew nothing of the attachment which had sprung up between his pupil and his niece; and even if he had, it is doubtful whether he would have regarded its existence as any serious obstruction to the wishes of Minheer Vanderhausen. Marriages were then and there matters of traffic and calculation; and it would have appeared as absurd in the eyes of the guardian to make a mutual attachment an essential element in a contract of the sort, as it would have been to draw up his bonds and receipts in the language of romance.

The painter, however, did not communicate to his niece the important step which he had taken in her behalf, a forebearance caused not by any anticipated opposition on her part, but solely by a ludicrous conscious-ness that if she were to ask him for a description of her destined bride-groom, he would be forced to confess that he had not once seen his face, and if called upon, would find it absolutely impossible to identify him. Upon the next day, Gerard Douw, after dinner, called his niece to him and having scanned her person with an air of satisfaction, he took her hand, and looking upon her pretty innocent face with a smile of kindness, he said:—

"Rose, my girl, that face of yours will make your fortune." Rose blushed and smiled. "Such faces and such tempers seldom go together, and when they do, the compound is a love charm, few heads or hearts can resist; trust me, you will soon be a bride, girl. But this is trifling, and I am pressed for time, so make ready the large room by eight o'clock to-night, and give directions for supper at nine. I expect a friend; and observe me, child, do you trick yourself out handsomely. I will not have him think us poor or sluttish."

With these words he left her, and took his way to the room in which his pupils worked.

When the evening closed in, Gerard called Schalken, who was about to take his departure to his own obscure and comfortless lodgings, and asked him to come home and sup with Rose and Vanderhausen. The invitation was, of course, accepted and Gerard Douw and his pupil soon found them-selves in the handsome and, even then, antique chamber, which had been prepared for the reception of the stranger. A cheerful wood fire blazed in the hearth, a little at one side of which an old-fashioned table, which shone in the fire-light like burnished gold, was awaiting the supper, for which preparations were going forward; and ranged with exact regularity, stood the tall-backed chairs, whose ungracefulness was more than com-pensated by their comfort. The little party, consisting of Rose, her uncle, and the artist, awaited the arrival of the expected visitor with considerable impatience. Nine o'clock at length came, and with it a summons at the street door, which being speedily answered, was followed by a slow and emphatic tread upon the staircase; the steps moved heavily across the lobby, the door of the room in which the party we have described were assembled slowly opened, and there entered a figure which startled, almost appalled, the phlegmatic Dutchmen, and nearly made Rose scream with terror. It was the form, and arrayed in the garb of Minheer Vanderhausen; the air, the gait, the height were the same, but the features had never been seen by any of the party before. The stranger stopped at the door of the room, and displayed his form and face completely. He wore a dark-coloured cloth cloak, which was short and full, not falling quite to his knees; his legs were cased in dark purple silk stockings, and his shoes were adorned with roses of the same colour. The opening of the cloak in front showed the under-suit to consist of some very dark, perhaps sable material, and his hands were enclosed in a pair of heavy leather gloves, which ran up considerably above the wrist, in the manner of a gauntlet. In one hand he carried his walking-stick and his hat, which he had removed, and the other hung heavily by his side. A quantity of grizzled hair descended in long tresses from his head, and rested upon the plaits of a stiff ruff, which effectually concealed his neck. So far all was well; but the face!—all the flesh of the face was coloured with the bluish leaden hue, which is sometimes produced by metallic medicines, administered in excessive quantities; the eyes showed an undue proportion of muddy white, and had a certain indefinable character of insanity; the hue of the lips bearing the usual relation to that of the face, was, consequently, nearly black; and the entire character of the face was sensual, malignant, and even satanic. It was remarkable that the worshipful stranger suffered as little as possible of his flesh to appear, and that during his visit he did not once remove his gloves. Having stood for some moments at the door, Gerard Douw at length found breath and collectedness to bid him welcome, and with a mute inclination of the head, the stranger stepped forward into the room. There was something indescribably odd, even horrible, about all his motions, something undefinable, that was unnatural, unhuman; it was as if the limbs were guided and directed by a spirit unused to the management of bodily machinery. The stranger spoke hardly at all during his visit, which did not exceed half an hour; and the host himself could scarcely muster courage enough to utter the few necessary salutations and courtesies; and, indeed, such was the nervous terror which the presence of Vanderhausen inspired, that very little would have

made all his entertainers fly in downright panic from the room. They had
not so far lost all self-possession, however, as to fail to observe two
strange peculiarities of their visitor. During his stay his eyelids did not
once close, or, indeed, move in the slightest degree; and farther, there was
a deathlike stillness in his whole person, owing to the absence of the
heaving motion of the chest, caused by the process of respiration. These
two peculiarities, though when told they may appear trifling, produced a
very striking and unpleasant effect when seen and observed. Vanderhausen at length relieved the painter of Leyden of his inauspicious presence; and with no trifling sense of relief the little party heard the street
door close after him.

"Dear uncle," said Rose, "what a frightful man! I would not see him
again for the wealth of the States."

"Tush, foolish girl," said Douw, whose sensations were anything but
comfortable. "A man may be as ugly as the devil, and yet, if his heart and
actions are good, he is worth all the pretty-faced perfumed puppies that
walk the Mall. Rose, my girl, it is very true he has not thy pretty face, but
I know him to be wealthy and liberal; and were he ten times more ugly,
these two virtues would be enough to counter balance all his deformity,
and if not sufficient actually to alter the shape and hue of his features, at
least enough to prevent one thinking them so much amiss."

"Do you know, uncle," said Rose, "when I saw him standing at the
door, I could not get it out of my head that I saw the old painted wooden
figure that used to frighten me so much in the Church of St. Laurence at
Rotterdam."

Gerard laughed, though he could not help inwardly acknowledging the
justness of the comparison. He was resolved, however, as far as he could,
to check his niece's disposition to dilate upon the ugliness of her intended
bridegroom, although he was not a little pleased, as well as puzzled, to
observe that she appeared totally exempt from that mysterious dread of
the stranger which, he could not disguise it from himself, considerably
affected him, as also his pupil Godfrey Schalken.

Early on the next day there arrived, from various quarters of the town,
rich presents of silks, velvets, jewellery, and so forth, for Rose; and also a
packet directed to Gerard Douw, which on being opened, was found to
contain a contract of marriage, formally drawn up, between Wilken Vanderhausen of the *Boom-quay*, in Rotterdam, and Rose Velderkaust of
Leyden, niece to Gerard Douw, master in the art of painting, also of the
same city; and containing engagements on the part of Vanderhausen to

make settlements upon his bride, far more splendid than he had before led her guardian to believe likely, and which were to be secured to her use in the most unexceptionable manner possible—the money being placed in the hand of Gerard Douw himself.

I have no sentimental scenes to describe, no cruelty of guardians, no magnanimity of wards, no agonies, or transport of lovers. The record I have to make is one of sordidness, levity, and heartlessness. In less than a week after the first interview which we have just described, the contract of marriage was fulfilled, and Schalken saw the prize which he would have risked existence to secure, carried off in solemn pomp by his repulsive rival. For two or three days he absented himself from the school; he then returned and worked, if with less cheerfulness, with far more dogged resolution than before; the stimulus of love had given place to that of ambition. Months passed away, and, contrary to his expectation, and, indeed, to the direct promise of the parties, Gerard Douw heard nothing of his niece or her worshipful·spouse. The interest of the money, which was to have been demanded in quarterly sums, lay unclaimed in his hands.

He began to grow extremely uneasy. Minheer Vanderhausen's direction in Rotterdam he was fully possessed of; after some irresolution he finally determined to journey thither—a trifling undertaking, and easily accomplished—and thus to satisfy himself of the safety and comfort of his ward, for whom he entertained an honest and strong affection. His search was in vain, however; no one in Rotterdam had ever heard of Minheer Vanderhausen. Gerard Douw left not a house in the Boom-quay untried, but all in vain. No one could give him any information whatever touching the object of his inquiry, and he was obliged to return to Leyden nothing wiser and far more anxious, than when he had left it.

On his arrival he hastened to the establishment from which Vanderhausen had hired the lumbering, though, considering the times, most luxurious vehicle, which the bridal party had employed to convey them to Rotterdam. From the driver of this machine he learned, that having proceeded by slow stages, they had late in the evening approached Rotterdam; but that before they entered the city, and while yet nearly a mile from it, a small party of men, soberly clad, and after the old fashion, with peaked beards and moustaches, standing in the centre of the road, obstructed the further progress of the carriage. The driver reined in his horses, much fearing, from the obscurity of the hour, and the loneliness, of the road, that some mischief was intended. His fears were, however, somewhat allayed by his observing that these strange men carried a large litter, of an antique shape, and which they immediately set down upon the pavement, whereupon the bridegroom, having opened the coach-door from within, descended, and having assisted his bride to do likewise, led her, weeping bitterly, and wringing her hands, to the litter, which they both entered. It was then raised by the men who surrounded it, and speedily carried towards the city, and before it had proceeded very far, the darkness concealed it from the view of the Dutch coachman. In the inside of the vehicle he found a purse, whose contents more than thrice paid the hire of the carriage and man. He saw and could tell nothing more of Minheer Vanderhausen and his beautiful lady.

This mystery was a source of profound anxiety and even grief to Gerard Douw. There was evidently fraud in the dealing of Vanderhausen with him, though for what purpose committed he could not imagine. He greatly doubted how far it was possible for a man possessing such a countenance to be anything but a villain, and every day that passed without his hearing from or of his niece, instead of inducing him to forget his fears, on the contrary tended more and more to aggravate them. The loss of her cheerful society tended also to depress his spirits; and in order to dispel the gloom, which often crept upon his mind after his daily occupations were over, he was wont frequently to ask Schalken to accompany him home, and share his otherwise solitary supper.

One evening, the painter and his pupil were sitting by the fire, having accomplished a comfortable meal, and had yielded to the silent and delicous melancholy of digestion, when their ruminations were disturbed by a loud sound at the street door, as if occasioned by some person rushing and scrambling vehemently against it. A domestic had run without delay to ascertain the cause of the disturbance, and they heard him twice or thrice interrogate the applicant for admission, but without eliciting any other answer but a sustained reiteration of sounds. They heard him then open the hall-door, and immediately there followed a light and rapid tread on the staircase. Schalken advanced towards the door. It opened before he reached it, and Rose rushed into the room. She looked wild, fierce and haggard with terror and exhaustion, but her dress surprised them as much as even her unexpected appearance. It consisted of a kind of white woollen wrapper, made close about the neck, and descending to the very ground. It was much deranged and travel-soiled. The poor creature had hardly entered the chamber when she fell senseless on the floor. With some difficulty they succeeded in reviving her, and on recovering her senses, she instantly exclaimed, in a tone of terror rather than mere impatience:—

"Wine! wine! quickly, or I'm lost!"

Astonished and almost scared at the strange agitation in which the call was made, they at once administered to her wishes, and she drank some wine with a haste and eagerness which surprised them. She had hardly swallowed it, when she exclaimed, with the same urgency:

"Food, for God's sake, food, at once, or I perish."

A considerable fragment of a roast joint was upon the table, and Schalken immediately began to cut some, but he was anticipated, for no sooner did she see it than she caught it, a more than mortal image of famine, and with her hands, and even with her teeth, she tore off the flesh, and swallowed it. When the paroxysm of hunger had been a little appeased, she appeared on a sudden overcome with shame, or it may have been that other more agitating thoughts overpowered and scared her, for she began to weep bitterly and to wring her hands.

"Oh, send for a minister of God," said she; "I am not safe till he comes; send for him speedily."

Gerard Douw despatched a messenger instantly, and prevailed on his niece to allow him to surrender his bed chamber to her use. He also persuaded her to retire to it at once to rest; her consent was extorted upon the condition that they would not leave her for a moment.

"Oh that the holy man were here," she said; "he can deliver me: the dead and the living can never be one: God has forbidden it."

With these mysterious words she surrendered herself to their guidance, and they proceeded to the chamber which Gerard Douw had assigned to her use.

"Do not, do not leave me for a moment," said she; "I am lost for ever if you do."

Gerard Douw's chamber was approached through a spacious apartment, which they were now about to enter. He and Schalken each carried a candle, so that a sufficiency of light was cast upon all surrounding objects. They were now entering the large chamber, which as I have said, communicated with Douw's apartment, when Rose suddenly stopped, and, in a whisper which thrilled them both with horror, she said:—

"Oh, God! he is here! he is here! See, see! there he goes!"

She pointed towards the door of the inner room, and Schalken thought he saw a shadowy and ill-defined form gliding into that apartment. He drew his sword, and, raising the candle so as to throw its light with increased distinctness upon the objects in the room, he entered the chamber into which the shadow had glided. No figure was there—nothing but the furniture which belonged to the room, and yet he could not be deceived as to the fact that something had moved before them into the chamber. A sickening dread came upon him, and the cold perspiration broke out in heavy drops upon his forehead; nor was he more composed, when he heard the increased urgency and agony of entreaty, with which Rose implored them not to leave her for a moment.

"I saw him," said she; "he's here. I cannot be deceived; I know him; he's by me; he is with me; he's in the room. Then, for God's sake, as you would save me, do not stir from beside me."

They at length prevailed upon her to lie down upon the bed, where she continued to urge them to stay by her. She frequently uttered incoherent sentences, repeating, again and again, "the dead and the living cannot be one: God has forbidden it." And then again, "Rest to the wakeful—sleep to the sleep-walkers." These and such mysterious and broken sentences, she continued to utter until the clergyman arrived. Gerard Douw began to fear, naturally enough, that terror or ill-treatment, had unsettled the poor girl's intellect, and he half suspected, by the suddenness of her appearance, the unseasonableness of the hour, and above all, from the wildness and terror of her manner, that she had made her escape from some place of confinement for lunatics, and was in imminent fear of pursuit. He resolved to summon medical advice as soon as the mind of his niece had been in some measure set at rest by the offices of the clergyman whose attendance she had so earnestly desired; and until this object had been attained, he did not venture to put any questions to her, which might possibly, by reviving painful or horrible recollections, increase her agitation. The clergyman soon arrived—a man of ascetic countenance and venerable age—one whom Gerard Douw respected very much, forasmuch as he was a veteran polemic, though one perhaps more dreaded as a combatant than beloved as a Christian—of pure morality, subtle brain, and frozen heart. He entered the chamber which communicated with that in which Rose reclined and immediately on his arrival, she requested him to pray for her, as for one who lay in the hands of Satan, and who could hope for deliverance only from heaven.

That you may distinctly understand all the circumstances of the event which I am going to describe, it is necessary to state the relative position of the parties who were engaged in it. The old clergyman and Schalken were in the anteroom of which I have already spoken; Rose lay in the inner chamber, the door of which was open; and by the side of the bed, at her urgent desire, stood her guardian; a candle burned in the bedchamber, and three were lighted in the outer apartment. The old man now cleared his voice as if about to commence, but before he had time to begin, a sudden gust of air blew out the candle which served to illuminate the room in which the poor girl lay, and she, with hurried alarm, exclaimed:—

"Godfrey, bring in another candle; the darkness is unsafe."

Gerard Douw forgetting for the moment her repeated injunctions, in the immediate impulse, stepped from the bedchamber into the other, in order to supply what she desired.

"Oh God! do not go, dear uncle," shrieked the unhappy girl—and at the same time she sprung from the bed, and darted after him, in order, by her grasp, to detain him. But the warning came too late, for scarcely had he passed the threshold, and hardly had his niece had time to utter the startling exclamation, when the door which divided the two rooms closed violently after him, as if swung by a strong blast of wind. Schalken and he both rushed to the door, but their united and desperate efforts could not avail so much as to shake it. Shriek after shriek burst from the inner chamber, with all the piercing loudness of despairing terror. Schalken and Douw applied every nerve to force open the door; but all in vain. There was no sound of struggling from within, but the screams seemed to increase in loudness, and at the same time they heard the bolts of the latticed window withdrawn, and the window itself grated upon the sill as if thrown open. One *last* shriek, so long and piercing and agonized as to be scarcely human, swelled from the room, and suddenly there followed a death-like silence. A light step was heard crossing the floor, as if from the bed to the window; and almost at the same instant the door gave way, and, yielding to the pressure of the external applicants, nearly precipitated them into the room. It was empty. The window was open, and Schalken sprung to a chair and gazed out upon the street and canal below. He saw no form, but he saw, or thought he saw, the waters of the broad canal beneath settling ring after ring in heavy circles, as if a moment before disturbed by the submission of some ponderous body.

No trace of Rose was ever after found, nor was anything certain respecting her mysterious wooer discovered or even suspected—no clue whereby to trace the intricacies of the labyrinth and to arrive at its solution, presented itself. But an incident occurred, which, though it will not be received by our rational readers in lieu of evidence, produced never-

theless a strong and a lasting impression upon the mind of Schalken.
Many years after the events which we have detailed, Schalken, then residing far away received an intimation of his father's death, and of his intended burial upon a fixed day in the church of Rotterdam. It was necessary that a very considerable journey should be performed by the funeral
procession, which as it will be readily believed, was not very numerously
attended. Schalken with difficulty arrived in Rotterdam late in the day
upon which the funeral was appointed to take place. It had not then arrived. Evening closed in, and still it did not appear.

Schalken strolled down to the church; he found it open; notice of the
arrival of the funeral had been given, and the vault in which the body was
to be laid had been opened. The sexton, on seeing a well-dressed gentleman, whose object was to attend the expected obsequies, pacing the aisle
of the church, hospitably invited him to share with him the comforts of a
blazing fire, which, as was his custom in winter time upon such occasions,
he had kindled in the hearth of a chamber in which he was accustomed to
await the arrival of such grisly guests and which communicated, by a
flight of steps, with the vault below. In this chamber, Schalken and his
entertainer seated themselves; and the sexton, after some fruitless
attempts to engage his guest in conversation, was obliged to apply himself
to his tobacco-pipe and can, to solace his solitude. In spite of his grief and
cares, the fatigues of a rapid journey of nearly forty hours gradually over-
came the mind and body of Godfrey Schalken, and he sank into a deep
sleep, from which he awakened by someone's shaking him gently by the
shoulder. He first thought that the old sexton had called him, but *he* was
no longer in the room. He roused himself, and as soon as he could clearly
see what was around him, he perceived a female form, clothed in a kind of
light robe of white, part of which was so disposed as to form a veil, and in
her hand she carried a lamp. She was moving rather away from him, in the
direction of the flight of steps which conducted towards the vaults.
Schalken felt a vague alarm at the sight of this figure and at the same time
an irresistible impulse to follow its guidance. He followed it towards the
vaults, but when it reached the head of the stairs, he paused; the figure
paused also, and, turning gently round, displayed, by the light of the lamp
it carried, the face and features of his first love, Rose Velderkaust. There
was nothing horrible, or even sad, in the countenance. On the contrary, it
wore the same arch smile which used to enchant the artist long before in
his happy days. A feeling of awe and interest, too intense to be resisted,
prompted him to follow the spectre, if spectre it were. She descended the

stairs—he followed—and turning to the left, through a narrow passage, she led him, to his infinite surprise, into what appeared to be an old-fashioned Dutch apartment, such as the pictures of Gerard Douw have served to immortalize. Abundance of costly antique furniture was disposed about the room, and in one corner stood a four-post bed, with heavy black cloth curtains around it; the figure frequently turned towards him with the same arch smile; and when she came to the side of the bed, she drew the curtains, and, by the light of the lamp, which she held towards its contents, she disclosed to the horror-stricken painter, sitting bolt upright in the bed, the livid and demoniac form of Vanderhausen. Schalken had hardly seen him, when he fell senseless upon the floor, where he lay until discovered, on the next morning, by persons employed in closing the passages into the vaults. He was lying in a cell of considerable size, which had not been disturbed for a long time, and he had fallen beside a large coffin, which was supported upon small pillars, a security against the attacks of vermin.

To his dying day Schalken was satisfied of the reality of the vision which he had witnessed, and he has left behind him a curious evidence of the impression which it wrought upon his fancy, in a painting executed shortly after the event I have narrated, and which is valuable as exhibiting not only the peculiarities which have made Schalken's pictures sought after, but even more so as presenting a portrait of his early love, Rose Velderkaust, whose mysterious fate must always remain matter of speculation.

⤳ GREEN TEA ⤳

PROLOGUE

Martin Hesselius, the German Physician

Though carefully educated in medicine and surgery, I have never practised either. The study of each continues, nevertheless, to interest me
profoundly. Neither idleness nor caprice caused my secession from the
honourable calling which I had just entered. The cause was a very trifling
scratch inflicted by a dissecting knife. This trifle cost me the loss of two
fingers, amputated promptly, and the more painful loss of my health, for I
have never been quite well since, and have seldom been twelve months
together in the same place.

In my wanderings I became acquainted with Dr. Martin Hesselius, a
wanderer like myself, like me a physician, and like me an enthusiast in his
profession. Unlike me in this, that his wanderings were voluntary, and he
a man, if not of fortune, as we estimate fortune in England, at least in
what our forefathers used to term "easy circumstances." He was an old
man when I first saw him; nearly five-and-thirty years my senior.

In Dr. Martin Hesselius, I found my master. His knowledge was immense, his grasp of a case was an intuition. He was the very man to inspire
a young enthusiast, like me, with awe and delight. My admiration has
stood the test of time and survived the separation of death. I am sure it
was well-founded.

For nearly twenty years I acted as his medical secretary. His immense
collection of papers he has left in my care, to be arranged, indexed and
bound. His treatment of some of these cases is curious. He writes in two
distinct characters. He describes what he saw and heard as an intelligent
layman might, and when in this style of narrative he had seen the patient
either through his own hall-door, to the light of day, or through the gates
of darkness to the caverns of the dead, he returns upon the narrative, and
in the terms of his art and with all the force and originality of genius, pro-
ceeds to the work of analysis, diagnosis and illustration.

Here and there a case strikes me as of a kind to amuse or horrify a lay
reader with an interest quite different from the peculiar one which it may

possess for an expert. With slight modifications, chiefly of language, and of course a change of names, I copy the following. The narrator is Dr. Martin Hesselius. I find it among the voluminous notes of cases which he made during a tour in England about sixty-four years ago.

It is related in a series of letters to his friend Professor Van Loo of Leyden. The professor was not a physician, but a chemist, and a man who read history and metaphysics and medicine, and had, in his day, written a play.

The narrative is therefore, if somewhat less valuable as a medical record, necessarily written in a manner more likely to interest an un-learned reader.

These letters, from a memorandum attached, appear to have been returned on the death of the professor, in 1819, to Dr. Hesselius. They are written, some in English, some in French, but the greater part in German. I am a faithful, though I am conscious, by no means a graceful translator, and although here and there I omit some passages, and shorten others, and disguise names, I have interpolated nothing.

CHAPTER I

Dr. Hesselius Relates How He Met the Rev. Mr. Jennings

The Rev. Mr. Jennings is tall and thin. He is middle-aged, and dresses with a natty, old-fashioned, high-church precision. He is naturally a little stately, but not at all stiff. His features without being handsome, are well formed, and their expression extremely kind, but also shy.

I met him one evening at Lady Mary Heyduke's. The modesty and benevolence of his countenance are extremely prepossessing.

We were but a small party, and he joined agreeably enough in the con-versation, He seems to enjoy listening very much more than contributing to the talk; but what he says is always to the purpose and well said. He is a great favourite of Lady Mary's, who it seems, consults him upon many things, and thinks him the most happy and blessed person on earth. Little knows she about him.

The Rev. Mr. Jennings is a bachelor, and has, they say sixty thousand pounds in the funds. He is a charitable man. He is most anxious to be actively employed in his sacred profession, and yet though always toler-ably well elsewhere, when he goes down to his vicarage in Warwickshire, to engage in the actual duties of his sacred calling, his health soon fails him, and in a very strange way. So says Lady Mary.

There is no doubt that Mr. Jennings' health does break down in, generally, a sudden and mysterious way, sometimes in the very act of officiating in his old and pretty church at Kenlis. It may be his heart, it may be his brain. But so it has happened three or four times, or oftener, that after proceeding a certain way in the service, he has on a sudden stopped short, and after a silence, apparently quite unable to resume, he has fallen into solitary, inaudible prayer, his hands and his eyes uplifted, and then pale as death, and in the agitation of a strange shame and horror, descended trembling, and got into the vestry-room, leaving his congregation, without explanation, to themselves. This occurred when his curate was absent. When he goes down to Kenlis now, he always takes care to provide a clergyman to share his duty, and to supply his place on the instant should he become thus suddenly incapacitated.

When Mr. Jennings breaks down quite, and beats a retreat from the vicarage, and returns to London, where, in a dark street off Piccadilly, he inhabits a very narrow house, Lady Mary says that he is always perfectly well. I have my own opinion about that. There are degrees of course. We shall see.

Mr. Jennings is a perfectly gentlemanlike man. People, however, remark something odd. There is an impression a little ambiguous. One thing which certainly contributes to it, people I think don't remember; or, perhaps, distinctly remark. But I did, almost immediately. Mr. Jennings has a way of looking sidelong upon the carpet, as if his eye followed the movements of something there. This, of course, is not always. It occurs now and then. But often enough to give a certain oddity, as I have said, to his manner, and in this glance travelling along the floor there is something both shy and anxious.

A medical philosopher, as you are good enough to call me, elaborating theories by the aid of cases sought out by himself, and by him watched and scrutinised with more time at command, and consequently infinitely more minuteness than the ordinary practitioner can afford, falls insensibly into habits of observation which accompany him everywhere, and are exercised, as some people would say, impertinently, upon every subject that presents itself with the least likelihood of rewarding inquiry.

There was a promise of this kind in the slight, timid, kindly, but reserved gentleman, whom I met for the first time at this agreeable little evening gathering. I observed, of course, more than I here set down; but I reserve all that borders on the technical for a strictly scientific paper.

I may remark, that when I here speak of medical science, I do so, as I hope some day to see it more generally understood, in a much more comprehensive sense than its generally material treatment would warrant. I believe the entire natural world is but the ultimate expression of that spiritual world from which, and in which alone, it has its life. I believe that the essential man is a spirit, that the spirit is an organised substance, but as different in point of material from what we ordinarily understand by matter, as light or electricity is; that the material body is, in the most literal sense, a vesture, and death consequently no interruption of the living man's existence, but simply his extrication from the natural body—a process which commences at the moment of what we term death, and the completion of which, at furthest a few days later, is the resurrection "in power."

The person who weighs the consequences of these positions will probably see their practical bearing upon medical science. This is, however, by no means the proper place for displaying the proofs and discussing the consequences of this too generally unrecognized state of facts.

In pursuance of my habit, I was covertly observing Mr. Jennings, with all my caution—I think he perceived it—and I saw plainly that he was as cautiously observing me. Lady Mary happening to address me by my name, as Dr. Hesselius, I saw that he glanced at me more sharply, and then became thoughtful for a few minutes.

After this, as I conversed with a gentleman at the other end of the room, I saw him look at me more steadily, and with an interest which I thought I understood. I then saw him take an opportunity of chatting with Lady Mary, and was, as one always is, perfectly aware of being the subject of a distant inquiry and answer.

This tall clergyman approached me by-and-by; and in a little time we had got into conversation. When two people, who like reading, and know books and places, having travelled, wish to discourse, it is very strange if they can't find topics. It was not accident that brought him near me, and led him into conversation. He knew German and had read my Essays on Metaphysical Medicine, which suggest more than they actually say.

This courteous man, gentle, shy, plainly a man of thought and reading, who moving and talking among us, was not altogether of us, and whom I already suspected of leading a life whose transactions and alarms were carefully concealed, with an impenetrable reserve from, not only the world, but his best beloved friends—was cautiously weighing in his own mind the idea of taking a certain step with regard to me.

I penetrated his thoughts without his being aware of it, and was careful to say nothing which could betray to his sensitive vigilance my suspicions respecting his position, or my surmises about his plans respecting myself.

We chatted upon indifferent subjects for a time, but at last he said:

"I was very much interested by some papers of yours, Dr. Hesselius, upon what you term Metaphysical Medicine—I read them in German, ten or twelve years ago—have they been translated?"

"No, I'm sure they have not—I should have heard. They would have asked my leave, I think."

"I asked the publishers here, a few months ago, to get the book for me in the original German; but they tell me it is out of print."

"So it is, and has been for some years; but it flatters me as an author to find that you have not forgotten my little book, although," I added, laughing, "ten or twelve years is a considerable time to have managed without it: but I suppose you have been turning the subject over again in your mind, or something has happened lately to revive your interest in it."

At this remark, accompanied by a glance of inquiry, a sudden embarrassment disturbed Mr. Jennings, analogous to that which makes a young lady blush and look foolish. He dropped his eyes, and folded his hands together uneasily, and looked oddly, and you would have said, guiltily, for a moment.

I helped him out of his awkwardness in the best way, by appearing not to observe it, and going straight on, I said: "Those revivals of interest in a subject happen to me often; one book suggests another, and often sends me back on a wild-goose chase over an interval of twenty years. But if you still care to possess a copy, I shall be only too happy to provide you; I have still got two or three by me—and if you allow me to present one I shall be very much honoured."

"You are very good indeed," he said, quite at his ease again, in a moment: "I almost despaired—I don't know how to thank you."

"Pray don't say a word; the thing is really so little worth that I am only ashamed of having offered it, and if you thank me any more I shall throw it into the fire in a fit of modesty."

Mr. Jennings laughed. He inquired where I was staying in London, and after a little more conversation on a variety of subjects, he took his departure.

CHAPTER II

The Doctor Questions Lady Mary and She Answers

"I like your vicar so much, Lady Mary," said I, as soon as he was gone.

"He has read, travelled, and thought, and having also suffered, he ought to be an accomplished companion."

"So he is, and, better still, he is a really good man," said she. "His advice is invaluable about my schools, and all my little undertakings at Dawlbridge, and he's so painstaking, he takes so much trouble—you have no idea—wherever he thinks he can be of use: he's so good-natured and so sensible."

"It is pleasant to hear so good an account of his neighbourly virtues. I can only testify to his being an agreeable and gentle companion, and in addition to what you have told me, I think I can tell you two or three things about him," said I.

"Really!"

"Yes, to begin with, he's unmarried."

"Yes, that's right—go on."

"He has been writing, that is he *was*, but for two or three years perhaps, he has not gone on with his work, and the book was upon some rather abstract subject—perhaps theology."

"Well, he was writing a book, as you say; I'm not quite sure what it was about, but only that it was nothing that I cared for; very likely you are right, and he certainly did stop—yes."

"And although he only drank a little coffee here to-night, he likes tea, at least, did like it extravagantly."

"Yes, that's *quite* true."

"He drank green tea, a good deal, didn't he?" I pursued.

"Well, that's very odd! Green tea was a subject on which we used almost to quarrel."

"But he has quite given that up," said I.

"So he has."

"And, now, one more fact. His mother or his father, did you know them?"

"Yes, both; his father is only ten years dead, and their place is near Dawlbridge. We knew them very well," she answered.

"Well, either his mother or his father—I should rather think his father, saw a ghost," said I.

"Well, you really are a conjurer, Dr. Hesselius."

"Conjurer or no, haven't I said right?" I answered merrily.

"You certainly have, and it *was* his father: he was a silent, whimsical man, and he used to bore my father about his dreams, and at last he told him a story about a ghost he had seen and talked with, and a very odd story it was. I remember it particularly, because I was so afraid of him. This story was long before he died—when I was quite a child—and his ways were so silent and moping, and he used to drop in sometimes, in the dusk, when I was alone in the drawing-room, and I used to fancy there were ghosts about him."

I smiled and nodded.

"And now, having established my character as a conjurer, I think I must say good-night," said I.

"But how *did* you find it out?"

"By the planets, of course, as the gipsies do," I answered, and so, gaily we said good-night.

Next morning I sent the little book he had been inquiring after, and a note to Mr. Jennings, and on returning late that evening, I found that he had called at my lodgings, and left his card. He asked whether I was at home, and asked at what hour he would be most likely to find me.

Does he intend opening his case, and consulting me "professionally," as they say? I hope so. I have already conceived a theory about him. It is supported by Lady Mary's answers to my parting questions. I should like much to ascertain from his own lips. But what can I do consistently with good breeding to invite a confession? Nothing. I rather think he meditates one. At all events, my dear Van L., I shan't make myself difficult of access; I mean to return his visit tomorrow. It will be only civil in return for his politeness, to ask to see him. Perhaps something may come of it. Whether much, little, or nothing, my dear Van L., you shall hear.

CHAPTER III

Dr. Hesselius Picks Up Something in Latin Books

Well, I have called at Blank Street.

On inquiring at the door, the servant told me that Mr. Jennings was engaged very particularly with a gentleman, a clergyman from Kenlis, his parish in the country. Intending to reserve my privilege, and to call again, I merely intimated that I should try another time, and turned to go, when the servant begged my pardon, and asked me, looking at me a little more attentively than well-bred persons of his order usually do, whether I was Dr. Hesselius; and, on learning that I was, he said, "Perhaps then, sir, you would allow me to mention it to Mr. Jennings, for I am sure he wishes to see you."

The servant returned in a moment, with a message from Mr. Jennings, asking me to go into his study, which was in effect his back drawing-room, promising to be with me in a very few minutes.

This was really a study—almost a library. The room was lofty with two tall slender windows, and rich dark curtains. It was much larger than I had expected, and stored with books on every side, from the floor to the ceiling. The upper carpet—for to my tread it felt that there were two or three—was a Turkey carpet. My steps fell noiselessly. The bookcases standing out, placed the windows, particularly narrow ones, in deep recesses. The effect of the room was, although extremely comfortable, and even luxurious, decidedly gloomy, and aided by the silence, almost oppressive. Perhaps, however, I ought to have allowed something for association. My mind had connected peculiar ideas with Mr. Jennings. I stepped into this perfectly silent room, of a very silent house, with a peculiar foreboding; and its darkness, and solemn clothing of books, for except where two narrow looking-glasses were set in the wall, they were everywhere, helped this sombre feeling.

While awaiting Mr. Jennings' arrival, I amused myself by looking into some of the books with which his shelves were laden. Not among these, but immediately under them, with their backs upward, on the floor, I lighted upon a complete set of Swedenborg's "Arcana Cælestia," in the original Latin, a very fine folio set, bound in the natty livery which theology affects, pure vellum, namely, gold letters, and carmine edges. There were paper markers in several of these volumes, I raised and placed them, one after the other, upon the table, and opening where these papers were placed, I read in the solemn Latin phraseology, a series of sentences indicated by a pencilled line at the margin. Of these I copy here a few, translating them into English.

"When man's interior sight is opened, which is that of his spirit, then there appear the things of another life, which cannot possibly be made visible to the bodily sight." . . . .

"By the internal sight it has been granted me to see the things that are in the other life, more clearly than I see those that are in the world. From these considerations, it is evident that external vision exists from interior vision, and this from a vision still more interior, and so on." . . . .

"There are with every man at least two evil spirits." . . . .

"With wicked genii there is also a fluent speech, but harsh and grating. There is also among them a speech which is not fluent, wherein the dissent of the thoughts is perceived as something secretly creeping along within it."

"The evil spirits associated with man are, indeed from the hells, but when with man they are not then in hell, but are taken out thence. The place where they then are, is in the midst between heaven and hell, and is called the world of spirits—when the evil spirits who are with man, are in that world, they are not in any infernal torment, but in every thought and affection of man, and so, in all that the man himself enjoys. But when they are remitted into their hell, they return to their former state." . . . .

"If evil spirits could perceive that they were associated with man, and yet they were spirits separate from him, and if they could flow in into the things of his body, they would attempt by a thousand means to destroy him; for they hate man with a deadly hatred." . . . .

"Knowing, therefore, that I was a man in the body, they were continually striving to destroy me, not as to the body only, but especially as to the soul; for to destroy any man or spirit is the very delight of the life of all who are in hell; but I have been continually protected by the Lord. Hence it appears how dangerous it is for man to be in a living consort with spirits, unless he be in the good of faith." . . . .

"Nothing is more carefully guarded from the knowledge of associate spirits than their being thus conjoint with a man, for if they knew it they would speak to him, with the intention to destroy him." . . . .

"The delight of hell is to do evil to man, and to hasten his eternal ruin."

A long note, written with a very sharp and fine pencil, in Mr. Jennings' neat hand, at the foot of the page, caught my eye. Expecting his criticism upon the text, I read a word or two, and stopped, for it was something quite different, and began with these words, *Deus misereatur mei*—"May God compassionate me." Thus warned of its private nature, I averted my eyes, and shut the book, replacing all the volumes as I had found them, except one which interested me, and in which, as men studious and solitary in their habits will do, I grew so absorbed as to take no cognisance of the outer world, nor to remember where I was.

I was reading some pages which refer to "representatives" and "correspondents," in the technical language of Swedenborg, and had arrived at a passage, the substance of which is, that evil spirits, when seen by other eyes than those of their infernal associates, present themselves, by "correspondence," in the shape of the beast (*fera*) which represents their particular lust and life, in aspect direful and atrocious. This is a long passage, and particularises a number of those bestial forms.

CHAPTER IV

Four Eyes Were Reading the Passage

I was running the head of my pencil-case along the line as I read it, and something caused me to raise my eyes.

Directly before me was one of the mirrors I have mentioned, in which I saw reflected the tall shape of my friend, Mr. Jennings, leaning over my shoulder, and reading the page at which I was busy, and with a face so dark and wild that I should hardly have known him.

I turned and rose. He stood erect also, and with an effort laughed a little, saying:

"I came in and asked you how you did, but without succeeding in awaking you from your book; so I could not restrain my curiosity, and very impertinently, I'm afraid, peeped over your shoulder. This is not your first time of looking into those pages. You have looked into Swedenborg, no doubt, long ago?"

"Oh dear, yes! I owe Swedenborg a great deal; you will discover traces of him in the little book on Metaphysical Medicine, which you were so good as to remember."

Although my friend affected a gaiety of manner, there was a slight flush in his face, and I could perceive that he was inwardly much perturbed.

"I'm scarcely yet qualified, I know so little of Swedenborg. I've only had them a fortnight," he answered, "and I think they are rather likely to make a solitary man nervous—that is, judging from the very little I have read—I don't say that they have made me so," he laughed; "and I'm so very much obliged for the book. I hope you got my note?"

I made all proper acknowledgments and modest disclaimers.

"I never read a book that I go with, so entirely, as that of yours," he continued. "I saw at once there is more in it than is quite unfolded. Do you know Dr. Harley?" he asked, rather abruptly.

In passing, the editor remarks that the physician here named was one of the most eminent who had ever practised in England.

I did, having had letters to him, and had experienced from him great courtesy and considerable assistance during my visit to England.

"I think that man one of the very greatest fools I ever met in my life," said Mr. Jennings.

This was the first time I had ever heard him say a sharp thing of anybody, and such a term applied to so high a name a little startled me.

"Really! and in what way?" I asked.

"In his profession," he answered.

I smiled.

"I mean this," he said: "he seems to me, one half, blind—I mean one
half of all he looks at is dark—preternaturally bright and vivid all the rest;
and the worst of it is, it seems *wilful.* I can't get him—I mean he won't—
I've had some experience of him as a physician, but I look on him as, in
that sense, no better than a paralytic mind, an intellect half dead. I'll tell
you—I know I shall some time—all about it," he said, with a little agitation. "You stay some months longer in England. If I should be out of
town during your stay for a little time, would you allow me to trouble you
with a letter?"

"I should be only too happy," I assured him.

"Very good of you. I am so utterly dissatisfied with Harley."

"A little leaning to the materialistic school," I said.

"A *mere* materialist," he corrected me; "you can't think how that sort
of thing worries one who knows better. You won't tell any one—any of
my friends you know—that I am hippish; now, for instance, no one
knows—not even Lady Mary—that I have seen Dr. Harley, or any other
doctor. So pray don't mention it; and, if I should have any threatening of
an attack, you'll kindly let me write, or, should I be in town, have a little
talk with you."

I was full of conjecture and unconsciously I found I had fixed my eyes
gravely on him, for he lowered his for a moment, and he said:

"I see you think I might as well tell you now, or else you are forming a
conjecture; but you may as well give it up. If you were guessing all the rest
of your life, you will never hit on it."

He shook his head smiling, and over that wintry sunshine a black cloud
suddenly came down, and he drew his breath in, through his teeth as men
do in pain.

"Sorry, of course, to learn that you apprehend occasion to consult any
of us; but, command me when and how you like, and I need not assure
you that your confidence is sacred."

He then talked of quite other things, and in a comparatively cheerful
way and after a little time, I took my leave.

CHAPTER V

Dr. Hesselius is Summoned to Richmond

We parted cheerfully, but he was not cheerful, nor was I. There are certain expressions of that powerful organ of spirit—the human face—which, although I have seen them often, and possess a doctor's nerve, yet disturb me profoundly. One look of Mr. Jennings haunted me. It had seized my imagination with so dismal a power that I changed my plans for the evening, and went to the opera, feeling that I wanted a change of ideas.

I heard nothing of or from him for two or three days, when a note in his hand reached me. It was cheerful, and full of hope. He said that he had been for some little time so much better—quite well, in fact—that he was going to make a little experiment, and run down for a month or so to his parish, to try whether a little work might not quite set him up. There was in it a fervent religious expression of gratitude for his restoration, as he now almost hoped he might call it.

A day or two later I saw Lady Mary, who repeated what his note had announced, and told me that he was actually in Warwickshire, having resumed his clerical duties at Kenlis; and she added, "I begin to think that he is really perfectly well, and that there never was anything the matter, more than nerves and fancy; we are all nervous, but I fancy there is nothing like a little hard work for that kind of weakness, and he has made up his mind to try it. I should not be surprised if he did not come back for a year."

Notwithstanding all this confidence, only two days later I had this note, dated from his house off Piccadilly:

> Dear Sir,—I have returned disappointed. If I should feel at all able to see you, I shall write to ask you kindly to call. At present, I am too low, and, in fact, simply unable to say all I wish to say. Pray don't mention my name to my friends. I can see no one. By-and-by, please God, you shall hear from me. I mean to take a run into Shropshire, where some of my people are. God bless you! May we, on my return, meet more happily than I can now write.

About a week after this I saw Lady Mary at her own house, the last person, she said, left in town, and just on the wing for Brighton, for the London season was quite over. She told me that she had heard from Mr. Jennings' niece, Martha, in Shropshire. There was nothing to be gathered from her letter, more than that he was low and nervous. In those words, of which healthy people think so lightly, what a world of suffering is sometimes hidden!

Nearly five weeks had passed without any further news of Mr. Jennings. At the end of that time I received a note from him. He wrote:

"I have been in the country, and have had change of air, change of scene, change of faces, change of everything—and in everything—but *myself*. I have made up my mind, so far as the most irresolute creature on earth can do it, to tell my case fully to you. If your engagements will permit, pray come to me to-day, to-morrow, or the next day; but, pray defer as little as possible. You know not how much I need help. I have a quiet house at Richmond, where I now am. Perhaps you can manage to come to dinner, or to luncheon, or even to tea. You shall have no trouble in finding me out. The servant at Blank Street, who takes this note, will have a carriage at your door at any hour you please; and I am always to be found. You will say that I ought not to be alone. I have tried everything. Come and see."

I called up the servant, and decided on going out the same evening, which accordingly I did.

He would have been much better in a lodging-house, or hotel, I thought, as I drove up through a short double row of sombre elms to a very old-fashioned brick house, darkened by the foliage of these trees, which overtopped, and nearly surrounded it. It was a perverse choice, for nothing could be imagined more triste and silent. The house, I found, belonged to him. He had stayed for a day or two in town, and, finding it for some cause insupportable, had come out here, probably because being furnished and his own, he was relieved of the thought and delay of selection, by coming here.

The sun had already set, and the red reflected light of the western sky illuminated the scene with the peculiar effect with which we are all familiar. The hall seemed very dark, but, getting to the back drawing-room, whose windows command the west, I was again in the same dusky light.

I sat down, looking out upon the richly-wooded landscape that glowed in the grand and melancholy light which was every moment fading. The corners of the room were already dark; all was growing dim, and the gloom was insensibly toning my mind, already prepared for what was sinister. I was waiting alone for his arrival, which soon took place. The door communicating with the front room opened, and the tall figure of

Mr. Jennings, faintly seen in the ruddy twilight, came, with quiet stealthy steps, into the room.

We shook hands, and, taking a chair to the window, where there was still light enough to enable us to see each other's faces, he sat down beside me, and, placing his hand upon my arm, with scarcely a word of preface began his narrative.

CHAPTER VI

How Mr. Jennings Met His Companion

The faint glow of the west, the pomp of the then lonely woods of Richmond, were before us, behind and about us the darkening room, and on the stony face of the sufferer—for the character of his face, though still gentle and sweet, was changed—rested that dim, odd glow which seems to descend and produce, where it touches, lights, sudden though faint, which are lost, almost without gradation, in darkness. The silence, too, was utter: not a distant wheel, or bark, or whistle from without; and within the depressing stillness of an invalid bachelor's house.

I guessed well the nature, though not even vaguely the particulars of the revelations I was about to receive, from that fixed face of suffering that so oddly flushed stood out, like a portrait of Schalken's, before its background of darkness.

"It began," he said, "on the 15th of October, three years and eleven weeks ago, and two days—I keep very accurate count, for every day is torment. If I leave anywhere a chasm in my narrative tell me.

"About four years ago I began a work, which had cost me very much thought and reading. It was upon the religious metaphysics of the ancients."

"I know," said I, "the actual religion of educated and thinking paganism, quite apart from symbolic worship? A wide and very interesting field."

"Yes, but not good for the mind—the Christian mind, I mean. Paganism is all bound together in essential unity, and, with evil sympathy, their religion involves their art, and both their manners, and the subject is a degrading fascination and the Nemesis sure. God forgive me!

"I wrote a great deal; I wrote late at night. I was always thinking on the subject, walking about, wherever I was, everywhere. It thoroughly infected me. You are to remember that all the material ideas connected with it were more or less of the beautiful, the subject itself delightfully interesting, and I, then, without a care."

He sighed heavily.

"I believe that every one who sets about writing in earnest does his work, as a friend of mine phrased it, *on* something—tea, or coffee, or tobacco. I suppose there is a material waste that must be hourly supplied in such occupations, or that we should grow too abstracted, and the mind, as it were, pass out of the body, unless it were reminded often enough of the connection by actual sensation. At all events, I felt the want, and I supplied it. Tea was my companion—at first the ordinary black tea, made in the usual way, not too strong: but I drank a good deal, and increased its strength as I went on. I never experienced an uncomfortable symptom from it. I began to take a little green tea. I found the effect pleasanter, it cleared and intensified the power of thought so. I had come to take it frequently, but not stronger than one might take it for pleasure. I wrote a great deal out here, it was so quiet, and in this room. I used to sit up very late, and it became a habit with me to sip my tea—green tea—every now and then as my work proceeded. I had a little kettle on my table, that swung over a lamp, and made tea two or three times between eleven o'clock and two or three in the morning, my hours of going to bed. I used to go into town every day. I was not a monk, and, although I spent an hour or two in a library, hunting up authorities and looking out lights upon my theme, I was in no morbid state as far as I can judge. I met my friends pretty much as usual and enjoyed their society, and, on the whole, existence had never been, I think, so pleasant before.

"I had met with a man who had some odd old books, German editions in mediæval Latin, and I was only too happy to be permitted access to them. This obliging person's books were in the City, a very out-of-the-way part of it. I had rather out-stayed my intended hour, and, on coming out, seeing no cab near, I was tempted to get into the omnibus which used to drive past this house. It was darker than this by the time the 'bus had reached an old house, you may have remarked, with four poplars at each side of the door, and there the last passenger but myself got out. We drove along rather faster. It was twilight now. I leaned back in my corner next the door ruminating pleasantly.

"The interior of the omnibus was nearly dark. I had observed in the corner opposite to me at the other side, and at the end next the horses, two small circular reflections, as it seemed to me, of a reddish light. They were about two inches apart, and about the size of those small brass but-

tons that yachting men used to put upon their jackets. I began to specu-
late, as listless men will, upon this trifle, as it seemed. From what centre
did that faint but deep red light come, and from what—glass beads, but-
tons, toy decorations—was it reflected? We were lumbering along gently,
having nearly a mile still to go. I had not solved the puzzle, and it became
in another minute more odd, for these two luminous points, with a sudden jerk, descended nearer and nearer the floor, keeping still their relative distance and horizontal position, and then, as suddenly, they rose to
the level of the seat on which I was sitting and I saw them no more.

"My curiosity was now really excited, and, before I had time to think,
I saw again these two dull lamps, again together near the floor; again they
disappeared, and again in their old corner I saw them.

"So, keeping my eyes upon them, I edged quietly up my own side,
towards the end at which I still saw these tiny discs of red.

"There was very little light in the 'bus. It was nearly dark. I leaned
forward to aid my endeavour to discover what these little circles really
were. They shifted position a little as I did so. I began now to perceive an
outline of something black, and I soon saw, with tolerable distinctness,
the outline of a small black monkey, pushing its face forward in mimicry
to meet mine; those were its eyes, and I now dimly saw its teeth grinning
at me.

"I drew back, not knowing whether it might not meditate a spring. I
fancied that one of the passengers had forgot this ugly pet, and wishing to
ascertain something of its temper, though not caring to trust my fingers
to it, I poked my umbrella softly towards it. It remained immovable—up
to it—*through* it. For through it, and back and forward it passed, without
the slightest resistance.

"I can't, in the least, convey to you the kind of horror that I felt. When
I had ascertained that the thing was an illusion, as I then supposed, there
came a misgiving about myself and a terror that fascinated me in im-
potence to remove my gaze from the eyes of the brute for some moments.
As I looked, it made a little skip back, quite into the corner, and I, in a
panic, found myself at the door, having put my head out, drawing deep
breaths of the outer air, and staring at the lights and trees we were passing, too glad to reassure myself of reality.

"I stopped the 'bus and got out. I perceived the man look oddly at me as
I paid him. I dare say there was something unusual in my looks and
manner, for I had never felt so strangely before."

CHAPTER VII

The Journey: First Stage

"When the omnibus drove on, and I was alone upon the road, I looked carefully round to ascertain whether the monkey had followed me. To my indescribable relief I saw it nowhere. I can't describe easily what a shock I had received, and my sense of genuine gratitude on finding myself, as I supposed, quite rid of it.

"I had got out a little before we reached this house, two or three hundred steps. A brick wall runs along the footpath, and inside the wall is a hedge of yew, or some dark evergreen of that kind, and within that again the row of fine trees which you may have remarked as you came.

"This brick wall is about as high as my shoulder, and happening to raise my eyes I saw the monkey, with that stooping gait, on all fours, walking or creeping, close beside me, on top of the wall. I stopped, looking at it with a feeling of loathing and horror. As I stopped so did it. It sat up on the wall with its long hands on its knees looking at me. There was not light enough to bring the peculiar light of its eyes into strong relief. I still saw, however, that red foggy light plainly enough. It did not show its teeth, nor exhibit any sign of irritation, but seemed jaded and sulky, and was observing me steadily.

"I drew back into the middle of the road. It was an unconscious recoil, and there I stood, still looking at it. It did not move.

"With an instinctive determination to try something—anything, I turned about and walked briskly towards town with askance look, all the time, watching the movements of the beast. It crept swiftly along the wall, at exactly my pace.

"Where the wall ends, near the turn of the road, it came down, and with a wiry spring or two brought itself close to my feet, and continued to keep up with me, as I quickened my pace. It was at my left side, so close to my leg that I felt every moment as if I should tread upon it.

"The road was quite deserted and silent, and it was darker every moment. I stopped dismayed and bewildered, turning as I did so, the other way—I mean, towards this house, away from which I had been walking. When I stood still, the monkey drew back to a distance of, I suppose, about five or six yards, and remained stationary, watching me.

"I had been more agitated than I have said. I had read, of course, as everyone has, something about 'spectral illusions,' as you physicians term the phenomena of such cases. I considered my situation, and looked my misfortune in the face.

"These affections, I had read, are sometimes transitory and sometimes obstinate. I had read of cases in which the appearance, at first harmless, had, step by step, degenerated into something direful and insupportable, and ended by wearing its victim out. Still as I stood there, but for my bestial companion, quite alone, I tried to comfort myself by repeating again and again the assurance, 'the thing is purely disease, a well-known physical affection, as distinctly as small-pox or neuralgia. Doctors are all agreed on that, philosophy demonstrates it. I must not be a fool. I've been sitting up too late, and I daresay my digestion is quite wrong, and, with God's help, I shall be all right, and this is but a symptom of nervous dyspepsia.' Did I believe all this? Not one word of it, no more than any other miserable being ever did who is once seized and riveted in this satanic captivity. Against my convictions, I might say my knowledge, I was simply bullying myself into a false courage.

"I now walked homeward. I had only a few hundred yards to go. I had forced myself into a sort of resignation, but I had not got over the sickening shock and the flurry of the first certainty of my misfortune.

"I made up my mind to pass the night at home. The brute moved close beside me, and I fancied there was the sort of anxious drawing toward the house, which one sees in tired horses or dogs sometimes as they come toward home.

"I was afraid to go into town, I was afraid of any one's seeing and recognizing me. I was conscious of an irrepressible agitation in my manner. Also, I was afraid of any violent change in my habits, such as going to a place of amusement, or walking from home in order to fatigue myself. At the hall door it waited till I mounted the steps, and when the door was opened entered with me.

"I drank no tea that night. I got cigars and some brandy and water. My idea was that I should act upon my material system, and by living for a while in sensation apart from thought, send myself forcibly, as it were, into a new groove. I came up here to this drawing-room. I sat just here. The monkey then got upon a small table that then stood *there*. It looked dazed and languid. An irrepressible uneasiness as to its movements kept my eyes always upon it. Its eyes were half closed, but I could see them glow. It was looking steadily at me. In all situations, at all hours, it is awake and looking at me. That never changes.

"I shall not continue in detail my narrative of this particular night. I shall describe, rather, the phenomena of the first year, which never varied, essentially. I shall describe the monkey as it appeared in daylight. In the dark, as you shall presently hear, there are peculiarities. It is a small monkey, perfectly black. It had only one peculiarity—a character of malignity—unfathomable malignity. During the first year it looked sullen and sick. But this character of intense malice and vigilance was always underlying that surly languor. During all that time it acted as if on a plan of giving me as little trouble as was consistent with watching me. Its eyes were never off me. I have never lost sight of it, except in my sleep, light or dark, day or night, since it came here, excepting when it withdraws for some weeks at a time, unaccountably.

"In total dark it is visible as in daylight. I do not mean merely its eyes. It is *all* visible distinctly in a halo that resembles a glow of red embers, and which accompanies it in all its movements.

"When it leaves me for a time, it is always at night, in the dark, and in the same way. It grows at first uneasy, and then furious, and then advances towards me, grinning and shaking, its paws clenched, and, at the same time, there comes the appearance of fire in the grate. I never have any fire. I can't sleep in the room where there is any, and it draws nearer and nearer to the chimney, quivering, it seems, with rage, and when its fury rises to the highest pitch, it springs into the grate, and up the chimney, and I see it no more.

"When first this happened, I thought I was released. I was now a new man. A day passed—a night—and no return, and a blessed week—a week—another week. I was always on my knees, Dr. Hesselius, always, thanking God and praying. A whole month passed of liberty, but on a sudden, it was with me again."

CHAPTER VIII

The Second Stage

"It was with me, and the malice which before was torpid under a sullen exterior, was not active. It was perfectly unchanged in every other respect. This new energy was apparent in its activity and its looks, and soon in other ways.

"For a time, you will understand, the change was shown only in an increased vivacity, and an air of menace, as if it were always brooding over some atrocious plan. Its eyes, as before, were never off me."

"Is it here now?" I asked.

"No," he replied, "it has been absent exactly a fortnight and a day—fifteen days. It has sometimes been away so long as nearly two months, once for three. Its absence always exceeds a fortnight, although it may be but by a single day. Fifteen days having past since I saw it last, it may return now at any moment."

"Is its return," I asked, "accompanied by any peculiar manifestation?"

"Nothing—no," he said. "It is simply with me again. On lifting my eyes from a book, or turning my head, I see it, as usual, looking at me, and then it remains, as before, for its appointed time. I have never told so much and so minutely before to any one."

I perceived that he was agitated, and looking like death, and he repeatedly applied his handkerchief to his forehead; I suggested that he might be tired, and told him that I would call, with pleasure, in the morning, but he said:

"No, if you don't mind hearing it all now. I have got so far, and I should prefer making one effort of it. When I spoke to Dr. Harley, I had nothing like so much to tell. You are a philosophic physician. You give spirit its proper rank. If this thing is real——"

He paused looking at me with agitated inquiry.

"We can discuss it by-and-by, and very fully. I will give you all I think," I answered, after an interval.

"Well—very well. If it is anything real, I say, it is prevailing, little by little, and drawing me more interiorly into hell. Optic nerves, he talked of. Ah! well—there are other nerves of communication. May God Almighty help me! You shall hear.

"Its power of action, I tell you, had increased. Its malice became, in a way, aggressive. About two years ago, some questions that were pending between me and the bishop having been settled, I went down to my parish in Warwickshire, anxious to find occupation in my profession. I was not prepared for what happened, although I have since thought I might have apprehended something like it. The reason of my saying so is this——"

He was beginning to speak with a great deal more effort and reluctance, and sighed often, and seemed at times nearly overcome. But at this time his manner was not agitated. It was more like that of a sinking patient, who has given himself up.

"Yes, but I will first tell you about Kenlis, my parish.

"It was with me when I left this place for Dawlbridge. It was my silent travelling companion, and it remained with me at the vicarage. When I entered on the discharge of my duties, another change took place. The thing exhibited an atrocious determination to thwart me. It was with me in the church—in the reading-desk—in the pulpit—within the communion rails. At last, it reached this extremity, that while I was reading to the congregation, it would spring upon the book and squat there, so that I was unable to see the page. This happened more than once.

"I left Dawlbridge for a time. I placed myself in Dr. Harley's hands. I did everything he told me. He gave my case a great deal of thought. It interested him, I think. He seemed successful. For nearly three months I was perfectly free from a return. I began to think I was safe. With his full assent I returned to Dawlbridge.

"I travelled in a chaise. I was in good spirits. I was more—I was happy and grateful. I was returning, as I thought, delivered from a dreadful hallucination, to the scene of duties which I longed to enter upon. It was a beautiful sunny evening, everything looked serene and cheerful, and I was delighted. I remember looking out of the window to see the spire of my church at Kenlis among the trees, at the point where one has the earliest view of it. It is exactly where the little stream that bounds the parish passes under the road by a culvert, and where it emerges at the road-side, a stone with an old inscription is placed. As we passed this point, I drew my head in and sat down, and in the corner of the chaise was the monkey.

"For a moment I felt faint, and then quite wild with despair and horror. I called to the driver, and got out, and sat down at the road-side, and prayed to God silently for mercy. A despairing resignation supervened. My companion was with me as I re-entered the vicarage. The same persecution followed. After a short struggle I submitted, and soon I left the place.

"I told you," he said, "that the beast has before this become in certain ways aggressive. I will explain a little. It seemed to be actuated by intense and increasing fury, whenever I said my prayers, or even meditated prayer. It amounted at last to a dreadful interruption. You will ask, how could a silent immaterial phantom effect that? It was thus, whenever I meditated praying; It was always before me, and nearer and nearer.

"It used to spring on a table, on the back of a chair, on the chimney-piece, and slowly to swing itself from side to side, looking at me all the time. There is in its motion an indefinable power to dissipate thought, and to contract one's attention to that monotony, till the ideas shrink, as it were, to a point, and at last to nothing—and unless I had started up, and shook off the catalepsy I have felt as if my mind were on the point of losing itself. There are other ways," he sighed heavily; "thus, for instance, while I pray with my eyes closed, it comes closer and closer, and I see it. I know it is not to be accounted for physically, but I do actually see it, though my lids are closed, and so it rocks my mind, as it were, and overpowers me, and I am obliged to rise from my knees. If you had ever yourself known this, you would be acquainted with desperation."

CHAPTER IX

The Third Stage

"I see, Dr. Hesselius, that you don't lose one word of my statement. I need not ask you to listen specially to what I am now going to tell you. They talk of the optic nerves, and of spectral illusions, as if the organ of sight was the only point assailable by the influences that have fastened upon me—I know better. For two years in my direful case that limitation prevailed. But as food is taken in softly at the lips, and then brought under the teeth, as the tip of the little finger caught in a mill crank will draw in the hand, and the arm, and the whole body, so the miserable mortal who has been once caught firmly by the end of the finest fibre of his nerve, is drawn in and in, by the enormous machinery of hell, until he is as I am. Yes, Doctor, as *I* am, for while I talk to you, and implore relief, I feel that my prayer is for the impossible, and my pleading with the inexorable."

I endeavoured to calm his visibly increasing agitation, and told him that he must not despair.

While we talked the night had overtaken us. The filmy moonlight was wide over the scene which the window commanded, and I said:

"Perhaps you would prefer having candles. This light, you know, is odd. I should wish you, as much as possible, under your usual conditions while I make my diagnosis, shall I call it—otherwise I don't care."

"All lights are the same to me," he said; "except when I read or write, I care not if night were perpetual. I am going to tell you what happened about a year ago. The thing began to speak to me."

"Speak! How do you mean—speak as a man does, do you mean?"

"Yes; speak in words and consecutive sentences, with perfect coherence and articulation; but there is a peculiarity. It is not like the tone of a human voice. It is not by my ears it reaches me—it comes like a singing through my head.

"This faculty, the power of speaking to me, will be my undoing. It won't let me pray, it interrupts me with dreadful blasphemies. I dare not go on, I could not. Oh! Doctor, can the skill, and thought, and prayers of man avail me nothing!"

"You must promise me, my dear sir, not to trouble yourself with unnecessarily exciting thoughts; confine yourself strictly to the narrative of *facts*; and recollect, above all, that even if the thing that infests you be, you seem to suppose a reality with an actual independent life and will, yet it can have no power to hurt you, unless it be given from above: its access to your senses depends mainly upon your physical condition—this is, under God, your comfort and reliance: we are all alike environed. It is only that in your case, the '*paries*,' the veil of the flesh, the screen, is a little out of repair, and sights and sounds are transmitted. We must enter on a new course sir,—be encouraged. I'll give to-night to the careful consideration of the whole case."

"You are very good, sir; you think it worth trying, you don't give me quite up; but, sir, you don't know, it is gaining such an influence over me: it orders me about, it is such a tyrant, and I'm growing so helpless. May God deliver me!"

"It orders you about—of course you mean by speech?"

"Yes, yes; it is always urging me to crimes, to injure others, or myself. You see, Doctor, the situation is urgent, it is indeed. When I was in Shropshire, a few weeks ago" (Mr. Jennings was speaking rapidly and trembling now, holding my arm with one hand, and looking in my face), "I went out one day with a party of friends for a walk: my persecutor, I tell you, was with me at the time. I lagged behind the rest: the country near the Dee, you know, is beautiful. Our path happened to lie near a coal mine, and at the verge of the wood is a perpendicular shaft, they say, a hundred and fifty feet deep. My niece had remained behind with me— she knows, of course nothing of the nature of my sufferings. She knew, however, that I had been ill, and was low, and she remained to prevent my being quite alone. As we loitered slowly on together, the brute that accompanied me was urging me to throw myself down the shaft. I tell you now—oh, sir, think of it!—the one consideration that saved me from that hideous death was the fear lest the shock of witnessing the occurrence should be too much for the poor girl. I asked her to go on and walk with her friends, saying that I could go no further. She made excuses, and the more I urged her the firmer she became. She looked doubtful and frightened. I suppose there was something in my looks or manner that alarmed her; but she would not go, and that literally saved me. You had no idea, sir, that a living man could be made so abject a slave of Satan," he said, with a ghastly groan and a shudder.

There was a pause here, and I said, "You *were* preserved nevertheless. It was the act of God. You are in His hands and in the power of no other being: be therefore confident for the future."

CHAPTER X

Home

I made him have candles lighted, and saw the room looking cheery and inhabited before I left him. I told him that he must regard his illness strictly as one dependent on physical, though *subtle* physical causes. I told him that he had evidence of God's care and love in the deliverance which he had just described, and that I had perceived with pain that he seemed to regard its peculiar features as indicating that he had been delivered over to spiritual reprobation. Than such a conclusion nothing could be, I insisted, less warranted; and not only so, but more contrary to facts, as disclosed in his mysterious deliverance from that murderous influence during his Shropshire excursion. First, his niece had been retained by his side without his intending to keep her near him; and, secondly, there had been infused into his mind an irresistible repugnance to execute the dreadful suggestion in her presence.

As I reasoned this point with him, Mr. Jennings wept. He seemed comforted. One promise I exacted, which was that should the monkey at any time return, I should be sent for immediately; and, repeating my assurance that I would give neither time nor thought to any other subject until I had thoroughly investigated his case, and that to-morrow he should hear the result, I took my leave.

Before getting into the carriage I told the servant that his master was far from well, and that he should make a point of frequently looking into his room.

My own arrangements I made with a view to being quite secure from interruption.

I merely called at my lodgings, and with a travelling-desk and carpet-bag, set off in a hackney carriage for an inn about two miles out of town, called "The Horns," a very quiet and comfortable house, with good thick walls. And there I resolved, without the possibility of intrusion or distraction, to devote some hours of the night, in my com-

fortable sitting-room, to Mr. Jennings' case, and so much of the morning
as it might require.

(There occurs here a careful note of Dr. Hesselius' opinion upon the
case, and of the habits, dietary, and medicines which he prescribed. It is
curious—some persons would say mystical. But, on the whole, I doubt
whether it would sufficiently interest a reader of the kind I am likely to
meet with, to warrant its being here reprinted. The whole letter was
plainly written at the inn where he had hid himself for the occasion. The
next letter is dated from his town lodgings.)

I left town for the inn where I slept last night at half-past nine, and did
not arrive at my room in town until one o'clock this afternoon. I found
a letter in Mr. Jennings' hand upon my table. It had not come by post,
and, on inquiry, I learned that Mr. Jennings' servant had brought it, and
on learning that I was not to return until to-day, and that no one could
tell him my address, he seemed very uncomfortable, and said his orders
from his master were that he was not to return without an answer.

I opened the letter and read:

> Dear Dr. Hesselius.—It is here. You had not been an hour gone when it re-
> turned. It is speaking. It knows all that has happened. It knows everything—it
> knows you, and is frantic and atrocious. It reviles. I send you this. It knows every
> word I have written—I write. This I promised, and I therefore write, but I fear very
> confused, very incoherently. I am so interrupted, disturbed.
>   Ever yours, sincerely yours,
>   Robert Lynder Jennings

"When did this come?" I asked.

"About eleven last night: the man was here again, and has been here
three times to-day. The last time is about an hour since."

Thus answered, and with the notes I had made upon his case in my
pocket, I was in a few minutes driving towards Richmond, to see Mr. Jennings.

I by no means, as you perceive, despaired of Mr. Jennings' case. He had
himself remembered and applied, though quite in a mistaken way, the
principle which I lay down in my Metaphysical Medicine, and which
governs all such cases. I was about to apply it in earnest. I was profoundly interested, and very anxious to see and examine him while the "enemy" was actually present.

I drove up to the sombre house, and ran up the steps, and knocked. The
door, in a little time, was opened by a tall woman in black silk. She looked
ill, and as if she had been crying. She curtseyed, and heard my question,

but she did not answer. She turned her face away, extending her hand towards two men who were coming down-stairs; and thus having, as it were, tacitly made me over to them, she passed through a side-door hastily and shut it.

The man who was nearest the hall, I at once accosted, but being now close to him, I was shocked to see that both his hands were covered with blood.

I drew back a little, and the man, passing downstairs, merely said in a low tone, "Here's the servant, sir."

The servant had stopped on the stairs, confounded and dumb at seeing me. He was rubbing his hands in a handkerchief, and it was steeped in blood.

"Jones, what is it? what has happened?" I asked, while a sickening suspicion overpowered me.

The man asked me to come up to the lobby. I was beside him in a moment, and, frowning and pallid, with contracted eyes, he told me the horror which I already half guessed.

His master had made away with himself.

I went upstairs with him to the room—what I saw there I won't tell you. He had cut his throat with his razor. It was a frightful gash. The two men had laid him on the bed, and composed his limbs. It had happened, as the immense pool of blood on the floor declared, at some distance between the bed and the window. There was carpet round his bed, and a carpet under his dressing-table, but none on the rest of the floor, for the man said he did not like a carpet on his bedroom. In this sombre and now terrible room, one of the great elms that darkened the house was slowly moving the shadow of one of its great boughs upon this dreadful floor.

I beckoned to the servant, and we went downstairs together. I turned off the hall into an old-fashioned panelled room, and there standing, I heard all the servant had to tell. It was not a great deal.

"I concluded, sir, from your words, and looks, sir, as you left last night, that you thought my master was seriously ill. I thought it might be that you were afraid of a fit, or something. So I attended very close to your directions. He sat up late, till past three o'clock. He was not writing or reading. He was talking a great deal to himself, but that was nothing unusual. At about that hour I assisted him to undress, and left him in his slippers and dressing-gown. I went back softly in about half-an-hour. He was in his bed, quite undressed, and a pair of candles lighted on the table beside his bed. He was leaning on his elbow, and looking out at the other side of the bed when I came in. I asked him if he wanted anything, and he said No.

"I don't know whether it was what you said to me, sir, or something a little unusual about him, but I was uneasy, uncommon uneasy about him last night.

"In another half hour, or it might be a little more, I went up again. I did not hear him talking as before. I opened the door a little. The candles were both out, which was not usual. I had a bedroom candle, and I let the light in, a little bit, looking softly round. I saw him sitting in that chair beside the dressing-table with his clothes on again. He turned round and looked at me. I thought it strange he should get up and dress, and put out the candles to sit in the dark, that way. But I only asked him again if I could do anything for him. He said, No, rather sharp, I thought. I asked him if I might light the candles, and he said, 'Do as you like, Jones.' So I lighted them, and I lingered about the room, and he said, "Tell me the truth, Jones; why did you come again—you did not hear anyone cursing?' 'No, sir,' I said, wondering what he could mean.

" 'No,' said he, after me, 'of course, no;' and I said to him, 'Wouldn't it be well, sir, you went to bed? It's just five o'clock;' and he said nothing, but, 'Very likely; good-night, Jones.' So I went, sir, but in less than an hour I came again. The door was fast, and he heard me, and called as I thought from the bed to know what I wanted, and he desired me not to disturb him again. I lay down and slept for a little. It must have been between six and seven when I went up again. The door was still fast, and he made no answer, so I did not like to disturb him, and thinking he was asleep, I left him till nine. It was his custom to ring when he wished me to come, and I had no particular hour for calling him. I tapped very gently, and getting no answer, I stayed away a good while, supposing he was getting some rest then. It was not till eleven o'clock I grew really uncomfortable about him—for at the latest he was never, that I could remember, later than half-past ten. I got no answer. I knocked and called, and still no answer. So not being able to force the door, I called Thomas from the stables, and together we forced it, and found him in the shocking way you saw."

Jones had no more to tell. Poor Mr. Jennings was very gentle, and very kind. All his people were fond of him. I could see that the servant was very much moved.

So, dejected and agitated, I passed from that terrible house, and its dark canopy of elms, and I hope I shall never see it more. While I write to you I feel like a man who has but half waked from a frightful and monotonous dream. My memory rejects the picture with incredulity and horror. Yet I know it is true. It is the story of the process of a poison, a poison which excites the reciprocal action of spirit and nerve, and paralyses the tissue that separates those cognate functions of the senses, the external and the interior. Thus we find strange bed-fellows, and the mortal and immortal prematurely make acquaintance.

CONCLUSION

A Word for Those Who Suffer

My dear Van L—, you have suffered from an affection similar to that which I have just described. You twice complained of a return of it.

Who, under God, cured you? Your humble servant, Martin Hesselius. Let me rather adopt the more emphasised piety of a certain good old French surgeon of three hundred years ago: "I treated, and God cured you."

Come, my friend, you are not to be hippish. Let me tell you a fact.

I have met with, and treated, as my book shows, fifty-seven cases of this kind of vision, which I term indifferently "sublimated," "precocious," and "interior."

There is another class of affections which are truly termed—though commonly confounded with those which I describe—spectral illusions. These latter I look upon upon as being no less simply curable than a cold in the head or a trifling dyspepsia.

It is those which rank in the first category that test our promptitude of thought. Fifty-seven such cases have I encounteed, neither more nor less. And in how many of these have I failed? In no one single instance.

There is no one affliction of mortality more easily and certainly reducible, with a little patience, and a rational confidence in the physician. With these simple conditions, I look upon the cure as absolutely certain.

You are to remember that I had not even commenced to treat Mr. Jennings' case. I have not any doubt that I should have cured him perfectly in eighteen months, or possibly it might have extended to two years. Some cases are very rapidly curable, others extremely tedious. Every intelligent physician who will give thought and diligence to the task, will effect a cure.

You know my tract on "The Cardinal Functions of the Brain." I there, by the evidence of innumerable facts, prove, as I think, the high probability of a circulation arterial and venous in its mechanism, through the nerves. Of this system, thus considered, the brain is the heart. The fluid, which is propagated hence through one class of nerves, returns in an altered state through another, and the nature of that fluid is spiritual, though not immaterial, any more than, as I before remarked, light or electricity are so.

By various abuses, among which the habitual use of such agents as green tea is one, this fluid may be affected as to its quality, but it is more frequently disturbed as to equilibrium. This fluid being that which we have in common with spirits, a congestion found upon the masses of brain or nerve, connected with the interior sense, forms a surface unduly exposed, on which disembodied spirits may operate: communication is thus more or less effectually established. Between this brain circulation and the heart circulation there is an intimate sympathy. The seat, or rather the instrument of exterior vision, is the eye. The seat of interior vision is the nervous tissue and brain, immediately about and above the eyebrow. You remember how effectually I dissipated your pictures by the simple application of iced eau-de-cologne. Few cases, however, can be treated exactly alike with anything like rapid success. Cold acts powerfully as a repellant of the nervous fluid. Long enough continued it will even produce that permanent insensibility which we call numbness, and a little longer, muscular as well as sensational paralysis.

I have not, I repeat, the slightest doubt that I should have first dimmed and ultimately sealed that inner eye which Mr. Jennings had inadvertently opened. The same senses are opened in delirium tremens, and entirely shut up again when the overaction of the cerebral heart, and the prodigious nervous congestions that attend it, are terminated by a decided change in the state of the body. It is by acting steadily upon the body, by a simple process, that this result is produced—and inevitably produced—I have never yet failed.

Poor Mr. Jennings made away with himself. But that catastrophe was the result of a totally different malady, which, as it were, projected itself upon the disease which was established. His case was in the distinctive manner a complication, and the complaint under which he really succumbed, was hereditary suicidal mania. Poor Mr. Jennings I cannot call a patient of mine, for I had not even begun to treat his case, and he had not yet given me, I am convinced, his full and unreserved confidence. If the patient do not array himself on the side of the disease, his cure is certain.

III.   THE ANTIQUARIAN GHOST STORY

M. R. JAMES

Count Magnus (1904)

The Ash-Tree (1904)

Montague Rhodes James was one of the most scrupulous and distinguished medieval scholars of the early twentieth century; he was also, according to poet John Betjeman, "the greatest master of the ghost story." More precisely, he was the master of the antiquarian ghost story, a subgenre he both inaugurated and developed to the ultimate degree of polish and refinement.

James's personae are upper-class British antiquaries whose scholarly enthusiasms get them into some very nasty, frequently fatal trouble. The antiquarian exotica with which they surround themselves—old books, engravings, coins, and even such things as ancient whistles and dolls' houses—give these Edwardian reactionaries an illusory sense of stability —illusory because it is precisely this collector's mania and obsession with the past that invokes intruders from the other side of the grave. It is ironic that James, himself a meticulous antiquary, consistently presented history and the antiquarian's preoccupation with it as a doorway to terror and tragedy.

Although James claimed to be merely an imitator of Le Fanu, whose works he revived in his famous edition of Le Fanu stories (*Madam Crowl's Ghost*, 1923), he was a distinctly original stylist. The "deliberateness" and "leisureliness" he praised in the introduction to *Madam Crowl's Ghost* were clearly inspirational, but his own style has an economy and a radical emphasis on unseen—or very briefly seen—horrors which Le Fanu never attempted. James was far more influential than he pretended to be, and the imprint of his sensibility can be clearly seen in the work of Malden, Swain, Wakefield, and other antiquarian writers.

"Count Magnus" is one of James's most refined yet most horrific tales. Among its many felicitous details are an amusingly described but terrifying engraving which prefigures the action; a sarcophagus that refuses to stay closed; and a terse ship's log, again both droll and frightening, which obliquely describes certain passengers' peculiar dining habits. As is often the case with James, the civilized stylistic veneer, filled with all manner of exotic and scholarly allusions, masks something truly monstrous. What ultimately happens to Mr. Wraxall, the besieged antiquary, is only hinted at in a landlord's grisly horror story from the past, but that tale within a tale, the key to the story, is explicit enough (indeed, more explicit than we might have liked) to explain the decidedly strange behavior of the jurors at the story's end.

The reader may well ask, as does the pitiable Mr. Wraxall in his cries to God, what he has done to merit the horror that overtakes him. Is the addiction to rare books really the moral explanation? Or is "over-inquisitiveness," like green tea in Le Fanu's tale, a cover story, a desperate attempt to explain the inexplicable? Mr. Wraxall may be close to the terrible truth when he implies, in the despairing pages of his journal, that doctors, policemen, and parsons, all principals of order and revelation, are impotent in the face of something totally disordered and mysterious.

In "The Ash-Tree" the connection between cause and effect is a bit tidier. The horror in the story, after all, is the result of a witch's curse. Nevertheless, Sir Matthew Fell, the object of the curse, is not guilty of hubris: he is not, as in a mummy tale, the rifler of a tomb or, as in an ecological horror story, a despoiler of nature. On the contrary, he is a decent man, one "not specially infected with the witch-hunting mania," whose only sin is telling the truth. The moral landscape may not be as bleak as in "Count Magnus," James's most uncompromising tale, but it is far from comforting.

The technique of "The Ash-Tree" is classically Jamesian. The tale opens with a deceptively amiable "digression" on English country houses, with not a single element of Gothic foreboding, then moves to "a curious series of events" recounted through an elaborate series of seventeenth- and eighteenth-century documents presented by a detached antiquarian narrator. The climax, one far more jolting than we get in "Count Magnus," grows out of tantalizing hints, usually prefaced by phrases like "the seemingly meaningless words . . . " or "though it sounded foolish . . .".

The basic form in each of these stories is a variation on an old theme, a technique James honed to perfection. Ostensibly, both are black-magic stories, one involving sorcery, the other witchcraft, but James's treatment of these traditional, somewhat trite subjects is so fiendishly original that the reader almost forgets the basic concept. Sorcerors and witches are far less interesting than what springs out of Count Magnus's sarcophagus or crawls out of Sir Matthew's ash-tree.

≋ COUNT MAGNUS ≋

By what means the papers out of which I have made a connected story came into my hands is the last point which the reader will learn from these pages. But it is necessary to prefix to my extracts from them a statement of the form in which I possess them.

They consist, then, partly of a series of collections for a book of travels, such a volume as was a common product of the forties and fifties. Horace Marryat's *Journal of a Residence in Jutland and the Danish Isles* is a fair specimen of the class to which I allude. These books usually treated of some unfamiliar district on the Continent. They were illustrated with woodcuts or steel plates. They gave details of hotel accommodation, and of means of communication, such as we now expect to find in any well-regulated guide-book, and they dealt largely in reported conversations with intelligent foreigners, racy innkeepers and garrulous peasants. In a word, they were chatty.

Begun with the idea of furnishing material for such a book, my papers as they progressed assumed the character of a record of one single personal experience, and this record was continued up to the very eve, almost, of its termination.

The writer was a Mr. Wraxall. For my knowledge of him I have to depend entirely on the evidence his writings afford, and from these I deduce that he was a man past middle age, possessed of some private means, and very much alone in the world. He had, it seems, no settled abode in England, but was a denizen of hotels and boarding-houses. It is probable that he entertained the idea of settling down at some future time which never came; and I think it also likely that the Pantechnicon fire in the early seventies must have destroyed a great deal that would have thrown light on his antecedents, for he refers once or twice to property of his that was warehoused at that establishment.

It is further apparent that Mr. Wraxall had published a book, and that it treated of a holiday he had once taken in Brittany. More than this I cannot say about his work, because a diligent search in bibliographical works has convinced me that it must have appeared either anonymously or under a pseudonym.

As to his character, it is not difficult to form some superficial opinion. He must have been an intelligent and cultivated man. It seems that he was near being a Fellow of his college at Oxford—Brasenose, as I judge from the Calendar. His besetting fault was pretty clearly that of over-inquisitiveness, possibly a good fault in a traveller, certainly a fault for which this traveller paid dearly enough in the end.

On what proved to be his last expedition, he was plotting another book. Scandinavia, a region not widely known to Englishmen forty years ago, had struck him as in interesting field. He must have lighted on some old books of Swedish history or memoirs, and the idea had struck him that there was room for a book descriptive of travel in Sweden, interspersed with episodes from the history of some of the great Swedish families. He procured letters of introduction, therefore, to some persons of quality in Sweden, and set out thither in the early summer of 1863.

Of his travels in the North there is no need to speak, nor of his residence of some weeks in Stockholm. I need only mention that some *savant* resident there put him on the track of an important collection of family papers belonging to the proprietors of an ancient manor-house in Vester-gothland, and obtained for him permission to examine them.

The manor-house, or *herrgård*, in question is to be called Råbäck (pronounced something like Roebeck), though that is not its name. It is one of the best buildings of its kind in all the country, and the picture of it in Dahlenberg's *Suecia antiqua et moderna*, engraved in 1694, shows it very much as the tourist may see it to-day. It was built soon after 1600, and is, roughly speaking, very much like an English house of that period in respect of material—red-brick with stone facings—and style. The man who built it was a scion of the great house of De la Gardie, and his descendants possess it still. De la Gardie is the name by which I will designate them when mention of them becomes necessary.

They received Mr. Wraxall with great kindness and courtesy, and pressed him to stay in the house as long as his researches lasted. But, preferring to be independent, and mistrusting his powers of conversing in Swedish, he settled himself at the village inn, which turned out quite sufficiently comfortable, at any rate during the summer months. This arrangement would entail a short walk daily to and from the manor-house of something under a mile. The house itself stood in a park, and was protected—we should say grown up—with large old timber. Near it you found the walled garden, and then entered a close wood fringing one of the small lakes with which the whole country is pitted. Then came the wall of the demesne, and you climbed a steep knoll—a knob of rock lightly covered with soil—and on the top of this stood the church, fenced in with tall dark trees. It was a curious building to English eyes. The nave and aisles were low, and filled with pews and galleries. In the western gallery stood the handsome old organ, gaily painted, and with silver pipes. The ceiling was flat, and had been adorned by a seventeenth-century artist with a strange and hideous "Last Judgment," full of lurid flames, falling cities, burning ships, crying souls, and brown and smiling demons. Handsome brass coronae hung from the roof; the pulpit was like a doll's-house, covered with little painted wooden cherubs and saints; a stand with three hour-glasses was hinged to the preacher's desk. Such sights as these may be seen in many a church in Sweden now, but what distinguished this one was an addition to the original building. At the eastern end of the north aisle the builder of the manor-house had erected a mausoleum for himself and his family. It was a largish eight-sided building, lighted by a series of oval windows, and it had a domed roof, topped by a kind of pumpkin-shaped object rising into a spire, a form in which Swedish architects greatly delighted. The roof was of copper externally, and was painted black, while the walls, in common with those of the church, were staringly white. To this mausoleum there was no access from the church. It had a portal and steps of its own on the northern side.

Past the churchyard the path to the village goes, and not more than three or four minutes bring you to the inn door.

On the first day of his stay at Råbäk Mr. Wraxall found the church door open, and made those notes of the interior which I have epitomized. Into the mausoleum, however, he could not make his way. He could by looking through the keyhole just descry that there were fine marble effigies and sarcophagi of copper, and a wealth of armorial ornament, which made him very anxious to spend some time in investigation.

The papers he had come to examine at the manor-house proved to be of just the kind he wanted for his book. There were family correspondence, journals, and account-books of the earliest owners of the estate, very carefully kept and clearly written, full of amusing and picturesque detail. The first De la Gardie appeared in them as a strong and capable man. Shortly after the building of the mansion there had been a period of distress in the district, and the peasants had risen and attacked several chateaux and done some damage. The owner of Råbäck took a leading part in suppressing the trouble, and there was reference to executions of ring-leaders and severe punishments inflicted with no sparing hand.

The portrait of this Magnus de la Gardie was one of the best in the house, and Mr. Wraxall studied it with no little interest after his day's work. He gives no detailed description of it, but I gather that the face impressed him rather by its power than by its beauty or goodness; in fact, he writes that Count Magnus was an almost phenomenally ugly man.

On this day Mr. Wraxall took his supper with the family, and walked back in the late but still bright evening.

"I must remember," he writes, "to ask the sexton if he can let me into the mausoleum at the church. He evidently has access to it himself, for I saw him to-night standing on the steps, and, as I thought, locking or unlocking the door."

I find that early on the following day Mr. Wraxall had some conversation with his landlord. His setting it down at such length as he does surprised me at first; but I soon realized that the papers I was reading were, at least in their beginning, the materials for the book he was meditating, and that it was to have been one of those quasi-journalistic productions which admit of the introduction of an admixture of conversational matter.

His object, he says, was to find out whether any traditions of Count Magnus de la Gardie lingered on in the scenes of that gentleman's activity, and whether the popular estimate of him were favourable or not. He found that the Count was decidedly not a favourite. If his tenants came late to their work on the days which they owed to him as Lord of the Manor, they were set on the wooden horse, or flogged and branded in the manor-house yard. One or two cases were of men who had occupied lands which encroached the lord's domain, and whose houses had been mysteriously burnt on a winter's night, with the whole family inside. But what seemed to dwell on the innkeeper's mind most—for he returned to the subject more than once—was that the Count had been on the Black Pilgrimage, and had brought something or someone back with him.

You will naturally inquire, as Mr. Wraxall did, what the Black Pilgrimage may have been. But your curiosity on the point must remain unsatisfied for the time being, just as his did. The landlord was evidently unwilling to give a full answer, or indeed any answer, on the point, and, being called out for a moment, trotted off with obvious alacrity, only putting his head in at the door a few minutes afterwards to say that he was called away to Skara, and could not be back till evening.

So Mr. Wraxall had to go unsatisfied to his day's work at the manor-house. The papers on which he was just then engaged soon put his thoughts into another channel, for he had to occupy himself with glancing over the correspondence between Sophia Albertina in Stockholm and her married cousin Ulrica Leonora at Råbäck in the years 1705-1710. The letters were of exceptional interest from the light they threw upon the culture of that period in Sweden, as anyone can testify who has read the full edition of them in the publications of the Swedish Historical Manuscripts Commission.

In the afternoon he had done with these, and after returning the boxes in which they were kept to their places on the shelf, he proceeded, very naturally, to take down some of the volumes nearest to them, in order to determine which of them had best be his principal subject of investigation next day. The shelf he had hit upon was occupied mostly by a collection of account-books in the writing of the first Count Magnus. But one among them was not an account-book, but a book of alchemical and other tracts in another sixteenth-century hand. Not being very familiar with alchemical literature, Mr. Wraxall spends much space which he might have spared in setting out the names and beginnings of the various treaties: The book of the Phœnix, book of the Thirty Words, book of the Toad, book of Miriam, Turba philosophorum, and so forth; and then he announces with a good deal of circumstances his delight at finding, on a leaf originally left blank near the middle of the book, some writing of Count Magnus himself headed "Liber nigræ peregrinationis." It is true that only a few lines were written, but there was quite enough to show that the landlord had that morning been referring to a belief at least as old as the time of Count Magnus, and probably shared by him. This is the English of what was written:

"If any man desires to obtain a long life, if he would obtain a faithful messenger and see the blood of his enemies, it is necessary that he should first go into the city of Chorazin, and there salute the prince. . . ." Here there was an erasure of one word, not very thoroughly done, so that Mr. Wraxall felt pretty sure that he was right in reading it as *aëris* ("of the air"). But there was no more of the text copied, only a line in Latin: "Quære reliqua hujus materiei inter secretiora" (See the rest of this matter among the more private things).

It could not be denied that this threw a rather lurid light upon the tastes and beliefs of the Count; but to Mr. Wraxall, separated from him by nearly three centuries, the thought that he might have added to his general forcefulness alchemy, and to alchemy something like magic, only made him a more picturesque figure; and when, after a rather prolonged

contemplation of his picture in the hall, Mr. Wraxall set out on his homeward way, his mind was full of the thought of Count Magnus. He had no
eyes for his surroundings, no perception of the evening scents of the
woods or the evening light on the lake; and when all of a sudden he pulled
up short, he was astonished to find himself already at the gate of the
churchyard, and within a few minutes of his dinner. His eyes fell on the
mausoleum.

"Ah," he said, "Count Magnus, there you are. I should dearly like to
see you."

"Like many solitary men," he writes, "I have a habit of talking to myself aloud; and, unlike some of the Greek and Latin particles, I do not expect an answer. Certainly, and perhaps fortunately in this case, there was
neither voice nor any that regarded: only the woman who, I suppose, was
cleaning up the church, dropped some metallic object on the floor, whose
clang startled me. Count Magnus, I think, sleeps sound enough."

That same evening the landlord of the inn, who had heard Mr. Wraxall
say that he wished to see the clerk or deacon (as he would be called in
Sweden) of the parish, introduced him to that official in the inn parlour.
A visit to the De la Gardie tombhouse was soon arranged for the next day,
and a little general conversation ensued.

Mr. Wraxall, remembering that one function of Scandinavian deacons
is to teach candidates for Confirmation, thought he would refresh his own
memory on a Biblical point.

"Can you tell me," he said, "anything about Chorazin?"

The deacon seemed startled, but readily reminded him how that village
had once been denounced.

"To be sure, " said Mr. Wraxall; "it is, I suppose, quite a ruin
now?"

"So I expect," replied the deacon. "I have heard some of our old
priests say that Antichrist is to be born there; and there are tales—"

"Ah! what tales are those?" Mr. Wraxall put in.

"Tales, I was going to say, which I have forgotten," said the deacon;
and soon after that he said good night.

The landlord was now alone, and at Mr. Wraxall's mercy; and that
inquirer was not inclined to spare him.

"Herr Nielsen," he said, "I have found out something about the Black
Pilgrimage. You may as well tell me what you know. What did the Count
bring back with him?"

Swedes are habitually slow, perhaps, in answering, or perhaps the land-

lord was an exception. I am not sure; but Mr. Wraxall notes that the landlord spent at least one minute in looking at him before he said anything at
all. Then he came close up to his guest, and with a good deal of effort he
spoke:

"Mr. Wraxall, I can tell you this one little tale, and no more—not any
more. You must not ask anything when I have done. In my grandfather's
time—that is, ninety-two years ago—there were two men who said: 'The
Count is dead; we do not care for him. We will go to-night and have a
free hunt in his wood'—the long wood on the hill that you have seen behind Råbäck. Well, those that heard them say this, they said: 'No, do not
go; we are sure you will meet with persons walking who should not be
walking. They should be resting, not walking.' These men laughed. There
were no forest-men to keep the wood, because no one wished to hunt
there. The family were not here at the house. These men could do what
they wished.

"Very well, they go to the wood that night. My grandfather was sitting
here in this room. It was the summer, and a light night. With the window
open, he could see out to the wood, and hear.

"So he sat there, and two or three men with him, and they listened. At
first they hear nothing at all; then they hear someone—you know how far
away it is—they hear someone scream, just as if the most inside part of his
soul was twisted out of him. All of them in the room caught hold of each
other, and they sat so for three-quarters of an hour. Then they hear someone else, only about three hundred ells off. They hear him laugh out loud:
it was not one of those two men that laughed, and, indeed, they have all of
them said that it was not any man at all. After that they hear a great door
shut.

"Then, when it was just light with the sun, they all went to the priest.
They said to him:

" 'Father, put on your gown and your ruff, and come to bury these
men, Anders Bjornsen and Hans Thorbjorn.'

"You understand that they were sure these men were dead. So they
went to the wood—my grandfather never forgot this. He said they were
all like so many dead men themselves. The priest, too, he was in a white
fear. He said when they came to him:

" 'I heard one cry in the night, and I heard one laugh afterwards. If I
cannot forget that, I shall not be able to sleep again.'

"So they went to the wood, and they found these men on the edge of
the wood. Hans Thorbjorn was standing with his back against a tree, and

all the time he was pushing with his hands—pushing something away from him which was not there. So he was not dead. And they led him away, and took him to the house at Nykjoping, and he died before the winter; but he went on pushing with his hands. Also Anders Bjornsen was there; but he was dead. And I tell you this about Anders Bjornsen, that he was once a beautiful man, but now his face was not there, because the flesh of it was sucked away off the bones. You understand that? My grandfather did not forget that. And they laid him on the bier which they brought, and they put a cloth over his head, and the priest walked before; and they began to sing the psalm for the dead as well as they could. So, as they were singing the end of the first verse, one fell down, who was carrying the head of the bier, and the others looked back, and they saw that the cloth had fallen off, and the eyes of Anders Bjornsen were looking up, because there was nothing to close over them. And this they could not bear. Therefore the priest laid the cloth upon him, and sent for a spade, and they buried him in that place."

The next day Mr. Wraxall records that the deacon called for him soon after his breakfast, and took him to the church and mausoleum. He noticed that the key of the latter was hung on a nail just by the pulpit, and it occurred to him that, as the church door seemed to be left unlocked as a rule, it would not be difficult for him to pay a second and more private visit to the monuments if there proved to be more of interest among them than could be digested at first. The building, when he entered it, he found not unimposing. The monuments, mostly large erections of the seventeenth and eighteenth centuries, were dignified if luxuriant, and the epitaphs and heraldry were copious. The central space of the domed room was occupied by three copper sarcophagi, covered with finely-engraved ornament. Two of them had, as is commonly the case in Denmark and Sweden, a large metal crucifix on the lid. The third, that of Count Magnus, as it appeared, had, instead of that, a full-length effigy engraved upon it, and round the edge were several bands of similar ornament representing various scenes. One was a battle, with cannon belching out smoke, and walled towns, and troops of pikemen. Another showed an execution. In a third, among trees, was a man running at full speed, with flying hair and outstretched hands. After him followed a strange form; it would be hard to say whether the artist had intended it for a man, and was unable to give the requisite similitude, or whether it was intentionally made as monstrous as it looked. In view of the skill with which the rest of the drawing was done, Mr. Wraxall felt inclined to adopt the latter idea.

The figure was unduly short, and was for the most part muffled in a hooded garment which swept the ground. The only part of the form which projected from that shelter was not shaped like any hand or arm. Mr. Wraxall compares it to the tentacle of a devil-fish, and continues: "On seeing this, I said to myself, 'This, then, which is evidently an allegorical representation of some kind—a fiend pursuing a hunted soul—may be the origin of the story of Count Magnus and his mysterious companion. Let us see how the huntsman is pictured: doubtless it will be a demon blowing his horn.' " But, as it turned out, there was no such sensational figure, only the semblance of a cloaked man on a hillock, who stood leaning on a stick, and watching the hunt with an interest which the engraver had tried to express in his attitude.

Mr. Wraxall noted the finely-worked and massive steel padlocks—three in number—which secured the sarcophagus. One of them, he saw, was detached, and lay on the pavement. And then, unwilling to delay the deacon longer or to waste his own working-time, he made his way onward to the manor-house.

"It is curious," he notes, "how on retracing a familiar path one's thoughts engross one to the absolute exclusion of surrounding objects. To-night, for the second time, I had entirely failed to notice where I was going (I had planned a private visit to the tomb-house to copy the epitaphs), when I suddenly, as it were, awoke to consciousness, and found myself (as before) turning in at the churchyard gate, and, I believe, singing or chanting some such words as, 'Are you awake, Count Magnus? Are you asleep, Count Magnus?' and then something more which I have failed to recollect. It seemed to me that I must have been behaving in this nonsensical way for some time."

He found the key of the mausoleum where he had expected to find it, and copied the greater part of what he wanted; in fact, he stayed until the light began to fail him.

"I must have been wrong," he writes, "in saying that one of the padlocks of my Count's sarcophagus was unfastened; I see to-night that two are loose. I picked both up, and laid them carefully on the window-ledge, after trying unsuccessfully to close them. The remaining one is still firm, and, though I take it to be a spring lock, I cannot guess how it is opened. Had I succeeded in undoing it, I am almost afraid I should have taken the liberty of opening the sarcophagus. It is strange, the interest I feel in the personality of this, I fear, somewhat ferocious and grim old noble."

The day following was, as it turned out, the last of Mr. Wraxall's stay at

Råbäck. He received letters connected with certain investments which made it desirable that he should return to England; his work among the papers was practically done, and travelling was slow. He decided, therefore, to make his farewells, put some finishing touches to his notes, and be off.

These finishing touches and farewells, as it turned out, took more time than he had expected. The hospitable family insisted on his staying to dine with them—they dined at three—and it was verging on half-past six before he was outside the iron gates of Råbäck. He dwelt on every step of his walk by the lake, determined to saturate himself, now that he trod it for the last time, in the sentiment of the place and hour. And when he reached the summit of the churchyard knoll, he lingered for many minutes, gazing at the limitless prospect of woods near and distant, all dark beneath a sky of liquid green. When at last he turned to go, the thought struck him that surely he must bid farewell to Count Magnus as well as the rest of the De la Gardies. The church was but twenty yards away, and he knew where the key of the mausoleum hung. It was not long before he was standing over the great copper coffin, and, as usual, talking to himself aloud. "You may have been a bit of a rascal in your time, Magnus," he was saying, "but for all that I should like to see you, or, rather—"

"Just at that instant," he says, "I felt a blow on my foot. Hastily enough I drew it back, and something fell on the pavement with a clash. It was the third, the last of the three padlocks which had fastened the sarcophagus. I stooped to pick it up, and—Heaven is my witness that I am writing only the bare truth—before I had raised myself there was a sound of metal hinges creaking, and I distinctly saw the lid shifting upwards. I may have behaved like a coward, but I could not for my life stay for one moment. I was outside that dreadful building in less time than I can write—almost as quickly as I could have said—the words; and what frightens me yet more, I could not turn the key in the lock. As I sit here in my room noting these facts, I ask myself (it was not twenty minutes ago) whether that noise of creaking metal continued, and I cannot tell whether it did or not. I only know that there was something more than I have written that alarmed me, but whether it was sound or sight I am not able to remember. What is this that I have done?"

Poor Mr. Wraxall! He set out on his journey to England on the next day, as he had planned, and he reached England in safety; and yet, as I gather from his changed hand and inconsequent jottings, a broken man. One of several small notebooks that have come to me with his papers gives, not a key to, but a kind of inkling of, his experiences. Much of his journey was made by canal-boat, and I find not less than six painful attempts to enumerate and describe his fellow-passengers. The entries are of this kind:

> "24 Pastor of village in Skåne. Usual black coat and soft black hat.
> "25. Commercial traveller from Stockholm going to Trollhättan. Black cloak, brown hat.
> "26. Man in long black cloak, broad-leafed hat, very old-fashioned."

This entry is lined out, and a note added: "Perhaps identical with No. 13. Have not yet seen his face." On referring to No. 13, I find that he is a Roman priest in a cassock.

The net result of the reckoning is always the same. Twenty-eight people appear in the enumeration, one being always a man in a long black cloak and broad hat, and the other a "short figure in dark cloak and hood." On the other hand, it is always noted that only twenty-six passengers appear at meals, and that the man in the cloak is perhaps absent, and the short figure is certainly absent.

On reaching England, it appears that Mr. Wraxall landed at Harwich, and that he resolved at once to put himself out of the reach of some person or persons whom he never specifies, but whom he had evidently come to regard as his pursuers. Accordingly he took a vehicle—it was a closed fly—not trusting the railway, and drove across country to the village of Belchamp St. Paul. It was about nine o'clock on a moonlight August night when he neared the place. He was sitting forward, and looking out of the window at the fields and thickets—there was little else to be seen—racing past him. Suddenly he came to a cross-road. At the corner two figures were standing motionless; both were in dark cloaks; the taller one wore a hat, the shorter a hood. He had no time to see their faces, nor did they make any motion that he could discern. Yet the horse shied violently and broke into a gallop, and Mr. Wraxall sank back into his seat in something like desperation. He had seen them before.

Arrived at Belchamp St. Paul, he was fortunate enough to find a decent furnished lodging, and for the next twenty-four hours he lived, comparatively speaking, in peace. His last notes were written on this day. They are too disjointed and ejaculatory to be given here in full, but the substance of them is clear enough. He is expecting a visit from his pursuers—how or when he knows not—and his constant cry is "What has he done?" and "Is there no hope?" Doctors, he knows, would call him mad, policemen would laugh at him. The parson is away. What can he do but lock his door and cry to God?

People still remembered last year at Belchamp St. Paul how a strange gentleman came one evening in August years back; and how the next morning but one he was found dead, and there was an inquest; and the jury that viewed the body fainted, seven of 'em did, and none of 'em wouldn't speak to what they see, and the verdict was visitation of God; and how the people as kep' the 'ouse moved out that same week, and went away from that part. But they do not, I think, know that any glimmer of light has ever been thrown, or could be thrown, on the mystery. It so happened that last year the little house came into my hands as part of a legacy. It had stood empty since 1863, and there seemed no prospect of letting it; so I had it pulled down, and the papers of which I have given you an abstract were found in a forgotten cupboard under the window in the best bedroom.

≈ THE ASH-TREE ≈

Everyone who has travelled over Eastern England knows the smaller country-houses with which it is studded—the rather dark little buildings, usually in the Italian style, surrounded with parks of some eighty to a hundred acres. For me they have always had a very strong attraction, with the grey paling of split oak, the noble trees, the meres with their reed-beds, and the line of distant woods. Then, I like the pillared portico—perhaps stuck on to a red-brick Queen Anne house which has been faced with stucco to bring it into line with the "Grecian" taste of the end of the eighteenth century; the hall inside, going up to the roof, which hall ought always to be provided with a gallery and a small organ. I like the library, too, where you may find anything from a Psalter of the thirteenth century to a Shakespeare quarto. I like the pictures, of course; and perhaps most of all I like fancying what life in such a house was when it was first built, and in the piping times of landlords' prosperity, and not least now, when, if money is not so plentiful, taste is more varied and life quite as interesting. I wish to have one of these houses and enough money to keep it together and entertain my friends in it modestly.

But this is a digression. I have to tell you of a curious series of events which happened in such a house as I have tried to describe. It is Castringham Hall in Suffolk. I think a good deal has been done to the building since the period of my story, but the essential features I have sketched are still there—Italian portico, square block of white house, older inside than out, park with fringe of woods, and mere. The one feature that marked out the house from a score of others is gone. As you looked at it from the park, you saw on the right a great old ash-tree growing within half a dozen yards of the wall, and almost or quite touching the building with its branches. I suppose it had stood there ever since Castringham ceased to be a fortified place, and since the moat was filled in and the Elizabethan dwelling-house built. At any rate, it had well-nigh attained its full dimensions in the year 1690.

In that year the district in which the Hall is situated was the scene of a number of witch-trials. It will be long, I think, before we arrive at a just estimate of the amount of solid reason—if there was any—which lay at the root of the universal fear of witches in old times. Whether the per-

sons accused of this offence really did imagine that they were possessed
of unusual power of any kind; or whether they had the will at least, if not
the power, of doing mischief to their neighbours; or whether all the con-
fessions, of which there are so many, were extorted by the mere cruelty of
the witch-finders—these are questions which are not, I fancy, yet solved.
And the present narrative gives me pause. I cannot altogether sweep it
away as mere invention. The reader must judge for himself.

Castringham contributed a victim to the *auto-da-fe*. Mrs. Mothersole
was her name, and she differed from the ordinary run of village witches
only in being rather better off and in a more influential position. Efforts
were made to save her by several reputable farmers of the parish. They did
their best to testify to her character, and showed considerable anxiety as
to the verdict of the jury.

But what seems to have been fatal to the woman was the evidence of
the then proprietor of Castringham Hall—Sir Matthew Fell. He deposed
to having watched her on three different occasions from his window, at
the full of the moon, gathering sprigs "from the ash-tree near my house."
She had climbed into the branches, clad only in her shift, and was cutting
off small twigs with a peculiarly curved knife, and as she did so she
seemed to be talking to herself. On each occasion Sir Matthew had done
his best to capture the woman, but she had always taken alarm at some
accidental noise he had made, and all he could see when he got down to
the garden was a hare running across the path in the direction of the
village.

On the third night he had been at the pains to follow at his best speed,
and had gone straight to Mrs. Mothersole's house; but he had had to wait
a quarter of an hour battering at her door, and then she had come out very
cross, and apparently very sleepy, as if just out of bed; and he had no good
explanation to offer of his visit.

Mainly on this evidence, though there was much more of a less striking
and unusual kind from other parishioners, Mrs Mothersole was found
guilty and condemned to die. She was hanged a week after the trial, with
five or six more unhappy creatures, at Bury St Edmunds.

Sir Matthew Fell, then Deputy-Sheriff, was present at the execution.
It was a damp, drizzly March morning when the cart made its way up the
rough grass hill outside Northgate, where the gallows stood. The other
victims were apathetic or broken down with misery; but Mrs Mothersole
was, as in life so in death, of a very different temper. Her "poysonous
Rage", as a reporter of the time puts it, "did so work upon the By-

standers—yea, even upon the Hangman—that it was constantly affirmed of all that saw her that she presented the living Aspect of a mad Divell. Yet she offer'd no Resistance to the Officers of the Law; onely she looked upon those that laid Hands upon her with so direfull and venomous an Aspect that—as one of them afterwards assured me—the meer Thought of it preyed inwardly upon his Mind for six Months after.''

However, all that she is reported to have said were the seemingly meaningless words: ''There will be guests at the Hall.'' Which she repeated more than once in an undertone.

Sir Matthew Fell was not unimpressed by the bearing of the woman. He had some talk upon the matter with the Vicar of his parish, with whom he travelled home after the assize business was over. His evidence at the trial had not been very willingly given; he was not specially infected with the witch-finding mania, but he declared, then and afterwards, that he could not give any other account of the matter than that he had given, and that he could not possibly have been mistaken as to what he saw. The whole transaction had been repugnant to him, for he was a man who liked to be on pleasant terms with those about him; but he saw a duty to be done in this business, and he had done it. That seems to have been the gist of his sentiments, and the Vicar applauded it, as any reasonable man must have done.

A few weeks after, when the moon of May was at the full, Vicar and Squire met again in the park, and walked to the Hall together. Lady Fell was with her mother, who was dangerously ill, and Sir Matthew was alone at home; so the Vicar, Mr Crome, was easily persuaded to take a late supper at the Hall.

Sir Matthew was not very good company this evening. The talk ran chiefly on family and parish matters, and, as luck would have it, Sir Matthew made a memorandum in writing of certain wishes or intentions of his regarding his estates, which afterwards proved exceedingly useful.

When Mr Crome thought of starting for home, about half past nine o'clock, Sir Matthew and he took a preliminary turn on the gravelled walk at the back of the house. The only incident that struck Mr Crome was this: they were in sight of the ash-tree which I described as growing near the windows of the building, when Sir Matthew stopped and said:

''What is that that runs up and down the stem of the ash? It is never a squirrel? They will all be in their nests by now.''

The Vicar looked and saw the moving creature, but he could make nothing of its colour in the moonlight. The sharp outline, however, seen for an instant, was imprinted on his brain, and he could have sworn, he said, though it sounded foolish, that, squirrel or not, it had more than four legs.

Still, not much was to be made of the momentary vision, and the two men parted. They may have met since then, but it was not for a score of years.

Next day Sir Matthew Fell was not downstairs at six in the morning, as was his custom, nor at seven, nor yet at eight. Hereupon the servants went and knocked at his chamber door. I need not prolong the description of their anxious listenings and renewed batterings on the panels. The door was opened at last from the outside, and they found their master dead and black. So much you have guessed. That there were any marks of violence did not at the moment appear; but the window was open.

One of the men went to fetch the parson, and then by his directions rode on to give notice to the coroner. Mr Crome himself went as quick as he might to the Hall, and was shown to the room where the dead man lay. He has left some notes among his papers which show how genuine a respect and sorrow was felt for Sir Matthew, and there is also this passage, which I transcribe for the sake of the light it throws upon the course of events, and also upon the common beliefs of the time:

"There was not any the least Trace of an Entrance having been forc'd to the Chamber: but the Casement stood open, as my poor Friend would always have it in this Season. He had his Evening Drink of small Ale in a silver vessel of about a pint measure, and tonight had not drunk it out. This Drink was examined by the Physician from Bury, a Mr Hodgkins, who could not, however, as he afterwards declar'd upon his Oath, before the Coroner's quest, discover that any matter of a venomous kind was present in it. For, as was natural, in the great Swelling and Blackness of the Corpse, there was talk made among the Neighbours of Poyson. The Body was very much Disorder'd as it laid in the Bed, being twisted after so extream a sort as gave too probable Conjecture that my worthy Friend and Patron had expir'd in great Pain and Agony. And what is as yet unexplain'd, and to myself the Argument of some Horrid and Artfull Designe in the Perpetrators of this Barbarous Murther, was this, that the Women which were entrusted with the laying-out of the Corpse and washing it, being both sad Pearsons and very well Respected in their Mournfull Profession, came to me in a great Pain and Distress both of Mind and Body, saying, what was indeed confirmed upon the first View, that they had no sooner touch'd the Breast of the Corpse with their naked Hands than they were sensible of a more than ordinary violent Smart and Acheing in their Palms, which, with their whole Forearms, in no long time swell'd so immoderately, the Pain still continuing, that, as afterwards proved, during many weeks they were forc'd to lay by the exercise of their Calling; and yet no mark seen on the Skin.

"Upon hearing this, I sent for the Physician, who was still in the House, and we made as carefull a Proof as we were able by the Help of a small Magnifying Lens of Crystal of the condition of the Skinn on this Part of the Body: but could not detect with the Instrument we had any Matter of Importance beyond a couple of small Punctures or Pricks, which we then concluded were the Spotts by which the Poyson might be introduced, remembering that Ring of *Pope Borgia*, with other known Specimens of the Horrid Art of the Italian Poysoners of the last age.

"So much is to be said of the Symptoms seen on the Corpse. As to what I am to add, it is meerly my own Experiment, and to be left to Posterity to judge whether there be anything of Value therein. There was on the Table by the Beddside a Bible of the small size, in which my Friend—punctuall as in Matters of less Moment, so in this more weighty one—used nightly, and upon his First Rising, to read a sett Portion. And I taking it up—not without a Tear duly paid to him wich from the Study of this poorer Adumbration was now pass'd to the contemplation of its great Originall—it came into my Thoughts, as at such moments of Helplessness we are prone to catch at any the least Glimmer that makes promise of Light, to make trial of that old and by many accounted Superstitious Practice of drawing the *Sortes*; of which a Principall Instance, in the case of his late Sacred Majesty the Blessed Martyr King *Charles* and my Lord *Falkland*, was now much talked of. I must needs admit that by my Trial not much Assistance was afforded me: yet, as the Cause and Origin of these Dreadfull Events may hereafter be search'd out, I set down the Results, in the case it may be found that they pointed the true Quarter of the Mischief to a quicker Intelligence than my own.

"I made, then, three trials, opening the Book and placing my Finger upon certain Words: which gave in the first these words, from Luke xiii. 7, *Cut it down*; in the second, Isaiah xiii. 20, *It shall never be inhabited*; and upon the third Experiment, Job xxxix. 30, *Her young ones also suck up blood*."

This is all that need be quoted from Mr Crome's papers. Sir Matthew Fell was duly coffined and laid into the earth, and his funeral sermon, preached by Mr Crome on the following Sunday, has been printed under

the title of "The Unsearchable Way; or, England's Danger and the
Malicious Dealings of Antichrist," it being the Vicar's view, as well as
that most commonly held in the neighbourhood, that the Squire was the
victim of a recrudescence of the Popish Plot.

His son, Sir Matthew the second, succeeded to the title and estates.
And so ends the first act of the Castringham tragedy. It is to be mentioned, though the fact is not surprising, that the new Baronet did not
occupy the room in which his father had died. Nor, indeed, was it slept in
by anyone but an occasional visitor during the whole of his occupation.
He died in 1735, and I do not find that anything particular marked his
reign, save a curiously constant mortality among his cattle and live-stock
in general, which showed a tendency to increase slightly as time went on.

Those who are interested in the details will find a statistical account in
a letter to the *Gentlemen's Magazine* of 1772, which draws the facts from
the Baronet's own papers. He put an end to it at last by a very simple ex-
pedient, that of shutting up all his beasts in sheds at night, and keeping no
sheep in his park. For he had noticed that nothing was ever attacked that
spent the night indoors. After that the disorder confined itself to wild
birds, and beasts of chase. But as we have no good account of the
symptoms, and as all-night watching was quite unproductive of any clue,
I do not dwell on what the Suffolk farmers called the "Castringham
sickness."

The second Sir Matthew died in 1735, as I said, and was duly succeeded
by his son, Sir Richard. It was in his time that the great family pew was
built out on the north side of the parish church. So large were the
Squire's ideas that several of the graves on that unhallowed side of the
building had to be disturbed to satisfy his requirements. Among them was
that of Mrs. Mothersole, the position of which was accurately known,
thanks to a note of a plan of the church and yard, both made by Mr Crome.

A certain amount of interest was excited in the village when it was
known that the famous witch, who was still remembered by a few, was to
be exhumed. And the feeling of surprise, and indeed disquiet, was very
strong when it was found that, though her coffin was fairly sound and unbroken, there was no trace whatever inside it of body, bones, or dust.
Indeed, it is a curious phenomenon, for at the time of her burying no such
things were dreamt of as resurrection-men, and it is difficult to conceive
any rational motive for stealing a body otherwise than for the uses of the
dissecting-room.

The incident revived for a time all the stories of witch-trials and of the exploits of the witches, dormant for forty years, and Sir Richard's orders that the coffin should be burnt were thought by a good many to be rather foolhardy, though they were duly carried out.

Sir Richard was a pestilent innovator, it is certain. Before his time the Hall had been a fine block of the mellowest red brick; but Sir Richard had travelled in Italy and become infected with the Italian taste, and, having more money than his predecessors, he determined to leave an Italian palace where he had found an English house. So stucco and ashlar masked the brick; some indifferent Roman marbles were planted about in the entrance-hall and gardens; a reproduction of the Sibyl's temple at Tivoli was erected on the opposite bank of the mere; and Castringham took an entirely new, and, I must say, a less engaging, aspect. But it was much admired, and served as a model to a good many of the neighbouring gentry in after-years.

One morning (it was in 1754) Sir Richard woke after a night of discomfort. It had been windy, and his chimney had smoked persistently, and yet it was so cold that he must keep up a fire. Also something had so rattled about the window that no man could get a moment's peace. Further, there was the prospect of several guests of position arriving in the course of the day, who would expect sport of some kind, and the inroads of the distemper (which continued among his game) had been lately so serious that he was afraid for his reputation as a game-preserver. But what really touched him most nearly was the other matter of his sleepless night. He could certainly not sleep in that room again.

That was the chief subject of his meditations at breakfast, and after it he began a systematic examination of the rooms to see which would suit his notions best. It was long before he found one. This had a window with an eastern aspect and that with a northern; this door the servants would be always passing, and he did not like the bedstead in that. No, he must have a room with a western look-out, so that the sun could not wake him early, and it must be out of the way of the business of the house. The housekeeper was at the end of her resources.

"Well, Sir Richard," she said, "you know that there is but the one room like that in the house."

"Which may that be?" said Sir Richard.

"And that is Sir Matthew's—the West Chamber."

"Well, put me in there, for there I'll lie tonight," said her master. "Which way is it? Here, to be sure"; and he hurried off.

"Oh, Sir Richard, but no one has slept there these forty years. The air has hardly been changed since Sir Matthew died there."

Thus she spoke, and rustled after him.

"Come, open the door, Mrs Chiddock. I'll see the chamber, at least."

So it was opened, and, indeed, the smell was very close and earthy. Sir Richard crossed to the window, and, impatiently, as was his wont, threw the shutters back, and flung open the casement. For this end of the house was one which the alterations had barely touched, grown up as it was with the great ash-tree, and being otherwise concealed from view.

"Air it, Mrs Chiddock, all today, and move my bed-furniture in in the afternoon. Put the Bishop of Kilmore in my old room."

"Pray, Sir Richard," said a new voice, breaking in on this speech, "might I have the favour of a moment's interview?"

Sir Richard turned round and saw a man in black in the doorway, who bowed.

"I must ask your indulgence for this intrusion, Sir Richard. You will, perhaps, hardly remember me. My name is William Crome, and my grandfather was Vicar in your grandfather's time."

"Well, sir," said Sir Richard, "the name of Crome is always a passport to Castringham. I am glad to renew a friendship of two generations' standing. In what can I serve you? for your hour of calling—and, if I do not mistake you, your bearing—shows you to be in some haste."

"That is no more than the truth, sir. I am riding from Norwich to Bury St Edmunds with what haste I can make, and I have called in on my way to leave with you some papers which we have but just come upon in looking over what my grandfather left at his death. It is thought you may find some matters of family interest in them."

"You are mighty obliging, Mr Crome, and, if you will be so good as to follow me to the parlour, and drink a glass of wine, we will take a first look at these same papers together. And you, Mrs Chiddock, as I said, be about airing this chamber . . . Yes, it is here my grandfather died . . . Yes, the tree, perhaps, does make the place a little dampish . . . No; I do not wish to listen to any more. Make no difficulties, I beg. You have your orders—go. Will you follow me, sir?"

They went to the study. The packet which young Mr Crome had brought—he was then just become a Fellow of Clare Hall in Cambridge, I may say, and subsequently brought out a respectable edition of Polyaenus—contained among other things the notes which the old Vicar had made upon the occasion of Sir Matthew Fell's death. And for the first time

Sir Richard was confronted with the enigmatical *Sortes Biblicae* which you have heard. They amused him a good deal.

"Well," he said, "my grandfather's Bible gave one prudent piece of advice—*Cut it down.* If that stands for the ash-tree, he may rest assured I shall not neglect it. Such a nest of catarrhs and agues was never seen."

The parlour contained the family books, which, pending the arrival of a collection which Sir Richard had made in Italy, and the building of a proper room to receive them, were not many in number.

Sir Richard looked up from the paper to the bookcase.

"I wonder," says he, "whether the old prophet is there yet? I fancy I see him."

Crossing the room, he took out a dumpy Bible, which, sure enough, bore on the flyleaf the inscription: "To Matthew Fell, from his Loving Godmother, Anne Aldous, 2 September 1659."

"It would be no bad plan to test him again, Mr Crome. I will wager we get a couple of names in the Chronicles. H'm! what have we here? 'Thou shalt seek me in the morning, and I shall not be.' Well, well! Your grandfather would have made a fine omen of that, hey? No more prophets for me! They are all in a tale. And now, Mr Crome, I am infinitely obliged to you for your packet. You will, I fear, be impatient to get on. Pray allow me—another glass."

So with offers of hospitality, which were genuinely meant (for Sir Richard thought well of the young man's address and manner), they parted.

In the afternoon came the guests—the Bishop of Kilmore, Lady Mary Hervey, Sir William Kentfield, etc. Dinner at five, wine, cards, supper, and dispersal to bed.

Next morning Sir Richard is disinclined to take his gun with the rest. He talks with the Bishop of Kilmore. This prelate, unlike a good many of the Irish Bishops of his day, had visited his see, and, indeed, resided there, for some considerable time. This morning, as the two were walking along the terrace and talking over the alterations and improvements in the house, the Bishop said, pointing to the window of the West Room:

"You could never get one of my Irish flock to occupy that room, Sir Richard."

"Why is that, my lord? It is, in fact, my own."

"Well, our Irish peasantry will always have it that it brings the worst of luck to sleep near an ash-tree, and you have a fine growth of ash not two yards from your chamber window. Perhaps," the Bishop went on, with a smile, "it has given you a touch of its quality already, for you do not seem, if I may say it, so much the fresher for your night's rest as your friends would like to see you."

"That, or something else, it is true, cost me my sleep from twelve to four, my lord. But the tree is to come down tomorrow, so I shall not hear much more from it."

"I applaud your determination. It can hardly be wholesome to have the air you breathe strained, as it were, through all that leafage."

"Your lordship is right there, I think. But I had not my window open last night. It was rather the noise that went on—no doubt from the twigs sweeping the glass—that kept me open-eyed."

"I think that can hardly be, Sir Richard. Here—you see it from this point. None of these nearest branches even can touch your casement unless there were a gale, and there was none of that last night. They miss the panes by a foot."

"No, sir, true. What, then, will it be, I wonder, that scratched and rustled so—ay, and covered the dust on my sill with lines and marks?"

At last they agreed that the rats must have come up through the ivy. That was the Bishop's idea, and Sir Richard jumped at it.

So the day passed quietly, and night came, and the party dispersed to their rooms, and wished Sir Richard a better night.

And now we are in his bedroom, with the light out and the Squire in bed. The room is over the kitchen, and the night outside still and warm, so the window stands open.

There is very little light about the bedstead, but there is a strange movement there; it seems as if Sir Richard were moving his head rapidly to and fro with only the slightest possible sound. And now you would guess, so deceptive is the half-darkness, that he had several heads, round and brownish which move back and forward, even as low as his chest. It is a horrible illusion. Is it nothing more? There! something drops off the bed with a soft plump, like a kitten, and is out of the window in a flash; another—four—and after that there is quiet again.

Thou shalt seek me in the morning, and I shall not be.

As with Sir Matthew, so with Sir Richard—dead and black in his bed!

A pale and silent party of guests and servants gathered under the window when the news was known. Italian poisoners, Popish emissaries, infected air—all these and more guesses were hazarded, and the Bishop of Kilmore looked at the tree, in the fork of whose lower boughs a white tom-cat was crouching, looking down the hollow which years had gnawed in the trunk. It was watching something inside the tree with great interest.

Suddenly it got up and craned over the hole. Then a bit of the edge on which it stood gave way, and it went slithering in. Everyone looked up at the noise of the fall.

It is known to most of us that a cat can cry; but few of us have heard, I hope, such a yell as came out of the trunk of the great ash. Two or three screams there were—the witnesses are not sure which—and then a slight and muffled noise of some commotion or struggling was all that came. But Lady Mary Hervey fainted outright, and the housekeeper stopped her ears and fled till she fell on the terrace.

The Bishop of Kilmore and Sir William Kentfield stayed. Yet even they were daunted, though it was only at the cry of a cat; and Sir William swallowed once or twice before he could say:

"There is something more than we know of in that tree, my lord. I am for an instant search."

And this was agreed upon. A ladder was brought, and one of the gardeners went up, and, looking down the hollow, could detect nothing but a few dim indications of something moving. They got a lantern, and let it down by a rope.

"We must get at the bottom of this. My life upon it, my lord, but the secret of these terrible deaths is there."

Up went the gardner again with the lantern, and let it down the hole cautiously. They saw the yellow light upon his face as he bent over, and saw his face struck with an incredulous terror and loathing before he cried out in a dreadful voice and fell back from the ladder—where, happily, he was caught by two of the men—letting the lantern fall inside the tree.

He was in a dead faint, and it was some time before any word could be got from him.

By then they had something else to look at. The lantern must have broken at the bottom, and the light in it caught upon dry leaves and rubbish that lay there, for in a few minutes a dense smoke began to come up, and then flame; and, to be short, the tree was in a blaze.

The bystanders made a ring at some yards' distance, and Sir William and the Bishop sent men to get what weapons and tools they could; for, clearly, whatever might be using the tree as its lair would be forced out by the fire.

So it was. First, at the fork, they saw a round body covered with fire—

the size of a man's head—appear very suddenly, then seem to collapse and fall back. This, five or six times; then a similar ball leapt into the air and fell on the grass, where after a moment it lay still. The Bishop went as near as he dared to it, and saw—what but the remains of an enormous spider, veinous and seared! And, as the fire burned lower down, more terrible bodies like this began to break out from the trunk, and it was seen that these were covered with greyish hair.

All that day the ash burned, and until it fell to pieces the men stood about it, and from time to time killed the brutes as they darted out. At last there was a long interval when none appeared, and they cautiously closed in and examined the roots of the tree.

"They found," says the Bishop of Kilmore, "below it a rounded hollow place in the earth, wherein were two or three bodies of these creatures that had plainly been smothered by the smoke; and, what is to me more curious, at the side of this den, against the wall, was crouching the anatomy or skeleton of a human being, with the skin dried upon the bones, having some remains of black hair, which was pronounced by those that examined it to be undoubtedly the body of a woman, and clearly dead for a period of fifty years."

WALTER DE LA MARE

A: B: O. (1895)*

An early de la Mare piece from an unknown magazine, "A: B: O." is at once the most antiquarian and the most Gothic of the many ghostly tales by this master of the macabre. The plot, involving a thing "neither man nor beast" foolishly unearthed and inadvertently unleashed by overeager antiquaries, is an early example of the M. R. James mode. The style, however, with its black cats, looming shadows, and grinning statues, has a ghoulishness more characteristic of such neo-Gothic writers as Bram Stoker and Vernon Lee.

Although the vibrant intensity of the narrative voice in "A: B: O." is uncharacteristic of the mature de la Mare (such as in the more delicately tuned "Bad Company," reprinted in the contemporary section of this book), the story nevertheless has elements that prefigure the later work. The narrator's need to hear the clatter of the railroad to "prove the reality of the world," for example, signals a preoccupation with isolation and alienation that permeates "Out of the Deep," "A Recluse," "Seaton's Aunt," and many other solipsistic later stories. Indeed the intense solitude and silence in "A: B: O."—culminating in the grotesquely humorous scene in which the narrator drags a caretaker and a derelict into his house to provide some desperately needed human companionship—is its most haunting characteristic.

For most readers, however, the most striking thing about "A: B: O." is likely to be the utterly weird and original *idea* of the story. What the antiquaries manage to dig up, a "child of disease and death," is both complicated in its spiritual symbolism and terribly simple in its gross physicality. It inspires not an "honest fear' but a "dim skulking horror of soul." Entirely real, it is seen by several characters, yet it is also a "vile symbol" of an inner guilt that is abstract and undefinable. Indeed, guilt clings to the very air in this story, yet there is no reason to distrust the narrator's statement that the man who accidently sets free the marauding creature is a "benevolent kindly gentleman" who "harmed no one." As in the stories of Le Fanu, religion is as powerless to thwart the powers of darkness as science. This powerlessness, the major theme of the English ghost story, is made unusually explicit here: "Science is slunk away shamefaced; religion is a withered flower."

Readers familiar with "The Minister's Black Veil" may detect a Hawthornian obsessiveness about "secret sin" in this story. Here, however, the secret sin has a physical life of its own; it emerges, not from the sinner's bosom, but from the earth. De la Mare was clearly interested in exploring spiritual evil, but he was also, like the Beowulf poet, interested in exciting us with a lively, old-fashioned monster story.

---

*This approximate date comes from Edward Wagenknecht, who, as far as he can remember, was alerted to the tale by de la Mare; it originally appeared in a nineteenth century magazine under a pseudonym, where it lay in oblivion until Wagenknecht's Arkham House reprint some seventy-five years later. (See bibliography.)

A: B: O.

I looked up over the top of my book at the portrait of my great-grand-
father and listened in astonishment to the sudden peal of the bell, which
clanged and clanged in straggling decisive strokes until, like a dog gone
back to his kennel, it slowed, slackened and fell silent again. A bell has an
unfriendly tongue; it is a router of wits, a messenger of alarms. Even in
the quiet of twilight it may resemble a sour virago's din. At a late hour,
when the world is snug in night-cap and snoring is the only harmony, it is
the devil's own discordancy. I looked over my book at my placid ancestor,
I say, and listened on even after the sound had been stilled.

To tell the truth, I was more than inclined to pay no heed to the summons, and, secure in the kind warmth and solitude of my room, to ignore
so rude a remembrancer of the world. Before I could decide either way,
yet again the metal tongue clattered, as icily as a martinet. It pulled me to
my feet. Then, my tranquillity, my inertia destroyed, it was useless and
profitless to take no heed. I vowed vengeance. I would pounce sourly
upon my visitor, thought I. I would send him back double-quick into the
darkness of the night, and, if this were some timid feminine body (which
God forefend) an antic and a grimace would effectually put such an one to
route.

I rose, opened the door, and slid cautiously in my slippers to the bolted
door. There I paused to climb up on a chair in an endeavour to spy out on
the late-comer from the fanlight, to take his size, to analyze his intentions, but standing there even on tiptoe I could see not so much as the
crown of a hat. I clambered down and, after a dismal rattling of chain and
shooting of bolts, flung open the door.

Upon my top step (eight steps run down from the door to the garden
and two more into the street) stood a little boy. A little boy with a ready
tongue in his head, I perceived by the smirk at the corner of his mouth; a
little boy of spirit too, for the knees of his knickerbockers were patched.
This I perceived by the light of a lamp-post which stands over against the
doctor's house. Grimaces were wasted on this sturdy youngster in his red
flannel neckerchief. I eyed him with pursed lips.

"Mr. Pelluther?" said the little boy, his fists deep in the pockets of his
jacket.

93

"Who asks for Mr. Pelluther?" said I pedagogically.

"Me," said the little boy.

"What does me want with Mr. Pelluther at so untoward an hour, eh, my little man? What the gracious do you mean by making clangour with my bell and waking the stars when all the world's asleep, and fetching me out of the warmth to this windy doorstep? I have a mind to pull your ear."

Such sudden eloquence somewhat astonished the little boy. His "boyness" seemed, I fancied, to leave him in the lurch; he was at school out of season; he retrogressed a few steps.

"Please sir, I've got a letter for Mr. Pelluther, the gentleman said," he turned his back on me, "but as he ain't here I'll take it back." He skipped down the step and at the bottom lustily set to whistling the *Marseillaise.*

My dignity was hurt. "Come, come, my little man," I called, "I myself am Mr. Pelluther."

"*Le jour de gloire . . .* " whistled the little boy.

"Give me the letter," said I peremptorily.

"I've got to give it into the gentleman's own hands," said the little boy.

"Come, give me the letter," said I persuasively.

"I've got to give it into the gentleman's own hands," said the little boy doggedly, "and you don't see a corner of the envelope."

"Come, my boy, here's a sixpence."

He eyed me suspiciously, "Chestnuts," said he, retiring a step or two.

"See, a silver sixpence for the honest messenger," said I.

"Honest be blowed!" said he. "Put it on the step and go behind the door. I'll come up for the tanner and put the letter on the step. Catch a weasel?"

I wanted the letter; I trusted my boy; so I put the sixpence on the top step and retired behind the door. He was true to his word. With a wary eye and a whoop of triumph he made the exchange. He doubled his fist on the sixpence and retired into the garden. I came like a felon out of the stocks for my letter.

The letter was addressed simply "Pelluther," in uncommon careless handwriting, so careless indeed that I hardly recognized the scholarly penmanship of my friend Dugdale. Forgetful of the messenger, who yet lingered upon my garden path, I shut the door and bustled into my study. I was reminded of his presence and of my discourtesy by a rattling shower of stones upon the panels of my door and by the sound of the *Marseillaise* startling the distant trees of the quiet square.

"Dear, dear me," said I, perching my spectacles most unskilfully. Indeed, I was not a little perturbed by this untimely letter. For only a few hours ago I had walked and smoked with dear old Dugdale in his own pleasant garden, in his own gentle twilight. For twilight seems to soothe to sleep the flowers of my old friend's garden with gentler hands than she can have vouchsafed even to the gardens of Solomon.

I opened my letter in trepidation, only a little reassured of Dugdale's safety by the superscription written in his own handwriting. This is the burden of the letter—"Dear Friend Pell. I am writing, in a fever. Come at once—*Antiquities!*—the lumber—a mere scrawl—Come at once, or I begin without you. R. D."

"Antiquities" was the peak of the climax of this summons—the golden word. All else might be meaningless; as indeed it was, "Come at once. *Antiquities!*"

I bustled into my coat and was pelting at perilous speed down my eight steps, before the *Marseillaise* had ceased to echo from the adjacent houses. Isolated wayfarers no doubt imagined me to be a doctor, bent on enterprise of life or death. Truly an unvenerable appearance was mine, but Dugdale was itching to begin, and haste spelt glory.

His white house lay not a mile distant, and soon the squeal of his gate upon its hinges comforted my heart and gave my lungs pause. Dugdale himself, also, the noise brought flying down into his drive to greet me. He was without his coat. Under his arm was clumsily tucked a spade, his cheeks were flushed with excitement. Even his firm lips, children of science, were trembling, and his grey eyes, wives of the microscope, were agog behind the golden-rimmed spectacles set awry on his magnificent nose.

I squeezed his left hand and thus together we hurried up the steps. "Have you begun?" said I.

"Just on the move when you came round the corner," said he. "Who would believe it, Old Roman, or Druidical, God knows."

Excitement and panting made me totter and I was dismayed at the thought of my digestion. We hurried down the passage to his study, which was in great disorder and filled with a vexing dust, hardly reminiscent of his admirable housemaid, and with a most unpleasant mouldy odour, of damp paper I conjecture.

Dugdale seized a ragged piece of parchment which lay upon the table and pressed it into my hand. He sank back into his well-worn leather armchair, the spade resting against his knee, and energetically set to polishing his glasses.

I looked fixedly at him. He flourished his long forefinger at me fussily, shaking his head, eager for me to get on.

Rudely scrawled upon the chart was a diagram rectangular in shape with divers scrawls in red ink, and crazy figures. I drove my brains into the open, with vain threats and cudgelling; no, I could make nothing of it. A small chest or coffer upon the floor, of a curious workmanship, overflowing with dusty and stained papers and parchments, betrayed whence the chart had come.

I looked at Dugdale. "What does it mean?" said I, a little disappointed, for many a trick of the foolish and of the fraudulent has sent me on an idle errand in search of "Antiquities."

"My garden," said Dugdale, sweeping his hand towards the window, then triumphantly pointing to the chart in my hand. "I have studied it. My uncle, the antiquarian; it *is* genuine. I have had suspicions, ah! yes, every one of yours; I'm not blind. It may be anything. I dig at once. Come and help or go to the—"

He shouldered his spade, in which action he shivered a precious little porcelain cup upon a cabinet. He never so much as blinked at the calamity. He slackened not an inch his triumphant march to the door. Well, what is a five-pound note in one's pocket to a sixpence discovered in a gutter?

I caught up the pick and another shovel. "Bravo, Pelluther," said he, and we strutted off arm and arm into the pleasant and spacious garden which lay at the back of the house. I felt proud as a drummer-boy.

In the garden Dugdale whipped out of his pocket a yard measure, and having lighted a wax candle stuck it with its own grease in a recess of the wall. After which he knelt down upon the mould with transparent sedateness and studied the chart by the candle-light, very clear and conspicuous in the darkness.

"Yes tree ten yards N. by seven E. three—semicir—um—square. It's mere A.B.C., 'pon my word."

He darted away to the bottom of the garden. I followed in a canter by the path between the darkened roses. All was blackness except where the candle-light bleached the old bricks of Dugdale's wall and glittered upon the dewy trees. At the squat old yew tree he beckoned me. I had repeatedly beseeched him to fell the ugly thing—but he would not.

"Hold the reel," said he, with trembling fingers offering me the yard-measure. Away we went. "Ten yards by how much?"

"Five, I think," said I.

"Spellicans," said Dugdale, and bustled away to the house for the chart. His shirt-sleeves winked between the bushes. He fetched back with him the chart and another candle stick.

"Do wake up, Pelluther, wake up! Oh, 'seven,' wake up?"

I was shivering with excitement and my teeth sounded like a skeleton swaying in the wind. He measured the yards and marked the place on the soil with his spade.

"Now then to work," said he, and set the example by a savage slash at a pensive *Gloire de Dijon*.

Exceedingly solemn, yet gurgling with self-conscious laughter, I also began to pick and dig. The sweat was cold upon my forehead after a quarter of an hour's hard labour. I sat on the grass and panted.

"City dinners, orgies," muttered Dugdale, slaving away like a man in search of his soul.

"No wind, thank goodness. See that flint flash? Good exercise! Gentenarians and all the better for it. I am no chicken either. Phugh! the place is black as a tiger's throat. I'll swear someone's been here before. Thumb that time!—bless the blister!"

Even in my own abject condition I had time to be amazed at his sinewy strokes and his fanatical energy. He was sexton, and I the owl! Exquisitely, suddenly, Dugdale's pick struck heavily and hollowly.

"Oh God!" said he scrambling like a rat out of the hole. He leaned heavily on his pick and peered at me with round eyes. A great silence was over the place. I seemed to hear the metallic ring of the pick cleaving its way to the stars. Dugdale crept very cautiously and extinguished the candle with damp fingers.

"Eh, now," whispered he, "you and I, old boy, d'ye hear. In the hole—it's desecration, it's as glum a trade as body-snatching. Hush! who's that?"

His hand pounced on my shoulder. We craned our necks. A plaintive howl grew out of the silence and faded into the silence. A black cat leapt the fence and disappeared with a flutter of leaves.

"That black beast!" said I, gazing into the wormy hole. "I would like to wait—and think."

"No time," said Dugdale, doubtfully bold. "The hole must be filled up before dawn or Jenkinson will make enquiries. Tut, tut, what's that noise of thumping. Oh, yes, all right!" He clapped his hand on his chest, "Now, Rattie, like mice!"

Rattie had been my nickname a very long time ago.

We set to work again, each tap of pick or shovel chased a shiver down my spine. And after great labour we excavated a metallic chest.

"Pell, you're a brick—I told you so!" said Dugdale.

We continued to gaze at our earthly spoil. One strange and inexplicable discovery we made was this: a thickly rusted iron tube ran out from the top of the chest into the earth, and thence by surmise we traced it to the trunk of the dwarfed yew tree; and, with the light of our candles eventually discovered its termination imbedded in a boss between two gnarled encrusted branches a few feet up. We were unable to drag out the chest without first disinterring the pipe.

I eyed it with perplexity.

"Come and get a saw," said Dugdale. "It's strange, eh?"

He turned a mottled face to me. The air seemed to be slightly phosphorescent. Whether he had suspicions that I should force open the lid in his absence I know not. At any rate, I willingly accompanied him to the tool-house. We brought back a handsaw, Dugdale greased it plentifully with the candle, and I held the pipe while he sawed. What the purpose or use of the pipe might be I puzzled my brains in vain to discover.

"Perhaps," said Dugdale, pausing, saw in hand, "perhaps it's delicate merchandise, eh, and needs fresh air."

"Perhaps it is not," said I, unaccountably vexed at his halting speech.

He seemed to expect no different answer and again set busily to work. The pipe vibrated at his vigour, dealing me little shocks and numbing my fingers. At last the chest was free, we tapped it with our fingers. We scraped off flakes of mould and rust with our nails. I knelt and put my eye to the end of the pipe. Dugdale pushed me aside and did likewise.

I am assured that passing in his brain was a sequence of ideas exactly similar to my own. We nursed our excitement, we conceived the wildest fantasies, we brought forth litters of surmises. Perhaps just the shadow of apprehension lurked about us. Possibly a familiar spirit may have tapped our shoulders.

Then, at the same instant we both began to pull and push vigorously at the chest; but, in such a confined space (for the hole was ragged and unequal) its weight was too great for our strength.

"A rope," said Dugdale, "let's go together again. Two 'old boys' in the plot." He laughed hypocritically.

"Certainly," said I, amused at his suspicions and wiles.

Again we stepped away to the tool-shed, and returned with a coil of rope. The pick being used as a lever, we were soon able to haul the chest out of its hole.

"Duty first," said Dugdale, shovelling the loose earth into the cavity. I imitated him. And over the place of the disturbance we planted the dying rose bush, already hanging drooping leaves.

"Jenkinson's eyes are not microscopes, but he's damned inquisitive."

Jenkinson, incidentally, was an old gentleman who lived in the house next to Dugdale. One who having no currants in his own bun must needs pick and steal his neighbours! But he is dumb in the grave now, and out of hearing of any cavilling tongue.

Dugdale swore, but a man would be a saint or a fool who could refrain from swearing under the circumstance. Even I displayed blasphemous knowledge and was not ashamed.

Dugdale took one end and I the other side of the chest. Together we carried it with immense difficulty (for the thing was prodigously weighty) to the study. We cleared away all the furniture to the sides of the room. We placed the chest in the middle of the floor so that we might gloat upon it at our ease. With the fire-shovel, for we had neglected to bring the spade, Dugdale scraped away mould and rust and upon the top of the chest appeared three letters, initial to a word, I conjectured, which originally ran the whole width of the side, but the greater part of which had been rendered illegible by the action of the soil. "A-B-O" were the letters.

"I have no idea," said Dugdale peering at this barely perceptible record. "I have no idea," I echoed vaguely.

And would to God we had forewith carried the chest unopened to the garden and buried it deeper than deep!

"Let us open it," said I, after arduous examination of the inscription.

The fire flames glittered upon dear old Dugdale's glasses. He was a chilly man and at a suggestion of east wind would have a fire set blazing. The room was snug and cozy. I remember the carved figure of a Chinese God grinning at me in a very palpable manner as I handed Dugdale his chisel. (May he forgive me!) The intense silence was ominous. In a cranny at the lid of the chest he inserted the tool. He looked at me queerly, at the second jerk the steel snapped.

"Dugdale," said I, eyeing the Chinese God, "let's leave well alone."

"Eh," said he in an unfamiliar voice.

"Have nought to do with the thing."

"What, eh?" said he sucking his finger, the nail of which he had broken in his digging. He hesitated an instant. "We must get another chisel," said he, laughing.

But somehow I cared for the laugh not at all. It was not the fair bleak laugh of Dugdale. He took my arm in his and for the third time we made our way to the tool-shed.

"It's fresh and sweet," said I, sniffing the air of the garden. My eyes beseeched Dugdale.

"Ay, so it is, it is," said he.

When he again set to work upon the chest he prised open the lid at the first effort. The scrap of broken steel rang upon the metal of the chest. A faint and unpleasant odour became perceptible. Dugdale remained in the position the sudden lift of the lid had given his body, his head bent slightly forward, over the open chest. I put one hand upon the side of the chest. My fingers touched a little cake of hard stuff. I looked into the chest. I took a step forward and looked in. Yellow cotton wool lined the leaden sides and was thrust into the interstices of the limbs of the creature which sat within. I will speak without emotion. I saw a flat mal-formed skull and meagre arms and shoulders clad in coarse fawn hair. I saw a face thrown back a little, bearing hideous and ungodly resemblance to the human face, its lids heavy blue and closely shut with coarse lashes and tangled eyebrows. This I saw, this the monstrous antiquity hid in the chest which Dugdale and I dug out of the garden. Only one glimpse I took at the thing, then Dugdale had replaced the lid, had sat down on the floor and was rocking to and fro with hands clasped over his knees.

I made my way to the window feeling stiff and sore with unaccustomed toil; I threw open the window and leaned far out into the scented air. The sweetness of the flowers eddied into the room. The night was very quiet. For many minutes so I stood counting a row of poplars at the far end of the garden. Then I returned to Dugdale.

"It's the end of the business," said I. "My gorge rises with despair of life. Swear it! my dear old Dugdale. I implore you to swear that this shall be the end of the business. We will go bury it now."

"I swear it, Pelluther. Pell! Pell!" The bitterness of his childish cry is venomous even now. "But hear me old friend," he said. "I am too weak now. Come tomorrow at this time and we will bury it together."

The chest stood in front of the fire. The metal was green with verdigris.

We went out of the room leaving the glittering candles to their watch, and in my presence Dugdale turned the key in the lock of the door. He walked with me to the Church and there we parted company.

"A damnable thing," said Dugdale, shaking my hand.

I wagged my head woefully.

The next day, being Wednesday, the charwomen invaded my house, as was customary upon that day, and to be free of the steam and the stench of soap I took my way to Kew. Throughout the day I wandered through the gardens striving to enjoy the luxuriance and the flowers.

In the first coolness of evening I turned my back upon the gorgeous west and made my way home again. I met the women red and flustered leaving the house.

"Has any one called?" said I.

"The butcher, sir," said Mrs. Rodd.

"Thank you," said I and entered my house.

Now in the twilight as I sat down at my own fireside, my surroundings recalled most vividly the scene of the night. I leaned heavily in my chair feeling faint and sick, and in so doing was much inconvenienced by some hard thing in the pocket of my jacket pressed to my side by the arm of the chair. I rummaged in my pocket and brought out the little cake of hard green substance which had been in the mouth of the chest. I suppose that my fingers had clutched it when they had come in contact with it the night before and unknowingly I had deposited it in my pocket.

Deeming it prudent to have care in the matter, I rose and locked up the stuff in my little medicine chest, which is hanged above the mantlepiece in the room which looks out upon the garden. For to analyze or examine the stuff I feared. This done I came again to my chair and composed myself to reading.

Supper had been prepared by the women and was set upon the table for me in my study. It has been my custom since the death of my sister to dine at mid-day at my club.

True! I sat with the book upon my knee but all my thoughts were with Dugdale. A rectangular shape obtruded itself upon my retina and floated upon the white page. The hours dragged wearily. My head drooped and my chin tapped my chest. In fact I was dreaming, when I was awakened by a doubtful knock upon the front door. My senses were alert in an instant. The sound, just as though something were scraping the paint, was repeated.

I rose stealthily. A vague desire to flee out into the garden seized upon me.

The sound was repeated.

I went very slowly to the door. Again I climbed the chair (I loved the little boy now.) But I could see nothing. I peeped through the keyhole but something obscured the opening upon the other side. A faint odour— unpleasant—was in the house. With desperation of terror I flung open the door. I fancied I heard the sound of panting. I fancied something brushing my arm; then I found myself staring down the hallway listening

to the echo of the click of the latch of the door of the room which overlooks my garden. In this unseemly rhythm and this succession of words I
write with intent. Thus my thoughts ran then; thus then I write now.
Many years ago when I was a young man I was nearly burnt alive. I felt
then an honest fear. This was a dim skulking horror of soul and an inhuman depravity. It is impossible for me to tell of my horrid strivings of
brain. I staggered into my room; I sat down in my chair; I took my book
upon my knee; I put my spectacles upon my nose; but all the time all my
senses were dead save that of hearing. Distinctly I felt my ears move and
twitch, with the help of some ancient muscle, I conjecture, long disused
by humanity. And as I sat, my brain cried out with fear.

For ten minutes (I slowly counted each sounding 'cluck' of my clock)
I sat so. At last my limbs began to quake, solitude was driving me to
perilous ravines of thought. I crept with guilty tread into the garden. I
climbed the fence which separates the next house from mine. This house,
No. 17, was inhabited by a caretaker, a rude uncouth fellow who used for
his living room only the kitchen, and who had tied all the bells together
so that he might not be disturbed. He was a cad of a man. But for companionship I cried out.

I went to the garden door keeping my eyes fixedly turned away from
the window. I hammered at the garden door of the house. I hammered
again. A sullen footstep resounded in the empty place and the door was
cautiously opened a few inches. A scared face looked out at me through
the chink.

"For God's sake," said I, "come and sup with me. I have a leg of good
meat, my dear fellow, come and sup with me."

The door opened wider. Curiosity took the place of apprehension.
"Say, Master, what is moving in the house?" said the fellow. "Why is my
'ead all damp, and my 'ands a shiverin'. I tell you there's a thing gone
wrong in the place. I sits with my back to the wall and somebody steps
quick and quiet on the other side. Why am I sick like so? I ask yer why?"

The man almost wept.

"You silly fellow! May a sick man not pace his mansion. I will give you
a five-pound note to come and sit with me," said I. "Be neighbourly, my
good fellow. I fear that a fit will overtake me. I am weak—the heat—
epileptical too. Rats crowd in the walls, I often hear their tumult. Come,
sup with me."

The cad shook his villainous head sagely.

"A five-pound note—two," said I.

"I was chaffin'," said he, and returned into the house to fetch a poker.

We climbed the fence and crept like thieves towards the house. But not an inch beyond my door would the fellow come. I expostulated. He blasphemed. He stubbornly stuck to his purpose.

"I don't budge till I've 'glimpsed' through that window," said he.

I argued and entreated; I doubled my bribe; I tapped him upon the shoulder and twitted him of cowardice; I performed a pirouette about him; I entreated him to sit with me.

"I don't budge till I've glimpsed through that window."

I fetched a little ladder from the greenhouse which stands to the left of the house, and the caretaker carried it to the window, the ledge of which is about five feet from the ground. He climbed laboriously step by step, stretching his neck so as to see into the black room beyond, while I, simply to be near him, climbed behind him.

He had got halfway and was breathing loudly when suddenly a long arm, thin as its bone, clad in tawny hair, pallid in the dim starlight, pounced across the window and dragged the curtains together—an arm thin as its bone. The fellow above me groaned, threw up his hands and tumbled headlong off the ladder, bringing me to the ground in his fall.

For a moment I lay dazed; then, lifting my head from the soil and the sweet lilies I perceived him clambering over the fence in savage hurry. I remember that the dew glistened upon his boots as he flung his heels over the fence.

Presently I was upon my feet and pelting after him, but he was a younger man, and when I reached the door at the back of his house he had already bolted and barred it. To all of my prayers and knockings he paid no attention. Notwithstanding, I feel certain that he sat listening upon the other side, for I discerned a hoarse breathing like the breathing of an asthmatic.

"You have left the poker. I bring you the poker," I bellowed, but he made no answer.

Again I climbed the fence, now determined to leave the house free for the thing to roam and to ravage, nor to return till daylight was come. I crept quietly through the haunted place. As I passed the room, I distinguished a sound—like the sound of a humming top—of incessant gabble. I ran and opened the front door and just then, as I peered out upon the street, a beggar clothed in rags shuffled past the garden gate. I leapt down the steps.

"Here my good man," said I speaking with difficulty for my tongue seemed stiff and glutinous.

He turned with an odd whine and shuffled towards me.

"Are you hungry?" said I. "Have you an appetite—just a stubborn yearning for a delicate snack of prime Welsh lamb?"

The scraggy wretch nodded and gesticulated with warty hands.

"Come in, come in," I screamed. "You shall eat a meal, poor man. How dire is civilization in rags—Evil fortune! Socialism! Millionaires! I'll be bound. Come in, come in."

I was weeping with delight. He squinted at me with suspicion and again waved his hands. By these movements and by his articulate cries, I fancied the man was dumb. (He was vexed with a serious impediment in his speech I now conjecture.) He was manifesting mistrust. He snuffled.

"No, no" said I. "Come in, my man and welcome. I am lonely—a Bohemian. Ancient books are musty company. Come sit and cheer me with an honest appetite. Take a glass of wine with me."

I patted the wretch on the back. I gripped his arm. In my tragic acting, moreover, I hummed a little song to prove my indifference. He tottered upon my steps in front of me—his shoes were mended with brown paper and the noise of his footsteps was like the rustle of a lady's silk dress. I blithely followed him into the house leaving the door wide open so that the clean night air might go through the house, so that the clatter of the railroad which lies behind the doctor's house might prove the reality of the world. I sat the beggar down in an arm-chair. I plied him with meat and drink. He luxuriated in the good fare, he guzzled my claret, he gnawed bones and crust like a bony beast, considering me the while, apprehensive of being reft of his meal. He snarled and he gobbled, he puffed, he mouthed and chawed. He was a bird of prey, a cat, a wild beast, and a man. His belly was the only truth. He had chanced on heaven, and awaited the archangel's trump of banishment. Yet in the midst of his ravenous feeding, terror was netting him, too. Full of my own fear, in watching his hands shivering, and the pallor overspreading his grimy face, I took delight. Still he ate furiously, flouting his fears.

All the while I was thinking desperately of the horrid creature which was in my house. The while I sat grinning at my guest, the while I was inciting him to eat, drink, and be merry, the while I analyzed each deplorable action of the rude fellow and sickened at his beastliness, the vile consciousness of that thing on its secret errand prowling within scent, never left me—that abortion—A-B-O, abortion; I knew then.

On a sudden, just as the tramp, having lifted the lamb bone, had set his teeth to gnawing at the gristly knuckle, there came to my ears the sound of breaking glass and then a rustling, (no extraordinary sound), a rustling sound of a hand wandering upon the panel of a door. But the beggar had heard what speech cannot make intelligible. I felt younger on that day than I have since my childhood. I was drunken with terror.

My beggar, dropping his tumbler of wine but still clutching the lamb bone, scrambled to his feet and eyed me with pale grey pupils set in circles of white. His dirty bleached face was stained with his meal. Dirt seamed his skin. I took his hand in mine. I caught up the lamp and held it on high. The beggar and I stood in the doorway gazing into the darkness; the lamp-light faintly lit the familiar passage. It gleamed on the door of the room whose window overlooks my garden. The handle of the door was silently turning. The door was opening—almost imperceptibly. The beggar's pulse throbbed furiously; my elbow was pressed against his arm. And a very thin abnormal thing—a fawn shadow—came out of the room and pattered past the beggar and me.

My jaws fell asunder, nor could I shut them so that I might speak. Tighter I clutched the beggar and we fled out together. Standing upon the topmost of the steps, we peered down the street; afar off with ponderous tread walked a policeman, playing the light of his lantern upon the windows of the houses and the doors. Presently he drew near to a lamp, to where flitted a monstrous shadow. I saw the policeman turn suddenly round about. With fluttering coat-tails he ran furiously down a little lane which leads to many bright shops.

The beggar and I spent the rest of the night upon the doorstep. Sometimes he made vain splutterings of speech and vexed gesticulations, but generally we waited speechless and motionless as two stuffed owls.

At the first faint ray of dawn, which leapt above the doctor's house opposite, the beggar flung away my hand, hopped blindly down the steps and, pausing not to open the gate, vaulted over it and was immediately gone. I scarcely felt surprise. The green-shaded lamp which stood upon the doorstep slowly burned itself out. The sun rose gladly, the sparrows made the morning noisy as they fluttered and fought in their busy foraging. I think my round eyes vaguely watched them.

Soon after eight the postman brought me a letter. And this was the letter—"God forgive me, friend, and help me to write sanely. A miserable curiosity has proved too strong for me. I went back to my house, now woefully strange to me. I could not sleep. Now pacing with me in my own bedroom, now wrapped in its unholy sleep, the thing as always with me. Each picture, indeed each chair, however severely I strove to discipline my thoughts, carried with it a pregnant suggestion. In the middle of the night

I took my way downstairs and opened the door of my study. My books seemed to me disconsolate friends offended. The case stood as we had left it—we, you and I, when we locked the door upon the tragedy. In fear and trembling I went a little farther into the room. Two steps had I taken when I discovered that the lid no longer shut the thing from the stars, that the lid was gaping open. Oh! Pelluther, how will you credit so astounding a statement. I saw (I say it solemnly though I have to labour vigorously to drive back a horde of thoughts) I saw the wretched creature, which you and I had raised from the belly of the earth, lying upon the floor; its meagre limbs were coiled in front of the fire. Had the heat roused him from his long sleep? I know not, I dare not think. He—he, Pelluther—lay upon the hearth-rug sunken in slumber soundlessly breathing. Oh, my friend, I stand eyeing insanity, face to face. My mind is mutinous. There lay the wretched abortion:—it seems to me that this thing is like a pestilent secret sin, which lies hid, festering, weaving snares, befouling the wholesome air, but which, some day, creeps out and goes stalking midst healthy men, a leprous child of the sinner. Ay, and like a sin perhaps of yours and of mine. Pelluther! But, being heavy with such a woesome burden it becomes us alone to bear it. I left the thing there in its sleep. Its history the world shall never know. I write this to warn you of the awful terror of the event which has come upon you and me. When you come,* we will make our plans to destroy utterly this horrid memory. And if this be not our lot we must exist but to hide our discovery from the eyes of the sane. If any suffer, it is you and I who must suffer. If murder can be just, the killing of this creature—neither man nor beast, this vile symbol—must be accounted to us a virtue. Fate has chosen her tools. Come, my old friend! I have sent away my servants and locked my door; and my prayer is that this thing may sleep until darkness comes down to cloak our horrid task from the eyes of the world. Science is slunk away shamefaced; religion is a withered flower. Oh, my friend, what shall I say! How shall I regain myself?"

From the slender record of this letter I leave you to deduce whatever conclusions you may. I may suppose that at some time of the second day (perhaps, while I was rambling through the green places of Kew!) Dugdale had again visited the thing and found it awake, alert, vigilant in his room. No man spied upon my friend in those hours. (Sometimes in the quietude, I fancy I hear an odd footfall upon my threshold!)

---

*I perceive that Dugdale omitted to post this letter in time to reach me on the second evening. I bitterly deplore the omission.

In the brilliant sunshine I drove in a four-wheeled cab to Dugdale's house, for my limbs were weak and would hardly bear my body. I limped up the garden path and the familiar steps with the help of two sticks. The door was ajar—I entered. I found Dugdale in his study. He was sitting in the chest with a Bible resting on one of the sides.

He looked at me. " 'For we are but of yesterday and know nothing because our days upon earth are a shadow.' What is life, Pelluther? A vain longing for death. What is beauty? A question of degree. And sin is in the air,—child of disease and death and springing-up and hatred of life. Fawn hair has beauty and as for bones; surely less for the worms. Worms! through lead? Pelluther, my dear old Pell. Through lead?"

He gazed at me like a child gazing at a bright light.

"Come!" said I, "the air is bland and the sun is fierce and warm. Come!" I could say no more.

"But the sunlight has no meaning to me now," said he. "That breeder of corruption, tall here and a monstrous being, walks under my skull strangling all the other beings, puny and sapless. I have one idea, conception, vivid faintness, a fierce red horrid idea—and a phenomenon, too. You see, it is when a deep abstract belief rots into loathing, when hope is eaten away by horrors of sleep and a mad longing for sleep—Mad! Yet fawn hair is not without beauty; provided, Pelluther, provided—through lead?" . . .

A vain idle report has been set about by the malicious. Oh, was there not reason and logical sequence in his conversation with me? I give it for demonstration's sake. I swear that he is not mad—a little eccentric (surely all clever men are eccentric), a little aged. I swear solemnly that my dear friend Dugdale was not mad. He was just a man. He wronged no one. He was a benevolent kindly gentleman and fine in intellect. Say you that he was eccentric—not mad. Tears ran down my cheeks as I looked at him.

L. P. HARTLEY

The Travelling Grave (1929)

In his introduction to Cynthia Asquith's *Third Ghost Book*, L. P. Hartley makes the point that a good ghost story has "a natural as well as supernatural interest." The characters, whether human beings or ghosts, have one thing in common: "Whether of flesh and blood or not of flesh and blood, humanity pervades them." Before it can truly frighten us, a ghost story, paradoxically, must do *more* than frighten us.

In antiquarian stories, the additional "natural interest" comes from the delights of art and the connoisseur's sensibility, just as in the visionary tale it comes from the delights of nature. In Hartley's stories, as his statement implies, the interest comes from character. All the people in "The Travelling Grave," from the vulnerable and foppish Hugh Curtis to the cruel and crafty Dick Munt, are drawn with sharpness and individuality. Another "natural" element in Hartley, indeed the most delicious and pleasurable one, is provided by humor, by dialogue and authorial observation that sting with irony and sparkle with wit. Hartley's settings are superb too, as is demonstrated by the elegant descriptions of Munt's house. The author of *The Go-Between* and *Eustace and Hilda*, Hartley was a recognized master of all the traditional elements of fiction, and his numerous ghost stories are among the most distinguished in the English tradition.

At the same time, Hartley recognized that sooner or later the tale of terror had to get down to business and deliver "a shock or surprise and horror, a tingling of the spine." In "The Travelling Grave," Hartley's most original tale, the horror comes not so much from the "ghost," a sinister but entirely mechanical contrivance, but from a coldness and ruthlessness in the world which can spring from surface gaiety. The travelling grave, a mobile killing machine that "has no settled direction" and moves "all ways at once, like a crab," suggests the mobility and capriciousness of death. To Dick Munt, the most villainous antiquary since Mr. Abney in M. R. James's "Lost Hearts," the self-propelled grave is a "charming toy"; to his victim, Hugh Curtis, it becomes a validation of

108

his post-World War I paranoia: " 'Whatever I've done,' he used to say to himself, 'they can't kill me.' With the war, this saving reservation had to be dropped: they could kill him, that was what they were there for." In the course of the story, Hugh finds himself in an absurd postwar world where they are still trying to kill him—in a lethal game of hide-and-seek.

In its basic outline, "The Travelling Grave" falls neatly into the antiquarian school: the dark caprice of the plot turns entirely on Dick Munt's jaded, unappeasable search for new antiquarian delights. In its attitude toward the supernatural, however, the story (which originally appeared in Cynthia Asquith's peerless 1929 anthology, *Shudders*) is difficult to classify. It is a rare example of a spook story which chills us without ever conjuring a real ghost, yet it is not a psychological piece: the travelling grave is manifestly real and is seen by several characters; it just happens to be a mechanical monster rather than a supernatural one. Nor is the tale in the irritating Gothic tradition of the explained-away supernatural: we know from the outset that the supernatural is absent from the story and thus don't feel tricked at the end. We readily accept the difficult challenge Hartley sets for himself of satisfying us *without* this vital ingredient because Hartley's seductive antiquarian atmosphere and glittering dialogue immediately draw us in. It is a measure of his artistry that he cheats without ever permitting us to feel cheated.

≈ THE TRAVELLING GRAVE ≈

Hugh Curtis was in two minds about accepting Dick Munt's invitation to spend Sunday at Lowlands. He knew little of Munt, who was supposed to be rich and eccentric and, like many people of that kind, a collector. Hugh dimly remembered having asked his friend Valentine Ostrop what it was that Munt collected, but he could not recall Valentine's answer. Hugh Curtis was a vague man with an unretentive mind, and the mere thought of a collection, with its many separate challenges to the memory, fatigued him. What he required of a week-end party was to be left alone as much as possible, and to spend the remainder of his time in the society of agreeable women. Searching his mind, though with distaste, for he hated to disturb it, he remembered Ostrop telling him that parties at Lowlands were generally composed entirely of men, and rarely exceeded four in number. Valentine didn't know who the fourth was to be, but he begged Hugh to come.

"You will enjoy Munt," he said. "He really doesn't pose at all. It's his nature to be like that."

"Like what?" his friend had enquired.

"Oh, original and—and queer, if you like," answered Valentine. "He's one of the exceptions—he's much odder than he seems, whereas most people are more ordinary than they seem."

Hugh Curtis agreed. "But I like ordinary people," he added. "So how shall I get on with Munt?"

"Oh," said his friend, "but you're just the type he likes. He prefers ordinary—it's a stupid word—I mean normal, people, because their reactions are more valuable."

"Shall I be expected to react?" asked Hugh with nervous facetiousness.

"Ha! Ha!" laughed Valentine, poking him gently—"we never quite know what he'll be up to. But you will come, won't you?"

Hugh Curtis had said he would.

All the same, when Saturday morning came he began to regret his decision and to wonder whether it might not honourably be reversed. He was a man in early middle life, rather set in his ideas, and, though not specially a snob, unable to help testing a new acquaintance by the

110

standards of the circle to which he belonged. This circle had never warmly welcomed Valentine Ostrop; he was the most unconventional of Hugh's friends. Hugh liked him when they were alone together, but directly Valentine fell in with kindred spirits he developed a kind of foppishness of manner that Hugh instinctively disliked. He had no curiosity about his friends, and thought it out of place in personal relationships, so he had never troubled to ask himself what this altered demeanour of Valentine's, when surrounded by his cronies, might denote. But he had a shrewd idea that Munt would bring out Valentine's less sympathetic side. Could he send a telegram saying he had been unexpectedly detained? Hugh turned the idea over; but partly from principle, partly from laziness (he hated the mental effort of inventing false circumstances to justify change of plans) he decided he couldn't. His letter of acceptance had been so unconditional. He also had the fleeting notion (a totally unreasonable one) that Munt would somehow find out and be nasty about it.

So he did the best he could for himself; looked out the latest train that would get him to Lowlands in decent time for dinner, and telegraphed that he would come by that. He would arrive at the house, he calculated, soon after seven. "Even if dinner is as late as half-past eight," he thought to himself, "they won't be able to do me much harm in an hour and a quarter." This habit of mentally assuring to himself periods of comparative immunity from unknown perils had begun at school. "Whatever I've done," he used to say to himself, "they can't kill me." With the war, this saving reservation had to be dropped: they could kill him, that was what they were there for. But now that peace was here the little mental amulet once more diffused its healing properties; Hugh had recourse to it more often than he would have admitted. Absurdly enough he invoked it now. But it annoyed him that he would arrive in the dusk of the September evening. He liked to get his first impression of a new place by daylight.

Hugh Curtis' anxiety to come late had not been shared by the other two guests. They arrived at Lowlands in time for tea. Though they had not travelled together, Ostrop motoring down, they met practically on the doorstep, and each privately suspected the other of wanting to have his host for a few moments to himself.

But it seemed unlikely that their wish would have been gratified even if they had not both been struck by the same idea. Tea came in, the water bubbled in the urn, but still Munt did not present himself, and at last Ostrop asked his fellow-guest to make the tea.

"You must be deputy-host," he said; "you know Dick so well, better than I do."

This was true. Ostrop had long wanted to meet Tony Bettisher who, after the death of someone vaguely known to Valentine as Squarchy, ranked as Munt's oldest and closest friend. He was a short, dark, thick-set man, whose appearance gave no clue to his character or pursuits. He had, Valentine knew, a job at the British Museum, but, to look at, he might easily have been a stockbroker.

"I suppose you know this place at every season of the year," Valentine said. "This is the first time I've been here in the autumn. How lovely everything looks."

He gazed out at the wooded valley and the horizon fringed with trees. The scent of burning garden-refuse drifted in through the windows.

"Yes, I'm a pretty frequent visitor," answered Bettisher, busy with the teapot.

"I gather from his letter that Dick has just returned from abroad," said Valentine. "Why does he leave England on the rare occasions when it's tolerable? Does he do it for fun, or does he have to?" He put his head on one side and contemplated Bettisher with a look of mock despair.

Bettisher handed him a cup of tea.

"I think he goes when the spirit moves him."

"Yet, but *what* spirit?" cried Valentine with an affected petulance of manner. "Of course, our Richard is a law unto himself: we all know that. But he must have some motive. I don't suppose he's *fond* of travelling. It's *so* uncomfortable. Now Dick cares for his comforts. That's why he travels with so much luggage."

"Oh does he?" enquired Bettisher. "Have you been with him?"

"No, but the Sherlock Holmes in me discovered that," declared Valentine triumphantly. "The trusty Franklin hadn't time to put it away. Two large crates. Now would you call that *personal* luggage?" His voice was for ever underlining: it pounced upon "personal" like a hawk on a dove.

"Perambulators, perhaps," suggested Bettisher laconically.

"Oh, do you think so? Do you think he collects perambulators? That would explain everything!"

"What would it explain?" asked Bettisher, stirring in his chair.

"Why, his collection, of course!" exclaimed Valentine, jumping up and bending on Bettisher an intensely serious gaze. "It would explain why he doesn't invite us to see it, and why he's so shy of talking about it. Don't you see? An unmarried man, a bachelor, sine prole as far as we know, with whole *attics-full* of perambulators! It would be *too* fantastic. The world would laugh, and Richard, much as we love him, is terribly serious. Do you imagine it's a kind of vice?"

"All collecting is a form of vice."

"Oh no, Bettisher, don't be hard, don't be cynical—a *substitute* for vice. But tell me before he comes—he *must* come soon, the laws of hospitality demand it—am I right in my surmise?"

"Which? You have made so many."

"I mean that what he goes abroad for, what he fills his house with, what he thinks about when we're not with him—in a word, what he collects, is perambulators?"

Valentine paused dramatically.

Bettisher did not speak. His eyelids flickered and the skin about his eyes made a sharp movement inwards. He was beginning to open his mouth when Valentine broke in—

"Oh no, of course, you're in his confidence, your lips are sealed. Don't tell me, you mustn't, I forbid you to!"

"What's that he's not to tell you?" said a voice from the other end of the room.

"Oh, Dick!" cried Valentine, "what a start you gave me! You must learn to move a little less like a dome of silence, mustn't he, Bettisher?"

Their host came forward to meet them, on silent feet and laughing soundlessly. He was a small, thin, slightly built man, very well turned out and with a conscious elegance of carriage.

"But I thought you didn't know Bettisher?" he said, when their greetings had been accomplished. "Yet when I come in I find you with difficulty stemming the flood of confidences pouring from his lips."

His voice was slightly ironical, it seemed at the same moment to ask a question and to make a statement.

"Oh, we've been together for hours," said Valentine airily, "and had the most enchanting conversation. Guess what we talked about."

"Not about me, I hope?"

"Well, about something very dear to you."

"About you, then?"

"Don't make fun of me. The objects I speak of are solid and useful."

"That does rather rule you out," said Munt meditatively. "What are they useful for?"

"Carrying bodies."

Munt glanced across at Bettisher, who was staring into the grate.

"And what are they made of?"

Valentine tittered, pulled a face, answered, "I've had little experience of them, but I should think chiefly of wood."

Munt got up and looked hard at Bettisher, who raised his eyebrows and said nothing.

"They perform at one time or another," said Valentine, enjoying himself enormously, "an essential service for us all."

There was a pause. Then Munt asked—

"Where do you generally come across them?"

"Personally I always try to avoid them," said Valentine. "But one meets them every day in the street and—and here, of course."

"Why do you try to avoid them?" asked Munt rather grimly.

"Since you think about them, and dote upon them, and collect them from all the corners of the earth, it pains me to have to say it," said Valentine with relish, "but I do not care to contemplate lumps of human flesh lacking the spirit that makes flesh tolerable."

He struck an oratorical attitude and breathed audibly through his nose. There was a prolonged silence. The dusk began to make itself felt in the room.

"Well," said Munt at last, in a hard voice. "You are the first person to guess my little secret, if I can give it so grandiose a name. I congratulate you."

Valentine bowed.

"May I ask how you discovered it? While I was detained upstairs, I suppose you—you—poked about?" His voice had a disagreeable ring; but Valentine, unaware of this, said loftily—

"It was unnecessary. They were in the hall, plain to be seen by anyone. My Sherlock Holmes sense (I have eight or nine) recognized them immediately."

Munt shrugged his shoulders, then said in a less constrained tone—

"At this stage of our acquaintance I did not really intend to enlighten you. But since you know already, tell me, as a matter of curiosity, were you horrified?"

"Horrified?" cried Valentine. "I think it a charming taste, so original, so—so human. It ravishes my aesthetic sense; it slightly offends my moral principles."

"I was afraid it might," said Munt.

"I am a believer in Birth Control," Valentine prattled on. "Every night I burn a candle to Stopes."

Munt looked puzzled. "But then, how can you object?" he began.

Valentine went on without heeding him.

"But of course by making a corner in the things, you *do* discourage the whole business. Being exhibits they have to stand idle, don't they? You keep them empty?"

Bettisher started up in his chair, but Munt held out a pallid hand and murmured in a stifled voice—

"Yes, that is, most of them are."

Valentine clapped his hands in ecstasy.

"But some are not? Oh, but that's too ingenious of you. To think of the darlings lying there quite still, not able to lift a finger, much less scream! A sort of mannequin parade!"

"They certainly seem more complete with an occupant," Munt observed.

"But who's to push them? They can't go of themselves."

"Listen," said Munt slowly. "I've just come back from abroad, and I've brought with me a specimen that does go by itself, or nearly. It's outside there where you saw, waiting to be unpacked."

Valentine Ostrop had been the life and soul of many a party. No one knew better than he how to breathe new life into a flagging joke. Privately he felt that this one was played out; but he had a social conscience; he realized his responsibility towards conversation, and summoning all the galvanic enthusiasm at his command he cried out—

"Do you mean to say that it looks after itself, it doesn't need a helping hand, and that a fond mother can entrust her precious charge to it without a nursemaid and without a tremor?"

"She can," said Munt, "and without an undertaker and without a sexton."

"Undertaker . . .? Sexton . . .?" echoed Valentine. "What have they to do with perambulators?"

There was a pause, during which the three figures, struck in their respective attitudes, seemed to have lost relationship with each other.

"So you didn't know," said Munt at length, "that it was coffins I collected."

An hour later the three men were standing in an upper room, looking down at a large oblong object that lay in the middle of a heap of shavings and seemed, to Valentine's sick fancy, to be burying its head among them. Munt had been giving a demonstration.

"Doesn't it look funny now it's still?" he remarked. "Almost as though it had been killed." He touched it pensively with his foot and it slid towards Valentine, who edged away. You couldn't quite tell where it was coming; it seemed to have no settled direction, and to move all ways at once, like a crab. "Of course the chances are really against it," sighed Munt. "But it's very quick, and it has that funny gift of anticipation. If it got a fellow up against a wall, I don't think he'd stand much chance. I didn't show you here, because I value my floors, but it can bury itself in wood in three minutes and in newly turned earth, say a flower-bed, in one. It has to be this squarish shape, or it couldn't dig. It just doubles the man up, you see, directly it catches him—backwards, so as to break the spine. The top of the head fits in just below the heels. The soles of the feet come uppermost. The spring sticks a bit." He bent down to adjust something. "Isn't it a charming toy?"

"Looking at it from the criminal's standpoint, not the engineer's," said Bettisher, "I can't see that it would be much use in a house. Have you tried it on a stone floor?"

"Yes, it screams in agony and blunts the blades."

"Exactly. Like a mole on paving-stones. And even on an ordinary carpeted floor it could cut its way in, but there would be a nice hole left in the carpet to show where it had gone."

Munt conceded this point, also. "But it's an odd thing," he added, "that in several of the rooms in this house it would really work, and baffle anyone but an expert detective. Below, of course, are the knives, but the top is inlaid with real parquet. The grave is so sensitive—you saw just now how it seemed to grope—that it can feel the ridges, and adjust itself perfectly to the pattern of the parquet. But of course I agree with you. It's not an indoor game, really: it's a field sport. You go on, will you, and leave me to clear up this mess. I'll join you in a moment."

Valentine followed Bettisher down into the library. He was very much subdued.

"Well, that was the funniest scene," remarked Bettisher, chuckling.

"Do you mean just now? I confess it gave me the creeps."

"Oh no, not that: when you and Dick were talking at cross-purposes."

"I'm afraid I made a fool of myself," said Valentine dejectedly. "I can't quite remember what we said. I know there was something I wanted to ask you."

"Ask away, but I can't promise to answer."

Valentine pondered a moment.

"Now I remember what it was."

"Spit it out."

"To tell you the truth, I hardly like to. It was something Dick said. I hardly noticed at the time. I expect he was just playing up to me."

"Well?"

"About these coffins. Are they real?"

"How do you mean 'real'?"

"I mean, could they be used as—?"

"My dear chap, they have been."

Valentine smiled, rather mirthlessly.

"Are they full-size—life-size, as it were?"

"The two things aren't quite the same," said Bettisher with a grin. "But there's no harm in telling you this: Dick's like all collectors. He prefers rarities, odd shapes, dwarfs, and that sort of thing. Of course any anatomical peculiarity has to have allowance made for it in the coffin. On the whole his specimens tend to be smaller than the general run— shorter, anyhow. Is that what you wanted to know?"

"You've told me a lot," said Valentine. "But there was another thing."

"Out with it."

"When I imagined we were talking about perambulators—"

"Yes, yes."

"I said something about their being empty. Do you remember?"

"I think so."

"Then I said something about them having mannequins inside, and he seemed to agree."

"Oh, yes."

"Well, he couldn't have meant that. It would be too—too realistic."

"Well, then, any sort of dummy."

"There are dummies and dummies. A skeleton isn't very talkative."

Valentine stared.

"He's been away," said Bettisher hastily. "I don't know what his latest idea is. But here's the man himself."

Munt came into the room.

"Children," he called out, "have you observed the time? It's nearly seven o'clock. And do you remember that we have another guest coming? He must be almost due."

"Who is he?" asked Bettisher.

"A friend of Valentine's. Valentine, you must be responsible for him. I asked him partly to please you. I scarcely know him. What shall we do to entertain him?"

"What sort of man is he?" Bettisher enquired.

"Describe him, Valentine. Is he tall or short? I don't remember."

"Medium."

"Dark or fair?"

"Mouse-coloured."

"Old or young?"

"About thirty-five."

"Married or single?"

"Single."

"What, has he no ties? No one to take an interest in him or bother what becomes of him?"

"He has no near relations."

"Do you mean to say that very likely nobody knows he is coming to spend Sunday here?"

"Probably not. He has rooms in London, and he wouldn't trouble to leave his address."

"Extraordinary the casual way some people live. Is he brave or timid?"

"Oh, come, what a question! About as brave as I am."

"Is he clever or stupid?"

"All my friends are clever," said Valentine, with a flicker of his old spirit. "He's not intellectual: he'd be afraid of difficult parlour games or brilliant conversation."

"He ought not to have come here. Does he play bridge?"

"I don't think he has much head for cards."

"Could Tony induce him to play chess?"

"Oh, no, chess needs too much concentration."

"Is he given to wool-gathering, then?" Munt asked. "Does he forget to look where he's going?"

"He's the sort of man," said Valentine, "who expects to find everything just so. He likes to be led by the hand. He is perfectly tame and confiding, like a nicely brought up child."

"In that case," said Munt, "we must find some childish pastime that won't tax him too much. Would he like Musical Chairs?"

"I think that would embarrass him," said Valentine. He began to feel a tenderness for his absent friend, and a wish to stick up for him. "I should leave him to look after himself. He's rather shy. If you try to make him come out of his shell, you'll scare him. He'd rather take the initiative himself. He doesn't like being pursued, but in a mild way he likes to pursue."

"A child with hunting instincts," said Munt pensively. "How can we accommodate him? I have it! Let's play Hide and Seek. We shall hide and he shall seek. Then he can't feel that we are forcing ourselves upon him. It will be the height of tact. He will be here in a few minutes. Let's go and hide now."

"But he doesn't know his way about the house."

"That will be all the more fun for him, since he likes to make discoveries on his own account."

"He might fall and hurt himself."

"Children never do. Now you run away and hide while I talk to Franklin," Munt continued quietly, "and mind you play fair, Valentine —don't let your natural affections lead you astray. Don't give yourself up because you're hungry for your dinner."

The motor that met Hugh Curtis was shiny and smart and glittered in the rays of the setting sun. The chauffeur was like an extension of it, and so quick in his movements that in the matter of stowing Hugh's luggage, putting him in and tucking the rug around him, he seemed to steal a march on time. Hugh regretted this precipitancy, this interference with the rhythm of his thoughts. It was a foretaste of the effort of adaptability he would soon have to make; the violent mental readjustment that every visit, and specially every visit among strangers entails: a surrender of the personality, the fanciful might call it a little death.

The car slowed down, left the main road, passed through white gate-posts and followed for two or three minutes a gravel drive shadowed by trees. In the dusk Hugh could not see how far to right and left these extended. But the house, when it appeared, was plain enough: a large regular, early nineteenth-century building, encased in cream-coloured stucco and pierced at generous intervals by large windows, some round-headed, some rectangular. It looked dignified and quiet, and in the twilight seemed to shine with a soft radiance of its own. Hugh's spirits began to rise. In his mind's ear he already heard the welcoming buzz of voices from a distant part of the house. He smiled at the man who opened the door. But the man didn't return his smile, and no sound came through the gloom that spread out behind him.

"Mr. Munt and his friends are playing 'Hide-and-Seek' in the house,

Sir," the man said, with a gravity that checked Hugh's impulse to laugh. "I was to tell you that the library is home, and you were to be 'He,' or I think he said, 'It,' Sir. Mr. Munt did not want the lights turned on till the game was over."

"Am I to start now?" asked Hugh, stumbling a little as he followed his guide—"or can I go to my room first?"

The Butler stopped and opened a door. "This is the library," he said. "I think it was Mr. Munt's wish that the game should begin immediately upon your arrival, Sir."

A faint coo-ee sounded through the house.

"Mr. Munt said you could go anywhere you liked," the man added as he went away.

Valentine's emotions were complex. The harmless frivolity of his mind had been thrown out of gear by its encounter with the harsher frivolity of his friend. Munt, he felt sure, had a heart of gold which he chose to hide beneath a slightly sinister exterior. With his travelling graves and charnel-talk he had hoped to get a rise out of his guest, and he had succeeded. Valentine still felt slightly unwell. But his nature was remarkably resilient, and the charming innocence of the pastime on which they were now engaged soothed and restored his spirits, gradually reaffirming his first impression of Munt as a man of fine mind and keen perceptions, a dilettante with the personal force of a man of action, a character with a vein of implacability, to be respected but not to be feared. He was conscious also of a growing desire to see Curtis; he wanted to see Curtis and Munt together, confident that two people he liked could not fail to like each other. He pictured the pleasant encounter after the mimic warfare of Hide-and-Seek—the captor and the caught laughing a little breathlessly over the diverting circumstances of their reintroduction. With every passing moment his mood grew more sanguine.

Only one misgiving remained to trouble it. He felt he wanted to confide in Curtis, tell him something of what had happened during the day; and this he could not do without being disloyal to his host. Try as he would to make light of Munt's behaviour about his collection, it was clear he wouldn't have given away the secret if it had not been surprised out of him. And Hugh would find his friend's bald statement of the facts difficult to swallow.

But what was he up to, letting his thoughts run on like this? He must hide, and quickly too. His acquaintance with the lie of the house, the fruits of two visits, was scanty, and the darkness did not help him. The house was long and symmetrical; its principal rooms lay on the first floor. Above were servants' rooms, attics, boxrooms, probably—plenty of natural hiding-places. The second story was the obvious refuge.

He had been there only once, with Munt that afternoon, and he did not specially want to revisit it; but he must enter into the spirit of the game. He found the staircase and went up, then paused: there was really no light at all.

"This is absurd," thought Valentine. "I must cheat." He entered the first room to the left, and turned down the switch. Nothing happened: the current had been cut off at the main. But by the light of a match he made out that he was in a combined bed-and-bathroom. In one corner was a bed, and in the other a large rectangular object with a lid over it, obviously a bath. The bath was close to the door.

As he stood debating he heard footsteps coming along the corridor. It would never do to be caught like this, without a run for his money. Quick as thought he raised the lid of the bath, which was not heavy, and slipped inside, cautiously lowering the lid.

It was narrower than the outside suggested, and it did not feel like a bath, but Valentine's enquiries into the nature of his hiding-place were suddenly cut short. He heard voices in the room, so muffled that he did not know at first whose they were. But they were evidently in disagreement.

Valentine lifted the lid. There was no light, so he lifted it farther. Now he could hear clearly enough.

"But I don't know what you really want, Dick," Bettisher was saying. "With the safety-catch it would be pointless, and without it would be damned dangerous. Why not wait a bit?"

"I shall never have a better opportunity than this," said Munt, but in a voice so unfamiliar that Valentine scarcely recognized it.

"Opportunity for what?" said Bettisher.

"To prove whether the Travelling Grave can do what Madrali claimed for it."

"You mean whether it can disappear? We know it can."

"I mean whether it can effect somebody else's disappearance."

There was a pause. Then Bettisher said—"Give it up. That's my advice."

"But he wouldn't leave a trace," said Munt half petulant, half pleading, like a thwarted child. "He has no relations. Nobody knows he's here. Perhaps he isn't here. We can tell Valentine he never turned up."

"We discussed all that," said Bettisher decisively, "and it won't wash."

There was another silence, disturbed by the distant hum of a motorcar.

"We must go," said Bettisher.

But Munt appeared to detain him. Half imploring, half whining, he said—

"Anyhow, you don't mind me having put it there with the safety-catch down."

"Where?"

"By the china-cabinet. He's certain to run into it."

Bettisher's voice sounded impatiently from the passage.

"Well, if it pleases you. But it's quite pointless."

Munt lingered a moment, chanting to himself in a high voice, greedy with anticipation: "I wonder which is up and which is down."

When he had repeated this three times he scampered away, calling out peevishly: "You might have helped me, Tony. It's so heavy for me to manage."

It was heavy indeed. Valentine, when he had fought down the hysteria that came upon him, had only one thought: to take the deadly object and put it somewhere out of Hugh Curtis' way. If he could drop it from a window, so much the better. In the darkness the vague outline of its bulk, placed just where one had to turn to avoid the china-cabinet, was dreadfully familiar. He tried to recollect the way it worked. Only one thing stuck in his mind. "The ends are dangerous, the sides are safe." Or should it be, "The sides are dangerous, the ends are safe?" While the two sentences were getting mixed up in his mind, he heard the sound of "coo-ee," coming first from one part of the house, then from another. He could also hear footsteps in the hall below him.

Then he made up his mind, and with a confidence that surprised him put his arms round the wooden cube and lifted it into the air. He hardly noticed its weight as he ran with it down the corridor. Suddenly he realized that he must have passed through an open door. A ray of moonlight showed him that he was in a bedroom, standing directly in front of an old-fashioned wardrobe, a towering majestic piece of furniture with three doors, the middle one holding a mirror. Dimly he saw himself reflected there, his burden in his arms. He deposited it on the parquet without making a sound; but on the way out he tripped over a footstool and nearly fell. He was relieved at making so much clatter, and the grating of the key, as he turned it in the lock, was music to his ears.

Automatically he put it in his pocket. But he paid the penalty for his clumsiness. He had not gone a step when a hand caught him by the elbow.

"Why, it's Valentine!" Hugh Curtis cried. "Now come quietly, and take me to my host. I must have a drink."

"I should like one too," said Valentine, who was trembling all over. "Why can't we have some light?"

"Turn it on, idiot," commanded his friend.

"I can't—it's cut off at the main. We must wait till Richard gives the word."

"Where is he?"

"I expect he's tucked away somewhere. Richard!" Valentine called out, "Dick!" He was too self-conscious to be able to give a good shout. "Bettisher! I'm caught! The game's over!"

There was silence a moment, then steps could be heard descending the stairs.

"Is that you, Dick?" asked Valentine of the darkness.

"No, Bettisher." The gaiety of the voice did not ring quite true.

"I've been caught," said Valentine again, almost as Atalanta might have done, and as though it was a wonderful achievement reflecting great credit upon everybody. "Allow me to present you to my captor. No, this is me. We've been introduced already."

It was a moment or two before the mistake was corrected, the two hands groping vainly for each other in the darkness.

"I expect it will be a disappointment when you see me," said Hugh Curtis in the pleasant voice that made many people like him.

"I want to see you," declared Bettisher. "I will, too. Let's have some light."

"I suppose it's no good asking you if you've seen Dick?" enquired Valentine facetiously. "He said we weren't to have any light till the game was finished. He's so strict with his servants; they have to obey him to the letter. I daren't even ask for a candle. But *you* know the faithful Franklin well enough."

"Dick will be here in a moment surely," Bettisher said, for the first time that day appearing undecided.

They all stood listening.

"Perhaps he's gone to dress," Curtis suggested. "It's past eight o'clock."

"How can he dress in the dark?" asked Bettisher.

Another pause.

"Oh, I'm tired of this," said Bettisher. "Franklin! Franklin!" His voice boomed through the house and a reply came almost at once from the hall, directly below them. "We think Mr. Munt must have gone to dress," said Bettisher. "Will you please turn on the light?"

"Certainly, Sir, but I don't think Mr. Munt is in his room."

"Well, anyhow—"

"Very good, Sir."

At once the corridor was flooded with light, and to all of them, in greater or less degree according to their familiarity with their surroundings, it seemed amazing that they should have had so much difficulty, half an hour before, in finding their way about. Even Valentine's harassed emotions experienced a moment's relaxation. They chaffed Hugh Curtis a little about the false impression his darkling voice had given them. Valentine, as always the more loquacious, swore it seemed to proceed from a large gaunt man with a hare-lip. They were beginning to move towards their rooms, Valentine had almost reached his, when Hugh Curtis called after them:

"I say, may I be taken to my room?"

"Of course," said Bettisher, turning back. "Franklin! Franklin! Franklin, show Mr. Curtis where his room is. I don't know myself." He disappeared and the butler came slowly up the stairs.

"It's quite near, Sir, at the end of the corridor," he said. "I'm sorry, with having no light we haven't got your things put out. But it'll only take a moment."

The door did not open when he turned the handle.

"Odd! It's stuck," he remarked: but it did not yield to the pressure of his knee and shoulder. "I've never known it to be locked before," he muttered, thinking aloud, obviously put out by this flaw in the harmony of the domestic arrangements. "If you'll excuse me, Sir, I'll go and fetch my key."

In a minute or two he was back with it. So gingerly did he turn the key in the lock he evidently expected another rebuff; but it gave a satisfactory click and the door swung open with the best will in the world.

"Now I'll go and fetch your suitcase," he said as Hugh Curtis entered.

"No, it's absurd to stay," soliloquized Valentine, fumbling feverishly with his front stud, "after all these warnings, it would be insane. It's what they do in a 'shocker,' linger on and on, disregarding revolvers and other palpable hints, while one by one the villain picks them off, all except the hero, who is generally the stupidest of all, but the luckiest. No doubt by staying I should qualify to be the hero: I should survive; but what about Hugh, and Bettisher, that close-mouthed rat-trap?" He studied his face in the glass: it looked flushed. "I've had an alarming increase in blood-pressure: I am seriously unwell; I must go away at once to a nursing home, and Hugh must accompany me." He gazed round wretchedly at the charmingly furnished room, with its chintz and polished furniture, so comfortable, safe, unsensational. And for the hundredth time his thoughts veered round and blew from the opposite quarter. It would equally be madness to run away at a moment's notice, scared by what was no doubt only an elaborate practical joke. Munt, though not exactly a jovial man, would have his joke, as witness the game of Hide-and-Seek. No doubt the Travelling Grave itself was just a take-in, a test of his and Bettisher's credulity. Munt was not popular, he had few friends, but that did not make him a potential murderer. Valentine had always liked him, and no one, to his knowledge, had ever spoken a word against him. What sort of figure would he, Valentine, cut, after this nocturnal flitting? He would lose at least two friends, Munt and Bettisher, and cover Hugh Curtis and himself with ridicule.

Poor Valentine! So perplexed was he that he changed his mind five times on the way down to the library. He kept repeating to himself the sentence, "I'm so sorry, Dick, I find my blood-pressure rather high, and I think I ought to go into a nursing home tonight—Hugh will see me safely there"—until it became meaningless, even its absurdity disappeared.

Hugh was in the library alone. It was now or never; but Valentine's opening words were swept aside by his friend who came running across the room to him.

"Oh, Valentine, the funniest thing has happened."

"Funny? Where? What?" Valentine asked.

"No, no, don't look as if you'd seen a ghost. It's not the least serious. Only it's so *odd*. This is a house of surprises. I'm glad I came."

"Tell me quickly."

"Don't look so alarmed. It's only very amusing. But I must show it you, or you'll miss the funny side of it. Come on up to my room; we've got five minutes."

But before they crossed the threshold Valentine pulled up with a start. "Is *this* your room?"

"Oh, yes. Don't look as if you had seen a ghost. It's a perfectly ordinary room, I tell you, except for one thing. No, stop a moment; wait here while I arrange the scene."

He darted in, and after a moment summoned Valentine to follow.

"Now, do you notice anything strange?"

"I see the usual evidences of untidiness."

A coat was lying on the floor and various articles of clothing were scattered about.

"You do? Well then—no deceit, gentlemen." With a gesture he snatched the coat up from the floor. "Now what do you see?"

"I see a further proof of slovenly habits—a pair of shoes where the coat was."

"Look well at those shoes. There's nothing about them that strikes you as peculiar?"

Valentine studied them. They were ordinary brown shoes, lying side by side, the soles uppermost, a short pace from the wardrobe. They looked as though someone had taken them off and forgotten to put them away, or taken them out, and forgotten to put them on.

"Well," pronounced Valentine at last, "I don't usually leave my shoes upside-down like that, but you might."

"Ah," said Hugh triumphantly, "your surmise is incorrect. They're *not* my shoes."

"Not yours? Then they were left here by mistake. Franklin should have taken them away."

"Yes, but that's where the coat comes in. I'm reconstructing the scene, you see, hoping to impress you. While he was downstairs fetching my bag, to save time I began to undress; I took my coat off and hurled it down there. After he had gone I picked it up. So he never saw the shoes."

"Well, why make such a fuss? They won't be wanted till morning. Or would you rather ring for Franklin and tell him to take them away?"

"Ah!" cried Hugh, delighted by this. "At last you've come to the heart of the matter. He *couldn't* take them away."

"Why couldn't he?"

"Because they're fixed to the floor!"

"Oh, rubbish!" said Valentine. "You must be dreaming."

He bent down, took hold of the shoes by the welts, and gave a little tug. They did not move.

"There you are!" cried Hugh. "Apologize. Own that it is unusual to find in one's room a strange pair of shoes adhering to the floor."

Valentine's reply was to give another heave. Still the shoes did not budge.

"No good," commented his friend. "They're nailed down, or gummed down, or something."

"The dinner-bell hasn't rung; we'll get Franklin to clear up the mystery."

The butler when he came looked uneasy, and surprised them by speaking first.

"Was it Mr. Munt you were wanting, Sir?" he said to Valentine. "I don't know where he is. I've looked everywhere and can't find him."

"Are these his shoes by any chance?" asked Valentine.

They couldn't deny themselves the mild entertainment of watching Franklin stoop down to pick up the shoes, and recoil in preplexity when he found them fast in the floor.

"These should be Mr. Munt's, Sir," he said doubtfully—"these should. But what's happened to them that they won't leave the floor?"

The two friends laughed gaily.

"That's what *we* want to know," Hugh Curtis chuckled. "That's why we called you: we thought you could help us."

"They're Mr. Munt's right enough," muttered the butler. "They must have got something heavy inside."

"Damned heavy," said Valentine, playfully grim.

Fascinated, the three men stared at the upturned soles, so close together that there was no room between for two thumbs set side by side.

Rather gingerly the butler stooped again, and tried to feel the uppers. This was not as easy as it seemed, for the shoes were flattened against the floor, as if a weight had pressed them down.

His face was white as he stood up.

"There *is* something in them," he said in a frightened voice.

"And his shoes were full of feet," carolled Valentine flippantly. "Trees, perhaps."

"It was not as hard as wood," said the butler. "You can squeeze it a bit if you try."

They looked at each other, and a tension made itself felt in the room.

"There's only one way to find out," declared Hugh Curtis suddenly, in a determined tone one could never have expected from him.

"How?"

"Take them off."

"Take what off?"

"His shoes off, you idiot."

"Off what?"

"That's what I don't know yet, you bloody fool!" Curtis almost screamed; and kneeling down, he tore apart the laces and began tugging and wrenching at one of the shoes.

"It's coming, it's coming," he cried. "Valentine, put your arms around me and pull, that's a good fellow. It's the heel that's giving the trouble."

Suddenly the shoe slipped off.

"Why, it's only a sock," whispered Valentine; "it's so thin."

"Yes, but the foot's inside it all right," cried Curtis in a loud strange voice, speaking very rapidly. "And here's the ankle, see, and here's where it begins to go down into the floor, see; he must have been a very small man; you see I never saw him, but it's all so crushed—"

The sound of a heavy fall made them turn.

Franklin had fainted.

E. G. SWAIN

The Man With the Roller (1912)

This charming variation on M. R. James's "Mezzotint," the greatest of all short stories about spooky pictures, is the lead story in the fabulously rare book *The Stoneground Ghost Tales,* one of several collections of antiquarian tales which have themselves become antiquarian items. Here Swain introduces us to the hero of the collection, Reverend Roland Batchel, the quintessential antiquary, a man who "disliked changes, even for the better," and who endlessly collects and arranges artifacts to create the pleasing illusion that nothing is ever out of its place. This introduction is brief, however, for the tale centers on a very odd photograph, one that has its own story to tell. As in the story that influenced it, "The Mezzotint," the present-tense story dissolves into the much darker tale re-created by the picture. Swain and James were Edwardians who possessed a lingering romantic impulse; they could accept modern gadgetry and chemical processes only if they could invest those processes with magical powers.

Swain's most striking departure from James, whom he affectionately called "the indulgent parent" of his ghostly tastes, is his renunciation of the Jamesian dictum that only malignant, lethal ghosts have any business in a ghost story. Swain's ghosts, with a few nasty exceptions (the exceptions invariably involving ghosts from the lower classes), are curiously civilized and well behaved. They want to be messy and disruptive, but they are victims of their genteel upbringings. Nevertheless, as "The Man With the Roller" illustrates, Swain's stories have their own quite special chill and poignance.

THE MAN WITH THE ROLLER

On the edge of that vast tract of East Anglia, which retains its ancient name of the Fens, there may be found, by those who know where to seek it, a certain village called Stoneground. It was once a picturesque village. To-day it is not to be called either a village, or picturesque. Man dwells not in one "house of clay," but in two, and the material of the second is drawn from the earth upon which this and the neighbouring villages stood. The unlovely signs of the industry have changed the place alike in aspect and in population. Many who have seen the fossil skeletons of great saurians brought out of the clay in which they have lain from pre-historic times, have thought that the inhabitants of the place have not since changed for the better. The chief habitations, however, have their foundations not upon clay, but upon a bed of gravel which anciently gave to the place its name, and upon the highest part of this gravel stands, and has stood for many centuries, the Parish Church, dominating the landscape for miles around.

Stoneground, however, is no longer the inaccessible village, which in the middle ages stood out above a waste of waters. Occasional floods serve to indicate what was once its ordinary outlook, but in more recent times the construction of roads and railways, and the drainage of the Fens, have given it freedom of communication with the world from which it was formerly isolated.

The Vicarage of Stoneground stands hard by the Church, and is re-nowned for its spacious garden, part of which, and that (as might be expected) the part nearest the house, of ancient date. To the original plot successive Vicars have added adjacent lands, so that the garden has gradually acquired the state in which it now appears.

The Vicars have been many in number. Since Henry de Greville was instituted in the year 1140 there have been 30, all of whom have lived, and most of whom have died, in successive vicarage houses upon the present site.

The present incumbent, Mr. Batchel, is a solitary man of somewhat studious habits, but is not too much enamoured of his solitude to receive visits, from time to time, from schoolboys and such. In the summer of the year 1906 he entertained two, who are the occasion of this narrative, though still unconscious of their part in it, for one of the two, celebrating his 15th birthday during his visit to Stoneground, was presented by Mr. Batchel with a new camera, with which he proceeded to photograph, with considerable skill, the surroundings of the house.

One of these photographs Mr. Batchel thought particularly pleasing. It was a view of the house with the lawn in the foreground. A few small copies, such as the boy's camera was capable of producing, were sent to him by his young friend, some weeks after the visit, and again Mr. Batchel was so much pleased with the picture, that he begged for the negative, with the intention of having the view enlarged.

The boy met the request with what seemed a needlessly modest plea. There were two negatives, he replied, but each of them had, in the same part of the picture, a small blur for which there was no accounting otherwise than by carelessness. His desire, therefore, was to discard these films, and to produce something more worthy of enlargement, upon a subsequent visit.

Mr. Batchel, however, persisted in his request, and upon receipt of the negative, examined it with a lens. He was just able to detect the blur alluded to; an examination under a powerful glass, in fact revealed something more than he had at first detected. The blur was like the nucleus of a comet as one sees it represented in pictures, and seemed to be connected with a faint streak which extended across the negative. It was, however, so inconsiderable a defect that Mr. Batchel resolved to disregard it. He had a neighbour whose favourite pastime was photography, one who was notably skilled in everything that pertained to the art, and to him he sent the negative, with the request for an enlargement, reminding him of a long-standing promise to do any such service, when as had now happened, his friend might see fit to ask it.

This neighbour who had acquired such skill in photography was one Mr. Groves, a young clergyman, residing in the Precincts of the Minster near at hand, which was visible from Mr. Batchel's garden. He lodged with a Mrs. Rumney, a superannuated servant of the Palace, and a strong-minded vigorous woman still, exactly such a one as Mr. Groves needed to have about him. For he was a constant trial to Mrs. Rumney, and but for the wholesome fear she begot in him, would have converted his rooms into a mere den. Her carpets and tablecloths were continually bespattered with chemicals; her chimney-piece ornaments had been unceremoniously stowed away and replaced by labelled bottles; even the bed of Mr.

Groves was, by day, strewn with drying films and mounts, and her old and favourite cat had a bald patch on his flank, the result of a mishap with the pyrogallic acid.

Mrs. Rumney's lodger, however, was a great favourite with her, as such helpless men are apt to be with motherly women, and she took no small pride in his work. A life-size portrait of herself, originally a peace-offering, hung in her parlour, and had long excited the envy of every friend who took tea with her.

"Mr. Groves," she was wont to say, "is a nice gentleman, AND a gentleman; and chemical though he may be, I'd rather wait on him for nothing than what I would on anyone else for twice the money."

Every new piece of photographic work was of interest to Mrs. Rumney, and she expected to be allowed both to admire and to criticise. The view of Stoneground Vicarage, therefore, was shown to her upon its arrival. "Well may it want enlarging," she remarked, "and it no bigger than a postage stamp; it looks more like a doll's house than a vicarage," and with this she went about her work, whilst Mr. Groves retired to his dark room with the film, to see what he could make of the task assigned to him.

Two days later, after repeated visits to his dark room, he had made something considerable; and when Mrs. Rumney brought him his chop for luncheon, she was lost in admiration. A large but unfinished print stood upon his easel, and such a picture of Stoneground Vicarage was in the making as was calculated to delight both the young photographer and the Vicar.

Mr. Groves spent only his mornings, as a rule, in photography. His afternoons he gave to pastoral work, and the work upon this enlargement was over for the day. It required little more than "touching up," but it was this "touching up" which made the difference between the enlargements of Mr. Groves and those of other men. The print, therefore, was to be left upon the easel until the morrow, when it was to be finished. Mrs. Rumney and he, together, gave it an admiring inspection as she was carrying away the tray, and what they agreed in admiring most particularly was the smooth and open stretch of lawn, which made so excellent a foreground for the picture. "It looks," said Mrs. Rumney, who had once been young, "as if it was waiting for someone to come and dance on it."

Mr. Groves left his lodgings—we must now be particular about the hours—at half-past two, with the intention of returning, as usual, at five. "As reg'lar as a clock," Mrs. Rumney was wont to say, "and a sight more reg'lar than some clocks I knows of."

Upon this day he was, nevertheless, somewhat late, some visit had detained him unexpectedly, and it was a quarter-past five when he inserted his latch-key in Mrs. Rumney's door.

Hardly had he entered, when his landlady, obviously awaiting him, appeared in the passage: her face, usually florid, was of the colour of parchment, and, breathing hurriedly and shortly, she pointed at the door of Mr. Groves' room.

In some alarm at her condition, Mr. Groves hastily questioned her; all she could say was: "The photograph! the photograph!" Mr. Groves could only suppose that his enlargement had met with some mishap for which Mrs. Rumney was responsible. Perhaps she had allowed it to flutter into the fire. He turned towards his room in order to discover the worst, but at this Mrs. Rumney laid a trembling hand upon his arm, and held him back. "Don't go in," she said, "have your tea in the parlour."

"Nonsense," said Mr. Groves, "if that is gone we can easily do another."

"Gone," said his landlady, "I wish to Heaven it was."

The ensuing conversation shall not detain us. It will suffice to say that after a considerable time Mr. Groves succeeded in quieting his landlady, so much so that she consented, still trembling violently, to enter the room with him. To speak truth, she was as much concerned for him as for herself, and she was not by nature a timid woman.

The room, so far from disclosing to Mr. Groves any cause for excitement, appeared wholly unchanged. In its usual place stood every article of his stained and ill-used furniture, on the easel stood the photograph, precisely where he had left it; and except that his tea was not upon the table, everything was in its usual state and place.

But Mrs. Rumney again became excited and tremulous, "It's there," she cried. "Look at the lawn."

Mr. Groves stepped quickly forward and looked at the photograph. Then he turned as pale as Mrs. Rumney herself.

There was a man, a man with an indescribably horrible suffering face, rolling the lawn with a large roller.

Mr. Groves retreated in amazement to where Mrs. Rumney had remained standing. "Has anyone been in here?" he asked.

"Not a soul," was the reply, "I came in to make up the fire, and turned to have another look at the picture, when I saw that dead-alive face at the edge. It gave me the creeps," she said, "particularly from not having noticed it before. If that's anyone in Stoneground, I said to myself, I wonder the Vicar has him in the garden with that awful face. It took that hold of me I thought I must come and look at it again, and at five o'clock I brought your tea in. And then I saw him moved along right in front, with a roller dragging behind him, like you see."

Mr. Groves was greatly puzzled. Mrs. Rumney's story, of course, was incredible, but this strange evil-faced man had appeared in the photograph somehow. That he had not been there when the print was made was quite certain.

The problem soon ceased to alarm Mr. Groves; in his mind it was investing itself with a scientific interest. He began to think of suspended chemical action, and other possible avenues of investigation. At Mrs. Rumney's urgent entreaty, however, he turned the photograph upon the easel, and with only its white back presented to the room, he sat down and ordered tea to be brought in.

He did not look again at the picture. The face of the man had about it something unnaturally painful: he could remember, and still see, as it were, the drawn features, and the look of the man had unaccountably distressed him.

He finished his slight meal, and having lit a pipe, began to brood over the scientific possibilities of the problem. Had any other photograph upon the original film become involved in the one he had enlarged? Had the image of any other face, distorted by the enlarging lens, become a part of this picture? For the space of two hours he debated this possibility, and that, only to reject them all. His optical knowledge told him that no conceivable accident could have brought into his picture a man with a roller. No negative of his had ever contained such a man; if it had, no natural causes would suffice to leave him, as it were, hovering about the apparatus.

His repugnance to the actual thing had by this time lost its freshness, and he determined to end his scientific musings with another inspection of the object. So he approached the easel and turned the photograph round again. His horror returned, and with good cause. The man with the roller had now advanced to the middle of the lawn. The face was stricken still with the same indescribable look of suffering. The man seemed to be appealing to the spectator for some kind of help. Almost, he spoke.

Mr. Groves was naturally reduced to a condition of extreme nervous excitement. Although not by nature what is called a nervous man, he trembled from head to foot. With a sudden effort, he turned away his head, took hold of the picture with his outstretched hand, and opening a drawer in his sideboard thrust the thing underneath a folded tablecloth which was lying there. Then he closed the drawer and took up an entertaining book to distract his thoughts from the whole matter.

In this he succeeded very ill. Yet somehow the rest of the evening passed, and as it wore away, he lost something of his alarm. At ten o'clock, Mrs. Rumney, knocking and receiving answer twice, lest by any chance she should find herself alone in the room, brought in the cocoa usually taken by her lodger at that hour. A hasty glance at the easel showed her that it stood empty, and her face betrayed her relief. She made no comment, and Mr. Groves invited none.

The latter, however, could not make up his mind to go to bed. The face he had seen was taking firm hold upon his imagination, and seemed to fascinate him and repel him at the same time. Before long, he found himself wholly unable to resist the impulse to look at it once more. He took it again, with some indecision, from the drawer and laid it under the lamp.

The man with the roller had now passed completely over the lawn, and was near the left of the picture.

The shock to Mr. Groves was again considerable. He stood facing the fire, trembling with excitement which refused to be suppressed. In this state his eye lighted upon the calendar hanging before him, and it furnished him with some distraction. The next day was his mother's birthday. Never did he omit to write a letter which should lie upon her breakfast-table, and the pre-occupation of this evening had made him wholly forgetful of the matter. There was a collection of letters, however, from the pillarbox near at hand, at a quarter before midnight, so he turned to his desk, wrote a letter which would at least serve to convey his affectionate greetings, and having written it, went out into the night and posted it.

The clocks were striking midnight as he returned to his room. We may be sure that he did not resist the desire to glance at the photograph he had left on his table. But the results of that glance, he, at any rate, had not anticipated. The man with the roller had disappeared. The lawn lay as smooth and clear as at first, "looking," as Mrs. Rumney had said, "as if it was waiting for someone to come and dance on it."

The photograph, after this, remained a photograph and nothing more. Mr. Groves would have liked to persuade himself that it had never undergone these changes which he had witnessed, and which we have endeavoured to describe, but his sense of their reality was too insistent. He kept the print lying for a week upon his easel. Mrs. Rumney, although she had ceased to dread it, was obviously relieved at its disappearance, when it was carried to Stoneground to be delivered to Mr. Batchel. Mr. Groves said nothing of the man with the roller, but gave the enlargement, without comment, into his friend's hands. The work of enlargement had been skillfully done, and was deservedly praised.

Mr. Groves, making some modest disclaimer, observed that the view, with its spacious foreground of lawn, was such as could not have failed to enlarge well. And this lawn, he added, as they sat looking out of the Vicar's study, looks as well from within your house as from without. It must give you a sense of responsibility, he added, reflectively, to be sitting where your predecessors have sat for so many centuries and to be continuing their peaceful work. The mere presence before your window, of the turf upon which good men have walked, is an inspiration.

The Vicar made no reply to these somewhat sententious remarks. For a moment he seemed as if he would speak some words of conventional assent. Then he abruptly left the room, to return in a few minutes with a parchment book.

"Your remark, Groves," he said as he seated himself again, "recalled to me a curious bit of history: I went up to the old library to get the book. This is the journal of William Longue who was Vicar here up to the year 1602. What you said about the lawn will give you an interest in a certain portion of the journal. I will read it."

Aug. 1, 1600.—I am now returned in haste from a journey to Brightelmstone whither I had gone with full intention to remain about the space of two months. Master Josiah Wilburton, of my dear College of Emmanuel, having consented to assume the charge of my parish of Stoneground in the meantime. But I had intelligence, after 12 days' absence, by a messenger from the Churchwardens, that Master Wilburton had disappeared last Monday sennight, and had been no more seen. So here I am again in my study to the entire frustration of my plans, and can do nothing in my perplexity but sit and look out from my window, before which Andrew Birch rolleth the grass with much persistence. Andrew passeth so many times over the same place with his roller that I have just now stepped without to demand why he so wasteth his labour, and upon this he hath pointed out a place which is not levelled, and hath continued his rolling.

Aug. 2.—There is a change in Andrew Birch since my absence, who hath indeed the aspect of one in great depression, which is noteworthy of so cheerful a man. He haply shares our common trouble in respect of Master Wilburton, of whom we remain without tidings. Having made part of a sermon upon the seventh Chapter of the former Epistle of St. Paul to the Corinthians and the 27th verse, I found Andrew again at his task, and bade him desist and saddle my horse, being minded to ride forth and take counsel with my good friend John Palmer at the Deanery, who bore Master Wilburton great affection.

Aug. 2 continued.—Dire news awaiteth me upon my return. The Sheriff's men have disinterred the body of poor Master W. from beneath the grass Andrew was rolling, and have arrested him on the charge of being his cause of death.

Aug. 10.—Alas! Andrew Birch hath been hanged, the Justice having mercifully ordered that he should hang by the neck until he should be dead, and not sooner molested. May the Lord have mercy on his soul. He made full confession before me, that he had slain Master Wilburton in heat upon his threatening to make me privy to certain peculation of which I should not have suspected so old a servant. The poor man bemoaned his evil temper in great contrition, and beat his breast, saying that he knew himself doomed for ever to roll the grass in the place where he had tried to conceal his wicked fact.

"Thank you," said Mr. Groves. "Has that little negative got the date upon it?" "Yes," replied Mr. Batchel, as he examined it with his glass. "The boy has marked it August 10." The Vicar seemed not to remark the coincidence with the date of Birch's execution. Needless to say that it did not escape Mr. Groves. But he kept silence about the man with the roller, who has been no more seen to this day.

Doubtless there is more in our photography than we yet know of. The camera sees more than the eye, and chemicals in a freshly prepared and active state, have a power which they afterwards lose. Our units of time, adopted for the convenience of persons dealing with the ordinary movements of material objects, are of course conventional. Those who turn the instruments of science upon nature will always be in danger of seeing more than they looked for. There is such a disaster as that of knowing too much, and at some time or another it may overtake each of us. May we then be as wise as Mr. Groves in our reticence, if our turn should come.

SIR ARTHUR GRAY ("INGULPHUS")

The Everlasting Club (1919)

The most deliberately remote story in this book, "The Everlasting Club" is the lead piece in Sir Arthur Gray's rare, virtually unknown *Tedious Brief Tales of Granta and Gramarye.* This delightful, cleverly illustrated volume, the contents of which have never appeared in the United States, is solidly in the M. R. James tradition. Gray, a Master of Jesus College, devotes his book to gracefully narrated stories involving imaginary ghostly and Satanic incidents from the college's history. These are period pieces, many of which are set farther back in the past than James's suggested thirty years, but Gray's unpretentious erudition and deft wit make history come to life.

"The Everlasting Club" is distanced by more than time. The narrative consists of quotations from the Minute Book of an eighteenth-century Libertine Club devoted to "unholy revelry." The reader must carefully piece these fragments together to create a tentative "story" about the hideous visitations of the club's "Incorporeal Members." With its meticulous eighteenth-century diction and elaborate antiquarian ambience, "The Everlasting Club" achieves a chilling objectivity and indirection. The Minute Book format has a curious double edge: it is hard and "factual," but diabolically suggestive.

≈ THE EVERLASTING CLUB ≈

There is a chamber in Jesus College the existence of which is probably known to few who are now resident, and fewer still have penetrated into it or even seen its interior. It is on the right hand of the landing on the top floor of the precipitous staircase in the angle of the cloister next the Hall—a staircase which for some forgotten story connected with it is traditionally called "Cow Lane." The padlock which secures its massive oaken door is very rarely unfastened, for the room is bare and unfurnished. Once it served as a place of deposit for superfluous kitchen ware, but even that ignominious use has passed from it, and it is now left to undisturbed solitude and darkness. For I should say that it is entirely cut off from the light of the outer day by the walling up, some time in the eighteenth century, of its single window, and such light as ever reaches it comes from the door, when rare occasion causes it to be opened.

Yet at no extraordinarily remote day this chamber has evidently been tenanted, and, before it was given up to darkness, was comfortably fitted, according to the standard of comfort which was known in college in the days of George II. There is still a roomy fireplace before which legs have been stretched and wine and gossip have circulated in the days of wigs and brocade. For the room is spacious and, when it was lighted by the window looking eastward over the fields and common, it must have been a cheerful place for a sociable don.

Let me state in brief, prosaic outline the circumstances which account for the gloom and solitude in which this room has remained now for nearly a century and a half.

In the second quarter of the eighteenth century the University possessed a great variety of clubs of a social kind. There were clubs in college parlours and clubs in private rooms, or in inns and coffee-houses: clubs flavoured with politics, clubs clerical, clubs purporting to be learned and literary. Whatever their professed particularity, the aim of each was convivial. Some of them, which included undergraduates as well as seniors, were dissipated enough, and in their limited provincial way aped the profligacy of such clubs as the Hell Fire Club of London notoriety.

Among these last was one which was at once more select and of more

139

evil fame than any of its fellows. By a singular accident, presently to be explained, the Minute Book of this Club, including the years from 1738 to 1766, came into the hands of a Master of Jesus College, and though, so far as I am aware, it is no longer extant, I have before me a transcript of it which, though it is in a recent handwriting, presents in a bald shape such a singular array of facts that I must ask you to accept them as veracious. The original book is described as a stout duodecimo volume bound in red leather and fastened with red silken strings. The writing in it occupied some 40 pages, and ended with the date November 2, 1766.

The Club in question was called the Everlasting Club—a name sufficiently explained by its rules, set forth in the pocket-book. Its number was limited to seven, and it would seem that its members were all young men, between 22 and 30. One of them was a Fellow-Commoner of Trinity: three of them were Fellows of Colleges, among whom I should specially mention a Fellow of Jesus, named Charles Bellasis: another was a landed proprietor in the county, and the sixth was a young Cambridge physician. The Founder and President of the Club was the Honourable Alan Dermot, who, as the son of an Irish peer, had obtained a nobleman's degree in the University, and lived in idleness in the town. Very little is known of his life and character, but that little is highly in his disfavour. He was killed in a duel at Paris in the year 1743, under circumstances which I need not particularise, but which point to an exceptional degree of cruelty and wickedness in the slain man.

I will quote from the first pages of the Minute Book some of the laws of the Club, which will explain its constitution:—

"1. This Society consisteth of seven Everlastings, who may be Corporeal or Incorporeal, as Destiny shall determine.

2. The rules of the Society, as herein written, are immutable and Everlasting.

3. None shall hereafter be chosen into the Society and none shall cease to be members.

4. The Honourable Alan Dermot is the Everlasting President of the Society.

5. The Senior Corporeal Everlasting, not being the President, shall be the Secretary of the Society, and in this Book of Minutes shall record its transactions, the date at which any Everlasting shall cease to be Corporeal, and all fines due to the Society. And when such Senior Everlasting shall cease to be Corporeal he shall, either in person or by some sure hand, deliver this Book of Minutes to him who shall be next Senior and at

the time Corporeal, and he shall in like manner record the transactions therein and transmit it to the next Senior. The neglect of these provisions shall be visited by the President with fine or punishment according to his discretion.

6. On the second day of November in every year, being the Feast of All Souls, at ten o'clock *post meridiem*, the Everlastings shall meet at supper in the place of residence of that Corporeal member of the Society to whom it shall fall in order of rotation to entertain them, and they shall all subscribe in this Book of Minutes their names and present place of abode.

7. It shall be the obligation of every Everlasting to be present at the yearly entertainment of the Society, and none shall allege for excuse that he has not been invited thereto. If any Everlasting shall fail to attend the yearly meeting, or in his turn shall fail to provide entertainment for the Society, he shall be mulcted at the discretion of the President.

8. Nevertheless, if in any year, in the month of October and not less than seven days before the Feast of All Souls, the major part of the Society, that is to say, four at the least, shall meet and record in writing in these Minutes that it is their desire that no entertainment be given in that year, then, notwithstanding the two rules last rehearsed, there shall be no entertainment in that year, and no Everlasting shall be mulcted on the ground of his absence."

The rest of the rules are either too profane or too puerile to be quoted here. They indicate the extraordinary levity with which the members entered on their preposterous obligations. In particular, to the omission of any regulation as to the transmission of the Minute Book after the last Everlasting ceased to be "Corporeal," we owe the accident that it fell into the hands of one who was not a member of the society, and the consequent preservation of its contents to the present day.

Low as was the standard of morals in all classes of the University in the first half of the eighteenth century, the flagrant defiance of public decorum by the members of the Everlasting Society brought upon it the stern censure of the authorities, and after a few years it was practically dissolved and its members banished from the University. Charles Bellasis, for instance, was obliged to leave the college, and, though he retained his fellowship, he remained absent from it for nearly twenty years. But the minutes of the society reveal a more terrible reason for its virtual extinction.

Between the years of 1738 and 1743 the minutes record many meetings of the Club, for it met on other occasions besides that of All Souls Day.

Apart from a great deal of impious jocularity on the part of the writers, they are limited to the formal record of the attendance of the members, fines inflicted, and so forth. The meeting on November 2nd in the latter year is the first about which there is any departure from the stereotyped forms. The supper was given in the house of the physician. One member, Henry Davenport, the former Fellow-Commoner of Trinity, was absent from the entertainment, as he was then serving in Germany, in the Dettingen campaign. The minutes contain an entry, "Mulctatus propter absentiam per Presidentem, Hen. Davenport." An entry on the next page of the book runs, "Henry Davenport by a Cannon-shot became an Incorporeal Member, November 3, 1743."

The minutes give in their own handwriting, under date November 2, the names and addresses of the six other members. First in the list, in a large bold hand, is the autograph of "Alan Dermot, President, at the Court of His Royal Highness." Now in October Dermot had certainly been in attendance on the Young Pretender at Paris, and doubtless the address which he gave was understood at the time by the other Everlastings to refer to the fact. But on October 28, five days *before* the meeting of the Club, he was killed, as I have already mentioned, in a duel. The news of his death cannot have reached Cambridge on November 2, for the Secretary's record of it is placed below that of Davenport, and with the date November 10: "this day was reported that the president was become an Incorporeal by the hands of a french chevalier." And in a sudden ebullition, which is in glaring contrast with his previous profanities, he has dashed down "The Good God shield us from ill."

The tidings of the President's death scattered the Everlastings like a thunderbolt. They left Cambridge and buried themselves in widely parted regions. But the Club did not cease to exist. The Secretary was still bound to his hateful records: the five survivors did not dare to neglect their fatal obligations. Horror of the presence of the President made the November gathering once and for ever impossible: but horror, too, forbade them to neglect the precaution of meeting in October of every year to put in writing their objection to the celebration. For five years five names are appended to that entry in the minutes, and that is all the business of the Club. Then another member died, who was not the Secretary.

For eighteen more years four miserable men met once each year to deliver the same formal protest. During those years we gather from the signatures that Charles Bellasis returned to Cambridge, now, to appearance, chastened and decorous. He occupied the rooms which I have described on the staircase in the corner of the cloister.

Then in 1766 comes a new handwriting and an altered minute: "Jan. 27, on this day Francis Witherington, Secretary, became an incorporeal Member. The same day this Book was delivered to me, James Harvey." Harvey lived only a month, and a similar entry on March 7 states that the book has descended, with the same mysterious celerity, to William Catherston. Then, on May 18, Charles Bellasis writes that on that day, being the date of Catherston's decease, the Minute Book has come to him as the last surviving Corporeal of the Club.

As it is my purpose to record fact only I shall not attempt to describe the feelings of the unhappy Secretary when he penned that fatal record. When Witherington died it must have come home to the three survivors that after twenty-three years' intermission the ghastly entertainment must be annually renewed, with the addition of fresh incorporeal guests, or that they must undergo the pitiless censure of the President. I think it likely that the terror of the alternative, coupled with the mysterious delivery of the Minute Book, was answerable for the speedy decease of the two first successors to the Secretaryship. Now that the alternative was offered to Bellasis alone, he was firmly resolved to bear the consequences, whatever they might be, of an infringement of the Club rules.

The graceless days of George II. had passed away from the University. They were succeeded by times of outward respectability, when religion and morals were no longer publicly challenged. With Bellasis, too, the petulance of youth had passed: he was discreet, perhaps exemplary. The scandal of his early conduct was unknown to most of the new generation, condoned by the few survivors who had witnessed it.

On the night of November 2nd, 1766, a terrible event revived in the older inhabitants of the College the memory of those evil days. From ten o'clock to midnight a hideous uproar went on in the chamber of Bellasis. Who were his companions none knew. Blasphemous outcries and ribald songs, such as had not been heard for twenty years past, aroused from sleep or study the occupants of the court; but among the voices was not that of Bellasis. At twelve a sudden silence fell upon the cloisters. But the Master lay awake all night, troubled at the relapse of a respected colleague and the horrible example of libertinism set to his pupils.

In the morning all remained quiet about Bellasis' chamber. When his door was opened, soon after daybreak, the early light creeping through the drawn curtains revealed a strange scene. About the table were drawn seven chairs, but some of them had been overthrown, and the furniture was in chaotic disorder, as after some wild orgy. In the chair at the foot of the table sat the lifeless figure of the Secretary, his head bent over his folded arms, as though he would shield his eyes from some horrible sight. Before him on the table lay pen, ink and the red Minute Book. On the last inscribed page, under the date of November 2nd, were written, for the first time since 1742, the autographs of the seven members of the Everlasting Club, but without address. In the same strong hand in which the President's name was written there was appended below the signatures the note "Mulctatus per Presidentem propter neglectum obsonii, Car. Bellasis."

The Minute Book was secured by the Master of the College and I believe that he alone was acquainted with the nature of its contents. The scandal reflected on the College by the circumstances revealed in it caused him to keep the knowledge rigidly to himself. But some suspicion of the nature of the occurrences must have percolated to students and servants, for there was a long-abiding belief in the College that annually on the night of November 2 sounds of unholy revelry were heard to issue from the chamber of Bellasis. I cannot learn that the occupants of the adjoining rooms have ever been disturbed by them. Indeed, it is plain from the minutes that owing to their improvident drafting no provision was made for the perpetuation of the All Souls entertainment after the last Everlasting ceased to be Corporeal. Such superstitious belief must be treated with contemptuous incredulity. But whether for that cause or another the rooms were shut up, and have remained tenantless from that day to this.

H. R. WAKEFIELD

"He Cometh and He Passeth By!" (1928)

Unlike the mistily ambiguous atmosphere pieces so prevalent in the English tradition of ghostly fiction, this is a rather straightforward, action-oriented story with real heroes and villains. The villain, one of the "Naughty Boys of the Nineties," a "man of evil power" who bears a more than passing resemblance to Aleister Crowley, is one of the most formidable and colorful in the literature. The heroes are charming and resourceful and know how to bear suffering gracefully. "Bluntly, I've been bothered," says one of them who is in mortal danger; "haunted perhaps is too strong a word—too pompous."

Nevertheless, " 'He Cometh and He Passeth By!' ", a story distinctly in the tradition of M. R. James's "Casting the Runes," has a highly relativistic sense of morality. In traditional stories with Faustian motifs, the man who acquires Satanic powers bargains away his soul. Here, the hero acquires them, uses them with authoritative, murderous precision, and seems to pay no price at all.

It is hoped that the inclusion of this exciting story will generate an interest in Wakefield's ghostly tales, which are sadly neglected. The author of seven supernatural collections, Wakefield was one of the genuine connoisseurs in the genre. As " 'He Cometh and He Passeth By!' " (from his forgotten first collection) illustrates, there is nothing murky or Gothic about Wakefield's style. His prose, like that of Shirley Jackson and Caroline Blackwood, is hard and clear. This very terseness can be a problem if the reader is not careful, for Wakefield is fond of throwing out frightening, precisely interconnected occult motifs but developing them only briefly. The ending to " 'He Cometh and He Passeth By!' " is a case in point: typically abrupt, it is nevertheless perfectly comprehensible if the reader carefully follows the deadly thread that leads to it.

145

◇ "HE COMETH AND HE PASSETH BY!" ◇

Edward Bellamy sat down at his desk, untied the ribbon round a formidable bundle of papers, yawned and looked out of the window.

On that glistening evening the prospect from Stone Buildings, Lincoln's Inn, was restful and soothing. Just below the motor mowing-machine placidly "chug-chugged" as it clipped the finest turf in London. The muted murmurs from Kingsway and Holborn roamed in placidly. One sleepy pigeon was scratching its poll and ruffling its feathers in a tree opposite, two others—one coyly fleeing, the other doggedly in pursuit—strutted the greensward. "A curious rite of courtship," thought Bellamy, "but they seem to enjoy it; more than I enjoy the job of reading this brief!"

Had these infatuated fowls gazed back at Mr. Bellamy they would have seen a pair of resolute and trustworthy eyes dominating a resolute, nondescript face—one that gave an indisputable impression of kindliness, candour and mental alacrity. No woman had etched lines upon it, nor were those deepening furrows ploughed by the highest exercise of the imagination marked thereon.

By his thirty-ninth birthday he had raised himself to the unchallenged position of the most brilliant junior at the Criminal Bar, though that is, perhaps, too flashy an epithet to describe that combination of inflexible integrity, impeccable common sense, perfect health and tireless industry which was Edward Bellamy. A modest person, he attributed his success entirely to that "perfect health," a view not lightly to be challenged by those who spend many of their days in those Black Holes of controversy, the Law Courts of London. And he had spent eight out of the last fourteen days therein. But the result had been a signal triumph, for the Court of Criminal Appeal had taken *his* view of Mr. James Stock's motives, and had substituted ten years' penal servitude for a six-foot drop. And he was very weary—and yet here was this monstrous bundle of papers! He had just succeeded in screwing his determination to the sticking point when his telephone bell rang.

He picked up the receiver languidly, and then his face lightened.

"I know that voice. How are you, my dear Philip? Why, what's the

146

matter? Yes, I'm doing nothing. Delighted! Brooks's at eight o'clock. Right you are!"

So Philip had not forgotten his existence. He had begun to wonder. His mind wandered back over his curious friendship with Franton. It had begun on the first morning of their first term at University, when they had both been strolling nervously about the quad. That it ever had begun was the most surprising thing about it, for superficially they had nothing in common. Philip, the best bat at Eton, almost too decorative, with a personal charm most people found irresistible, the heir to great possessions. He, the crude product of an obscure Grammar School, destined to live precariously on his scholarships, gauche, shy, taciturn. In the ordinary way they would have graduated to different worlds, for the economic factor alone would have kept their paths all through their lives at Oxford inexorably apart. They would have had little more in common with each other than they had with their scouts. And yet they had spent a good part of almost every day together during term time, and during every vacation he had spent some time at Franton Hall, where he had had first revealed to him those many and delicate refinements of life which only great wealth, allied with traditional taste, can secure. Why had it been so? He had eventually asked Philip.

"Because," he replied, "you have a first-class brain, I have a second or third. I have always had things made too easy for me. You have had most things made too hard. *Ergo*, you have a first-class character. I haven't. I feel a sense of respectful shame towards you, my dear Teddie, which alone would keep me trotting at your heels. I feel I can rely on you as on no one else. You are at once my superior and my complement. Anyway, it has happened, why worry? Analysing such things often spoils them, it's like over-rehearsing."

And then the War—and even the Defence of Civilisation entailed subtle social distinctions.

Philip was given a commission in a regiment of cavalry (with the best will in the world Bellamy never quite understood the privileged role of the horse in the higher ranks of English society); he himself enlisted in a line regiment, and rose through his innate common sense and his unflagging capacity for finishing a job to the rank of Major, D.S.O. and bar, and a brace of wound-stripes. Philip went to Mesopotamia and was eventually invalided out through the medium of a gas-shell. His right lung seriously affected, he spent from 1917 to 1924 on a farm in Arizona.

They had written to each other occasionally—the hurried, flippant, shadow-of-death letters of the time, but somehow their friendship had dimmed and faded and become more than a little pre-War by the end of it, so that Bellamy was not more than mildly disappointed when he heard casually that Philip was back in England, yet had had but the most casual, damp letter from him.

But there had been all the old cordiality and affection in his voice over the telephone—and something more—not so pleasant to hear.

At the appointed hour he arrived in St. James's Street, and a moment later Philip came up to him.

"Now, Teddie," he said, "I know what you're thinking, I know I've been a fool and the rottenest sort of type to have acted as I have, but there is a kind of explanation."

Bellamy surrendered at once to that absurd sense of delight at being in Philip's company, and his small resentment was rent and scattered. None the less he regarded him with a veiled intentness. He was looking tired and old—forcing himself—there was something seriously the matter.

"My very dear Philip," he said, "you don't need to explain things to me. To think it is eight years since we met!"

"First of all let's order something," said Philip. "You have what you like, I don't want much, except a drink." Whereupon he selected a reasonable collation for Bellamy and a dressed crab and asparagus for himself. But he drank two Martinis in ten seconds, and these were not the first—Bellamy knew—that he had ordered since five-thirty (there *was* something wrong).

For a little while the conversation was uneasily, stalely reminiscent. Suddenly Philip blurted out, "I can't keep it in any longer. You're the only really reliable, unswerving friend I've ever had. You will help me, won't you?"

"My dear Philip," said Bellamy, touched, "I always have and always will be ready to do anything you want me to do and at any time—you know that."

"Well, then, I'll tell you my story. First of all, have you ever heard of a man called Oscar Clinton?"

"I seem to remember the name. It is somehow connected in my mind with the nineties, raptures and roses, absinthe and poses; and the *other* Oscar. I believe his name cropped up in a case I was in. I have an impression he's a wrong 'un."

"That's the man," said Philip. "He stayed with me for three months at Franton."

"Oh," said Bellamy sharply, "how was that?"

"Well, Teddie, anything the matter with one's lungs affects one's mind —not always for the worse, however. I know that's true, and it affected mine. Arizona is a moon-dim region, very lovely in its way and stark and old, but I had to leave it. You know I was always a sceptic, rather a wooden one, as I remember; well, that ancient, lonely land set my lung-polluted mind working. I used to stare and stare into the sky. One is brought right up against the vast enigmas of time and space and eternity when one lung is doing the work of two, and none too well at that."

Edward realised under what extreme tension Philip had been living, but felt that he could establish a certain control over him. He felt more in command of the situation and resolved to keep that command.

"Well," continued Philip, filling up his glass, "when I got back to England I was so frantically nervous that I could hardly speak or think. I felt insane, unclean—mentally. I felt I was going mad, and could not bear to be seen by anyone who had known me—that is why I was such a fool as not to come to you. You have your revenge! I can't tell you, Teddie, how depression roared through me! I made up my mind to die, but I had a wild desire to know to what sort of place I should go. And then I met Clinton. I had rushed up to London one day just to get the inane anodyne of noise and people, and I suppose I was more or less tight, for I walked into a club of sorts called the 'Chorazin' in Soho. The door-keeper tried to turn me out, but I pushed him aside, and then someone came up and led me to a table. It was Clinton.

"Now there is no doubt he has great hypnotic power. He began to talk, and I at once felt calmer and started to tell him all about myself. I talked wildly for an hour, and he was so deft and delicate in his handling of me that I felt I could not leave him. He has a marvellous insight into abnormal mental—psychic—whatever you like to call them—states. Some time I'll describe what he looks like—he's certainly like no one else in the world.

"Well, the upshot was that he came down to Franton next day and stayed on. Now, I know that his motives were entirely mercenary, but none the less he saved me from suicide, and to a great extent gave back peace to my mind.

"Never could I have imagined such an irresistible and brilliant talker. Whatever he may be, he's also a poet, a profound philosopher and amazingly versatile and erudite. Also, when he likes, his charm of manner carries one away. At least, in my case it did—for a time—though he borrowed twenty pounds or more a week from me.

"And then one day my butler came to me, and with the hushed gusto appropriate to such revelations murmured that two of the maids were in the family way and that another had told him an hysterical little tale—floating in floods of tears—about how Clinton had made several attempts to force his way into her bedroom.

"Well, Teddie, that sort of thing is that sort of thing, but I felt such a performance couldn't possibly be justified, that taking advantage of a trio of rustics in his host's house was a dastardly and unforgivable outrage.

"Other people's morals are chiefly their own affair, but I had a personal responsibility towards these buxom victims—well, you can realise just how I felt.

"I had to speak about it to Clinton, and did so that night. No one ever saw him abashed. He smiled at me in a superior and patronising way, and said he quite understood that I was almost bound to hold such feudal and socially primitive views, suggesting, of course, that my chief concern in the matter was that he had infringed my *droit de seigneur* in these cases. As for him, he considered it was his duty to disseminate his unique genius as widely as possible, and that it should be considered the highest privilege for anyone to bear his child. He had to his knowledge seventy-four offspring alive, and probably many more—the more the better for the future of humanity. But, of course, he understood and promised for the future—bowing to my rights and my prejudices—to allow me to plough my pink and white pastures—and much more to the same effect.

"Though still under his domination, I felt there was more lust than logic in these specious professions, so I made an excuse and went up to London the next day. As I left the house I picked up my letters, which I read in the car on the way up. One was a three-page catalogue raisonné from my tailor. Not being as dressy as all that, it seemed unexpectedly grandiose, so I paid him a visit. Well, Clinton had forged a letter from me authorising him to order clothes at my expense, and a lavish outfit had been provided.

"It then occurred to me to go to my bank to discover precisely how much I had lent Clinton during the last three months. It was four hundred and twenty pounds. All these discoveries—telescoping—caused me to review my relationship with Clinton. Suddenly I felt it had better end. I might be mediaeval, intellectually costive, and the possessor of much scandalously unearned increment, but I could not believe that the pursuit and contemplation of esoteric mysteries necessarily implied the lowest possible standards of private decency. In other words, I was recovering.

"I still felt that Clinton was the most remarkable person I had ever met. I do to this day—but I felt I was unequal to squaring such magic circles.

"I told him so when I got back. He was quite charming, gentle, understanding, commiserating, and he left the next morning, after pronouncing some incantation whilst touching my forehead. I missed him very much. I believe he's the devil, but he's that sort of person.

"Once I had assured the prospective mothers of his children that they would not be sacked and that their destined contributions to the population would be a charge upon me—there is a codicil to my will to this effect —they brightened up considerably, and rather too frequently snatches of the Froth-Blowers' Anthem cruised down to me as they went about their duties. In fact, I had a discreditable impression that the Immaculate Third would have shown less lachrymose integrity had the consequences of surrender been revealed *ante factum*. Eventually a brace of male infants came to contribute their falsettos to the dirge—for whose appearance the locals have respectfully given me the credit. These brats have searching malign eyes, and when they reach the age of puberty I should not be surprised if the birth statistics for East Surrey began to show a remarkable— even a magical—rise.

"Oh, how good it is to talk to you, Teddie, and get it all off my chest! I feel almost light-hearted, as though my poor old brain had been curetted. I feel I can face and fight it now.

"Well, for the next month I drowsed and read and drowsed and read until I felt two-lunged again. And several times I almost wrote to you, but I felt such lethargy and yet such a certainty of getting quite well again that I put everything off. I was content to lie back and let that blessed healing process work its quiet kindly way with me.

"And then one day I got a letter from a friend of mine, Melrose, who was at the House when we were up. He is the Secretary of 'Ye Ancient Mysteries,' a dining club I joined before the War. It meets once a month and discusses famous mysteries of the past—the *Mary Celeste*, the McLachlan Case, and so on—with a flippant yet scholarly zeal; but that doesn't matter. Well, Melrose said that Clinton wanted to become a member, and had stressed the fact that he was a friend of mine. Melrose was a little upset, as he had heard vague rumours about Clinton. Did I think he was likely to be an acceptable member of the club?

"Well, what was I to say? On the one side of the medal were the facts that he had used my house as his stud-farm, that he had forged my name and sponged on me shamelessly. On the reverse was the fact that he was a genius and knew more about Ancient Mysteries than the rest of the world put together. But my mind was soon made up; I could not recommend him. A week later I got a letter—a charming letter, a most understanding letter from Clinton. He realised, so he said, that I had been bound to give the secretary of the Ancient Mysteries the advice I had—no doubt I considered he was not a decent person to meet my friends. He was naturally disappointed, and so on.

"How the devil, I wondered, did he know—not only that I had put my thumbs down against him, but also the very reason for which I had put them down!

"So I asked Melrose, who told me he hadn't mentioned the matter to a soul, but had discreetly removed Clinton's name from the list of candidates for election. And no one should have been any the wiser; but how much wiser Clinton was!

"A week later I got another letter from him, saying that he was leaving England for a month. He enclosed a funny little paper pattern thing, an outline cut out with scissors with a figure painted on it, a beastly-looking thing. Like this!"

And he drew a quick sketch on the table cloth.

Certainly it was unpleasant, thought Bellamy. It appeared to be a crouching figure in the posture of pursuit. The robes it wore seemed to rise and billow above its head. Its arms were long—too long—scraping the ground with curved and spiked nails. Its head was not quite human, its expression devilish and venomous. A horrid, hunting thing, its eyes encarnadined and infinitely evil, glowing animal eyes in the foul dark face. And those long vile arms—not pleasant to be in their grip. He hadn't realised Philip could draw as well as that. He straightened himself, lit a cigarette, and rallied his fighting powers. For the first time he realised, why, that Philip was in serious trouble! Just a rather beastly little sketch on a table cloth. And now it was up to him!

"Clinton told me," continued Philip, "that this was a most powerful symbol which I should find of the greatest help in my mystical studies. I must place it against my forehead, and pronounce at the same time a certain sentence. And, Teddie, suddenly, I found myself doing so. I remember I had a sharp feeling of surprise and irritation when I found I had placarded this thing on my head and repeated this sentence."

"What was the sentence?" asked Bellamy.

"Well, that's a funny thing," said Philip. "I can't remember it, and both the slip of paper on which it was written and the paper pattern had disappeared the next morning. I remember putting them in my pocket book, but they completely vanished. And, Teddie, things haven't been the same since." He filled his glass and emptied it, lit a cigarette, and at once pressed the life from it in an ash tray and then lit another.

"Bluntly, I've been bothered, haunted perhaps is too strong a word—too pompous. It's like this. That same night I had read myself tired in the study, and about twelve o'clock I was glancing sleepily around the room when I noticed that one of the bookcases was throwing out a curious and unaccountable shadow. It seemed as if something was hiding behind the bookcase, and that this was that something's shadow. I got up and walked over to it, and it became just a bookcase shadow, rectangular and reassuring. I went to bed.

"As I turned on the light on the landing I noticed the same sort of shadow coming from the grandfather clock. I went to sleep all right, but suddenly found myself peering out of the window, and there was that shadow stretching out from the trees and in the drive. At first there was about that much of it showing." and he drew a line down the sketch on the table cloth, "about a sixth. Well, it's been a simple story since then. Every night that shadow has grown a little. It is now almost visible. And it comes out suddenly from different places. Last night it was on the wall beside the door into the Dutch Garden. I never know where I'm going to see it next."

"And how long has this been going on?" asked Bellamy.

"A month to-morrow. You sound as if you thought I was mad. I probably am."

"No, you're as sane as I am. But why don't you leave Franton and come to London?"

"And see it on the wall of the club bedroom! I've tried that, Teddie, but one's as bad as the other. Doesn't it sound ludicrous? But it isn't to me."

"Do you usually eat as little as this?" asked Bellamy.

" 'And drink as much?' you were too polite to add. Well, there's more to it than indigestion, and it isn't incipient D.T. It's just I don't feel very hungry nowadays."

Bellamy got that rush of tip-toe pugnacity which had won him so many desperate cases. He had had a Highland grandmother from whom he had inherited a powerful visualising imagination, by which he got a fleeting

yet authentic insight into the workings of men's minds. So now he knew
in a flash how he would feel if Philip's ordeal had been his.

"Whatever it is, Philip," he said, "there are two of us now."

"Then you do believe in it," said Philip. "Sometimes I can't. On a
sunny morning with starlings chattering and buses swinging up Waterloo
Place—then how can such things be? But at night I know they are."

"Well," said Bellamy, after a pause, "let us look at it coldly and precisely. Ever since Clinton sent you a certain painted paper pattern you've
seen a shadowed reproduction of it. Now I take it he has—as you suggested—unusual hypnotic power. He has studied mesmerism?"

"I think he's studied every bloody thing," said Philip.

"Then that's a possibility."

"Yes," agreed Philip, "it's a possibility. And I'll fight it, Teddie, now
that I have you, but can you minister to a mind diseased?"

"Throw quotations to the dogs," replied Bellamy. "What one man has
done another can undo—there's one for you."

"Teddie," said Philip, "will you come down to Franton to-night?"

"Yes," said Bellamy. "But why?"

"Because I want you to be with me at twelve o'clock to-night when I
look out from the study window and think I see a shadow flung on the
flagstones outside the drawing-room window."

"Why not stay up here for to-night?"

"Because I want to get it settled. Either I'm mad or—— Will you
come?"

"If you really mean to go down to-night I'll come with you."

"Well, I've ordered the car to be here by nine-fifteen," said Philip.
"We'll go to your rooms, and you can pack a suitcase and we'll be there
by half past ten." Suddenly he looked up sharply, his shoulders drew together and his eyes narrowed and became intent. It happened at that
moment no voice was busy in the dining-room of the Brooks's Club. No
doubt they were changing over at the Power Station, for the lights dimmed for a moment. It seemed to Bellamy that someone was developing
wavy, wicked little films far back in his brain, and a voice suddenly
whispered in his ear with a vile sort of shyness, "He cometh and he
passeth by!"

As they drove down through the night they talked little. Philip
drowsed and Bellamy's mind was busy. His preliminary conclusion was
that Philip was neither mad nor going mad, but that he was not normal.
He had always been very sensitive and highly strung, reacting too quickly

and deeply to emotional stresses—and this living alone and eating nothing—the worst thing for him.

And this Clinton. He had the reputation of being an evil man of power, and such persons' hypnotic influence was absurdly underrated. He'd get on his track.

"When does Clinton get back to England?" he asked.

"If he kept to his plans he'll be back about now," said Philip sleepily.

"What are his haunts?"

"He lives near the British Museum in rooms, but he's usually to be found at the Chorazin Club after six o'clock. It's in Larn Street, just off Shaftesbury Avenue. A funny place with some funny members."

Bellamy made a note of this.

"Does he know you know me?"

"No, I think not, there's no reason why he should."

"So much the better," said Bellamy.

"Why?" asked Philip.

"Because I'm going to cultivate his acquaintance."

"Well, do look out, Teddie, he has a marvellous power of hiding the fact, but he's dangerous, and I don't want you to get into any trouble like mine."

"I'll be careful," said Bellamy.

Ten minutes later they passed the gates of the drive of Franton Manor, and Philip began glancing uneasily about him and peering sharply where the elms flung shadows. It was a perfectly still and cloudless night, with a quarter moon. It was just a quarter to eleven as they entered the house. They went up to the library on the first floor which looked out over the Dutch Garden to the Park. Franton is a typical Georgian house, with charming gardens and Park, but too big and lonely for one nervous person to inhabit, thought Bellamy.

The butler brought up sandwiches and drinks, and Bellamy thought he seemed relieved at their arrival. Philip began to eat ravenously, and gulped down two stiff whiskies. He kept looking at his watch, and his eyes were always searching the walls.

"It comes, Teddie, even when it ought to be too light for shadows."

"Now then," replied the latter, "I'm with you, and we're going to keep quite steady. It may come, but I shall not leave you until it goes and for ever." And he managed to lure Philip on to another subject, and for a time he seemed quieter, but suddenly he stiffened, and his eyes became rigid and staring. "It's there," he cried, "I know it!"

"Steady, Philip!" said Bellamy sharply. "Where?"

"Down below," he whispered, and began creeping towards the window.

Bellamy reached it first and looked down. He saw it at once, knew what it was, and set his teeth.

He heard Philip shaking and breathing heavily at his side.

"It's there," he said, "and it's complete at last!"

"Now, Philip," said Bellamy, "we're going down, and I'm going out first, and we'll settle the thing once and for all."

They went down the stairs and into the drawingroom. Bellamy turned the light on and walked quickly to the French window and began to try to open the catch. He fumbled with it for a moment.

"Let me do it," said Philip, and put his hand to the catch, and then the window opened and he stepped out.

"Come back, Philip!" cried Bellamy. As he said it the lights went dim, a fierce blast of burning air filled the room, the window came crashing back. Then through the glass Bellamy saw Philip suddenly throw up his hands, and something huge and dark lean from the wall and envelop him. He seemed to writhe for a moment in its folds. Bellamy strove madly to thrust the window open, while his soul strove to withstand the mighty and evil power he felt was crushing him, and then he saw Philip flung down with awful force, and he could hear the foul, crushing thud as his head struck the stone.

And then the window opened and Bellamy dashed out into a quiet and scented night.

At the inquest the doctor stated he was satisfied that Mr. Franton's death was due to a severe heart attack—he had never recovered from the gas, he said, and such a seizure was always possible.

"Then there are no peculiar circumstances about the case?" asked the Coroner.

The doctor hesitated. "Well, there is one thing," he said slowly. "The pupils of Mr. Franton's eyes were—well, to put it simply to the jury—instead of being round, they were drawn up so that they resembled half-moons—in a sense they were like the pupils in the eyes of a cat."

"Can you explain that?" asked the Coroner.

"No, I have never seen a similar case," replied the doctor. "But I am satisfied the cause of death was as I have stated."

Bellamy was, of course, called as a witness, but he had little to say.

*   *   *   *

About eleven o'clock on the morning after these events Bellamy rang up the Chorazin Club from his chambers and learned from the manager that Mr. Clinton had returned from abroad. A little later he got a Sloane number and arranged to lunch with Mr. Solan at the United Universities Club. And then he made a conscientious effort to estimate the chances in Rex *v.* Tipwinkle.

But soon he was restless and pacing the room. He could not exorcise the jeering demon which told him sniggeringly that he had failed Philip. It wasn't true, but it pricked and penetrated. But the game was not yet played out. If he had failed to save he might still avenge. He would see what Mr. Solan had to say.

The personage was awaiting him in the smoking room. Mr. Solan was an original and looked it. Just five feet and two inches—a tiny body, a mighty head with a dominating forehead studded with a pair of thrusting frontal lobes. All this covered with a thick, greying thatch. Veiled, restless little eyes, a perky, tilted, little nose and a very thin-lipped, fighting mouth from which issued the most curious, resonant, high and piercing voice. This is a rough and ready sketch of one who is universally accepted to be the greatest living Oriental Scholar—a mystic—once upon a time a Senior Wrangler, a philosopher of European repute, a great and fascinating personality, who lived alone, save for a brace of tortoiseshell cats and a housekeeper, in Chester Terrace, Sloane Square. About every six years he published a masterly treatise on one of his special subjects; otherwise he kept to himself with the remorseless determination he brought to bear upon any subject which he considered worth serious consideration, such as the Chess Game, the works of Bach, the paintings of Van Gogh, the poems of Housman, and the short stories of P. G. Wodehouse and Austin Freeman.

He entirely approved of Bellamy, who had once secured him substantial damages in a copyright case. The damages had gone to the Society for the Prevention of Cruelty to Animals.

"And what can I do for you, my dear Bellamy?" he piped, when they were seated.

"First of all, have you ever heard of a person called Oscar Clinton? Secondly, do you know anything of the practice of sending an enemy a painted paper pattern?"

Mr. Sloan smiled slightly at the first question, and ceased to smile when he heard the second.

"Yes," he said, "I have heard of both, and I advise you to have nothing whatsoever to do with either."

"Unfortunately," replied Bellamy, "I have already had to do with both. Two nights ago my best friend died—rather suddenly. Presently I will tell you how he died. But first of all, tell me something about Clinton."

"It is characteristic of him that you know so little about him," replied Mr. Solan, "for although he is one of the most dangerous and intellectually powerful men in the world he gets very little publicity nowadays. Most of the much-advertised Naughty Boys of the Nineties harmed no one but themselves—they merely canonised their own and each other's dirty linen, but Clinton was in a class by himself. He was—and no doubt still is—an accomplished corrupter, and he took, and no doubt still takes, a jocund delight in his hobby. Eventually he left England—by request—and went out East. He spent some years in a Tibetan Monastery, and then some other years in less reputable places—his career is detailed very fully in a file in my study—and then he applied his truly mighty mind to what I may loosely call magic—for what I loosely call magic, my dear Bellamy, most certainly exists. Clinton is highly psychic, with great natural hypnotic power. He then joined an esoteric and little-known sect—Satanists —of which he eventually became High Priest. And then he returned to what we call civilisation, and has since been 'moved on' by the Civil Powers of many countries, for his forte is the extraction of money from credulous and timid individuals—usually female—by methods highly ingenious and peculiarly his own. It is a boast of his that he has never yet missed his revenge. He ought to be stamped out with the brusque ruthlessness meted out to a spreading fire in a Californian forest.

"Well, there is a short inadequate sketch of Oscar Clinton, and now about these paper patterns."

*   *   *   *

Two hours later Bellamy got up to leave. "I can lend you a good many of his books," said Mr. Solan, "and you can get the rest at Lilley's. Come to me from four till six on Wednesdays and Fridays, and I'll teach you all I think essential. Meanwhile, I will have a watch kept upon him, but I want you, my dear Bellamy, to do nothing decisive till you are qualified. It would be a pity if the Bar were to be deprived of your great gifts prematurely."

"Many thanks," said Bellamy. "I have now placed myself in your hands, and I'm in this thing till the end—some end or other."

Mr. Plank, Bellamy's clerk, had no superior in his profession, one which is the most searching test of character and adaptability. Not one of the devious and manifold tricks of his trade was unpracticed by him, and his income was twelve hundred and fifty pounds per annum, a fact which the Inland Revenue Authorities strongly suspected but were quite unable to establish. He liked Mr. Bellamy, personally well enough, financially very much indeed. It was not surprising, therefore, that many seismic recording instruments registered sharp shocks at 4 P.M. on June 12, 192—, a disturbance caused by the precipitous descent of Mr. Plank's jaw when Mr. Bellamy instructed him to accept no more briefs for him for the next three months. "But," continued that gentleman, "here is a cheque which will, I trust, reconcile you to the fact."

Mr. Plank scrutinised the numerals and *was* reconciled.

"Taking a holiday, sir?" he asked.

"I rather doubt it," replied Bellamy. "But you might suggest to any inquisitive enquirers that that is the explanation."

"I understand, sir."

From then till midnight, with one short pause, Bellamy was occupied with a pile of exotically bound volumes. Occasionally he made a note on his writing pad. When his clock struck twelve he went to bed and read *The Wallet of Kai-Lung* till he felt sleepy enough to turn out the light.

At eight o'clock the next morning he was busy once more with an exotically bound book, and making an occasional note on his writing pad.

Three weeks later he was bidding a temporary farewell to Mr. Solan, who remarked, "I think you'll do now. You are an apt pupil; pleading has given you a command of convincing bluff, and you have sufficient psychic insight to make it possible for you to succeed. Go forth and prosper! At all times I shall be fighting for you. He will be there at nine tonight."

At a quarter past that hour Bellamy was asking the door-keeper of the Chorazin Club to tell Mr. Clinton that a Mr. Bellamy wished to see him.

Two minutes later the official reappeared and led him downstairs into an ornate and gaudy cellar decorated with violence and indiscretion—the work, he discovered later, of a neglected genius who had died of neglected cirrhosis of the liver. He was led up to a table in the corner, where someone was sitting alone.

Bellamy's first impression of Oscar Clinton remained vividly with him till his death. As he got up to greet him he could see that he was physically gigantic—six foot five at least, with a massive torso—the build of a champion wrestler. Topping it was a huge, square, domed head. He had a

white yet mottled face, thick, tense lips, the lower one protruding fan-
tastically. His hair was clipped close, save for one twisted and oiled lock
which curved down to meet his eyebrows. But what impressed Bellamy
most was a pair of the hardest, most penetrating and merciless eyes—one
of which seemed soaking wet and dripping slowly.

Bellamy "braced his belt about him"—he was in the presence of a
power.

"Well, sir," said Clinton in a beautifully musical voice with a slight
drawl, "I presume you are connected with Scotland Yard. What can I do
for you?"

"No," replied Bellamy, forcing a smile, "I'm in no way connected with
that valuable institution."

"Forgive the suggestion," said Clinton, "but during a somewhat ad-
venturous career I have received so many unheralded visits from more or
less polite police officials. What then, is your business?"

"I haven't any, really," said Bellamy. "It's simply that I have long
been a devoted admirer of your work, the greatest imaginative work of our
time in my opinion. A friend of mine mentioned casually that he had seen
you going into this club, and I could not resist taking the liberty of
forcing, just for a moment, my company upon you."

Clinton stared at him, and seemed not quite at his ease.

"You interest me," he said at length. "I'll tell you why. Usually I know
decisively by certain methods of my own whether a person I meet comes
as an enemy or a friend. These tests have failed in your case, and this, as
I say, interests me. It suggests things to me. Have you been in the East?"

"No," said Bellamy.

"And made no study of its mysteries?"

"None whatever, but I can assure you I come merely as a most humble
admirer. Of course, I realise you have enemies—all great men have; it is
the privilege and penalty of their pre-eminence, and I know you to be a
great man."

"I fancy," said Clinton, "that you are perplexed by the obstinate hu-
midity of my left eye. It is caused by the rather heavy injection of heroin I
took this afternoon. I may as well tell you I use all drugs, but am the slave
of none. I take heroin when I desire to contemplate. But tell me—since
you profess such an admiration for my books—which of them most meets
with your approval?"

"That's a hard question," replied Bellamy, "but *A Damsel with a
Dulcimer* seems to me exquisite."

Clinton smiled patronisingly.

"It has merits," he said, "but is immature. I wrote it when I was living with a Bedouin woman aged fourteen in Tunis. Bedouin women have certain natural gifts"—and here he became remarkably obscene, before returning to the subject of his works—"my own opinion is that I reached my zenith in *The Songs of Hamdonna*. Hamdonna was a delightful companion, the fruit of the raptures of an Italian gentleman and a Persian lady. She had the most naturally—the most brilliantly vicious mind of any woman I ever met. She required hardly any training. But she was unfaithful to me, and died soon after."

"The *Songs* are marvellous," said Bellamy, and he began quoting from them fluently.

Clinton listened intently. "You have a considerable gift for reciting poetry," he said. "May I offer you a drink? I was about to order one for myself."

"I'll join you on one condition—that I may be allowed to pay for both of them—to celebrate the occasion."

"Just as you like," said Clinton, tapping the table with his thumb, which was adorned with a massive jade ring curiously carved. "I always drink brandy after heroin, but you order what you please."

It may have been the whisky, it may have been the pressing nervous strain or a combination of both, which caused Bellamy now to regard the mural decorations with a much modified sangfroid. Those distorted and tortured patches of flat colour, how subtly suggestive they were of something sniggeringly evil!

"I gave Valin the subject for those panels," said Clinton. "They are meant to represent an impression of the stages in the Black Mass, but he drank away his original inspiration, and they fail to do that majestic ceremony justice."

Bellamy flinched at having his thoughts so easily read.

"I was thinking the same thing," he replied; "that unfortunate cat they're slaughtering deserved a less ludicrous memorial to its fate."

Clinton looked at him sharply and sponged his oozing eye.

"I have made these rather flamboyant references to my habits purposely. Not to impress you, but to see *how* they impressed you. Had you appeared disgusted, I should have known it was useless to pursue our acquaintanceship. All my life I have been a law unto myself, and that is probably why the Law has always shown so much interest in me. I know myself to be a being apart, one to whom the codes and conventions of the herd can never be applied. I have sampled every so-called 'vice,' including every known drug. Always, however, with an object in view. Mere purposeless debauchery is not in my character. My art, to which you have so kindly referred, must always come first. Sometimes it demands that I sleep with a negress, that I take opium or hashish; sometimes it dictates rigid asceticism, and I tell you, my friend, that if such an instruction came again tomorrow, as it has often come in the past, I could, without the slightest effort, lead a life of complete abstinence from drink, drugs and women for an indefinite period. In other words, I have gained absolute control over my senses after the most exhaustive experiments with them. How many can say the same? Yet one does not know what life can teach till that control is established. The man of superior power—there are no such women—should not flinch from such experiments, he should seek to learn every lesson evil as well as good has to teach. So will he be able to extend and multiply his personality, but always he must remain absolute master of himself. And then he will have many strange rewards, and many secrets will be revealed to him. Some day, perhaps, I will show you some which have been revealed to me."

"Have you absolutely no regard for what is called 'morality'?" asked Bellamy.

"None whatever. If I wanted money I should pick your pocket. If I desired your wife—if you have one—I should seduce her. If someone obstructs me—something happens to him. You must understand this clearly—for I am not bragging—I do nothing purposelessly nor from what I consider a bad motive. To me 'bad' is synonymous with 'unnecessary.' I do nothing unnecessary."

"Why is revenge necessary?" asked Bellamy.

"A plausible question. Well, for one thing I like cruelty—one of my unpublished works is a defence of Super-Sadism. Then it is a warning to others, and lastly it is a vindication of my personality. All excellent reasons. Do you like my *Thus Spake Eblis?*"

"Masterly," replied Bellamy. "The perfection of prose, but, of course, its magical significance is far beyond my meagre understanding."

"My dear friend, there is only one man in Europe about whom that would not be equally true."

"Who is that?" asked Bellamy.

Clinton's eyes narrowed venomously.

"His name is Solan," he said. "One of these days, perhaps——" and he paused. "Well, now, if you like I will tell you of some of my experiences."

* * * *

An hour later a monologue drew to its close.

"And now, Mr. Bellamy, what is your role in life?"

"I'm a barrister."

"Oh, so you *are* connected with the Law?"

"I hope," said Bellamy smiling, "you'll find it possible to forget it."

"It would help me to do so," replied Clinton, "if you would lend me ten pounds. I have forgotten my note-case—a frequent piece of negligence on my part—and a lady awaits me. Thanks very much. We shall meet again, I trust."

"I was just about to suggest that you dine with me one day this week?"

"This is Tuesday," said Clinton. "What about Thursday?"

"Excellent, will you meet me at the Gridiron about eight?"

"I will be there," said Clinton, mopping his eye. "Good night."

* * * *

"I can understand now what happened to Franton," said Bellamy to Mr. Solan the next evening. "He is the most fascinating and catholic talker I have met. He has a wicked charm. If half to which he lays claim is true, he has packed ten lives into sixty years."

"In a sense," said Mr. Solan, "he has the best brain of any man living. He has also a marvellous histrionic sense and he is *deadly*. But he is vulnerable. On Thursday encourage him to talk of other things. He will consider you an easy victim. You must make the most of the evening—it may rather revolt you—he is sure to be suspicious at first."

* * * *

"It amuses and reassures me," said Clinton at ten-fifteen on Thursday evening in Bellamy's room, "to find you have a lively appreciation of obscenity."

He brought out a snuff box, an exquisite little masterpiece with an inexpressibly vile design enamelled on the lid, from which he took a pinch of white powder which he sniffed up from the palm of his hand.

"I suppose," said Bellamy, "that all your magical lore would be quite beyond me."

"Oh yes, quite," replied Clinton, "but I can show you what sort of power a study of that lore has given me, by a little experiment. Turn round, look out of the window, and keep quite quiet till I speak to you."

It was a brooding night. In the south-west the clouds made restless, quickly shifting patterns—the heralds of coming storm. The scattered sound of the traffic in Kingsway rose and fell with the gusts of the rising wind. Bellamy found a curious picture forming in his brain. A wide lonely waste of snow and a hill with a copse of fir trees, out from which someone came running. Presently this person halted and looked back, and then out from the wood appeared another figure (of a shape he had seen before). And then the one it seemed to be pursuing began to run on, staggering through the snow, over which the Shape seemed to skim lightly and rapidly, and gain on its quarry. Then it appeared as if the one in front could go no further. He fell and rose again, and faced his pursuer. The Shape came swiftly on and flung itself hideously on the one in front, who fell to his knees. The two seemed intermingled for a moment . . .

"Well," said Clinton, "and what did you think of that?"

Bellamy poured out a whisky and soda and drained it.

"Extremely impressive," he replied. "It gave me a feeling of great horror."

"The individual whose rather painful end you have just witnessed once did me a dis-service. He was found in a remote part of Norway. Why he chose to hide himself there is rather difficult to understand."

"Cause and effect?" asked Bellamy, forcing a smile.

Clinton took another pinch of white powder.

"Possibly a mere coincidence," he replied. "And now I must go, for I have a 'date,' as they say in America, with a rather charming and profligate young woman. Could you possibly lend me a little money?"

When he had gone Bellamy washed his person very thoroughly in a hot bath, brushed his teeth with zeal, and felt a little cleaner. He tried to read in bed, but between him and Mr. Jacobs's *Night-Watchman* a bestial and persistent phantasmagoria forced its way. He dressed again, went out, and walked the streets till dawn.

Some time later Mr. Solan happened to overhear a conversation in the club smoking-room.

"I can't think what's happened to Bellamy," said one. "He does no work and is always about with that incredible swine Clinton."

"A kink somewhere, I suppose," said another, yawning. "Dirty streak probably."

"Were you referring to Mr. Edward Bellamy, a friend of mine?" asked Mr. Solan.

"We were," said one.

"Have you ever known him do a discreditable thing?"

"Not till now," said another.

"Or a stupid thing?"

"I'll give you that," said one.

"Well," said Mr. Solan, "you have my word for it that he has not changed," and he passed on.

"Funny old devil that," said one.

"Rather shoves the breeze up me," said another. "He seems to know something. I like Bellamy, and I'll apologise to him for taking his name in vain when I see him next. But that bastard Clinton!——"

* * * *

"It will have to be soon," said Mr. Solan. "I heard to-day that he will be given notice to quit any day now. Are you prepared to go through with it?"

"He's the devil incarnate," said Bellamy. "If you knew what I've been through in the last month!"

"I have a shrewd idea of it," replied Mr. Solan. "You think he trusts you completely?"

"I don't think he has any opinion of me at all, except that I lend him money whenever he wants it. Of course, I'll go through with it. Let it be Friday night. What must I do? Tell me exactly. I know that but for you I should have chucked my hand in long ago."

"My dear Bellamy, you have done marvellously well, and you will finish the business as resolutely as you have carried it through so far. Well, this is what you must do. Memorise it flawlessly."

* * * *

"I will arrange it that we arrive at his rooms just about eleven o'clock. I will ring up five minutes before we leave."

"I shall be doing my part," said Mr. Solan.

Clinton was in high spirits at the Café Royal on Friday evening.

"I like you, my dear Bellamy," he observed, "not merely because you have a refined taste in pornography and have lent me a good deal of money, but for a more subtle reason. You remember when we first met I was puzzled by you. Well, I still am. There is some psychic power surrounding you. I don't mean that you are conscious of it, but there is some very powerful influence working for you. Great friends though we are, I sometimes feel that this power is hostile to myself. Anyhow, we have had many pleasant times together."

"And," replied Bellamy, "I hope we shall have many more. It has certainly been a tremendous privilege to have been permitted to enjoy so much of your company. As for that mysterious power you refer to, I am entirely unconscious of it, and as for hostility—well, I hope I've convinced you during the last month that I'm not exactly your enemy."

"You have, my dear fellow," replied Clinton. "You have been a charming and generous companion. All the same, there is an enigmatic side to you. What shall we do to-night?"

"Whatever you please," said Bellamy.

"I suggest we go round to my rooms," said Clinton, "bearing a bottle of whisky, and that I show you another little experiment. You are now sufficiently trained to make it a success."

"Just what I should have hoped for," replied Bellamy enthusiastically. "I will order the whisky now." He went out of the grill-room for a moment and had a few words with Mr. Solan over the telephone. And then he returned, paid the bill, and they drove off together.

Clinton's rooms were in a dingy street about a hundred yards from the British Museum. They were drab and melancholy, and contained nothing but the barest necessities and some books.

It was exactly eleven o'clock as Clinton took out his latchkey, and it was just exactly then that Mr. Solan unlocked the door of a curious little room leading off from his study.

Then he opened a bureau and took from it a large book bound in plain white vellum. He sat down at a table and began a bizarre procedure. He took from a folder at the end of the book a piece of what looked like crumpled tracing paper, and, every now and again consulting the quarto, drew certain symbols upon the paper, while repeating a series of short sentences in a strange tongue. The ink into which he dipped his pen for this exercise was a smoky sullen scarlet.

Presently the atmosphere of the room became intense, and charged with suspense and crisis. The symbols completed, Mr. Solan became rigid and taut, and his eyes were those of one passing into trance.

* * * *

"First of all a drink, my dear Bellamy," said Clinton.

Bellamy pulled the cork and poured out two stiff pegs. Clinton drank his off. He gave the impression of being not quite at his ease.

"Some enemy of mine is working against me to-night," he said. "I feel an influence strongly. However, let us try the little experiment. Draw up your chair to the window, and do not look round till I speak."

Bellamy did as he was ordered, and peered at a dark facade across the street. Suddenly it was as if wall after wall rolled up before his eyes and passed into the sky, and he found himself gazing into a long faintly-lit room. As his eyes grew more used to the dimness he could pick out a number of recumbent figures, apparently resting on couches. And then from the middle of the room a flame seemed to leap and then another and another until there was a fiery circle playing round one of those figures, which slowly rose to its feet and turned and stared at Bellamy; and its haughty, evil face grew vast, till it was thrust, dazzling and fiery, right into his own. He put up his hands to thrust back its scorching menace— and there was the wall of the house opposite, and Clinton was saying, "Well?"

"Your power terrifies me!" said Bellamy. "Who was that One I saw?"

"The one you saw was myself," said Clinton, smiling, "during my third reincarnation, about 1750 B.C. I am the only man in the world who can perform that quite considerable feat. Give me another drink."

Bellamy got up (it was time!). Suddenly he felt invaded by a mighty re-assurance. His ghostly terror left him. Something irresistible was sinking into his soul, and he knew that at the destined hour the promised succour had come to sustain him. He felt thrilled, resolute, exalted.

He had his back to Clinton as he filled the glasses and with a lightning motion he dropped a pellet into Clinton's which fizzed like a tiny comet down through the bubbles and was gone.

"Here's to many more pleasant evenings," said Clinton. "You're a brave man, Bellamy," he exclaimed, putting the glass to his lips. "For what you have seen might well appal the devil!"

"I'm not afraid because I trust you," replied Bellamy.

"By Eblis, this is a strong one," said Clinton, peering into his glass.

"Same as usual," said Bellamy, laughing. "Tell me something. A man I knew who'd been many years in the East told me about some race out there who cut out paper patterns and paint them and sent them to their enemies. Have you ever heard of anything of the sort?"

Clinton dropped his glass on the table sharply. He did not answer for a moment, but shifted uneasily in his chair.

"Who was this friend of yours?" he asked, in a voice already slightly thick.

"A chap called Bond," said Bellamy.

"Yes, I've heard of that charming practice. In fact, I can cut them my-self."

"Really, how's it done? I should be fascinated to see it."

Clinton's eyes blinked and his head nodded.

"I'll show you one," he said, "but it's dangerous and you must be very careful. Go to the bottom drawer of that bureau and bring me the piece of straw paper you'll find there. And there are some scissors on the writing table and two crayons in the tray." Bellamy brought them to him.

"Now," said Clinton, "this thing, as I say, is dangerous. If I wasn't drunk I wouldn't do it. And why am I drunk?" He leaned back in his chair and put his hand over his eyes. And then he sat up and, taking the scis-sors, began running them with extreme dexterity round the paper. And then he made some marks with the coloured pencils.

The final result of these actions was not unfamiliar in appearance to Bellamy.

"There you are," said Clinton. "That, my dear Bellamy, is potentially the most deadly little piece of paper in the world. Would you please take it to the fireplace and burn it to ashes?"

Bellamy burnt a piece of paper to ashes.

Clinton's head had dropped into his hands.

"Another drink?" asked Bellamy.

"My God, no," said Clinton, yawning and reeling in his chair. And then his head went down again. Bellamy went up to him and shook him. His right hand hovered a second over Clinton's coat pocket.

"Wake up," he said. "I want to know what could make that piece of paper actually deadly?"

Clinton looked up blearily at him and then rallied slightly.

"You'd like to know, wouldn't you?"

"Yes," said Bellamy. "Tell me."

"Just repeating six words," said Clinton, "but I shall not repeat them." Suddenly his eyes became intent and fixed on a corner of the room.

"What's that?" he asked sharply. "There! there! there! in the corner." Bellamy felt again the presence of a power. The air of the room seemed rent and sparking.

"That, Clinton," he said, "is the spirit of Philip Franton, whom you murdered." And then he sprang at Clinton, who was staggering from the chair. He seized him and pressed a little piece of paper fiercely to his forehead.

"Now, Clinton," he cried, "say those words!"

And then Clinton rose to his feet, and his face was working hideously. His eyes seemed bursting from his head, their pupils stretched and curved, foam streamed from his lips. He flung his hands above his head and cried in a voice of agony:

"He cometh and he passeth by!"

And then he crashed to the floor.

As Bellamy moved towards the door the lights went dim, in from the window poured a burning wind, and then from the wall in the corner a shadow began to grow. When he saw it, swift icy ripples poured through him. It grew and grew, and began to lean down towards the figure on the floor. As Bellamy took a last look back it was just touching it. He shuddered, opened the door, closed it quickly, and ran down the stairs and out into the night.

SIR HUGH WALPOLE

The Silver Mask (1933)

This neglected *conte cruel* by Sir Hugh Walpole, a noted novelist and a descendant of Horace Walpole, is a powerful example of how much ghostly terror can be achieved with only the wispiest hint of the supernatural. Indeed, there are no ghosts at all in this tale, only a preternatural foreshadowing of doom radiated by an antiquarian art object, one that seems to transform itself in a mysterious and altogether threatening way. Even without a ghost, this story of a middle-aged woman's obsession with a sinister and beautiful young man has an aura of evil about it that the reader will not easily forget.

Unlike the situation in most antiquarian tales, the art object here is only a motif rather than the center of interest. The focus is on character, on the twisted relationship between Miss Herries and her young man. Miss Herries is a memorable and skillfully drawn character. Solid, independent, and self-aware, she nevertheless has a tragic flaw, one she is not at all blind to and which, in other contexts, would be rather admirable. Here, it is the occasion for a somber allegory about the ways in which people participate in their own victimization.

A touch of much needed, if bleak, comedy is provided by the young man's bizarre entourage of family and relations, who behave and communicate very much like characters in a Harold Pinter play. Still, it is only a touch: the reader should be warned that "The Silver Mask" is the cruelest story in this book, although its cruelty has nothing whatever to do with the gross or the gruesome.

⇒ THE SILVER MASK ⇐

Miss Sonia Herries, coming home from a dinner-party at the Westons', heard a voice at her elbow.

'If you please—only a moment——'

She had walked from the Westons' flat because it was only three streets away, and now she was only a few steps from her door, but it was late, there was no one about and the King's Road rattle was muffled and dim.

'I am afraid I can't——' she began. It was cold, and the wind nipped her cheeks.

'If you would only——' he went on.

She turned and saw one of the handsomest young men possible. He was the handsome young man of all romantic stories, tall, dark, pale, slim, distinguished—oh! everything!—and he was wearing a shabby blue suit and shivering with the cold just as he should have been.

'I'm afraid I can't——' she repeated, beginning to move on.

'Oh, I know,' he interrupted quickly. 'Everyone says the same, and quite naturally. I should if our positions were reversed. But I *must* go on with it. I *can't* go back to my wife and baby with simply nothing. We have no fire, no food, nothing except the ceiling we are under. It is my fault, all of it. I don't want your pity, but I *have* to attack your comfort.'

He trembled. He shivered as though he were going to fall. Involuntarily she put out her hand to steady him. She touched his arm and felt it quiver under the thin sleeve.

'It's all right . . . ' he murmured. 'I'm hungry . . . I can't help it.'

She had had an excellent dinner. She had drunk perhaps just enough to lead to recklessness—in any case, before she realised it, she was ushering him in, through her dark-blue painted door. A crazy thing to do! Nor was it as though she were too young to know any better, for she was fifty if she was a day and, although sturdy of body and as strong as a horse (except for a little unsteadiness of the heart), intelligent enough to be thin, neurotic and abnormal; but she was none of these.

Although intelligent she suffered dreadfully from impulsive kindness. All her life she had done so. The mistakes that she had made—and there had been quite a few—had all arisen from the triumph of her heart over her brain. She knew it—how well she knew it!—and all her friends were for ever dinning it into her. When she reached her fiftieth birthday she said to herself, 'Well, now at last I'm too old to be foolish any more.' And here she was, helping an entirely unknown young man into her house at dead of night, and he in all probability the worst sort of criminal.

Very soon he was sitting on her rose-coloured sofa, eating sandwiches and drinking a whisky and soda. He seemed to be entirely overcome by the beauty of her possessions. 'If he's acting he's doing it very well,' she thought to herself. But he had taste and he had knowledge. He knew that the Utrillo was an early one, the only period of importance in that master's work, he knew that the two old men talking under a window belonged to Sickert's 'Middle Italian,' he recognised the Dobson head and the wonderful green bronze Elk of Carl Milles.

'You are an artist,' she said. 'You paint?'

'No, I am a pimp, a thief, a what you like—anything bad,' he answered fiercely. 'And now I must go,' he added, springing up from the sofa.

He seemed most certainly invigorated. She could scarcely believe that he was the same young man who only half an hour before had had to lean on her arm for support. And he was a gentleman. Of that there could be no sort of question. And he was astoundingly beautiful in the spirit of a hundred years ago, a young Byron, a young Shelley, not a young Ramón Novarro or a young Ronald Colman.

Well, it was better that he should go, and she did hope (for his own sake rather than hers) that he would not demand money and threaten a scene. After all, with her snow-white hair, firm broad chin, firm broad body, she did not look like someone who could be threatened. He had not apparently the slightest intention of threatening her. He moved towards the door.

'Oh!' he murmured with a little gasp of wonder. He had stopped before one of the loveliest things that she had—a mask in silver of a clown's face, the clown smiling, gay, joyful, not hinting at perpetual sadness as all clowns are traditionally supposed to do. It was one of the most successful efforts of the famous Sorat, greatest living master of Masks.

'Yes. Isn't that lovely?' she said. 'It was one of Sorat's earliest things, and still, I think, one of his best.'

'Silver is the right material for that clown,' he said.

'Yes, I think so too,' she agreed. She realised that she had asked him nothing about his troubles, about his poor wife and baby, about his past history. It was better perhaps like this.

'You have saved my life,' he said to her in the hall. She had in her hand a pound note.

'Well,' she answered cheerfully, 'I was a fool to risk a strange man in my house at this time of night—or so my friends would tell me. But such an old woman like me—where's the risk?'

'I could have cut your throat,' he said quite seriously.

'So you could,' she admitted. 'But with horrid consequences to yourself.'

'Oh no,' he said. 'Not in these days. The police are never able to catch anybody.'

'Well, good-night. Do take this. It can get you some warmth at least.'

He took the pound. 'Thanks,' he said carelessly. Then at the door he remarked: 'That mask. The loveliest thing I ever saw.'

When the door had closed and she went back into the sitting-room she sighed:

'What a good-looking young man!' Then she saw that her most beautiful white jade cigarette-case was gone. It had been lying on the little table by the sofa. She had seen it just before she went into the pantry to cut the sandwiches. He had stolen it. She looked everywhere. No, undoubtedly he had stolen it.

'What a good-looking young man!' she thought as she went up to bed.

Sonia Herries was a woman of her time in that outwardly she was cynical and destructive while inwardly she was a creature longing for affection and appreciation. For though she had white hair and was fifty she was outwardly active, young, could do with little sleep and less food, could dance and drink cocktails and play bridge to the end of all time. Inwardly she cared neither for cocktails nor bridge. She was above all things maternal and she had a weak heart, not only a spiritual weak heart but also a physical one. When she suffered, must take her drops, lie down and rest, she allowed no one to see her. Like all the other women of her period and manner of life she had a courage worthy of a better cause.

She was a heroine for no reason at all.

But, beyond everything else, she was maternal. Twice at least she would have married had she loved enough, but the man she had really loved had not loved her (that was twenty-five years ago), so she had pretended to despise matrimony. Had she had a child her nature would have

been fulfilled; as she had not had that good fortune she had been maternal
(with outward cynical indifference) to numbers of people who had made
use of her, sometimes laughed at her, never deeply cared for her. She
was named 'a jolly good sort,' and was always 'just outside' the real life of
her friends. Her Herries relations, Rockages and Cards and Newmarks,
used her to take odd places at table, to fill up spare rooms at house-parties,
to make purchases for them in London, to talk to when things went wrong
with them or people abused them. She was a very lonely woman.

She saw her young thief for a second time a fortnight later. She saw
him because he came to her house one evening when she was dressing for
dinner.

'A young man at the door,' said her maid Rose.

'A young man? Who?' But she knew.

'I don't know, Miss Sonia. He won't give his name.'

She came down and found him in the hall, the cigarette-case in his
hand. He was wearing a decent suit of clothes, but he still looked hungry,
haggard, desperate and incredibly handsome. She took him into the room
where they had been before. He gave her the cigarette-case. 'I pawned it,'
he said, his eyes on the silver mask.

'What a disgraceful thing to do!' she said. 'And what are you going to
steal next?'

'My wife made some money last week,' he said. 'That will see us
through for a while.'

'Do you never do any work?' she asked him.

'I paint,' he answered. 'But no one will touch my pictures. They are not
modern enough.'

'You must show me some of your pictures,' she said, and realised how
weak she was. It was not his good looks that gave him his power over her,
but something both helpless and defiant, like a wicked child who hates his
mother but is always coming to her for help.

'I have some here,' he said, went into the hall, and returned with
several canvases. He displayed them. They were very bad—sugary landscapes and sentimental figures.

'They are very bad,' she said.

'I know they are. You must understand that my aesthetic taste is very
fine. I appreciate only the best things in art, like your cigarette-case, that
mask there, the Utrillo. But I can paint nothing but these. It is very ex-
asperating.' He smiled at her.

'Won't you buy one?' he asked her.

'Oh, but I don't want one,' she answered. 'I should have to hide it.' She was aware that in ten minutes her guests would be here.

'Oh, do buy one.'

'No, but of course not——'

'Yes, please.' He came nearer and looked up into her broad kindly face like a beseeching child.

'Well . . . how much are they?'

'This is twenty pounds. This twenty-five——'

'But how absurd! They are not worth anything at all.'

'They may be one day. You never know with modern pictures.'

'I am quite sure about these.'

'Please buy one. That one with the cows is not so bad.'

She sat down and wrote a cheque.

'I'm a perfect fool. Take this, and understand I never want to see you again. Never! You will never be admitted. It is no use speaking to me in the street. If you bother me I shall tell the police.'

He took the cheque with quiet satisfaction, held out his hand and pressed hers a little.

'Hang that in the right light and it will not be so bad——'

'You want new boots,' she said. 'Those are terrible.'

'I shall be able to get some now,' he said and went away.

All that evening while she listened to the hard and crackling ironies of her friends she thought of the young man. She did not know his name. The only thing that she knew about him was that by his own confession he was a scoundrel and had at his mercy a poor young wife and a starving child. The picture that she formed of these three haunted her. It had been, in a way, honest of him to return the cigarette-case. Ah, but he knew, of course, that did he not return it he could never have seen her again. He had discovered at once that she was a splendid source of supply, and now that she had bought one of his wretched pictures—— Nevertheless he could not be altogether bad. No one who cared so passionately for beautiful things could be quite worthless. The way that he had gone straight to the silver mask as soon as he entered the room and gazed at it as though with his very soul! And, sitting at her dinner-table, uttering the most cynical sentiments, she was all softness as she gazed across to the wall upon whose pale surface the silver mask was hanging. There was, she thought, a certain look of the young man in that jolly shining surface. But where? The clown's cheek was fat, his mouth broad, his lips thick—and yet, and yet——

For the next few days as she went about London she looked in spite of herself at the passers-by to see whether he might not be there. One thing she soon discovered, that he was very much more handsome than anyone else whom she saw. But it was not for his handsomeness that he haunted her. It was because he wanted her to be kind to him, and because she wanted—oh, so terribly—to be kind to someone!

The silver mask, she had the fancy, was gradually changing, the rotundity thinning, some new light coming into the empty eyes. It was most certainly a beautiful thing.

Then, as unexpectedly as on the other occasions, he appeared again. One night as she, back from a theatre smoking one last cigarette, was preparing to climb the stairs to bed, there was a knock on the door. Everyone of course rang the bell—no one attempted the old-fashioned knocker shaped like an owl that she had bought, one idle day, in an old curiosity shop. The knock made her sure that it was he. Rose had gone to bed, so she went herself to the door. There he was—and with him a young girl and a baby. They all came into the sitting-room and stood awkwardly by the fire. It was at that moment when she saw them in a group by the fire that she felt her first sharp pang of fear. She knew suddenly how weak she was—she seemed to be turned to water at sight of them, she, Sonia Herries, fifty years of age, independent and strong, save for that little flutter of the heart—yes, turned to water! She was afraid as though someone had whispered a warning in her ear.

The girl was striking, with red hair and a white face, a thin graceful little thing. The baby, wrapped in a shawl, was soaked in sleep. She gave them drinks and the remainder of the sandwiches that had been put there for herself. The young man looked at her with his charming smile.

'We haven't come to cadge anything this time,' he said. 'But I wanted you to see my wife and I wanted her to see some of your lovely things.'

'Well,' she said sharply, 'you can only stay a minute or two. It's late. I'm off to bed. Besides, I told you not to come here again.'

'Ada made me,' he said, nodding at the girl. 'She was so anxious to see you.'

The girl never said a word but only stared sulkily in front of her.

'All right. But you must go soon. By the way, you've never told me your name.'

'Henry Abbott, and that's Ada, and the baby's called Henry too.'

'All right. How have you been getting on since I saw you?'

'Oh, fine! Living on the fat of the land.' But he soon fell into silence and the girl never said a word. After an intolerable pause Sonia Herries suggested that they should go. They didn't move. Half an hour later she insisted. They got up. But, standing by the door, Henry Abbott jerked his head towards the writing-desk.

'Who writes your letters for you?'

'Nobody. I write them myself.'

'You ought to have somebody. Save a lot of trouble. I'll do them for you.'

'Oh no, thank you. That would never do. Well, good-night, good-night——'

'Of course I'll do them for you. And you needn't pay me anything either. Fill up my time.'

'Nonsense . . . good-night, good-night.' She closed the door on them. She could not sleep. She lay there thinking of him. She was moved, partly by a maternal tenderness for them that warmed her body (the girl and the baby had looked so helpless sitting there), partly by a shiver of apprehension that chilled her veins. Well, she hoped that she would never see them again. Or did she? Would she not to-morrow, as she walked down Sloane Street, stare at everyone to see whether by chance that was he?

Three mornings later he arrived. It was a wet morning and she had decided to devote it to the settling of accounts. She was sitting there at her table when Rose showed him in.

'I've come to do your letters,' he said.

'I should think not,' she said sharply. 'Now, Henry Abbott, out you go. I've had enough——'

'Oh no, you haven't,' he said, and sat down at her desk.

She would be ashamed for ever, but half an hour later she was seated in the corner of the sofa telling him what to write. She hated to confess it to herself, but she liked to see him sitting there. He was company for her, and to whatever depths he might by now have sunk, he was most certainly a gentleman. He behaved very well that morning; he wrote an excellent hand. He seemed to know just what to say.

A week later she said, laughing, to Amy Weston: 'My dear, would you believe it? I've had to take on a secretary. A very good-looking young man—but you needn't look down your nose. You know that good-looking young men are nothing to *me*—and he does save me endless bother.'

For three weeks he behaved very well, arriving punctually, offering her no insults, doing as she suggested about everything. In the fourth week, about a quarter to one on a day, his wife arrived. On this occasion she looked astonishingly young, sixteen perhaps. She wore a simple grey cotton dress. Her red bobbed hair was strikingly vibrant about her pale face.

The young man already knew that Miss Herries was lunching alone. He had seen the table laid for one with its simple appurtenances. It seemed to be very difficult not to ask them to remain. She did, although she did not wish to. The meal was not a success. The two of them together were tiresome, for the man said little when his wife was there, and the woman said nothing at all. Also the pair of them were in a way sinister.

She sent them away after luncheon. They departed without protest. But as she walked, engaged on her shopping that afternoon, she decided that she must rid herself of them, once and for all. It was true that it had been rather agreeable having him there; his smile, his wicked humorous remarks, the suggestion that he was a kind of malevolent gamin who preyed on the world in general but spared her because he like her—all this had attracted her—but what really alarmed her was that during all these weeks he had made no request for money, made indeed no request for anything. He must be piling up a fine account, must have some plan in his head with which one morning he would balefully startle her! For a moment there in the bright sunlight, with the purr of the traffic, the rustle of trees about her, she saw herself in surprising colour. She was behaving with a weakness that was astonishing. Her stout, thick-set, resolute body, her cheery rosy face, her strong white hair—all these disappeared, and in their place, there almost clinging for support to the Park railings, was a timorous little old woman with frightened eyes and trembling knees. What was there to be afraid of? She had done nothing wrong. There were the police at hand. She had never been a coward before. She went home, however, with an odd impulse to leave her comfortable little house in Walpole Street and hide herself somewhere, somewhere that no one could discover.

That evening they appeared again, husband, wife and baby. She had settled herself down for a cosy evening with a book and an 'early to bed.' There came the knock on the door.

On this occasion she was most certainly firm with them. When they were gathered in a little group she got up and addressed them.

'Here is five pounds,' she said, 'and this is the end. If one of you shows his or her face inside this door again I call the police. Now go.'

The girl gave a little gasp and fell in a dead faint at her feet. It was a perfectly genuine faint. Rose was summoned. Everything possible was done.

'She has simply not had enough to eat,' said Henry Abbott. In the end (so determined and resolved was the faint) Ada Abbott was put to bed in the spare room and a doctor was summoned. After examining her he said that she needed rest and nourishment. This was perhaps the critical moment of the whole affair. Had Sonia Herries been at this crisis properly resolute and bundled the Abbott family, faint and all, into the cold unsympathising street, she might at this moment be a hale and hearty old woman enjoying bridge with her friends. It was, however, just here that her maternal temperament was too strong for her. The poor young thing lay exhausted, her eyes closed, her cheeks almost the colour of her pillow. The baby (surely the quietest baby ever known) lay in a cot beside the bed. Henry Abbott wrote letters to dictation downstairs. Once Sonia Herries, glancing up at the silver mask, was struck by the grin on the clown's face. It seemed to her now a thin sharp grin—almost derisive.

Three days after Ada Abott's collapse there arrived her aunt and her uncle, Mr. and Mrs. Edwards. Mr. Edwards was a large red-faced man with a hearty manner and a bright waistcoat. He looked like a publican. Mrs. Edwards was a thin sharp-nosed woman with a bass voice. She was very, very thin, and wore a large old-fashioned brooch on her flat but emotional chest. They sat side by side on the sofa and explained that they had come to enquire after Ada, their favourite niece. Mrs. Edwards cried, Mr. Edwards was friendly and familiar. Unfortunately Mrs. Weston and a friend came and called just then. They did not stay very long. They were frankly amazed at the Edwards couple and deeply startled by Henry Abbott's familiarity. Sonia Herries could see that they drew the very worst conclusions.

A week later Ada Abbott was still in bed in the upstairs room. It seemed to be impossible to move her. The Edwardses were constant visitors. On one occasion they brought Mr. and Mrs. Harper and their girl Agnes. They were profoundly apologetic, but Miss Herries would understand that 'with the interest they took in Ada it was impossible to stay passive.' They all crowded into the spare bedroom and gazed at the pale figure with the closed eyes sympathetically.

Then two things happened together. Rose gave notice and Mrs. Weston came and had a frank talk with her friend. She began with that most sinister opening: 'I think you ought to know, dear, what everyone is saying——' What everyone was saying was that Sonia Herries was living with a young ruffian from the streets, young enough to be her son.

'You must get rid of them all and at once,' said Mrs. Weston, 'or you won't have a friend left in London, darling.'

Left to herself, Sonia Herries did what she had not done for years, she burst into tears. What had happened to her? Not only had her will and determination gone but she felt most unwell. Her heart was bad again; she could not sleep; the house, too, was tumbling to pieces. There was dust over everything. How was she ever to replace Rose? She was living in some horrible nightmare. This dreadful handsome young man seemed to have some authority over her. Yet he did not threaten her. All he did was to smile. Nor was she in the very least in love with him. This must come to an end or she would be lost.

Two days later, at tea-time, her opportunity arrived. Mr. and Mrs. Edwards had called to see how Ada was; Ada was downstairs at last, very weak and pale. Henry Abbott was there, also the baby. Sonia Herries, although she was feeling dreadfully unwell, addressed them all with vigour. She especially addressed the sharp-nosed Mrs. Edwards.

'You must understand,' she said. 'I don't want to be unkind, but I have my own life to consider. I am a very busy woman, and this has all been forced on me. I don't want to seem brutal. I'm glad to have been of some assistance to you, but I think Mrs. Abbott is well enough to go home now —and I wish you all good-night.'

'I am sure,' said Mrs. Edwards, looking at her from the sofa, 'that you've been kindness itself, Miss Herries. Ada recognises it, I'm sure. But to move her now would be to kill her, that's all. Any movement and she'll drop at your feet.'

'We have nowhere to go,' said Henry Abbott.

'But, Mrs. Edwards——' began Miss Herries, her anger rising.

'We have only two rooms,' said Mrs. Edwards quietly. 'I'm sorry, but just now, what with my husband coughing all night——'

'Oh, but this is monstrous!' Miss Herries cried. 'I have had enough of this. I have been generous to a degree——'

'What about my pay,' said Henry, 'for all these weeks?'

'Pay! Why, of course——' Miss Herries began. Then she stopped. She realised several things. She realised that she was alone in the house, the cook having departed that afternoon. She realised that none of them had moved. She realised that her 'things'—the Sickert, the Utrillo, the sofa— were alive with apprehension. She was fearfully frightened of their silence, their immobility. She moved towards her desk, and her heart turned, squeezed itself dry, shot through her body the most dreadful agony.

'Please,' she gasped. 'In the drawer—the little green bottle—oh, quick! Please, please!'

The last thing of which she was aware was the quiet handsome features of Henry Abbott bending over her.

When, a week later, Mrs. Weston called, the girl, Ada Abbott, opened the door to her.

'I came to enquire for Miss Herries,' she said. 'I haven't seen her about. I have telephoned several times and received no answer.'

'Miss Herries is very ill.'

'Oh, I'm so sorry. Can I not see her?'

Ada Abbott's quiet gentle tones were reassuring her. 'The doctor does not wish her to see anyone at present. May I have your address? I will let you know as soon as she is well enough.'

Mrs. Weston went away. She recounted the event. 'Poor Sonia, she's pretty bad. They seem to be looking after her. As soon as she's better we'll go and see her.'

The London life moves swiftly. Sonia Herries had never been of very great importance to anyone. Herries relations enquired. They received a very polite note assuring them that so soon as she was better——

Sonia Herries was in bed, but not in her own room. She was in the little attic bedroom but lately occupied by Rose the maid. She lay at first in a strange apathy. She was ill. She slept and woke and slept again. Ada Abbott, sometimes Mrs. Edwards, sometimes a woman she did not know, attended to her. They were all very kind. Did she need a doctor? No, of course she did not need a doctor, they assured her. They would see that she had everything that she wanted.

Then life began to flow back into her. Why was she in this room? Where were her friends? What was this horrible food that they were bringing her? What were they doing here, these women?

She had a terrible scene with Ada Abbott. She tried to get out of bed. The girl restrained her—and easily, for all the strength seemed to have gone from her bones. She protested, she was as furious as her weakness allowed her, then she cried. She cried most bitterly. Next day she was alone and she crawled out of bed; the door was locked; she beat on it. There was no sound but her beating. Her heart was beginning again that terrible strangled throb. She crept back into bed. She lay there, weakly, feebly crying. When Ada arrived with some bread, some soup, some water, she demanded that the door should be unlocked, that she should get up, have her bath, come downstairs to her own room.

'You are not well enough,' Ada said gently.

'Of course I am well enough. When I get out I will have you put in prison for this——'

'Please don't get excited. It is so bad for your heart.'

Mrs. Edwards and Ada washed her. She had not enough to eat. She was always hungry.

Summer had come. Mrs. Weston went to Etretat. Everyone was out of town.

'What's happened to Sonia Herries?' Mabel Newmark wrote to Agatha Benson. 'I haven't seen her for ages. . . .'

But no one had time to enquire. There were so many things to do. Sonia was a good sort, but she had been nobody's business. . . .

Once Henry Abbott paid her a visit. 'I am so sorry that you are not better,' he said smiling. 'We are doing everything we can for you. It is lucky we were around when you were so ill. You had better sign these papers. Someone must look after your affairs until you are better. You will be downstairs in a week or two.'

Looking at him with wide-open terrified eyes, Sonia Herries signed the papers.

The first rains of autumn lashed the streets. In the sitting-room the gramophone was turned on. Ada and young Mr. Jackson, Maggie Trent and stout Harry Bennett were dancing. All the furniture was flung against the walls. Mr. Edwards drank his beer; Mrs. Edwards was toasting her toes before the fire.

Henry Abbott came in. He had just sold the Utrillo. His arrival was greeted with cheers.

He took the silver mask from the wall and went upstairs. He climbed to the top of the house, entered, switched on the naked light.

'Oh! Who—what——?' A voice of terror came from the bed.

'It's all right,' he said soothingly. 'Ada will be bringing your tea in a minute.'

He had a hammer and nail and hung the silver mask on the speckled, mottled wall-paper where Miss Herries could see it.

'I know you're fond of it,' he said. 'I thought you'd like it to look at.'

She made no reply. She only stared.

'You'll want something to look at,' he went on. 'You're too ill, I'm

THE ANTIQUARIAN GHOST STORY

183

afraid, ever to leave this room again. So it'll be nice for you. Something to look at.'

He went out, gently closing the door behind him.

E. F. BENSON

The Bath-Chair (1934)

One of the most fascinating quirks in the history of the ghost story is the phenomenon of the Benson brothers—E. F., R. H., and A. C.—each of whom, in addition to his mainstream career, wrote ghost stories on the side and each of whom wrote exceptionally good ones. The most prolific was Edward Frederic, who published five collections of spook stories, enough to make him one of the major figures in the field.

Benson's stories are of two types: visionary out-of-door tales in the tradition of Blackwood and grim, claustrophobic tales involving haunted houses and artifacts. "The Bath-Chair," a rare item that has apparently never appeared in America, is in the latter category. With its "tenseness" and "oppression in the air," its relentless rain, its ruthlessly vengeful characters, and its merciless focus on family hatred, it is one of Benson's most gray and severe offerings.

Benson's sardonic humor (abundantly displayed in the opening paragraph) and interest in talismanic artifacts and furniture give him an affinity with M. R. James. Here, however, the haunted furniture, an old bath-chair, is just an excuse to get the story going. What Benson is really interested in is human relationships, especially unpleasant ones. To be sure, the victim in "The Bath-Chair" is faced with an occult conspiracy, but Benson makes it clear that the main force pursuing him is "the dynamo of hate" in his family.

Family ghosts, of course, are nothing new. Indeed, as Yi-fu Tuan recently pointed out in his book *Landscapes of Fear* (Pantheon, 1980), the pervasive fear of the living dead reflected in folklore frequently crawls up from a profound dread and distrust of family members and the very loved ones with whom people surround themselves for security. In both Eastern and Western societies, a witch is often an untrustworthy or hateful relative; a ghost is a dead parent who inspires fear, anger, and guilt. In fiction, family embroilments are ideal material for ghost stories: the fantastic emotional intensity generated in family squabbles can seem almost surreal and supernatural to begin with, so that the introduction of ghosts

184

and demons is experienced by the reader as merely another raising of the emotional ante.

Benson was well known for his ability to capture family dynamics, and in "The Bath-Chair" he turns his talents to rather nasty use. His narrative conciseness is such that we know after only a couple of pages why Edmund Faraday's family despises him so much. Nevertheless, despite Edmund's villainy and misogyny, there is still something deeply, deliciously shocking about the ghost of a furious father who is as gleefully intent on murdering his son as this one is. Edmund may get what he deserves, but evil is clearly not exorcised.

≋ THE BATH-CHAIR ≋

Edmund Faraday, at the age of fifty, had every reason to be satisfied with life: he had got all he really wanted, and plenty of it. Health was among the chief causes of his content, and he often reflected that the medical profession would have a very thin time of it, if everyone was as fortunate as he. His appreciation of his good fortune was apt at times to be a little trying: he ate freely, he absorbed large (but in no way excessive) quantities of mixed alcoholic liquors, pleasantly alluding to his immunity from any disagreeable effects, and he let it be widely known that he had a cold bath in the morning, spent ten minutes before an open window doing jerks and flexings, and had a fine appetite for breakfast. Not quite so popular was his faint contempt for those who had to be careful of themselves. It was not expressed in contemptuous terms, indeed he was jovially sympathetic with men perhaps ten years younger than himself who found it more prudent to be abstemious. "Such a bore for you, old man," he would comment, "but I expect you're wise."

In addition to these physical advantages, he was master of a very considerable income, derived from shares in a very sound company of general stores, which he himself had founded, and of which he was chairman: this and his accumulated savings enabled him to live precisely as he pleased. He had a house near Ascot, where he spent most week-ends from Friday to Monday, playing golf all day, and another in Massington Square, conveniently close to his business. He might reasonably look forward to a robust and prosperous traverse of that table-land of life which with healthy men continues till well after they have passed their seventieth year. In London he was accustomed to have a couple of hours' bridge at his club before he went back to his bachelor home where his sister kept house for him, and from morning to night his life was spent in enjoying or providing for his own pleasures.

Alice Faraday was, in her own department, one of the clues of his prosperous existence, for it was she who ran his domestic affairs for him. He saw little of her, for he always breakfasted by himself, and encountered her in the morning only for a moment when he came downstairs to set out for his office, and told her whether there would be some of his friends to dinner, or whether he would be out; she would then interview the cook and telephone to the tradesmen, and make her tour of the house to see that all was tidy and speckless. At the end of the day again it was but seldom that they spent a domestic evening together: either he dined out leaving her alone, or three friends or perhaps seven were his guests and made up a table or two tables of bridge. On these occasions Alice was never of the party. She was no card player, she was rather deaf, she was silent and by no means decorative, and she was best represented by the admirable meal she had provided for him and his friends. At the house at Ascot she performed a similar role, finding her way there by train on Friday morning, so as to have the house ready for him when he motored down later in the day.

Sometimes he wondered whether he would not be more comfortable if he married and gave Alice a modest home of her own with an income to correspond, for, though he saw her but seldom, her presence was slightly repugnant to him. But marriage was something of a risk, especially for a man of his age who had kept out of it so long, and he might find himself with a wife who had a will of her own, and who did not understand, as Alice certainly did, that the whole reason of her existence was to make him comfortable. Again he wondered whether perfectly-trained servants like his would not run the house as efficiently as his sister, in which case she would be better away; he would, indefinably, be more at his ease if she were not under his roof. But then his cook might leave, or his housemaid do her work badly, and there would be bills to go through, and wages to be paid, and catering to be thought of. Alice did all that, and his only concern was to draw her a monthly cheque, with a grumble at the total. As for his occasional evenings with her, though it was a bore to dine with this rather deaf, this uncouth and bony creature, such evenings were rare, and when dinner was over, he retired to his own den, and spent a tolerable hour or two over a book or a crossword puzzle. What she did with herself he had no idea, nor did he care, provided she did not intrude on him. Probably she read those gruesome books about the subconscious mind and occult powers which interested her. For him the conscious mind was sufficient, and she had little place in it. A secret unsavoury woman: it was odd that he, so spick and span and robust, should be of the same blood as she.

This regime, the most comfortable that he could devise for himself, had been practically forced on Alice. Up till her father's death she had kept house for him, and in his old age he had fallen on evil days. He had gambled away in stupid speculation on the Stock Exchange a very decent

capital, and for the last five years of his life he had been entirely dependent on his son, who housed them both in a dingy little flat just around
the corner from Massington Square. Then the old man had had a stroke
and was partially paralysed, and Edmund, always contemptuous of the
sick and the inefficient, had grudged every penny of the few hundred
pounds which he annually allowed him. At the same time he admired the
powers of management and economy that his sister manifested in con-
triving to make her father comfortable on his meagre pittance. For instance she even got him a second-hand bath-chair, shabby and shiny with
much usage, and on warm days she used to have him wheeled up and
down the garden in Massington Square, or sit there reading to him. Certainly she had a good idea of how to use money, and so, on her father's
death, since she had to be provided for somehow, he offered her a
hundred pounds a year, with board and lodging, to come and keep house
for him. If she did not accept this munificence she would have to look out
for herself, and as she was otherwise penniless, it was not in her power to
refuse. She brought the bath-chair with her, and it was stored away in a
big shed in the garden behind her brother's house. It might come into use
again some day.

Edmund Faraday was an exceedingly shrewd man, but he never
guessed that there was any psychical reason, beyond the material necessity, why Alice so eagerly accepted his offer. Briefly, this reason was that
his sister regarded him with a hatred that prospered and burned bright in
his presence. She hugged it to her, she cherished and fed it, and for that
she must be with him: otherwise it might die down and grow cold. To hear
him come in of an evening thrilled her with the sense of his nearness, to
sit with him in silence at their rare solitary meals, to watch him, to serve
him was a feast to her. She had no definite personal desire to injure him,
even if that had been possible, but she must be near him, waiting for some
inconjecturable doom, which, long though it might tarry, would surely
overtake him, provided only that she kept the dynamo of her hatred
ceaselessly at work. All vivid emotion, she knew, was a force in the world,
and sooner or later it worked out its fulfillment. In her solitary hours,
when her housekeeping work was accomplished, she directed her mind on
him like a searchlight, she studied books of magic and occult lore that
revealed or hinted at the powers which concentration can give. Witches
and sorcerers, in the old days, ignorant of the underlying cause, made
spells and incantations, they fashioned images of wax to represent their
victims, and bound and stabbed them with needles in order to induce

physical illness and torturing pains, but all this was child's play, dealing with symbols: the driving force behind them, which was much better left alone to do its will in its own way without interference, was hate. And it was no use being impatient: it was patience that did its perfect work. Perhaps when the doom began to shape itself, a little assistance might be given: fears might be encouraged, despair might be helped to grow, but nothing more than that. Just the unwearied waiting, the still intense desire, the black unquenchable flame. . . .

Often she felt that her father's spirit was in touch with her, for he, too, had loathed his son and when he lay paralysed, without power of speech, she used to make up stories about Edmund for his amusement, how he would lose all his money, how he would be detected in some gross dishonesty in his business, how his vaunted health would fail him, and how cancer or some crippling ailment would grip him; and then the old man's eyes would brighten with merriment, and he cackled wordlessly in his beard and twitched with pleasure. Since her father's death, Alice had no sense that he had gone from her, his spirit was near her, and its malevolence was undiminished. She made him partner of her thoughts: sometimes Edmund was late returning from his work, and as the minutes slipped by and still he did not come, it was as if she still made stories for her father, and told him that the telephone bell would soon ring, and she would find that she was being rung up from some hospital where Edmund had been carried after a street accident. But then she would check her thoughts; she must not allow herself to get too definite or even to suggest anything to the force that was brewing and working round him. And though at present all seemed well with him, and the passing months seemed but to endow him with new prosperities, she never doubted that fulfilment would fail, if she was patient and did her part in keeping the dynamo of hate at work.

Edmund Faraday had only lately moved into the house he now occupied. Previously he had lived in another in the same square, a dozen doors off, but he had always wanted this house: it was more spacious, and it had behind it a considerable plot of garden, lawn and flower-beds, with a high brick wall surrounding it. But the other house was still unlet, and the house agent's board on it was an eyesore to him: there was money unrealized while it stood empty. But to-night, as he approached it, walking briskly back from his office, he saw that there was a man standing on the balcony outside the drawing-room windows: evidently then there was someone seeing over it. As he drew nearer, the man turned, took a few steps towards the long open window and passed inside. Faraday noticed that he limped heavily, leaning on a stick and swaying his body forward as he advanced his left leg, as if the joint was locked. But that was no concern of his, and he was pleased to think that somebody had come to inspect his vacant property. Next morning on his way to business he looked in at the agent's, in whose hands was the disposal of the house, and asked who had been enquiring about it. The agent knew nothing of it: he had not given the keys to anyone.

"But I saw a man standing on the balcony last night," said Faraday. "He must have got hold of the keys."

But the keys were in their proper place, and the agent promised to send round at once to make sure that the house was duly locked up. Faraday took the trouble to call again on his way home, only to learn that all was in order, front door locked, and back door and area gate locked, nor was there any sign that the house had been burglariously entered.

Somehow this trumpery incident stuck in Faraday's mind, and more than once that week it was oddly recalled to him. One morning he saw in the street a little ahead of him a man who limped and leaned on his stick, and instantly he bethought himself of that visitor to the empty house for his build and his movement were the same, and he quickened his step to have a look at him. But the pavement was crowded, and before he could catch him up the man had stepped into the roadway, and dodged through the thick traffic, and Edmund lost sight of him. Once again, as he was coming up the Square to his own house, he was sure that he saw him walking in the opposite direction, down the other side of the Square, and now he turned back in order to come round the end of the garden and meet him face to face. But by the time he had got to the opposite pavement there was no sign of him. He looked up and down the street beyond; surely that limping crippled walk would have been visible a long way off. A big man, broad-shouldered and burly in make: it should have been easy to pick him out. Faraday felt certain he was not a householder in the Square, or surely he must have noticed him before. And what had he been doing in his locked house: and why, suddenly, should he himself now catch sight of him almost every day? Quite irrationally, he felt that this obtrusive and yet elusive stranger had got something to do with him.

He was going down to Ascot to-morrow, and to-night was one of those rare occasions when he dined alone with his sister. He had little appetite, he found fault with the food, and presently the usual silence descended. Suddenly she gave her little bleating laugh. "Oh, I forgot to tell you," she said. "There was a man who called to-day—didn't give any name—who wished to see you about the letting of the other house. I said it was in the agent's hands: I gave him the address. Was that right, Edmund?"

"What was he like?" he rapped out.

"I never saw his face clearly at all. He was standing in the hall with his back to the window, when I came down. But a big man, like you in build, but crippled. Very lame, leaning heavily on his stick."

"What time was this?"

"A few minutes only before you came in."

"And then?"

"Well, when I told him to apply to the agent, he turned and went out, and, as I say, I never saw his face. It was odd somehow. I watched him from the window, and he walked round the top of the Square and down the other side. A few minutes afterwards I heard you come in."

She watched him as she spoke, and saw trouble in his face.

"I can't make out who the fellow is," he said. "From your description he seems like a man I saw a week ago, standing on the balcony of the other house. Yet when I enquired at the agent's, no one had asked for the keys, and the house was locked up all right. I've seen him several times since, but never close. Why didn't you ask his name, or get his address?"

"I declare I never thought of it," she said.

"Don't forget, if he calls again. Now if you've finished you can be off. You'll go down to Ascot to-morrow morning, and let us have something fit to eat. Three men coming down for the week-end."

Faraday went out to his morning round of golf on Saturday in high good spirits: he had won largely at bridge the night before, and he felt brisk and clear-eyed. The morning was very hot, the sun blazed, but a bastion of black cloud coppery at the edges was pushing up the sky from the east, threatening a downpour, and it was annoying to have to wait at one of the short holes while the couple in front delved among the bunkers that guarded the green. Eventually they holed out, and Faraday waiting for them to quit saw that there was watching them a big man, leaning on a stick, and limping heavily as he moved. "That's he," he thought to himself, "so now I'll get a look at him." But when he arrived at the green the stranger had gone, and there was no sign of him anywhere. However, he knew the couple who were in front, and he could ask them when he got to the clubhouse who their friend was. Presently the rain began, short in duration but violent, and his partner went to change his clothes when they got in. Faraday scorned any such precaution: he never caught cold, and never yet in his life had he had a twinge of rheumatism, and while he waited for his less robust partner he made enquiries of the couple who had been playing in front of him as to who their lame companion was. But they knew nothing of him: neither of them had seen him.

Somehow this took the edge off his sense of well-being, for indeed it was a queer thing. But Sunday dawned, bright and sparkling, and waking early he jumped out of bed with the intention of a walk in the garden before his bath. But instantly he had to clutch at a chair to save himself a fall. His left leg had given way under his weight, and a stabbing pain shot through his hip-joint. Very annoying: perhaps he should have changed his wet clothes yesterday. He dressed with difficulty, and limped downstairs. Alice was there arranging fresh flowers for the table.

"Why, Edmund, what's the matter?" she asked.

"Touch of rheumatism," he said. "Moving about will put it right."

But moving about was not so easy: golf was out of the question, and he sat all day in the garden, cursing this unwonted affliction, and all day the thought of the lame man, in build like himself, scratched about underground in his brain, like a burrowing mole.

Arrived back in London Faraday saw a reliable doctor, who, learning of his cold baths and his undisciplined use of the pleasures of the cellar and the table, put him on a regime which was a bitter humiliation to him, for he had joined the contemptible army of the careful. "Moderation, my dear sir," said his adviser. "No more cold baths or port for you, and a curb on your admirable appetite. A little more quiet exercise, too, during the week, and a good deal less on your week-ends. Do your work and play your games and see your friends. But moderation, and we'll soon have you all right."

It was in accordance with this distasteful advice that Faraday took to walking home if he had been dining out in the neighbourhood, or, if at home, took a couple of turns round the Square before going to bed. Contrary to use, he was without guests several nights this week, and on the last of them, before going down into the country again, he limped out about eleven o'clock feeling ill at ease and strangely apprehensive of the future. Though the violence of his attack had abated, walking was painful and difficult, and his halting steps, he felt sure, must arrest a contemptuous compassion in all who knew what a brisk, strong mover he had been. The night was cloudy and sweltering hot, there was a tenseness and an oppression in the air that matched his mood. All pleasure had been sucked out of life for him by this indisposition, and he felt with some inward and quaking certainty that it was but the shadow of some more dire visitant who was drawing near. All this week, too, there had been something strange about Alice. She seemed to be expecting something, and that expectation filled her with a secret glee. She watched him, she took note, she was alert. . . .

He had made the complete circuit of the Square, and now was on his second round, after which he would turn in. A hundred yards of pavement lay between him and his own house, and it and the roadway were absolutely empty. Then, as he neared his own door, he saw that a figure was advancing in his direction; like him it limped and leaned on a stick. But though a week ago he had wanted to meet this man face to face, something in his mind had shifted, and now the prospect of the encounter filled him with some quaking terror. A meeting, however, was not to be avoided, unless he turned back again, and the thought of being followed by him was even more intolerable than the encounter. Then, while he was still a dozen yards off, he saw that the other had paused opposite his door, as if waiting for him.

Faraday held his latchkey in his hand ready to let himself in. He would not look at the fellow at all, but pass him with averted head. When he was now within a foot or two of him, the other put out his hand with a detaining gesture, and involuntarily Faraday turned. The man was standing close to the street lamp, and his face was in vivid light. And that face was Faraday's own: it was as if he beheld his own image in a looking-glass. . . . With a gulping breath he let himself into his house, and banged the door. There was Alice standing close within, waiting for him surely.

"Edmund," she said— and just as surely her voice trembled with some secret suppressed glee—"I went to post a letter just now, and that man who called about the other house was loitering outside. So odd."

He wiped the cold dews from his forehead.

"Did you get a look at him?" he asked. "What was he like?"

She gave her bleating laugh, and her eyes were merry.

"A most extraordinary thing!" she said. "He was so like you that I actually spoke to him before I saw my mistake. His walk, his build, his face: everything. Most extraordinary! Well, I'll go up to bed now. It's late for me, but I thought you would like to know that he was about, in case you wanted to speak to him. I wonder who he is, and what he wants. Sleep well!"

In spite of her good wishes, Faraday slept far from well. According to his usual custom, he had thrown the windows wide before he got into bed, and he was just dozing off, when he heard from outside an uneven tread and the tap of a stick on the pavement, his own tread he would have thought, and the tap of his own stick. Up and down it went, in a short patrol, in front of his house. Sometimes it ceased for a while, but no sooner did sleep hover near him than it began again. Should he look out, he asked himself, and see if there was anyone there? He recoiled from that, for the thought of looking again on himself, his own face and figure, brought the sweat to his forehead. At last, unable to bear this haunted vigil any longer, he went to the window. From end to end, as far as he could see, the Square was empty, but for a policeman moving noiselessly on his rounds, and flashing his light into areas.

Dr. Inglis visited him next morning. Since seeing him last, he had examined the X-ray photograph of the troublesome joint, and he could give him good news about that. There was no sign of arthritis; a muscular rheumatism, which no doubt would yield to treatment and care, was all that ailed him. So off went Faraday to his work, and the doctor remained to have a talk to Alice, for, jovially and encouragingly, he had told him that he suspected he was not a very obedient patient, and must tell his sister that his instructions as to food and tabloids must be obeyed.

"Physically there's nothing much wrong with him, Miss Faraday," he said, "but I want to consult you. I found him very nervous and I am sure he was wanting to tell me something, but couldn't manage it. He ought to have thrown off his rheumatism days ago, but there's something on his mind, sapping his vitality. Have you any idea—strict confidence of course—what it is?"

She gave her little bleat of laughter.

"Wrong of me to laugh, I know, Dr. Inglis," she said, "but it's such a relief to be told there's nothing really amiss with dear Edmund. Yes: he has something on his mind—dear me, it's so ridiculous that I can hardly speak of it."

"But I want to know."

"Well, it's a lame man, whom he has seen several times. I've seen him, too, and the odd thing is he is exactly like Edmund. Last night he met him just outside the house, and he came in, well, really looking like death."

"And when did he see him first? After this lameness came upon him, I'll be bound."

"No: before. We both saw him before. It was as if—such nonsense it sounds!—it was as if this sort of double of himself showed what was going to happen to him."

There was glee and gusto in her voice. And how slovenly and uncouth she was with that lock of grey hair loose across her forehead, and her uncared-for hands. Dr. Inglis felt a distaste for her: he wondered if she was quite right in the head.

She clasped one knee in her long bony fingers.

"That's what troubles him—oh, I understand him so well," she said. "Edmund's terrified of this man. He doesn't know *what* he is. Not *who* he is, but *what* he is."

"But what is there to be afraid about?" asked the doctor. "This lame fellow, so like him, is no disordered fancy of his own brain, since you've seen him too. He's an ordinary living human being."

She laughed again, she clapped her hands like a pleased child. "Why, of course, that must be so!" she said. "So there's nothing for him to be afraid of. That's splendid! I must tell Edmund that. What a relief! Now about the rules you've laid down for him, his food and all that. I will be very strict with him. I will see that he does what you tell him. I will be quite relentless."

For a week or two Faraday saw no more of this unwelcome visitor, but he did not forget him, and somewhere deep down in his brain there remained that little cold focus of fear. Then came an evening when he had been dining out with friends: the food and the wine were excellent, they chaffed him about his abstemiousness, and loosening his restrictions he made a jolly evening of it, like one of the old days. He seemed to himself to have escaped out of the shadow that had lain on him, and he walked home in high good humour, limping and leaning on his stick, but far more brisk than was his wont. He must be up betimes in the morning, for the annual general meeting of his company was soon coming on, and to-morrow he must finish writing his speech to the shareholders. He would be giving them a pleasant half-hour; twelve percent free of tax and a five per cent bonus was what he had to tell them about Faraday's Stores.

He had taken a short cut through the dingy little thoroughfare where his father had lived during his last stricken years, and his thoughts flitted back, with the sense of a burden gone, to the last time he had seen him alive, sitting in his bath-chair in the garden of the Square, with Alice reading to him. Edmund had stepped into the garden to have a word with him, but his father only looked at him malevolently from his sunken eyes, mumbling and muttering in his beard. He was like an old monkey, Edmund thought, toothless and angry and feeble, and then suddenly he had struck out at him with the hand that still had free movement. Edmund had given him the rough side of his tongue for that; told him he

must behave more prettily unless he wanted his allowance cut down. A
nice way to behave to a son who gave him every penny he had!

Thus pleasantly musing he came out of this mean alley, and crossed into the Square. There were people about to-night, motors were moving this
way and that, and a taxi was standing at the house next his, obstructing
any further view of the road. Passing it, he saw that directly under the
lamp-post opposite his own door there was drawn up an empty bath-chair.
Just behind it, as if waiting to push it, when its occupant was ready, there
was standing an old man with a straggling white beard. Peering at him Edmund saw his sunken eyes and his mumbling mouth, and instantly came
recognition. His latchkey slipped from his hand, and without waiting to
pick it up, he stumbled up the steps, and, in an access of uncontrollable
panic, was plying bell and knocker and beating with his hands on the
panel of his door. He heard a step within, and there was Alice, and he
pushed by her collapsing on to a chair in the hall. Before she closed the
door and came to him, she smiled and kissed her hand to someone outside.

It was with difficulty that they got him up to his bedroom, for though
just now he had been so brisk, all power seemed to have left him, his
thigh-bones would scarce stir in their sockets, and he went up the stairs
crab-wise or corkscrew-wise sidling and twisting as he mounted each step.
At his direction, Alice closed and bolted his windows and drew the curtains across them; not a word did he say about what he had seen, but indeed there was no need for that.

Then leaving him she went to her own room, alert and eager, for who
knew what might happen before day? How wise she had been to leave the
working out of this in other hands: she had but concentrated and
thought, and, behold, her thoughts and the force that lay behind them
were taking shape of their own in the material world. Fear, too, that great
engine of destruction, had Edmund in its grip, he was caught in its invisible machinery, and was being drawn in among the relentless wheels.
And still she must not interfere: she must go on hating him and wishing
him ill. That had been a wonderful moment when he battered at the door
in a frenzy of terror, and when, opening it, she saw outside the shabby
old bath-chair and her father standing behind it. She scarcely slept that
night, but lay happy and nourished and tense, wondering if at any
moment now the force might gather itself up for some stroke that would
end all. But the short summer night brightened into day, and she went
about her domestic duties again, so that everything should be comfortable for Edmund.

Presently his servant came down with his master's orders to ring up
Dr. Inglis. After the doctor had seen him, he again asked to speak to
Alice. This repetition of his interview was lovely to her mind: it was like
the re-entry of some musical motif in a symphony, and now it was decorated and amplified, for he took a much graver view of his patient. This
sudden stiffening of his joints could not be accounted for by any physical
cause, and there accompanied it a marked loss of power, which no bodily
lesion explained. Certainly he had had some great shock, but of that he
would not speak. Again the doctor asked her whether she knew anything
of it, but all she could tell him was that he came in last night in a frightful
state of terror and collapse. Then there was another thing. He was worrying himself over the speech he had to make at this general meeting. It was
highly important that he should get some rest and sleep, and while that
speech was on his mind, he evidently could not. He was therefore getting
up, and would come down to his sitting-room where he had the necessary
papers. With the help of his servant he could manage to get there, and
when his job was done, he could rest quietly there, and Dr. Inglis would
come back during the afternoon to see him again: probably a week or two
in a nursing home would be advisable. He told Alice to look in on him occasionally, and if anything alarmed her she must send for him. Soon he
went upstairs again to help Edmund to come down, and there were the
sounds of heavy treads, and the creaking of banisters, as if some dead
weight was being moved. That brought back to Alice the memory of her
father's funeral and the carrying of the coffin down the narrow stairs of
the little house which his son's bounty had provided for him.

She went with her brother and the doctor into his sitting-room and
established him at the table. The room looked out on to the high-walled
garden at the back of the house, and a long French window, opening to
the ground, communicated with it. A plane-tree in full summer foliage
stood just outside, and on this sultry overcast morning the room was dim
with the dusky green light that filters through a screen of leaves. His
table was strewn with his papers, and he sat in a chair with its back to the
window. In that curious and sombre light his face looked strangely
colourless, and the movements of his hands among his papers seemed to
falter and stumble.

Alice came back an hour later and there he sat still busy and without a
word for her, and she turned on the electric light, for it had grown darker,
and she closed the open window, for now rain fell heavily. As she fastened
the bolts, she saw that the figure of her father was standing just outside,

not a yard away. He smiled and nodded to her, he put his finger to his lips, as if enjoining silence; then he made a little gesture of dismissal to her, and she left the room, just looking back as she shut the door. Her brother was still busy with his work, and the figure outside had come close up to the window. She longed to stop, she longed to see with her own eyes what was coming, but it was best to obey that gesture and go. The hall outside was very dark, and she stood there a moment, listening intently. Then from the door which she had just shut there came, unmistakably, the click of a turned key, and again there was silence but for the drumming of the rain, and the splash of overflowing gutters. Something was imminent: would the silence be broken by some protest of mortal agony, or would the gutters continue to gurgle till all was over?

And then the silence within was shattered. There came the sound of Edmund's voice rising higher and more hoarse in some incoherent babble of entreaty, and suddenly, as it rose to a scream, it ceased as if a tap had been turned off. Inside there, something fell with a thump that shook the solid floor, and up the stairs from below came Edmund's servant.

"What was that, miss?" he said in a scared whisper, and he turned the handle of the door. "Why, the master's locked himself in."

"Yes, he's busy," said Alice, "perhaps he doesn't want to be disturbed. But I heard his voice, too, and then the sound of something falling. Tap at the door and see if he answers."

The man tapped and paused, and tapped again. Then from inside came the click of a turned key and they entered.

The room was empty. The light still burned on his table but the chair where she had left him five minutes before was pushed back, and the window she had bolted was wide. Alice looked out into the garden, and that was as empty as the room. But the door of the shed where her father's bath-chair was kept stood open, and she ran out into the rain and looked in. Edmund was lying in it with head lolling over the side.

R. H. MALDEN

Between Sunset and Moonrise (1943)

A completely forgotten writer of ghost stories, the Reverend Richard
Henry Malden, Canon of Ripon and Dean of Wells, states in the preface
to his collected tales that his purpose is to "continue the tradition" of
M. R. James, his friend and colleague of thirty years. Of his own tales, he
writes, "Anyone familiar with *Ghost Stories of an Antiquary* will have no
difficulty in recognizing their *provenance.*"

Yet, as "Between Sunset and Moonrise" delightfully illustrates,
Malden had a voice of his own. To be sure, the requisite hero "of antiquarian knowledge and artistic perception" appears on cue, as do the
threatening intimations from an old book, in this case the Bible. The
suaveness and reticence of Malden's diction are also identifiably
Jamesian. The real power and charm in the story, however, derive from
Malden's sense of place, his marvelous evocation of the bleak Fen district,
as somber and ghostly a setting as one could desire and certainly wilder
than the typically bookish James setting. The surprisingly elaborate apparition scene is also memorable and entirely original. Indeed, Malden
manages a toad image at the end of the scene that would have made the
master white with envy.

~~ BETWEEN SUNSET AND MOONRISE ~~

During the early part of last year it fell to me to act as executor for an old friend. We had not seen much of each other of late, as he had been living in the west of England, and my own time had been fully occupied elsewhere. The time of our intimacy had been when he was vicar of a large parish not very far from Cambridge. I will call it Yaxholme, though that is not its name.

The place had seemed to suit him thoroughly. He had been on the best of terms with his parishioners, and with the few gentry of the neighbour-hood. The church demanded a custodian of antiquarian knowledge and artistic perception, and in these respects too my friend was particularly well qualified for his position. But a sudden nervous breakdown had compelled him to resign. The cause of it had always been a mystery to his friends, for he was barely middle-aged when it took place and had been a man of robust health. His parish was neither particularly laborious nor harassing; and, as far as was known, he had no special private anxieties of any kind. But the collapse came with startling suddenness, and was so severe that, for a time, his reason seemed to be in danger. Two years of rest and travel enabled him to lead a normal life again, but he was never the man he had been. He never revisited his old parish, or any of his friends in the county; and seemed to be ill at ease if conversation turned upon the part of England in which it lay. It was perhaps not unnatural that he should dislike the place which had cost him so much. But his friends could not but regard as childish the length to which he carried his aversion.

He had had a distinguished career at the University, and had kept up his intellectual interests in later life. But, except for an occasional *succès d'estime* in a learned periodical, he had published nothing. I was not with-out hope of finding something completed among his papers which would secure for him a permanent place in the world of learning. But in this I was disappointed. His literary remains were copious, and a striking testi-mony to the vigour and range of his intellect. But they were very frag-mentary. There was nothing which could be made fit for publication, ex-cept one document which I should have preferred to suppress. But he had left particular instructions in his will that it was to be published when he

200

had been dead for a year. Accordingly I subjoin it exactly as it left his hand. It was dated two years after he had left Yaxholme, and nearly five before his death. For reasons which will be apparent to the reader I make no comment of any kind upon it.

The solicitude which my friends have displayed during my illness has placed me under obligations which I cannot hope to repay. But I feel that I owe it to them to explain the real cause of my breakdown. I have never spoken of it to anyone, for, had I done so, it would have been impossible to avoid questions which I should not wish to be able to answer. Though I have only just reached middle-age I am sure that I have not many more years to live. And I am therefore confident that most of my friends will survive me, and be able to hear my explanation after my death. Nothing but a lively sense of what I owe to them could have enabled me to undergo the pain of recalling the experience which I am now about to set down.

Yaxholme lies, as they will remember, upon the extreme edge of the Fen district. In shape it is a long oval, with a main line of railway cutting one end. The church and vicarage were close to the station, and round them lay a village containing nearly five-sixths of the entire population of the parish. On the other side of the line the Fen proper began, and stretched for many miles. Though it is now fertile corn land, much of it had been permanently under water within living memory, and would soon revert to its original condition if it were not for the pumping stations. In spite of these it is not unusual to see several hundred acres flooded in winter.

My own parish ran for nearly six miles, and I had therefore several scattered farms and cottages so far from the village that a visit to one of them took up the whole of a long afternoon. Most of them were not on any road, and could only be reached by means of droves. For the benefit of those who are not acquainted with the Fen I may explain that a drove is a very imperfect sketch of the idea of a road. It is bounded by hedges or dykes, so that the traveller cannot actually lose his way, but it offers no further assistance to his progress. The middle is simply a grass track, and as cattle have to be driven along it the mud is sometimes literally knee-deep in winter. In summer the light peaty soil rises in clouds of sable dust. In fact I seldom went down one without recalling Hesiod's unpatriotic description of his native village in Boeotia. 'Bad in winter; intolerable in summer; good at no time.'

At the far end of one of these lay a straggling group of half a dozen cottages, of which the most remote was inhabited by an old woman whom I will call Mrs. Vries. In some ways she was the most interesting of all my parishioners, and she was certainly the most perplexing. She was not a native, but had come to live there some twenty years before, and it was hard to see what had tempted a stranger to so unattractive a spot. It was the last house in the parish: her nearest neighbour was a quarter of a mile away, and she was fully three miles from a hard road or a shop. The house itself was not at all a good one. It had been unoccupied, I was told, for some years before she came to it, and she had found it in a semi-ruinous condition. Yet she had not been driven to seek a very cheap dwelling by poverty, as she had a good supply of furniture of very good quality, and, apparently, as much money as she required. She never gave the slightest hint as to where she had come from or what her previous history had been. As far as was known she never wrote or received any letters. She must have been between fifty and sixty when she came. Her appearance was striking, as she was tall and thin, with an aquiline nose, and a pair of very brilliant dark eyes, and a quantity of hair—snow-white by the time I knew her. At one time she must have been handsome; but she had grown rather forbidding, and I used to think that, a couple of centuries before, she might have had some difficulty in proving that she was not a witch. Though her neighbours, not unnaturally, fought rather shy of her, her conversation showed that she was a clever woman who had at some time received a good deal of education, and had lived in cultivated surroundings. I used to think that she must have been an upper servant—most probably lady's maid—in a good house, and, despite the ring on her finger, suspected that the 'Mrs.' was brevet rank.

One New Year's Eve I thought it my duty to visit her. I had not seen her for some months, and a few days of frost had made the drove more passable than it had been for several weeks. But, in spite of her interesting personality, I always found that it required a considerable moral effort to call at her cottage. She was always civil, and expressed herself pleased to see me. But I could never get rid of the idea that she regarded civility to me in the light of an insurance, which might be claimed elsewhere. I always told myself that such thoughts were unfounded and unworthy, but I could never repress them altogether, and whenever I left her cottage it was with a strong feeling that I had no desire to see her again. I used, however, to say to myself that that was really due to personal pique (because I could never discover that she had any religion, nor could I instil any into her), and that the fault was therefore more mine than hers.

On this particular afternoon the prospect of seeing her seemed more than usually distasteful, and my disinclination increased curiously as I made my way along the drove. So strong did it become that if any reasonable excuse for turning back had presented itself I am afraid I should have seized it. However, none did: so I held on, comforting myself with the thought that I should begin the New Year with a comfortable sense of having discharged the most unpleasant of my regular duties in a conscientious fashion.

When I reached the cottage I was a little surprised at having to knock three times, and by hearing the sound of bolts cautiously drawn back. Presently the door opened and Mrs. Vries peered out. As soon as she saw who it was she made me very welcome as usual. But it was impossible not to feel that she had been more or less expecting some other visitor, whom she was not anxious to see. However, she volunteered no statement, and I thought it better to pretend to have noticed nothing unusual. On a table in the middle of the room lay a large book in which she had obviously been reading. I was surprised to see that it was a Bible, and that it lay open at the Book of Tobit. Seeing that I had noticed it Mrs. Vries told me—with a little hesitation, I thought—that she had been reading the story of Sarah and the fiend Asmodeus. Then—the ice once broken—she plied me almost fiercely with questions. 'To what cause did I attribute Sarah's obsession, in the first instance?' 'Did the efficacy of Tobias' remedy depend upon the fact that it had been prescribed by an angel?' and much more to the same effect. Naturally my answers were rather vague, and her good manners could not conceal her disappointment. She sat silent for a minute or two, while I looked at her—not, I must confess, without some alarm, for her manner had been very strange—and then said abruptly, 'Well, will you have a cup of tea with me?' I assented gladly, for it was nearly half-past four, and it would take me nearly an hour and a half to get home. She took some time over the preparations and during the meal talked with even more fluency than usual. I could not help thinking that she was trying to make it last as long as possible.

Finally, at about half-past five, I got up and said that I must go, as I had a good many odds and ends waiting me at home. I held out my hand, and as she took it said, 'You must let me wish you a very happy New Year.' She stared at me for a moment, and then broke into a harsh laugh, and said 'If wishes were horses beggars might ride. Still, I thank you for your good will. Good-bye.' About thirty yards from her house there was an elbow in the drove. When I reached it I looked back and saw that she was still standing in her doorway, with her figure sharply silhouetted against the red glow of the kitchen fire. For one instant the play of shadow made it look as if there were another, taller, figure behind her, but the illusion passed directly. I waved my hand to her and turned the corner.

It was a fine, still, starlight night. I reflected that the moon would be up before I reached home, and my walk would not be unpleasant. I had naturally been rather puzzled by Mrs. Vries' behaviour, and decided that I must see her again before long, to ascertain whether, as seemed possible, her mind were giving way.

When I had passed the other cottages of the group. I noticed that the stars were disappearing, and a thick white mist was rolling up. This did not trouble me. The drove now ran straight until it joined the high-road, and there was no turn into it on either side. I had therefore no chance of losing my way, and anyone who lives in the Fens is accustomed to fogs. It soon grew very thick, and I was conscious of the slightly creepy feeling which a thick fog very commonly inspires. I had been thinking of a variety of things, in somewhat desultory fashion, when suddenly— almost as if it had been whispered into my ear—a passage from the Book of Wisdom came into my mind and refused to be dislodged. My nerves were good then, and I had often walked up a lonely drove in a fog before; but still just at that moment I should have preferred to have recalled almost anything else. For this was the extract with which my memory was pleased to present me. 'For neither did the dark recesses that held them guard them from fears, but sounds rushing down rang around them; and phantoms appeared, cheerless with unsmiling faces. And no force of fire prevailed to give them light, neither were the brightest flames of the stars strong enough to illumine that gloomy night. And in terror they deemed the things which they saw to be worse than that sight on which they could not gaze. And they lay helpless, made the sport of magic art.' (*Wisdom* xvii. 4-6).

Suddenly I heard a loud snort, as of a beast, apparently at my elbow. Naturally I jumped and stood still for a moment to avoid blundering into a stray cow, but there was nothing there. The next moment I heard what sounded exactly like a low chuckle. This was more disconcerting: but common sense soon came to my aid. I told myself that the cow must have been on the other side of the hedge and not really so close as it had seemed to be. What I had taken for a chuckle must have been the squelching of her feet in a soft place. But I must confess that I did not find this explanation as convincing as I could have wished.

I plodded on, but soon began to feel unaccountably tired. I say 'unaccountably' because I was a good walker and often covered much more ground than I had done that day.

I slackened my pace, but, as I was not out of breath, that did not relieve me. I felt as if I were wading through water up to my middle, or through very deep soft snow, and at last was fairly compelled to stop. By this time I was thoroughly uneasy, wondering what could be the matter with me. But as I had still nearly two miles to go there was nothing for it but to push on as best I might.

When I started again I saw that the fog seemed to be beginning to clear, though I could not feel a breath of air. But instead of thinning in the ordinary way it merely rolled back a little on either hand, producing an effect which I had never seen before. Along the sides of the drove lay two solid banks of white, with a narrow passage clear between them. This passage seemed to stretch for an interminable distance, and at the far end I 'perceived' a number of figures. I say advisedly 'perceived,' rather than 'saw,' for I do not know whether I saw them in the ordinary sense of the word or not. That is to say—I did not know then, and have never been able to determine since, whether it was still dark. I only know that my power of vision seemed to be independent of light or darkness. I perceived the figures, as one sees the creatures of a dream, or the mental pictures which sometimes come when one is neither quite asleep nor awake.

They were advancing rapidly in orderly fashion, almost like a body of troops. The scene recalled very vividly a picture of the Israelites marching across the Red Sea between two perpendicular walls of water, in a set of Bible pictures which I had had as a child. I suppose that I had not thought of that picture for more than thirty years, but now it leapt into my mind, and I found myself saying aloud, 'Yes: of course it must have been exactly like that. How glad I am to have seen it.'

I suppose it was the interest of making the comparison that kept me from feeling the surprise which would otherwise have been occasioned by meeting a large number of people marching down a lonely drove after dark on a raw December evening.

At first I should have said there were thirty or forty in the party, but when they had drawn a little nearer they seemed to be not more than ten or a dozen strong. A moment later I saw to my surprise that they were reduced to five or six. The advancing figures seemed to be melting into one another, something after the fashion of dissolving views. Their speed and stature increased as their numbers diminished, suggesting that the survivors had, in some horrible fashion, absorbed the personality of their companions. Now there appeared to be only three, then one solitary figure of gigantic stature rushing down the drove towards me at a fearful pace, without a sound. As he came the mist closed behind him, so that his dark figure was thrown up against a solid background of white: much as mountain climbers are said sometimes to see their own shadows upon a bank of cloud. On and on he came, until at last he towered above me and I saw his face. It has come to me once or twice since in troubled dreams, and may come again. But I am thankful that I have never had any clear picture of it in my waking moments. If I had I should be afraid for my reason. I know that the impression which it produced upon me was that of intense malignity long baffled, and now at last within reach of its desire. I believe I screamed aloud. Then after a pause, which seemed to last for hours, he broke over me like a wave. There was a rushing and a streaming all round me, and I struck out with my hands as if I were swimming. The sensation was not unlike that of rising from a deep dive: there was the same feeling of pressure and suffocation, but in this case coupled with the the most intense physical loathing. The only comparison which I can suggest is that I felt as a man might feel if he were buried under a heap of worms or toads.

Suddenly I seemed to be clear, and fell forward on my face. I am not sure whether I fainted or not, but I must have lain there for some minutes. When I picked myself up I felt a light breeze upon my forehead and the mist was clearing away as quickly as it had come. I saw the rim of the moon above the horizon, and my mysterious fatigue had disappeared. I hurried forward as quickly as I could without venturing to look behind me. I only wanted to get out of that abominable drove on to the high-road, where there were lights and other human beings. For I knew that what I had seen was a creature of darkness and waste places, and that among my fellows I should be safe. When I reached home my housekeeper looked at me oddly. Of course my clothes were muddy and disarranged, but I suspect that there was something else unusual in my appearance. I merely said that I had had a fall coming up a drove in the dark, and was not feeling particularly well. I avoided the looking-glass when I went to my room to change.

Coming downstairs I heard through the open kitchen door some scraps of conversation—or rather of a monologue delivered by my housekeeper —to the effect that no one ought to be about the droves after dark as much as I was, and that it was a providence that things were no worse. Her own mother's uncle had—it appeared—been down just such another drove on just such another night, forty-two years ago come next Christmas Eve. 'They brought 'im 'ome on a barrow with both 'is eyes drawed down, and every drop of blood in 'is body turned. But 'e never would speak to what 'e see, and wild cats couldn't ha' scratched it out of him.'

An inaudible remark from one of the maids was met with a long sniff, and the statement: 'Girls seem to think they know everything nowadays.' I spent the next day in bed, as besides the shock which I had received I had caught a bad cold. When I got up on the second I was not surprised to hear that Mrs. Vries had been found dead on the previous afternoon. I had hardly finished breakfast when I was told that the policeman, whose name was Winter, would be glad to see me.

It appeared that on New Year's morning a half-witted boy of seventeen, who lived at one of the other cottages down the drove, had come to him and said that Mrs. Vries was dead, and that he must come and enter her house. He declined to explain how he had come by the information: so at first Mr. Winter contented himself with pointing out that it was the first of January not of April. But the boy was so insistent that finally he went. When repeated knockings at Mrs. Vries' cottage produced no result he had felt justified in forcing the back-door. She was sitting in a large wooden armchair quite dead. She was leaning forward a little and her hands were clasping the arms so tightly that it proved to be a matter of some difficulty to unloose her fingers. In front of her was another chair, so close that if anyone had been sitting in it his knees must have touched those of the dead woman. The seat cushions were flattened down as if it had been occupied recently by a solid personage. The tea-things had not been cleared away, but the kitchen was perfectly clean and tidy. There was no suspicion of foul play, as all the doors and windows were securely fastened on the inside. Winter added that her face made him feel 'quite sickish like,' and that the house smelt very bad for all that it was so clean.

A post-mortem examination of the body showed that her heart was in a very bad state, and enabled the coroner's jury to return a verdict of 'Death from Natural Causes.' But the doctor told me privately that she must have had a shock of some kind. 'In fact,' he said, 'if anyone ever died of fright, she did. But goodness knows what can have frightened her in her own kitchen unless it was her own conscience. But that is more in your line than mine.'

He added that he had found the examination of the body peculiarly trying: though he could not, or would not, say why.

As I was the last person who had seen her alive, I attended the inquest, but gave only formal evidence of an unimportant character. I did not mention that the second armchair had stood in a corner of the room during my visit, and that I had not occupied it.

The boy was of course called and asked how he knew she was dead. But nothing satisfactory could be got from him. He said that there was right houses and there was wrong houses—not to say persons—and that 'they' had been after her for a long time. When asked whom he meant by 'they' he declined to explain, merely adding as a general statement that he could see further into a milestone than what some people could, for all they thought themselves so clever. His own family deposed that he had been absolutely silent, contrary to his usual custom, from tea-time on New Year's Eve to breakfast-time next day. Then he had suddenly announced that Mrs. Vries was dead; and ran out of the house before they could say anything to him. Accordingly he was dismissed, with a warning to the effect that persons who were disrespectful to Constituted Authorities always came to a bad end.

It naturally fell to me to conduct the funeral, as I could have given no reason for refusing her Christian burial. The coffin was not particularly weighty, but as it was being lowered into the grave the ropes supporting it parted, and it fell several feet with a thud. The shock dislodged a quantity of soil from the sides of the cavity, so that the coffin was completely covered before I had had time to say 'Earth to earth: Ashes to ashes: Dust to dust.'

Afterwards the sexton spoke to me apologetically about the occurrence. 'I'm fair put about, Sir, about them ropes,' he said. 'Nothing o' that sort ever 'appened afore in my time. They was pretty nigh new too and I thought they'd a done us for years. But just look 'ere, Sir.' Here he showed two extraordinarily ravelled ends. 'I never see a rope part like that afore. Almost looks as if it 'ad been scratted through by a big cat or something.'

That night I was taken ill. When I was better my doctor said that rest and change of scene were imperative. I knew that I could never go down a drove alone by night again, so tendered my resignation to my Bishop. I hope that I have still a few years of usefulness before me: but I know that I can never be as if I had not seen what I have seen. Whether I met with my adventure through any fault of my own I cannot tell. But of one thing I am sure. There are powers of darkness which walk abroad in waste places: and that man is happy who has never had to face them.

If anyone who reads this should ever have a similar experience and should feel tempted to try to investigate it further, I commend to him the counsel of Jesus-ben-Sira.

'My son, seek not things that are too hard for thee: and search not out things that are above thy strength.'

IV. THE VISIONARY GHOST STORY

H. G. WELLS

The Plattner Story (1897)

Those who think of H. G. Wells exclusively as a science-fiction writer
are in for a chilling surprise with this story. Although Wells is certainly
the premier science-fiction writer of the period (for many of us, of any
period), he also wrote some of the most skillfully wrought ghost and
horror stories in English. Wells could write stories that were surpassingly
grim ("Plollock and the Porroh Man," about a man pursued by a decapi-
tated head) or splendidly witty ("The Strange Orchid," about a man
pursued by a vampiric orchid). In his darkest moods he could write in a
conte cruel mode ("The Cone") or unleash an attack of octopoid creatures
("The Sea Raiders") as loathsome as anything in H. P. Lovecraft. For a
man who spent so many years writing essays about scientific and metaphysical subjects, Wells was surprisingly good about keeping his story
moving and keeping essay-like explanations to a minimum.

Science does sometimes appear in Wells's more weird and unearthly
stories, but it is merely an excuse, a springboard to get his imagination
moving into the realm of awe and terror. "The Plattner Story," which
has not one, but countless ghosts, begins with a dryly technical explanation of the fourth dimension, then moves quickly into the otherworld of
the "Watchers of the Living," with its spectral lights and tomblike cities.
Wells's treatment of this material becomes increasingly less technical
and more metaphorical and ghostly, until "inhabitants of another dimension" becomes just a fancy way of saying "ghosts." There is certainly
nothing "scientific" about the shadowy personification of Death at the
story's climax: the almost medieval starkness and intensity of this scene
is the last thing we might expect from this propagandist for "scientific
materialism."

Of all the many writers of the Victorian and Edwardian periods who
attempted the fashionable exercise of reconciling science with mystical
experience (Bulwer-Lytton, Hichens, Doyle, Machen, Hodgson, to name
a few), Wells was the most graceful, witty, and (since he was widely read)
influential. Wells offers a pleasant combination: he has the cultivated,
careful sensibility of an antiquarian writer, but his ideas are visionary and
transcendental.

≈ THE PLATTNER STORY ≈

Whether the story of Gottfried Plattner is to be credited or not, is a pretty question in the value of evidence. On the one hand, we have seven witnesses—to be perfectly exact, we have six and a half pairs of eyes, and one undeniable fact; and on the other we have—what is it?—prejudice, common sense, the inertia of opinion. Never were there seven more honest-seeming witnesses; never was there a more undeniable fact that the inversion of Gottfried Plattner's anatomical structure, and—never was there a more preposterous story than the one they have to tell! The most preposterous part of the story is the worthy Gottfried's contribution (for I count him as one of the seven). Heaven forbid that I should be led into giving countenance to superstition by a passion for impartiality, and so come to share the fate of Eusapia's patrons! Frankly, I believe there is something crooked about this business of Gottfried Plattner; but what that crooked factor is, I will admit as frankly, I do not know. I have been surprised at the credit accorded to the story in the most unexpected and authoritative quarters. The fairest way to the reader, however, will be for me to tell it without further comment.

Gottfried Plattner is, in spite of his name, a free-born Englishman. His father was an Alsatian who came to England in the Sixties, married a respectable English girl of unexceptionable antecedents, and died, after a wholesome and uneventful life (devoted, I understand, chiefly to the laying of parquet flooring), in 1887. Gottfried's age is seven-and-twenty. He is, by virtue of his heritage of three languages, Modern Languages Master in a small private school in the South of England. To the casual observer he is singularly like any other Modern Languages Master in any other small private school. His costume is neither very costly nor very fashionable, but, on the other hand, it is not markedly cheap or shabby; his complexion, like his height and his bearing, is inconspicuous. You would notice perhaps that, like the majority of people, his face was not absolutely symmetrical, his right eye a little larger than the left, and his jaw a trifle heavier on the right side. If you, as an ordinary careless person, were to bare his chest and feel his heart beating, you would probably find it quite like the heart of anyone else. But here you and the trained observer would part company. If you found his heart quite ordinary, the trained observer would find it quite otherwise. And once the thing was pointed out to you, you too would perceive the peculiarity easily enough. It is that Gottfried's heart beats on the right side of his body.

Now that is not the only singularity of Gottfried's structure, although it is the only one that would appeal to the untrained mind. Careful sounding of Gottfried's internal arrangements, by a well-known surgeon, seems to point to the fact that all the other unsymmetrical parts of his body are similarly misplaced. The right lobe of his liver is on the left side, the left on his right; while his lungs, too, are similarly contraposed. What is still more singular, unless Gottfried is a consummate actor we must believe that his right hand has recently become his left. Since the occurrences we are about to consider (as impartially as possible), he has found the utmost difficulty in writing except from right to left across the paper with his left hand. He cannot throw with his right hand, he is perplexed at meal times between knife and fork, and his ideas of the rule of the road—he is a cyclist—are still a dangerous confusion. And there is not a scrap of evidence to show that before these occurrences Gottfried was at all left-handed.

There is yet another wonderful fact in this preposterous business. Gottfried produces three photographs of himself. You have him at the age of five or six, thrusting fat legs at you from under a plaid frock, and scowling. In that photograph his left eye is a little larger than his right, and his jaw is a trifle heavier on the left side. This is the reverse of his present living conditions. The photograph of Gottfried at fourteen seems to contradict these facts, but that is because it is one of those cheap "Gem" photographs that were then in vogue, taken direct upon metal, and therefore reversing things just as a looking-glass would. The third photograph represents him at one-and-twenty, and confirms the record of the others. There seems here evidence of the strongest confirmatory character that Gottfried has exchanged his left side for his right. Yet how a human being can be so changed, short of a fantastic and pointless miracle, it is exceedingly hard to suggest.

In one way, of course, these facts might be explicable on the supposition that Plattner has undertaken an elaborate mystification on the strength of his heart's displacement. Photographs may be fudged, and left-handedness imitated. But the character of the man does not lend itself to any such theory. He is quiet, practical, unobtrusive, and thoroughly sane from the Nordau standpoint. He likes beer and smokes moderately, takes walking exercise daily, and has a healthily high estimate of the value of his teaching. He has a good but untrained tenor voice, and takes a pleasure in singing airs of a popular and cheerful character. He is fond, but not morbidly fond, of reading—chiefly fiction pervaded with a vaguely pious optimism,—sleeps well, and rarely dreams. He is, in fact, the very last person to evolve a fantastic fable. Indeed, so far from forcing this story upon the world, he has been singularly reticent on the matter. He meets inquirers with a certain engaging—bashfulness is almost the word, that disarms the most suspicious. He seems genuinely ashamed that anything so unusual has occurred to him.

It has to be regretted that Plattner's aversion to the idea of post-mortem dissection may postpone, perhaps for ever, the positive proof that his entire body has had its left and right sides transposed. Upon that fact mainly the credibility of his story hangs. There is no way of taking a man and moving him about *in space*, as ordinary people understand space, that will result in our changing his sides. Whatever you do, his right is still his right, his left his left. You can do that with a perfectly thin and flat thing, of course. If you were to cut a figure of paper, any figure with a right and left side, you could change its sides simply by lifting it up and turning it over. But with a solid it is different. Mathematical theorists tell us that the only way in which the right and left sides of a solid body can be changed is by taking that body clean out of space as we know it,—taking it out of ordinary existence, that is, and turning it somewhere outside space. This is a little abstruse, no doubt, but anyone with a slight knowledge of mathematical theory will assure the reader of its truth. To put the thing in technical language, the curious inversion of Plattner's right and left sides is proof that he has moved out of our space into what is called the Fourth Dimension, and that he has returned again to our world. Unless we choose to consider ourselves the victims of an elaborate and motiveless fabrication, we are almost bound to believe that this has occurred.

So much for the tangible facts. We come now to the account of the phenomena that attended his temporary disappearance from the world. It appears that in the Sussexville Proprietary School, Plattner not only discharged the duties of Modern Language Master, but also taught chemistry, commercial geography, bookkeeping, shorthand, drawing, and any other additional subject to which the changing fancies of the boys' parents might direct attention. He knew little or nothing of these various subjects, but in secondary as distinguished from Board or elementary schools, knowledge in the teacher is, very properly, by no means so necessary as high moral character and gentlemanly tone. In chemistry he was particularly deficient, knowing, he says, nothing beyond the Three Gases (whatever the three gasses may be). As, however, his pupils began by knowing nothing, and derived all their information from him, this caused him (or anyone) but little inconvenience for several terms. Then a little boy named Whibble joined the school, who had been educated, it seems, by some mischievous relative into an inquiring habit of mind. This little boy followed Plattner's lessons with marked and sustained interest, and in order to exhibit his zeal on the subject, brought at various times substances for Plattner to analyse. Plattner, flattered by this evidence of his power to awaken interest and trusting to the boy's ignorance, analysed these and even made general statements as to their composition. Indeed he was so far stimulated by his pupil as to obtain a work upon analytical chemistry, and study it during his supervision of the evening's preparation. He was surprised to find chemistry quite an interesting subject.

So far the story is absolutely commonplace. But now the greenish powder comes upon the scene. The source of that greenish powder seems, unfortunately, lost. Master Whibble tells a tortuous story of finding it done up in a packet in a disused limekiln near the Downs. It would have been an excellent thing for Plattner, and possibly for Master Whibble's family, if a match could have been applied to that powder there and then. The young gentleman certainly did not bring it to school in a packet, but in a common eight-ounce graduated medicine bottle, plugged with masticated newspaper. He gave it to Plattner at the end of the afternoon school. Four boys had been detained after school prayers in order to complete some neglected tasks, and Plattner was supervising these in the small classroom in which the chemical teaching was conducted. The appliances for the practical teaching of chemistry in the Sussexville Proprietary School, as in most private schools in this country, are characterised by a severe simplicity. They are kept in a cupboard standing in a recess and having about the same capacity as a common travelling trunk. Plattner, being bored with his passive superintendence, seems to have welcomed the intervention of Whibble with his green powder as an agreeable diversion, and, unlocking this cupboard, proceeded at once with his analytical experiments. Whibble sat, luckily for himself, at a safe distance, regarding him. The four malefactors, feigning a profound absorption in their work, watched him furtively with the keenest interest. For even within the limits of the Three Gases, Plattner's practical chemistry was, I understand, temerarious.

They are practically unanimous in their account of Plattner's proceedings. He poured a little of the green powder into a test-tube, and tried the substance with water, hydrochloric acid, nitric acid, and sulphuric acid in succession. Getting no result, he emptied out a little heap—nearly half the bottleful, in fact—upon a slate and tried a match. He held the medicine bottle in his left hand. The stuff began to smoke and melt, and then—exploded with deafening violence and a blinding flash.

The five boys, seeing the flash and being prepared for catastrophes, ducked below their desks, and were none of them seriously hurt. The window was blown out into the playground, and the blackboard on its easel was upset. The slate was smashed to atoms. Some plaster fell from the ceiling. No other damage was done to the school edifice or appliances, and the boys at first, seeing nothing of Plattner, fancied he was knocked down and lying out of their sight below the desks. They jumped out of their places to go to his assistance, and were amazed to find the space empty. Being still confused by the sudden violence of the report, they hurried to the open door, under the impression that he must have been hurt, and have rushed out of the room. But Carson, the foremost, nearly collided in the doorway with the principal, Mr. Lidgett.

Mr. Lidgett is a corpulent, excitable man with one eye. The boys describe him as stumbling into the room mouthing some of those tempered expletives irritable schoolmasters accustom themselves to use— lest worse befall. "Wretched mumchancer!" he said. "Where's Mr. Plattner?" The boys are agreed on the very words. ("Wobbler," "snivelling puppy," and "mumchancer" are, it seems, among the ordinary small change of Mr. Lidgett's scholastic commerce.)

Where's Mr. Plattner? That was a question that was to be repeated many times in the next few days. It really seemed as though that frantic hyperbole, "blown to atoms," had for once realised itself. There was not a visible particle of Plattner to be seen; not a drop of blood nor a stitch of clothing to be found. Apparently he had been blown clean out of existence and left not a wrack behind. Not so much as would cover a sixpenny piece, to quote a proverbial expression! The evidence of his absolute disappearance, as a consequence of that explosion, is indubitable.

It is not necessary to enlarge here upon the commotion excited in the Sussexville Proprietary School, and in Sussexville and elsewhere, by this event. It is quite possible, indeed, that some of the readers of these pages may recall the hearing of some remote and dying version of that excitement during the last summer holidays. Lidgett, it would seem, did everything in his power to suppress and minimise the story. He instituted a penalty of twenty-five lines for any mention of Plattner's name among the boys, and stated in the schoolroom that he was clearly aware of his assistant's whereabouts. He was afraid, he explains, that the possibility of an explosion happening, in spite of the elaborate precautions taken to minimise the practical teaching of chemistry, might injure the reputation of the school; and so might any mysterious quality in Plattner's departure. Indeed, he did everything in his power to make the occurrence seem as ordinary as possible. In particular, he cross-examined the five eye-witnesses of the occurrence so searchingly that they began to doubt the plain evidence of their senses. But, in spite of these efforts, the tale, in a magnified and distorted state, made a nine days' wonder in the district, and several parents withdrew their sons on colourable pretexts. Not the least remarkable point in the matter is the fact that a large number of people in the neighbourhood dreamed singularly vivid dreams of Plattner during the period of excitement before his return, and that these dreams had a curious uniformity. In almost all of them Plattner was seen, sometimes singly, sometimes in company. wandering about through a coruscating iridescence. In all cases his face was pale and distressed, and in some he gesticulated towards the dreamer. One or two of the boys, evidently under the influence of nightmare, fancied that Plattner approached them with remarkable swiftness, and seemed to look closely into their very eyes. Others fled with Plattner from the pursuit of vague and extraordinary creatures of a globular shape. But all these fancies were forgotten in inquiries and speculations when, on the Wednesday next but one after the Monday of the explosion, Plattner returned.

The circumstances of his return were as singular as those of his departure. So far as Mr. Lidgett's somewhat choleric outline can be filled in from Plattner's hesitating statements, it would appear that on Wednesday evening, towards the hour of sunset, the former gentleman, having dismissed evening preparation, was engaged in his garden, picking and eating strawberries, a fruit of which he is inordinately fond. It is a large old-fashioned garden, secured from observation, fortunately, by a high and ivy-covered red-brick wall. Just as he was stooping over a particularly prolific plant, there was a flash in the air and a heavy thud, and before he could look round, some heavy body struck him violently from behind. He was pitched forward, crushing the strawberries he held in his hand, and with such force that his silk hat—Mr. Lidgett adheres to the older ideas of scholastic costume—was driven violently down upon his forehead, and almost over one eye. This heavy missile, which slid over him sideways and collapsed into a sitting posture among the strawberry plants, proved to be our long-lost Mr. Gottfried Plattner, in an extremely dishevelled condition. He was collarless and hatless, his linen was dirty, and there was blood upon his hands. Mr. Lidgett was so indignant and surprised that he remained on all-fours, and with his hat jammed down on his eye, while he expostulated vehemently with Plattner for his disrespectful and unaccountable conduct.

This scarcely idyllic scene completes what I may call the exterior version of the Plattner story—its exoteric aspect. It is quite unnecessary to enter here into all the details of his dismissal by Mr. Lidgett. Such details, with the full names and dates and references, will be found in the larger report of these occurrences that was laid before the Society for the Investigation of Abnormal Phenomena. The singular transposition of Plattner's right and left sides was scarcely observed for the first day or so, and then first in connection with his disposition to write from right to left across the blackboard. He concealed rather than ostended this curious confirmatory circumstance, as he considered it would unfavourably affect his prospects in a new situation. The displacement of his heart was discovered some months after, when he was having a tooth extracted under anæsthetics. He then, very unwillingly, allowed a cursory surgical examination to be made of himself, with a view to a brief account in the *Journal of Anatomy*. That exhausts the statement of the material facts; and we may now go on to consider Plattner's account of the matter.

But first let us clearly differentiate between the preceding portion of this story and what is to follow. All I have told thus far is established by such evidence as even a criminal lawyer would approve. Every one of the witnesses is still alive; the reader, if he have the leisure, may hunt the lads out to-morrow, or even brave the terrors of the redoubtable Lidgett, and cross-examine and trap and test to his heart's content; Gottfried Plattner, himself, and his twisted heart and his three photographs are producible. It may be taken as proved that he did disappear for nine days as the consequence of an explosion; that he returned almost as violently, under circumstances in their nature annoying to Mr. Lidgett, whatever the details of those circumstances may be; and that he returned inverted, just as a reflection returns from a mirror. From the last fact, as I have already stated, it follows almost inevitably that Plattner, during those nine days, must have been in some state of existence altogether out of space. The evidence of these statements is, indeed, far stronger than that upon which most murderers are hanged. But for his own particular account of where he had been, with its confused explanations and well-nigh self-contradictory details, we have only Mr. Gottfried Plattner's word. I do not wish to discredit that, but I must point out—what so many writers upon obscure psychic phenomena fail to do—that we are passing here from the practically undeniable to that kind of matter which any reasonable man is entitled to believe or reject as he thinks proper. The previous statements render it plausible; its discordance with common experience tilts it towards the incredible. I would prefer not to sway the beam of the reader's judgment either way, but simply to tell the story as Plattner told it me.

He gave me his narrative, I may state, at my house at Chislehurst; and so soon as he had left me that evening, I went into my study and wrote down everything as I remembered it. Subsequently he was good enough to read over a type-written copy, so that its substantial correctness is undeniable.

He states that at the moment of the explosion he distinctly thought he was killed. He felt lifted off his feet and driven forcibly backward. It is a curious fact for psychologists that he thought clearly during his backward flight, and wondered whether he should hit the chemistry cupboard or the blackboard easel. His heels struck ground, and he staggered and fell heavily into a sitting position on something soft and firm. For a moment the concussion stunned him. He became aware at once of a vivid scent of singed hair, and he seemed to hear the voice of Lidgett asking for him. You will understand that for a time his mind was greatly confused.

At first he was distinctly under the impression that he was still in the classroom. He perceived quite distinctly the surprise of the boys and the entry of Mr. Lidgett. He is quite positive upon that score. He did not hear their remarks, but that he ascribed to the deafening effect of the experiment. Things about him seemed curiously dark and faint, but his mind explained that on the obvious but mistaken idea that the explosion had engendered a huge volume of dark smoke. Through the dimness the figures of Lidgett and the boys moved, as faint and silent as ghosts. Plattner's face still tingled with the stinging heat of the flash. He was, he says, "all muddled." His first definite thoughts seem to have been of his personal safety. He thought he was perhaps blinded and deafened. He felt his limbs and face in a gingerly manner. Then his perceptions grew clearer, and he was astonished to miss the old familiar desks and other schoolroom furniture about him. Only dim, uncertain, grey shapes stood in the place of these. Then came a thing that made him shout aloud, and awoke his stunned faculties to instant activity. *Two of the boys, gesticulating, walked one after the other clean through him!* Neither manifested the slightest consciousness of his presence. It is difficult to imagine the sensation he felt. They came against him, he says, with no more force than a wisp of mist.

Plattner's first thought after that was that he was dead. Having been brought up with thoroughly sound views in these matters, however, he was a little surprised to find his body still about him. His second conclusion was that he was not dead, but that the others were: that the explosion had destroyed Sussexville Proprietary School and every soul in it except himself. But that, too, was scarcely satisfactory. He was thrown back upon astonished observation.

Everything about him was extraordinarily dark: at first it seemed to have an altogether ebony blackness. Overhead was a black firmament. The only touch of light in the scene was a faint greenish glow at the edge of the sky in one direction, which threw into prominence a horizon of undulating black hills. This, I say, was his impression at first. As his eye grew accustomed to the darkness, he began to distinguish a faint quality of differentiating greenish colour in the circumambient night. Against this background the furniture and occupants of the classroom, it seems, stood out like phosphorescent spectres, faint and impalpable. He extended his hand, and thrust it without an effort through the wall of the room by the fireplace.

He describes himself as making a strenuous effort to attract attention. He shouted to Lidgett, and tried to seize the boys as they went to and fro. He only desisted from these attempts when Mrs. Lidgett, whom he as an Assistant Master naturally disliked, entered the room. He says the sensation of being in the world, and yet not a part of it, was an extraordinarily disagreeable one. He compared his feelings not inaptly to those of a cat watching a mouse through a window. Whenever he made a motion to communicate with the dim, familiar world about him, he found an invisible, incomprehensible barrier preventing intercourse.

He then turned his attention to his solid environment. He found the medicine bottle still unbroken in his hand, with the remainder of the green powder therein. He put this in his pocket, and began to feel about him. Apparently, he was sitting on a boulder of rock covered with a velvety moss. The dark country about him he was unable to see, the faint, misty picture of the schoolroom blotting it out, but he had a feeling (due perhaps to a cold wind) that he was near the crest of a hill, and that a

steep valley fell away beneath his feet. The green glow along the edge of
the sky seemed to be growing in extent and intensity. He stood up,
rubbing his eyes.

It would seem that he made a few steps, going steeply downhill, and
then stumbled, nearly fell, and sat down again upon a jagged mass of rock
to watch the dawn. He became aware that the world about him was absolutely silent. It was as still as it was dark, and though there was a cold
wind blowing up the hill-face, the rustle of grass, the sighing of the
boughs that should have accompanied it, were absent. He could hear,
therefore, if he could not see, that the hillside upon which he stood was
rocky and desolate. The green grew brighter every moment, and as it did
so a faint, transparent blood-red mingled with, but did not mitigate, the
blackness of the sky overhead and the rocky desolations about him.
Having regard to what follows, I am inclined to think that that redness
may have been an optical effect due to contrast. Something black fluttered momentarily against the livid yellow-green of the lower sky, and
then the thin and penetrating voice of a bell rose out of the black gulf
below him. An oppressive expectation grew with the growing light.

It is probable that an hour or more elapsed while he sat there, the
strange green light growing brighter every moment, and spreading slowly,
in flamboyant fingers, upwards towards the zenith. As it grew, the spectral vision of *our* world became relatively or absolutely fainter. Probably
both, for the time must have been about that of our earthly sunset. So far
as his vision of our world went, Plattner by his few steps downhill, had
passed through the floor of the classroom, and was now, it seemed, sitting
in mid-air in the larger schoolroom downstairs. He saw the boarders distinctly, but much more faintly than he had seen Lidgett. They were preparing their evening tasks, and he noticed with interest that several were
cheating with their Euclid riders by means of a crib, a compilation whose
existence he had hitherto never suspected. As the time passed they faded
steadily, as steadily as the light of the green dawn increased.

Looking down into the valley, he saw that the light had crept far down
its rocky sides, and that the profound blackness of the abyss was now
broken by a minute green glow, like the light of a glow-worm. And almost
immediately the limb of a huge heavenly body of blazing green rose over
the basaltic undulations of the distant hills, and the monstrous hill-
masses about him came out gaunt and desolate, in green light and deep,
ruddy black shadows. He became aware of a vast number of ball-shaped
objects drifting as thistledown drifts over the high ground. There were

none of these nearer to him than the opposite side of the gorge. The bell below twanged quicker and quicker, with something like impatient insistence, and several lights moved hither and thither. The boys at work at their desks were now almost imperceptibly faint.

This extinction of our world, when the green sun of this other universe rose, is a curious point upon which Plattner insists. During the Other-World night it is difficult to move about, on account of the vividness with which the things of this world are visible. It becomes a riddle to explain why, if this is the case, we in this world catch no glimpse of the Other-World. It is due, perhaps, to the comparatively vivid illumination of this world of ours. Plattner describes the midday of the Other-World, at its brightest, as not being nearly so bright as this world at full moon, while its night is profoundly black. Consequently, the amount of light, even in an ordinary dark room, is sufficient to render the things of the Other-World invisible, on the same principle that faint phosphorescence is only visible in the profoundest darkness. I have tried, since he told me his story, to see something of the Other-World by sitting for a long space in a photographer's dark room at night. I have certainly seen indistinctly the form of greenish slopes and rocks, but only, I must admit, very indistinctly indeed. The reader may possibly be more successful. Plattner tells me that since his return he has seen and recognised places in the Other-World in his dreams, but this is probably due to his memory of these scenes. It seems quite possible that people with unusually keen eyesight may occasionally catch a glimpse of this strange Other-World about us.

However, this is a digression. As the green sun rose, a long street of black buildings became perceptible, though only darkly and indistinctly, in the gorge, and, after some hesitation, Plattner began to clamber down the precipitous descent towards them. The descent was long and exceedingly tedious, being so not only by the extraordinary steepness, but also by reason of the looseness of the boulders with which the whole face of the hill was strewn. The noise of his descent—now and then his heels struck fire from the rocks—seemed now the only sound in the universe, for the beating of the bell had ceased. As he drew nearer he perceived that the various edifices had a singular resemblance to tombs and mausoleums and monuments, saving only that they were all uniformly black instead of being white as most sepulchres are. And then he saw, crowding out of the largest building very much as people disperse from church, a number of pallid, rounded, pale-green figures. These scattered in several directions about the broad street of the place, some going through side alleys and reappearing upon the steepness of the hill, others entering some of the small black buildings which lined the way.

At the sight of these things drifting up towards him, Plattner stopped, staring. They were not walking, they were indeed limbless; and they had the appearance of human heads beneath which a tadpole-like body swung. He was too astonished at their strangeness, too full indeed of strangeness, to be seriously alarmed by them. They drove towards him, in front of the chill wind that was blowing uphill, much as soap-bubbles drive before a draught. And as he looked at the nearest of those approaching, he saw it was indeed a human head, albeit with singularly large eyes, and wearing such an expression of distress and anguish as he had never seen before upon mortal countenance. He was surprised to find that it did not turn to regard him, but seemed to be watching and following some unseen moving thing. For a moment he was puzzled, and then it occurred to him that this creature was watching with its enormous eyes something that was happening in the world he had just left. Nearer it came, and nearer, and he was too astonished to cry out. It made a very faint fretting sound as it came close to him. Then it struck his face with a gentle pat—its touch was very cold—and drove past him, and upward towards the crest of the hill.

An extraordinary conviction flashed across Plattner's mind that this head had a strong likeness to Lidgett. Then he turned his attention to the other heads that were now swarming thickly up the hillside. None made the slightest sign of recognition. One or two, indeed, came close to his head and almost followed the example of the first, but he dodged convulsively out of the way. Upon most of them he saw the same expression of unavailing regret he had seen upon the first and heard the same faint sounds of wretchedness from them. One or two wept, and one rolling swiftly uphill wore an expression of diabolical rage. But others were cold, and several had a look of gratified interest in their eyes. One, at least, was almost in an ecstasy of happiness. Plattner does not remember that he recognized any more likenesses in those he saw at this time.

For several hours, perhaps, Plattner watched these strange things dispersing themselves over the hills, and not till long after they had ceased to issue from the clustering black buildings in the gorge did he resume his downward climb. The darkness about him increased so much that he had a difficulty in stepping true. Overhead the sky was now a bright pale green. He felt neither hunger nor thirst. Later, when he did, he found a chilly stream running down the centre of the gorge, and the rare moss upon the boulders, when he tried it at last in desperation, was good to eat.

He groped about among the tombs that ran down the gorge, seeking vaguely for some clue to these inexplicable things. After a long time he came to the entrance of the big mausoleum-like building from which the heads had issued. In this he found a group of green lights burning upon a kind of basaltic altar, and a bell-rope from a belfry overhead hanging down into the centre of the place. Round the wall ran a lettering of fire in a character unknown to him. While he was still wondering at the purport of these things, he heard the receding tramp of heavy feet echoing far down the street. He ran out into the darkness again, but he could see nothing. He had a mind to pull the bell-rope, and finally decided to follow the footsteps. But although he ran far, he never overtook them; and his shouting was of no avail. The gorge seemed to extend an interminable distance. It was as dark as earthly starlight throughout its length, while the ghastly green day lay along the upper edges of its precipices. There were none of the heads, now, below. They were all, it seemed, busily occupied along the upper slopes. Looking up, he saw them drifting hither and thither, some hovering stationary, some flying swiftly through the air. It reminded him, he said, of "big snowflakes"; only these were black and pale green.

In pursuing the firm, undeviating footsteps that he never overtook, in groping into new regions of this endless devil's dyke, in clambering up and down the pitiless heights, in wandering about the summits, and in watching the drifting faces, Plattner states that he spent the better part of seven or eight days. He did not keep count, he says. Though once or twice he found eyes watching him, he had word with no living soul. He slept among the rocks on the hillside. In the gorge things earthly were invisible, because, from the earthly standpoint, it was far underground. On the altitudes, so soon as the earthly day began, the world became visible to him. He found himself sometimes stumbling over the dark green rocks, or arresting himself on a precipitous brink, while all about him the green branches of the Sussexville lanes were swaying; or, again, he seemed to be walking through the Sussexville streets, or watching unseen the private business of some household. And then it was he discovered, that to almost every human being in our world there pertained some of these drifting heads; that everyone in the world is watched intermittently by these helpless disembodiments.

What are they—these Watchers of the Living? Plattner never learned. But two that presently found and followed him, were like his childhood's memory of his father and mother. Now and then other faces turned their eyes upon him: eyes like those of dead people who had swayed him, or injured him, or helped him in his youth and manhood. Whenever they looked at him, Plattner was overcome with a strange sense of responsibility. To his mother he ventured to speak; but she made no answer. She looked sadly, steadfastly, and tenderly—a little reproachfully, too, it seemed—into his eyes.

He simply tells this story: he does not endeavour to explain. We are left to surmise who these Watchers of the Living may be, or if they are indeed the Dead, why they should so closely and passionately watch a world they have left for ever. It may be—indeed to my mind it seems just —that, when our life has closed, when evil or good is no longer a choice for us, we may still have to witness the working out of the train of consequences we have laid. If human souls continue after death, then surely human interests continue after death. But that is merely my own guess at the meaning of the things seen. Plattner offers no interpretation, for none was given him. It is well the reader should understand this clearly. Day after day, with his head reeling, he wandered about this green-lit world outside the world, weary and, towards the end, weak and hungry. By day—by our earthly day, that is—the ghostly vision of the old familiar scenery of Sussexville, all about him, irked and worried him. He could not see where to put his feet, and ever and again with a chilly touch one of these Watching Souls would come against his face. And after dark the multitude of these Watchers about him, and their intent distress, confused his mind beyond describing. A great longing to return to the earthly life that was so near and yet so remote consumed him. The unearthliness of things about him produced a positively painful mental distress. He was worried beyond describing by his own particular followers. He would shout at them to desist from staring at him, scold at them, hurry away from them. They were always mute and intent. Run as he might over the uneven ground they followed his destinies.

On the ninth day, towards evening, Plattner heard the invisible footsteps approaching, far away down the gorge. He was then wandering over the broad crest of the same hill upon which he had fallen in his entry into this strange Other-World of his. He turned to hurry down into the gorge, feeling his way hastily, and was arrested by the sight of the thing that was happening in a room in a back street near the school. Both of the people in the room he knew by sight. The windows were open, the blinds up, and the setting sun shone clearly into it, so that it came out quite brightly at first, a vivid oblong of room, lying like a magic-lantern picture upon the black landscape and the livid green dawn. In addition to the sunlight, a candle had just been lit in the room.

On the bed lay a lank man, his ghastly white face terrible upon the tumbled pillow. His clenched hands were raised above his head. A little table beside the bed carried a few medicine bottles, some toast and water, and an empty glass. Every now and then the lank man's lips fell apart, to indicate a word he could not articulate. But the woman did not notice that he wanted anything, because she was busy turning out papers from an old-fashioned bureau in the opposite corner of the room. At first the picture was very vivid indeed, but as the green dawn behind it grew brighter and brighter, so it became fainter and more and more transparent.

As the echoing footsteps paced nearer and nearer, those footsteps that sound so loud in that Other-World and come so silently in this, Plattner perceived about him a great multitude of dim faces gathering together out of the darkness and watching the two people in the room. Never before had he seen so many of the Watchers of the Living. A multitude had eyes only for the sufferer in the room, another multitude, in infinite anguish, watched the woman as she hunted with greedy eyes for something she could not find. They crowded about Plattner, they came across his sight and buffeted his face, the noise of their unavailing regrets was all about him. He saw clearly only now and then. At other times the pictures quivered dimly, through the veil of green reflections upon their movements. In the room it must have been very still, and Plattner says the candle flame streamed up into a perfectly vertical line of smoke, but in his ears each footfall and its echoes beat like a clap of thunder. And the faces! Two more particularly, near the woman's: one a woman's also, white and clear-featured, a face which might have once been cold and hard but which was now softened by the touch of a wisdom strange to earth. The other might have been the woman's father. Both were evidently absorbed in the contemplation of some act of hateful meanness, so it seemed, which they could no longer guard against and prevent. Behind were others, teachers it may be who had taught ill, friends whose influence had failed. And over the man, too—a multitude, but none that seemed to be parents or teachers! Faces that might once have been coarse, now purged to strength by sorrow! And in the forefront one face, a girlish one, neither

angry nor remorseful but merely patient and weary, and, as it seemed to
Plattner, waiting for relief. His powers of description fail him at the
memory of this multitude of ghastly countenances. They gathered on the
stroke of the bell. He saw them all in the space of a second. It would seem
that he was so worked upon by his excitement that quite involuntarily his
restless fingers took the bottle of green powder out of his pocket and held
it before him. But he does not remember that.

Abruptly the footsteps ceased. He waited for the next and there was
silence, and then suddenly, cutting through the unexpected stillness like
a keen, thin blade, came the first stroke of the bell. At that the multitudi-
nous faces swayed to and fro, and a louder crying began all about him. The
woman did not hear; she was burning something now in the candle flame.
At the second stroke everything grew dim, and a breath of wind, icy cold,
blew through the host of watchers. They swirled about him like an eddy of
dead leaves in the spring, and at the third stroke something was extended
through them to the bed. You have heard of a beam of light. This was like
a beam of darkness, and looking again at it, Plattner saw that it was a
shadowy arm and hand.

The green sun was now topping the black desolations of the horizon,
and the vision of the room was very faint. Plattner could see that the
white of the bed struggled, and was convulsed; and that the woman looked
round over her shoulder at it, startled.

The cloud of watchers lifted high like a puff of green dust before the
wind, and swept swiftly downward towards the temple in the gorge. Then
suddenly Plattner understood the meaning of the shadowy black arm that
stretched across his shoulder and clutched its prey. He did not dare turn
his head to see the Shadow behind the arm. With a violent effort, and
covering his eyes, he set himself to run, made perhaps twenty strides,
then slipped on a boulder and fell. He fell forward on his hands; and the
bottle smashed and exploded as he touched the ground.

In another moment he found himself, stunned and bleeding, sitting
face to face with Lidgett in the old walled garden behind the school.

There the story of Plattner's experiences ends. I have resisted, I believe successfully, the natural disposition of a writer of fiction to dress
up incidents of this sort. I have told the thing as far as possible in the
order in which Plattner told it to me. I have carefully avoided any attempt
at style, effect, or construction. It would have been easy, for instance, to
have worked the scene of the death-bed into a kind of plot in which

Plattner might have been involved. But quite apart from the objection-ableness of falsifying a most extraordinary true story, any such trite de-vices would spoil, to my mind, the peculiar effect of this dark world, with its livid green illumination and its drifting Watchers of the Living, which, unseen and unapproachable to us, is yet lying all about us.

It remains to add, that a death did actually occur in Vincent Terrace, just beyond the school garden, and, so far as can be proved, at the moment of Plattner's return. Deceased was a rate-collector and insurance agent. His widow, who was much younger than himself, married last month a Mr. Whymper, a veterinary surgeon of Allbeeding. As the portion of this story given here has in various forms circulated orally in Sussexville, she has consented to my use of her name, on condition that I make it dis-tinctly known that she emphatically contradicts every detail of Plattner's account of her husband's last moments. She burnt no will, she says, al-though Plattner never accused her of doing so: her husband made but one will, and that just after their marriage. Certainly, from a man who had never seen it, Plattner's account of the furniture of the room was curiously accurate.

One other thing, even at the risk of an irksome repetition, I must in-sist upon lest I seem to favour the credulous superstitious view. Platt-ner's absence from the world for nine days is, I think, proved. But that does not prove his story. It is quite conceivable that even outside space hallucinations may be possible. That, at least, the reader must bear distinctly in mind.

ARTHUR MACHEN

The White People (1899)

Along with Algernon Blackwood, his fellow member in the Order of the Golden Dawn, Arthur Machen was the most sumptuous and visionary writer of ghost stories in English. The possessor of trancelike imagery and rhythm, Machen had a strong empathy with wild nature, an ability to make landscapes come alive with singing prose. One of his most original devices is a powerful dissonance in which beauty and terror ring out at precisely the same moment. Another is his central organizing mythos, fragments of which appear in several stories, which tells of an ancient otherworldly race of "White People," or "Little People," who practice an ancient evil science and who periodically emerge from the earth to worship the Great God Pan.

"The White People," a horror story in the form of a fairy tale, is Machen's most radical and inventive work. Told from the rapturous point of view of a young girl who is initiated into the diabolical "secrets" of the White People, its central narrative, entitled "The Green Book," consists of nonchronological memories within memories and stories within stories. There is little in the way of a central story, however, and the reader should be warned not to look for one. This is an experiment in language, one often bordering on surrealism, which disrupts physical time to put us in touch with a world beyond space and time.

The sentences are remarkable: lengthy, sinuous, and lyrical, they have surprisingly few metaphors and rely almost exclusively on *and* as a connective. They are vibrant and childlike but also strangely austere, like the pagan chants they invoke. We never quite know where we will be taken by these intoxicating sentences, any more than we know at any given moment where the present tense of the story is. At once the most intense and the most oblique story in this anthology, "The Green Book" dramatizes Machen's mysticism in its very structure and poetry rather than in the heavy-handed pronouncements of occultist characters. Form and content dissolve into one as the story suggests a terrifying connectedness between the childlike and the diabolical.

"The Green Book" is enclosed by an occultist prologue and epilogue, consisting of two adult characters discussing the relationship between "sorcery and sanctity" at considerable length. Although these esoteric discussions are highly provocative in themselves, suggesting as they do that evil and holiness are only two sides of the same "ecstasy," their main function is to provide a prosaic counterpoint to the wonderful mistiness of the central tale. They do go on a bit too long, however, and my advice to the reader the first time through the story is to move briskly through the prologue and get to the spellbinding "Green Book" as soon as possible. Even with its structural oddities, "The White People" remains the most authentically pagan work in the literature.

THE WHITE PEOPLE

PROLOGUE

"Sorcery and sanctity," said Ambrose, "these are the only realities. Each is an ecstasy, a withdrawal from the common life."

Cotgrave listened, interested. He had been brought up by a friend to this mouldering house in a northern suburb, through an old garden to the room where Ambrose the recluse dozed and dreamed over his books.

"Yes," he went on, "magic is justified of her children. There are many, I think, who eat dry crusts and drink water, with a joy infinitely sharper than anything within the experience of the 'practical' epicure."

"You are speaking of the saints?"

"Yes, and of the sinners, too. I think you are falling into the very general error of confining the spiritual world to the supremely good; but the supremely wicked, necessarily, have their portion in it. The merely carnal, sensual man can no more be a great sinner than he can be a great saint. Most of us are just indifferent, mixed-up creatures; we muddle through the world without realizing the meaning and the inner sense of things, and, consequently, our wickedness and our goodness are alike second-rate, unimportant."

"And you think the great sinner, then, will be an ascetic, as well as the great saint?"

"Great people of all kinds forsake the imperfect copies and go to the perfect originals. I have no doubt but that many of the very highest among the saints have never done a 'good action' (using the words in their ordinary sense). And, on the other hand, there have been those who have sounded the very depths of sin, who all their lives have never done an 'ill deed.' "

He went out of the room for a moment, and Cotgrave, in high delight, turned to his friend and thanked him for the introduction.

"He's grand," he said. "I never saw that kind of lunatic before."

Ambrose returned with more whisky and helped the two men in a liberal manner. He abused the teetotal sect with ferocity, as he handed the seltzer, and pouring out a glass of water for himself, was about to resume his monologue, when Cotgrave broke in——

"I can't stand it, you know," he said, "your paradoxes are too monstrous. A man may be a great sinner and yet never do anything sinful! Come!"

"You're quite wrong," said Ambrose. "I never make paradoxes; I wish I could. I merely said that a man may have an exquisite taste in Romanée Conti, and yet never have even smelt four ale. That's all, and it's more like a truism than a paradox, isn't it? Your surprise at my remark is due to the fact that you haven't realized what sin is. Oh, yes, there is a sort of connexion between Sin with the capital letter, and actions which are commonly called sinful: with murder, theft, adultery, and so forth. Much the same connexion that there is between the A, B, C and fine literature. But I believe that the misconception—it is all but universal—arises in great measure from our looking at the matter through social spectacles. We think that a man who does evil to *us* and to his neighbours must be very evil. So he is, from a social standpoint; but can't you realize that Evil in its essence is a lonely thing, a passion of the solitary, individual soul? Really, the average murderer, *qua* murderer, is not by any means a sinner in the true sense of the word. He is simply a wild beast that we have to get rid of to save our own necks from his knife. I should class him rather with tigers than with sinners."

"It seems a little strange."

"I think not. The murderer murders not from positive qualities, but from negative ones; he lacks something which non-murderers possess. Evil, of course, is wholly positive—only it is on the wrong side. You may believe me that sin in its proper sense is very rare; it is probable that there have been far fewer sinners than saints. Yes, your standpoint is all very well for practical, social purposes; we are naturally inclined to think that a person who is very disagreeable to us must be a very great sinner! It is very disagreeable to have one's pocket picked, and we pronounce the thief to be a very great sinner. In truth, he is merely an undeveloped man. He cannot be a saint, of course; but he may be, and often is, an infinitely better creature than thousands who have never broken a single commandment. He is a great nuisance to *us*, I admit, and we very properly lock him up if we catch him; but between his troublesome and unsocial action and evil—Oh, the connexion is of the weakest."

It was getting very late. The man who had brought Cotgrave had probably heard all this before, since he assisted with a bland and judicious smile, but Cotgrave began to think that his "lunatic" was turning into a sage.

"Do you know," he said, "you interest me immensely? You think, then, that we do not understand the real nature of evil?"

"No, I don't think we do. We over-estimate it and we under-estimate it. We take the very numerous infractions of our social 'bye-laws'—the very necessary and very proper regulations which keep the human company together—and we get frightened at the prevalence of 'sin' and 'evil.' But this is really nonsense. Take theft, for example. Have you any *horror* at the thought of Robin Hood, of the Highland caterans of the seventeenth century, of the moss-troopers, of the company promoters of our day?

"Then, on the other hand, we underrate evil. We attach such an enormous importance to the 'sin' of meddling with our pockets (and our wives) that we have quite forgotten the awfulness of real sin."

"And what is sin?" said Cotgrave.

"I think I must reply to your question by another. What would your feelings be, seriously, if your cat or your dog began to talk to you, and to dispute with you in human accents? You would be overwhelmed with horror. I am sure of it. And if the roses in your garden sang a weird song, you would go mad. And suppose the stones in the road began to swell and grow before your eyes, and if the pebble that you noticed at night had shot out stony blossoms in the morning?

"Well, these examples may give you some notion of what sin really is."

"Look here," said the third man, hitherto placid, "you two seem pretty well wound up. But I'm going home. I've missed my tram, and I shall have to walk."

Ambrose and Cotgrave seemed to settle down more profoundly when the other had gone out into the early misty morning and the pale light of the lamps.

"You astonish me," said Cotgrave. "I had never thought of that. If that is really so, one must turn everything upside down. Then the essence of sin really is——"

"In the taking of heaven by storm, it seems to me," said Ambrose. "It appears to me that it is simply an attempt to penetrate into another and higher sphere in a forbidden manner. You can understand why it is so rare. There are few, indeed, who wish to penetrate into other spheres, higher or lower, in ways allowed or forbidden. Men, in the mass, are amply content with life as they find it. Therefore there are few saints, and sinners (in the proper sense) are fewer still, and men of genius, who partake sometimes of each character are rare also. Yes; on the whole, it is, perhaps, harder to be a great sinner than a great saint."

"There is something profoundly unnatural about sin? Is that what you mean?"

"Exactly. Holiness requires as great, or almost as great, an effort; but holiness works on lines that *were* natural once; it is an effort to recover the ecstasy that was before the Fall. But sin is an effort to gain the ecstasy and the knowledge that pertain alone to angels, and in making this effort man becomes a demon. I told you that the mere murderer is not *therefore* a sinner; that is true, but the sinner is sometimes a murderer. Gilles de Rais is an instance. So you see that while the good and the evil are unnatural to man as he now is—to man the social, civilized being—evil is unnatural in a much deeper sense than good. The saint endeavours to recover a gift which he has lost; the sinner tries to obtain something which was never his. In brief, he repeats the Fall."

"But are you a Catholic?" said Cotgrave.

"Yes; I am a member of the persecuted Anglican Church."

"Then, how about those texts which seem to reckon as sin that which you would set down as a mere trivial dereliction?"

"Yes; but in one place the word 'sorcerers' comes in the same sentence, doesn't it? That seems to me to give the key-note. Consider: can you imagine for a moment that a false statement which saves an innocent man's life is a sin? No; very good, then, it is not the mere liar who is excluded by those words; it is, above all, the 'sorcerers' who use the material life, who use the failings incidental to material life as instruments to obtain their infinitely wicked ends. And let me tell you this: our higher senses are so blunted, we are so drenched with materialism, that we should probably fail to recognize real wickedness if we encountered it."

"But shouldn't we experience a certain horror—a terror such as you hinted we would experience if a rose tree sang—in the mere presence of an evil man?"

"We should if we were natural: children and women feel this horror you speak of, even animals experience it. But with most of us convention and civilization and education have blinded and deafened and obscured the natural reason. No, sometimes we may recognize evil by its hatred of the good—one doesn't need much penetration to guess at the influence which dictated, quite unconsciously, the 'Blackwood' review of Keats—but this is purely incidental; and, as a rule, I suspect that the

Hierarchs of Tophet pass quite unnoticed, or, perhaps, in certain cases, as good but mistaken men."

"But you used the word 'unconscious' just now, of Keats' reviewers. Is wickedness ever unconscious?"

"Always. It must be so. It is like holiness and genius in this as in other points; it is a certain rapture or ecstasy of the soul; a transcendent effort to surpass the ordinary bounds. So, surpassing these, it surpasses also the understanding, the faculty that takes note of that which comes before it. No, a man may be infinitely and horribly wicked and never suspect it. But I tell you, evil in this, its certain and true sense, is rare, and I think it is growing rarer."

"I am trying to get hold of it all," said Cotgrave. "From what you say, I gather that the true evil differs generically from that which we call evil?"

"Quite so. There is, no doubt, an analogy between the two; a resemblance such as enables us to use, quite legitimately, such terms as the 'foot of the mountain' and the 'leg of the table.' And, sometimes, of course, the two speak, as it were, in the same language. The rough miner, or 'puddler,' the untrained, undeveloped 'tiger-man,' heated by a quart or two above his usual measure, comes home and kicks his irritating and injudicious wife to death. He is a murderer. And Gilles de Rais was a murderer. But you see the gulf that separates the two? The 'word,' if I may so speak, is accidentally the same in each case, but the 'meaning' is utterly different. It is flagrant 'Hobson Jobson' to confuse the two, or rather, it is as if one supposed that Juggernaut and the Argonauts had something to do etymologically with one another. And no doubt the same weak likeness, or analogy, runs between all the 'social' sins and the real spiritual sins, and in some cases, perhaps, the lesser may be 'schoolmaster' to lead one on to the greater—from the shadow to the reality. If you are anything of a theologian, you will see the importance of all this."

"I am sorry to say," remarked Cotgrave, "that I have devoted very little of my time to theology. Indeed, I have often wondered on what grounds theologians have claimed the title of Science of Sciences for their favourite study; since the 'theological' books I have looked into have always seemed to me to be concerned with feeble and obvious pieties, or with the kings of Israel and Judah. I do not care to hear about those kings."

Ambrose grinned.

"We must try to avoid theological discussion," he said. "I perceive that you would be a bitter disputant. But perhaps the 'dates of the kings' have as much to do with theology as the hobnails of the murderous puddler with evil."

"Then, to return to our main subject, you think that sin is an esoteric, occult thing?"

"Yes. It is the infernal miracles as holiness is the supernal. Now and then it is raised to such a pitch that we entirely fail to suspect its existence; it is like the note of the great pedal pipes of the organ, which is so deep that we cannot hear it. In other cases it may lead to the lunatic asylum, or to still stranger issues. But you must never confuse it with mere social misdoing. Remember how the Apostle, speaking of the 'other side,' distinguishes between 'charitable' actions and charity. and as one may give all one's goods to the poor, and yet lack charity; so, remember, one may avoid every crime and yet be a sinner."

"Your psychology is very strange to me," said Cotgrave, "but I confess I like it, and I suppose that one might fairly deduce from your premises the conclusion that the real sinner might very possibly strike the observer as a harmless personage enough?"

"Certainly; because the true evil has nothing to do with social life or social laws, or if it has, only incidentally and accidentally. It is a lonely passion of the soul—or a passion of the lonely soul—whichever you like. If, by chance, we understand it, and grasp its full significance, then, indeed, it will fill us with horror and with awe. But this emotion is widely distinguished from the fear and the disgust with which we regard the ordinary criminal, since this latter is largely or entirely founded on the regard which we have for our own skins or purses. We hate a murderer, because we know that we should hate to be murdered, or to have any one that we like murdered. So, on the 'other side,' we venerate the saints, but we don't 'like' them as we like our friends. Can you pursuade yourself that you would have 'enjoyed' St. Paul's company? Do you think that you and I would have 'got on' with Sir Galahad?

"So with the sinners, as with the saints. If you met a very evil man, and recognized his evil; he would, no doubt, fill you with horror and awe; but there is no reason why you should 'dislike' him. On the contrary, it is quite possible that if you could succeed in putting the sin out of your mind you might find the sinner capital company, and in a little while you might have to reason yourself back into horror. Still, how awful it is. If the roses and the lilies suddenly sang on this coming morning; if the furniture began to move in procession, as in De Maupassant's tale!"

"I am glad you have come back to that comparison," said Cotgrave, "because I wanted to ask you what it is that corresponds in humanity to these imaginary feats of inanimate things. In a word—what is sin? You have given me, I know, an abstract definition, but I should like a concrete example."

"I told you it was very rare," said Ambrose, who appeared willing to avoid the giving of a direct answer. "The materialism of the age, which has done a good deal to suppress sanctity, has done perhaps more to suppress evil. We find the earth so very comfortable that we have no inclination either for ascents or descents. It would seem as if the scholar who decided to 'specialize' in Tophet, would be reduced to purely antiquarian researches. No palaeontologist could show you a *live* pterodactyl."

"And yet you, I think, have 'specialized,' and I believe that your researches have descended to our modern times."

"You are really interested, I see. Well, I confess that I have dabbled a little, and if you like I can show you something that bears on the very curious subject we have been discussing."

Ambrose took a candle and went away to a far, dim corner of the room. Cotgrave saw him open a venerable bureau that stood there, and from some secret recess he drew out a parcel, and came back to the window where they had been sitting.

Ambrose undid a wrapping of paper, and produced a green book.

"You will take care of it?" he said. "Don't leave it lying about. It is one of the choicer pieces in my collection, and I should be very sorry if it were lost."

He fondled the faded binding.

"I knew the girl who wrote this," he said. "When you read it, you will see how it illustrates the talk we have had to-night. There is a sequel, too, but I won't talk of that."

"There was an odd article in one of the reviews some months ago," he began again, with the air of a man who changes the subject. "It was written by a doctor—Dr. Coryn, I think, was the name. He says that a lady, watching her little girl playing at the drawing-room window, suddenly saw the heavy sash give way and fall on the child's fingers. The lady fainted, I think, but at any rate the doctor was summoned, and when he had dressed the child's wounded and maimed fingers he was summoned to the mother. She was groaning with pain, and it was found that three fingers of her hand, corresponding with those that had been injured on the child's hand, were swollen and inflamed, and later, in the doctor's language, purulent sloughing set in."

Ambrose still handled delicately the green volume.

"Well, here it is," he said at last, parting with difficulty, it seemed, from his treasure.

"You will bring it back as soon as you have read it," he said, as they went out into the hall, into the old garden, faint with the odour of white lilies.

There was a broad red band in the east as Cotgrave turned to go, and from the high ground where he stood he saw that awful spectacle of London in a dream.

THE GREEN BOOK

The morocco binding of the book was faded, and the colour had grown faint, but there were no stains nor bruises nor marks of usage. The book looked as if it had been bought "on a visit to London" some seventy or eighty years ago, and had somehow been forgotten and suffered to lie away out of sight. There was an old, delicate, lingering odour about it, such an odour as sometimes haunts an ancient piece of furniture for a century or more. The end-papers, inside the binding, were oddly decorated with coloured patterns and faded gold. It looked small, but the paper was fine, and there were many leaves, closely covered with minute, painfully formed characters.

I found this book (the manuscript began) in a drawer in the old bureau that stands on the landing. It was a very rainy day and I could not go out, so in the afternoon I got a candle and rummaged in the bureau. Nearly all the drawers were full of old dresses, but one of the small ones looked empty, and I found this book hidden right at the back. I wanted a book like this, so I took it to write in. It is full of secrets. I have a great many other books of secrets I have written, hidden in a safe place, and I am going to write here many of the old secrets and some new ones; but there are some I shall not put down at all. I must not write down the real names of the days and months which I found out a year ago, nor the way to make the Aklo letters, or the Chian language, or the great beautiful circles, nor the Mao Games, nor the chief songs. I may write something about all these things but not the way to do them, for peculiar reasons. And I must not say who the Mymphs are, or the Dôls, or Jeelo, or what voolas mean. All these are most secret secrets, and I am glad when I remember what they are, and how many wonderful languages I know, but there are some things that I call the secrets of the secrets of the secrets that I dare not think of unless I am quite alone, and then I shut my eyes, and put my hands over them and whisper the word, and the Alala comes. I only do this at night in my room or in certain woods that I know, but I must not describe them, as they are secret woods. Then there are the Ceremonies, which are all of them important, but some are more delightful than others —there are the White Ceremonies, and the Green Ceremonies, and the Scarlet Ceremonies. The Scarlet Ceremonies are the best, but there is only one place where they can be performed properly, though there is a very nice imitation which I have done in other places. Besides these, I have the dances, and the Comedy, and I have done the Comedy sometimes when the others were looking, and they didn't understand anything about it. I was very little when I first knew about these things.

When I was very small, and mother was alive, I can remember remembering things before that, only it has all got confused. But I remember when I was five or six I heard them talking about me when they thought I was not noticing. They were saying how queer I was a year or two before, and how nurse had called my mother to come and listen to me talking all to myself, and I was saying words that nobody could understand. I was speaking the Xu language, but I only remember a very few of the words, as it was about the little white faces that used to look at me when I was lying in my cradle. They used to talk to me, and I learnt their language and talked to them in it about some great white place where they lived, where the trees and the grass were all white, and there were white hills as high up as the moon, and a cold wind. I have often dreamed of it afterwards, but the faces went away when I was very little. But a wonderful thing happened when I was about five. My nurse was carrying me on her shoulder; there was a field of yellow corn, and we went through it, it was very hot. Then we came to a path through a wood, and a tall man came after us, and went with us till we came to a place where there was a deep pool, and it was very dark and shady. Nurse put me down on the soft moss under a tree, and she said: "She can't get to the pond now." So they left me there, and I sat quite still and watched, and out of the water and out of the wood came two wonderful white people, and they began to play and dance and sing. They were a kind of creamy white like the old ivory figure in the drawing-room; one was a beautiful lady with kind dark eyes, and a grave face, and long black hair, and she smiled such a strange sad smile at the other, who laughed and came to her. They played together, and danced round and round the pool, and they sang a song till I fell asleep. Nurse woke me up when she came back, and she was looking something like the lady had looked, so I told her all about it, and asked her why she looked like that. At first she cried, and then she looked very frightened, and turned quite pale. She put me down on the grass and stared at me, and I could see she was shaking all over. Then she said I had been dreaming, but I knew I hadn't. Then she made me promise not to say a word about it to anybody, and if I did I should be thrown into the black pit. I was not frightened at all, though nurse was, and I never forgot about it, because when I shut my eyes and it was quite quiet, and I was all alone, I could see them again, very faint and far away, but very splendid; and little bits of the song they sang came into my head, but I couldn't sing it.

I was thirteen, nearly fourteen, when I had a very singular adventure, so strange that the day on which it happened is always called the White Day. My mother had been dead for more than a year, and in the morning I had lessons, but they let me go out for walks in the afternoon. And this afternoon I walked a new way, and a little brook led me into a new country, but I tore my frock getting through many bushes, and beneath the low branches of trees, and up thorn thickets on the hills, and by dark woods full of creeping thorns. And it was a long, long way. It seemed as if I was going on for ever and ever, and I had to creep by a place like a tunnel where a brook must have been, but all the water had dried up, and the floor was rocky, and the bushes had grown overhead till they met, so that it was quite dark. And I went on and on through that dark place; it was a long, long way. And I came to a hill that I never saw before. I was in a dismal thicket full of black twisted boughs that tore me as I went through them, and I cried out because I was smarting all over, and then I found that I was climbing, and I went up and up a long way, till at last the thicket stopped and I came out crying just under the top of a big bare place, where there were ugly grey stones lying all about on the grass, and here and there a little twisted, stunted tree came out from under a stone, like a snake. And I went up, right to the top, a long way. I never saw such big ugly stones before; they came out of the earth some of them, and some looked as if they had been rolled to where they were, and they went on and on as far as I could see, a long, long way. I looked out from them and saw the country, but it was strange. It was winter time, and there were black terrible woods hanging from the hills all round; it was like seeing a large room hung with black curtains, and the shape of the trees seemed quite

different from any I had ever seen before. I was afraid. Then beyond the
woods there were other hills round in a great ring, but I had never seen
any of them; it all looked black, and everything had a voor over it. It was
all so still and silent, and the sky was heavy and grey and sad, like a wicked
voorish dome in Deep Dendo. I went on into the dreadful rocks. There
were hundreds and hundreds of them. Some were like horrid-grinning
men; I could see their faces as if they would jump at me out of the stone,
and catch hold of me, and drag me with them back into the rock, so that I
should always be there. And there were other rocks that were like animals, creeping, horrible animals, putting out their tongues, and others
were like words that I could not say, and others like dead people lying on
the grass. I went on among them, though they frightened me, and my
heart was full of wicked songs that they put into it; and I wanted to make
faces and twist myself about in the way they did, and I went on and on a
long way till at last I liked the rocks, and they didn't frighten me any
more. I sang the songs I thought of; songs full of words that must not be
spoken or written down. Then I made faces like the faces on the rocks,
and I twisted myself about like the twisted ones, and I lay down flat on
the ground like the dead ones, and I went up to one that was grinning, and
put my arms round him and hugged him. And so I went on and on through
the rocks till I came to a round mound in the middle of them. It was higher
than a mound, it was nearly as high as our house, and it was like a great
basin turned upside down, all smooth and round and green, with one
stone, like a post, sticking up at the top. I climbed up the sides, but they
were so steep I had to stop or I should have rolled all the way down again,
and I should have knocked against the stones at the bottom, and perhaps
been killed. But I wanted to get up to the very top of the big round mound,
so I lay down flat on my face, and took hold of the grass with my hands
and drew myself up, bit by bit, till I was at the top. Then I sat down on the
stone in the middle, and looked all round about. I felt I had come such a
long, long way, just as if I were a hundred miles from home, or in some
other country, or in one of the strange places I had read about in the *Tales
of the Genie* and the *Arabian Nights*, or as if I had gone across the sea, far
away, for years and I had found another world that nobody had ever seen
or heard of before, or as if I had somehow flown through the sky and
fallen on one of the stars I had read about where everything is dead and
cold and grey, and there is no air, and the wind doesn't blow. I sat on the
stone and looked all round and down and round about me. It was just as if
I was sitting on a tower in the middle of a great empty town, because I

could see nothing all around but the grey rocks on the ground. I couldn't make out their shapes any more, but I could see them on and on for a long way, and I looked at them, and they seemed as if they had been arranged into patterns, and shapes, and figures. I knew they couldn't be, because I had seen a lot of them coming right out of the earth, joined to the deep rocks below, so I looked again, but still I saw nothing but circles, and small circles inside big ones, and pyramids, and domes, and spires, and they seemed all to go round and round the place where I was sitting, and the more I looked, the more I saw great big rings of rocks, getting bigger and bigger, and I stared so long that it felt as if they were all moving and turning, like a great wheel, and I was turning, too, in the middle. I got quite dizzy and queer in the head, and everything began to be hazy and not clear, and I saw little sparks of blue light, and the stones looked as if they were springing and dancing and twisting as they went round and round and round. I was frightened again, and I cried out loud, and jumped up from the stone I was sitting on, and fell down. When I got up I was so glad they all looked still, and I sat down on the top and slid down the mound, and went on again. I danced as I went in the peculiar way the rocks had danced when I got giddy, and I was so glad I could do it quite well, and I danced and danced along, and sang extraordinary songs that came into my head. At last I came to the edge of that great flat hill, and there were no more rocks, and the way went again through a dark thicket in a hollow. It was just as bad as the other one I went through climbing up, but I didn't mind this one, because I was so glad I had seen those singular dances and could imitate them. I went down, creeping through the bushes, and a tall nettle stung me on my leg, and made me burn, but I didn't mind it, and I tingled with the boughs and the thorns, but I only laughed and sang. Then I got out of the thicket into a close valley, a little secret place like a dark passage that nobody ever knows of, because it was so narrow and deep and the woods were so thick round it. There is a steep bank with trees hanging over it, and there the ferns keep green all through the winter, when they are dead and brown upon the hill, and the ferns there have a sweet, rich smell like what oozes out of fir trees. There was a little stream of water running down this valley, so small that I could easily step across it. I drank the water with my hand, and it tasted like bright, yellow wine, and it sparkled and bubbled as it ran down over beautiful red and yellow stones, so that it seemed alive and all colours at once. I drank it, and I drank more with my hand, but I couldn't drink enough, so I lay down and bent my head and sucked the water up with my lips. It tasted much better, drinking it that way, and a ripple would come up to my mouth and give me a kiss, and I laughed, and drank again, and pretended there was a nymph, like the one in the old picture at home, who lived in the water and was kissing me. So I bent low down to the water, and put my lips softly to it, and whispered to the nymph that I would come again. I felt sure it would not be common water, I was so glad when I got up and went on; and I danced again and went up and up the valley, under hanging hills. And when I came to the top, the ground rose up in front of me, tall and steep as a wall, and there was nothing but the green wall and the sky. I thought of "for ever and for ever, world without end, Amen"; and I thought I must have really found the end of the world, because it was like the end of everything, as if there could be nothing at all beyond, except the kingdom of Voor, where the light goes when it is put out, and the water goes when the sun takes it away. I began to think of all the long, long way I had journeyed, how I had found a brook and followed it, and followed it on, and gone through bushes and thorny thickets, and dark woods full of creeping thorns. Then I had crept up a tunnel under trees, and climbed a thicket, and seen all the grey rocks, and sat in the middle of them when they turned round, and then I had gone on through the grey rocks and come down the hill through the stinging thicket and up the dark valley, all a long, long way. I wondered how I should get home again, if I could ever find the way, and if my home was there any more, or if it were turned and everybody in it into grey rocks, as in the *Arabian Nights.* So I sat down on the grass and thought what I should do next. I was tired, and my feet were hot with walking, and as I looked about I saw there was a wonderful well just under the high, steep wall of grass. All the ground round it was covered with bright, green, dripping moss; there was every kind of moss there, moss like beautiful little ferns, and like palms and fir trees, and it was all green as jewellery, and drops of water hung on it like diamonds. And in the middle was the great well, deep and shining and beautiful, so clear it looked as if I could touch the red sand at the bottom, but it was far below. I stood by it and looked in, as if I were looking in a glass. At the bottom of the well, in the middle of it, the red grains of sand were moving and stirring all the time, and I saw how the water bubbled up, but at the top it was quite smooth, and full and brimming. It was a great well, large like a bath, and with the shining, glittering green moss about it, it looked like a great white jewel, with green jewels all round. My feet were so hot and tired that I took off my boots and stockings, and let my feet down into the water, and the water was soft and cold, and when I got up I wasn't tired any more, and I felt I must go on, farther and farther, and see what was on the other side of the wall. I climbed up it very slowly, going sideways all the time, and when I got to the top and looked over, I was in the queerest country I had seen, stranger even than the hill of the grey rocks. It looked as if earth-children had been playing there with their spades, as it was all hills and hollows, and castles and walls made of earth and covered with grass. There were two mounds like big beehives, round and great and solemn, and then hollow basins, and then a steep mounting wall like the ones I saw once by the seaside where the big guns and the soldiers were. I nearly fell into one of the round hollows, it went away from under my feet so suddenly, and I ran fast down the side and stood at the bottom and looked up. It was strange and solemn to look up. There was nothing but the grey, heavy sky and the sides of the hollow; everything else had gone away, and the hollow was the whole world, and I thought that at night it must be full of ghosts and moving shadows and pale things when the moon shone down to the bottom at the dead of night, and the wind wailed up above. It was so strange and solemn and lonely, like a hollow temple of dead heathen gods. It reminded me of a tale my nurse had told me when I was quite little; it was the same nurse that took me into the wood where I saw the beautiful white people. And I remembered how nurse had told me the story one winter night, when the wind was beating the trees against the wall, and crying and moaning in the nursery chimney. She said there was, somewhere or other, a hollow pit, just like the one I was standing in, everybody was afraid to go into it or near it, it was such a bad place. But once upon a time there was a poor girl who said she would go into the hollow pit, and everybody tried to stop her, but she would go. And she went down into the pit and came back laughing, and said there was nothing there at all, except green grass and red stones, and white stones and yellow flowers. And soon after people saw she had most beautiful emerald earrings, and they asked how she got them, as she and her mother were quite poor. But she laughed, and said her earrings were not made of emeralds at all, but only of green grass. Then, one day, she wore on her breast the reddest ruby that any one had ever seen, and it was as big as a hen's egg, and glowed and sparkled like a hot burning coal of fire. And they asked how she got it, as she and her mother were quite poor. But she laughed, and said it was not a ruby at all, but only a red stone. Then one day she wore round her neck the loveliest necklace that any one had ever seen, much finer than the queen's finest, and it was made of great bright diamonds, hundreds of them, and they shone like all

the stars on a night in June. So they asked her how she got it, as she and
her mother were quite poor. But she laughed, and said they were not diamonds at all, but only white stones. And one day she went to the court,
and she wore on her head a crown of pure angel-gold, so nurse said, and it
shone like the sun, and it was much more splendid than the crown the
king was wearing himself, and in her ears she wore the emeralds, and the
big ruby was the brooch on her breast, and the great diamond necklace
was sparkling on her neck. And the king and queen thought she was some
great princess from a long way off, and got down from their thrones and
went to meet her, but somebody told the king and queen who she was, and
that she was quite poor. So the king asked why she wore a gold crown, and
how she got it, as she and her mother were so poor. And she laughed,
and said it wasn't a gold crown at all, but only some yellow flowers she
had put in her hair. And the king thought it was very strange, and said she
should stay at the court, and they would see what would happen next.
And she was so lovely that everybody said that her eyes were greener
than the emeralds, that her lips were redder than the ruby, that her skin
was whiter than the diamonds, and that her hair was brighter than the
golden crown. So the king's son said he would marry her, and the king
said he might. And the bishop married them, and there was a great supper,
and afterwards the king's son went to his wife's room. But just when he
had his hand on the door, he saw a tall, black man, with a dreadful face,
standing in front of the door, and a voice said——

> Venture not upon your life,
> This is mine own wedded wife.

Then the king's son fell down on the ground in a fit. And they came and
tried to get into the room, but they couldn't, and they hacked at the door
with hatchets, but the wood had turned hard as iron, and at last everybody ran away, they were so frightened at the screaming and laughing and
shrieking and crying that came out of the room. But next day they went
in, and found there was nothing in the room but thick black smoke, because the black man had come and taken her away. And on the bed there
were two knots of faded grass and red stone, and some white stones, and
some faded yellow flowers. I remembered this tale of nurse's while I was
standing at the bottom of the deep hollow; it was so strange and solitary
there, and I felt afraid. I could not see any stones or flowers, but I was
afraid of bringing them away without knowing, and I thought I would do a

charm that came into my head to keep the black man away. So I stood right in the very middle of the hollow, and I made sure that I had none of those things on me, and then I walked round the place, and touched my eyes, and my lips, and my hair in a peculiar manner, and whispered some queer words that nurse taught me to keep bad things away. Then I felt safe and climbed up out of the hollow, and went on through all those mounds and hollows and walls, till I came to the end, which was high above all the rest, and I could see that all the different shapes of the earth were arranged in patterns, something like the grey rocks, only the pattern was different. It was getting late, and the air was indistinct, but it looked from where I was standing something like two great figures of people lying on the grass. And I went on, and at last I found a certain wood, which is too secret to be described, and nobody knows of the passage into it, which I found out in a very curious manner, by seeing some little animal run into the wood through it. So I went after the animal by a very narrow dark way, under thorns and bushes, and it was almost dark when I came to a kind of open place in the middle. And there I saw the most wonderful sight I have ever seen, but it was only for a minute, as I ran away directly, and crept out of the wood by the passage I had come by, and ran and ran as fast as ever I could, because I was afraid, what I had seen was so wonderful and so strange and beautiful. But I wanted to get home and think of it, and I did not know what might not happen if I stayed by the wood. I was hot all over and trembling, and my heart was beating, and strange cries that I could not help came from me as I ran from the wood. I was glad that a great white moon came up from over a round hill and showed me the way, so I went back through the mounds and hollows and down the close valley, and up through the thicket over the place of the grey rocks, and so at last I got home again. My father was busy in his study, and the servants had not told about my not coming home, though they were frightened, and wondered what they ought to do, so I told them I had lost my way, but I did not let them find out the real way I had been. I went to bed and lay awake all through the night, thinking of what I had seen. When I came out of the narrow way, and it looked all shining, though the air was dark, it seemed so certain, and all the way home I was quite sure that I had seen it, and I wanted to be alone in my room, and be glad over it all to myself, and shut my eyes and pretend it was there, and do all the things I would have done if I had not been so afraid. But when I shut my eyes the sight would not come, and I began to think about my adventures all over again, and I remembered how dusky and queer it was at the end, and I was afraid it must be all a mistake, because it seemed impossible it could happen. It seemed like one of nurse's tales, which I didn't really believe in, though I was frightened at the bottom of the hollow; and the stories she told me when I was little came back into my head, and I wondered whether it was really there what I thought I had seen, or whether any of her tales could have happened a long time ago. It was so queer; I lay awake there in my room at the back of the house, and the moon was shining on the other side towards the river, so the bright light did not fall upon the wall. And the house was quite still. I had heard my father come upstairs, and just after the clock struck twelve, and after the house was still and empty, as if there was nobody alive in it. And though it was all dark and indistinct in my room, a pale glimmering kind of light shone in through the white blind, and once I got up and looked out, and there was a great black shadow of the house covering the garden, looking like a prison where men are hanged; and then beyond it was all white; and the wood shone white with black gulfs between the trees. It was still and clear, and there were no clouds in the sky. I wanted to think of what I had seen but I couldn't, and I began to think of all the tales that nurse had told me so long ago that I thought I had forgotten, but they all came back, and mixed up with the thickets and the grey rocks and the hollows in the earth and the secret wood, till I hardly knew what was new and what was old, or whether it was not all dreaming. And then I remembered that hot summer afternoon, so long ago, when nurse left me by myself in the shade, and the white people came out of the water and out of the wood, and played, and danced, and sang, and I began to fancy that nurse told me about something like it before I saw them, only I couldn't recollect exactly what she told me. Then I wondered whether she had been the white lady, as I remembered she was just as white and beautiful, and had the same dark eyes and black hair; and sometimes she smiled and looked like the lady had looked, when she was telling me some of her stories, beginning with "Once on a time," or "In the time of the fairies." But I thought she couldn't be the lady, as she seemed to have gone a different way into the wood, and I didn't think the man who came after us could be the other, or I couldn't have seen that wonderful secret in the secret wood. I thought of the moon: but it was afterwards when I was in the middle of the wild land, where the earth was made into the shape of great figures, and it was all walls, and mysterious hollows, and smooth round mounds, that I saw the great white moon come up over a round hill. I was wondering about all these things, till at last I got quite frightened, because I was afraid something had happened to me, and I remembered nurse's tale of the poor girl who went into the hollow pit, and was carried away at last by the black man. I knew I had gone into a hollow pit too, and perhaps it was the same, and I had done something dreadful. So I did the charm over again, and touched my eyes and my lips and my hair in a peculiar manner, and said the old words from the fairy language, so that I might be sure I had not been carried away. I tried again to see the secret wood, and to creep up the passage and see what I had seen there, but somehow I couldn't, and I kept on thinking of nurse's stories. There was one I remembered about a young man who once upon a time went hunting, and all the day he and his hounds hunted everywhere, and they crossed the rivers and went into all the woods, and went round the marshes, but they couldn't find anything at all, and they hunted all day till the sun sank down and began to set behind the mountain. And the young man was angry because he couldn't find anything, and he was going to turn back, when just as the sun touched the mountain, he saw come out of a brake in front of him a beautiful white stag. And he cheered to his hounds, but they whined and would not follow, and he cheered to his horse, but it shivered and stood stock still, and the young man jumped off the horse and left the hounds and began to follow the white stag all alone. And soon it was quite dark, and the sky was black, without a single star shining in it, and the stag went away into the darkness. And though the man had brought his gun with him he never shot at the stag, because he wanted to catch it, and he was afraid he would lose it in the night. But he never lost it once, though the sky was so black and the air was so dark, and the stag went on and on till the young man didn't know a bit where he was. And they went through enormous woods where the air was full of whispers and a pale, dead light came out from the rotten trunks that were lying on the ground, and just as the man thought he had lost the stag, he would see it all white and shining in front of him, and he would run fast to catch it, but the stag always ran faster, so he did not catch it. And they went through the enormous woods, and they swam across rivers, and they waded through black marshes where the ground bubbled, and the air was full of will-o'-the-wisps, and the stag fled away down into rocky narrow valleys, where the air was like the smell of a vault, and the man went after it. And they went over the great mountains, and the man heard the wind come down from the sky, and the stag went on and the man went after. At last the sun rose and the young man found he was in a country that he had never seen before; it was a beautiful valley with a bright stream running through it, and a great, big round hill in the middle. And the stag went down the valley, towards the hill, and it seemed to be getting tired and went slower and slower, and though the man was tired, too, he began to run faster, and he was sure he would catch the stag at last. But just as they got to the bottom of the hill, and the man stretched out his hand to catch the stag, it vanished into the earth, and the man began to cry; he was so sorry that he had lost it after all his long hunting. But as he was crying he saw there was a door in the hill, just in front of him, and he went in, and it was quite dark, but he went on, as he thought he would find the white stag. And all of a sudden it got light, and there was the sky, and the sun shining, and birds singing in the trees, and there was a beautiful fountain. And by the fountain a lovely lady was sitting, who was the queen of the fairies, and she told the man that she had changed herself into a stag to bring him there because she loved him so much. Then she brought out a great gold cup, covered with jewels, from her fairy palace, and she offered him wine in the cup to drink. And he drank, and the more he drank the more he longed to drink, because the wine was enchanted. So he kissed the lovely lady, and she became his wife, and he stayed all that day and all that night in the hill where she lived, and when he woke he found he was lying on the ground, close to where he had seen the stag first, and his horse was there and his hounds were there waiting, and he looked up, and the sun sank behind the mountain. And he went home and lived a long time, but he would never kiss any other lady because he had kissed the queen of the fairies, and he would never drink common wine any more, because he had drunk enchanted wine. And sometimes nurse told me tales that she had heard from her great-grandmother, who was very old, and lived in a cottage on the mountain all alone, and most of these tales were about a hill where people used to meet at night long ago, and they used to play all sorts of strange games and do queer things that nurse told me of, but I couldn't understand, and now, she said, everybody but her great-grandmother had forgotten all about it, and nobody knew where the hill was, not even her great-grandmother. But she told me one very strange story about the hill, and I trembled when I remembered it. She said that people always went there in summer, when it was very hot, and they had to dance a good deal. It would be all dark at first, and there were trees there, which made it much darker, and people would come, one by one, from all directions, by a secret path which nobody else knew, and two persons would keep the gate, and every one as they came up had to give a very curious sign, which nurse showed me as well as she could, but she said she couldn't show me properly. And all kinds of people would come; there would be gentle folks and village folks, and some old people and boys and girls, and quite small children, who sat and watched. And it would all be dark as they came in, except in one corner where some one was burning something that smelt strong and sweet, and made them laugh, and there one would see a glaring of coals, and the smoke mounting up red. So they would all come in, and when the last had come there was no door any more, so that no one else could get in, even if they knew there was anything beyond. And once a gentleman who was a stranger and had ridden a long way, lost his path at night, and his horse took him into the very middle of the wild country, where everything was upside down, and there were dreadful marshes and great stones everywhere, and holes underfoot, and the trees looked like gibbet-posts, because they had great black arms that stretched out across the way. And this strange gentleman was very frightened, and his horse began to shiver all over, and at last it stopped and wouldn't go any farther, and the gentleman got down and tried to lead the horse, but it wouldn't move, and it was all covered with a sweat, like death. So the gentleman went on all alone, going farther and farther into the wild country, till at last he came to a dark place, where he heard shouting and singing and crying, like nothing he had ever heard before. It all sounded quite close to him, but he couldn't get in, and so he began to call, and while he was calling, something came behind him, and in a minute his mouth and arms and legs were all bound up, and he fell into a swoon. And when he came to himself, he was lying by the roadside, just where he had first lost his way, under a blasted oak with a black trunk, and his horse was tied beside him. So he rode on to the town and told the people there what had happened, and some of them were amazed; but others knew. So when once everybody had come, there was no door at all for anybody else to pass in by. And when they were all inside, round in a ring, touching each other, some one began to sing in the darkness, and some one else would make a noise like thunder with a thing they had on purpose, and on still nights people would hear the thundering noise far, far away beyond the wild land, and some of them, who thought they knew what it was, used to make a sign on their breasts when they woke up in their beds at dead of night and heard that terrible deep noise, like thunder on the mountains. And the noise and the singing would go on and on for a long time, and the people who were in a ring swayed a little to and fro; and the song was in an old, old language that nobody knows now, and the tune was queer. Nurse said her great-grandmother had known some one who remembered a little of it, when she was quite a little girl, and nurse tried to sing some of it to me, and it was so strange a tune that I turned all cold and my flesh crept as if I had put my hand on something dead. Sometimes it was a man that sang and sometimes it was a woman, and sometimes the one who sang it did it so well that two or three of the people who were there fell to the ground shrieking and tearing with their hands. The singing went on, and the people in the ring kept swaying to and fro for a long time, and at last the moon would rise over a place they called the Tole Deol, and came up and showed them swinging and swaying from side to side, with the sweet thick smoke curling up from the burning coals, and floating in circles all around them. Then they had their supper. A boy and a girl brought it to them; the boy carried a great cup of wine, and the girl carried a cake of bread, and they passed the bread and wine round and round, but they tasted quite different from common bread and common wine, and changed everybody that tasted them. Then they all rose up and danced, and secret things were brought out of some hiding place, and they played extraordinary games, and danced round and round and round in the moonlight, and sometimes people would suddenly disappear and never be heard of afterwards, and nobody knew what had happened to them. And they drank more of that curious wine, and they made images and worshipped them, and nurse showed me how the images were made one day when we were out for a walk, and we passed by a place where there was a lot of wet clay. So nurse asked me if I would like to know what those things were like that they made on the hill, and I said yes. Then she asked me if I would promise never to tell a living soul a word about it, and if I did I was to be thrown into a black pit with the dead people, and I said I wouldn't tell anybody, and she said the same thing again and again, and I promised. So she took my wooden spade and dug a big lump of clay and put it in my tin bucket, and told me to say if any one met us that I was going to make pies when I went home. Then we went on a little way till we came to a little brake growing right down into the road, and nurse stopped, and looked up the road and down it, and then peeped through the hedge into the field on the other side, and then she said "Quick!" and we ran into the brake, and crept in and out among the bushes till we had gone a good way from the road. Then we sat down under a bush, and I wanted so much to know what nurse was going to make with the clay, but before she would begin she made me promise again not to say a word about it, and she went again and peeped through the bushes on every side, though the lane was so small and deep that hardly anybody ever went there. So we sat down, and nurse took the clay out of the bucket, and began to knead it with her hands, and do queer things with it, and turn it about. And she hid it under a big dock-leaf for a minute or two and then she brought it out again, and then she stood up and sat down, and walked round the clay in a peculiar manner, and all the time she was softly singing a sort of rhyme, and her face got very red. Then she sat down again, and took the clay in her hands and began to shape it into a doll, but not like the dolls I have at home, and she made the queerest doll I had ever seen, all out of the wet clay, and hid it under a bush to get dry and hard, and all the time she was making it she was singing these rhymes to herself, and her face got redder and redder. So we left the doll there, hidden away in the bushes where nobody would ever find it. And a few days later we went the same walk, and when we came to that narrow, dark part of the lane where the brake runs down to the bank, nurse made me promise all over again, and she looked about, just as she had done before, and we crept into the bushes till we got to the green place where the little clay man was hidden. I remember it all so well, though I was only eight, and it is eight years ago now as I am writing it down, but the sky was a deep violet blue, and in the middle of the brake where we were sitting there was a great elder tree covered with blossoms, and on the other side there was a clump of meadowsweet, and when I think of that day the smell of the meadow-sweet and elder blossom seems to fill the room, and if I shut my eyes I can see the glaring sky, with little clouds very white floating across it, and nurse who went away long ago sitting opposite me and looking like the beautiful white lady in the wood. So we sat down and nurse took out the clay doll from the secret place where she had hidden it, and she said we must "pay our respects," and she would show me what to do, and I must watch her all the time. So she did all sorts of queer things with the little clay man, and I noticed she was all streaming with perspiration, though we had walked so slowly, and then she told me to "pay my respects," and I did everything she did because I liked her, and it was such an odd game. And she said that if one loved very much, the clay man was very good, if one did certain things with it, and if one hated very much, it was just as good, only one had to do different things, and we played with it a long time, and pretended all sorts of things. Nurse said her great-grandmother had told her all about these images, but what we did was no harm at all, only a game. But she told me a story about these images that frightened me very much, and that was what I remembered that night when I was lying awake in my room in the pale, empty darkness, thinking of what I had seen and the secret wood. Nurse said there was once a young lady of the high gentry, who lived in a great castle. And she was so beautiful that all the gentlemen wanted to marry her, because she was the loveliest lady that anybody had ever seen, and she was kind to everybody, and everybody thought she was very good. But though she was polite to all the gentlemen who wished to marry her, she put them off, and said she couldn't make up her mind, and she wasn't sure she wanted to marry anybody at all. And her father, who was a very great lord, was angry, though he was so fond of her, and he asked why she wouldn't choose a bachelor out of all the handsome young men who came to the castle. But she only said she didn't love any of them very much, and she must wait, and if they pestered her, she said she would go and be a nun in a nunnery. So all the gentlemen said they would go away and wait for a year and a day, and when a year and a day were gone, they would come back again and ask her to say which one she would marry. So the day was appointed and they all went away; and the lady had promised that in a year and a day it would be her wedding day with one of them. But the truth was, that she was the queen of the people who danced on the hill on summer nights, and on the proper nights she would lock the door of her room, and she and her maid would steal out of the castle by a secret passage that only they knew of, and go away up to the hill in the wild land. And she knew more of the secret things than any one else, and more than any one knew before or after, because she would not tell anybody the most secret secrets. She knew how to do all the awful things, how to destroy young men, and how to put a curse on people, and other things that I could not understand. And her real name was the Lady Avelin, but the dancing people called her Cassap, which meant somebody very wise, in the old language. And she was whiter than any of them and taller, and her eyes shone in the dark like burning rubies; and she could sing songs that none of the others could sing, and when she sang they all fell down on their faces and worshipped her. And she could do what they called the shib-show, which was a very wonderful enchantment. She would tell the great lord, her father, that she wanted to go into the woods to gather flowers, so he let her go, and she and her maid went into the woods where nobody came, and the maid would keep watch. Then the lady would lie down under the trees and begin to sing a particular song, and she stretched out her arms, and from every part of the wood great serpents would come, hissing and gliding in and out among the trees, and shooting out their forked tongues as they crawled up to the lady. And they all came to her, and twisted round her, round her body, and her arms, and her neck, till she was covered with writhing serpents, and there was only her head to be seen. And she whispered to them, and she sang to them, and they writhed round and round, faster and faster, till she told them to go. And they all went away directly, back to their holes, and on the lady's breast there would be a most curious, beautiful stone, shaped something like an egg, and coloured dark blue and yellow, and red, and green, marked like a serpent's scales. It was called a glame stone, and with it one could do all sorts of wonderful things, and nurse said her great-grandmother had seen a glame stone with her own eyes, and it was for all the world shiny and scaly like a snake. And the lady could do a lot of other things as well, but she was quite fixed that she would not be married. And there were a great many gentlemen who wanted to marry her, but there were five of them who were chief, and their names were Sir Simon, Sir John, Sir Oliver, Sir Richard, and Sir Rowland. All the others believed she spoke the truth, and that she would choose one of them to be her man when a year and a day was done; it was only Sir Simon, who was very crafty, who thought she was deceiving them all, and he vowed he would watch and try if he could find out anything. And though he was very wise he was very young, and he had a smooth, soft face like a girl's, and he pretended, as the rest did, that he would not come to the castle for a year and a day, and he said he was going away beyond the sea to foreign parts. But he really only went a very little way, and came back dressed like a servant girl, and so he got a place in the castle to wash the dishes. And he waited and watched, and he listened and said nothing, and he hid in dark places, and woke up at night and looked out, and he heard things and he saw things that he thought were very strange. And he was so sly that he told the girl that waited on the lady that he was really a young man, and that he had dressed up as a girl because he loved her so very much and wanted to be in the same house with her, and the girl was so pleased that she told him many things, and he was more than ever certain that the Lady Avelin was deceiving him and the others. And he was so clever, and told the servant so many lies, that one night he managed to hide in the Lady Avelin's room behind the curtains. And he stayed quite still and never moved, and at last the lady came. And she bent down under the bed, and raised up a stone, and there was a hollow place underneath, and out of it she took a waxen image, just like the clay one that I and nurse had made in the brake. And all the time her eyes were burning like rubies. And she took the little wax doll up in her arms and held it to her breast, and she whispered and she murmured, and she took it up and she laid it down again, and she held it high, and she held it low, and she laid it down again. And she said, "Happy is he that begat the bishop, that ordered the clerk, that married the man, that had the wife, that fashioned the hive, that harboured the bee, that gathered the wax that my own true love was made of." and she brought out of an aumbry a great golden bowl, and she brought out of a closet a great jar of wine, and she poured some of the wine into the bowl, and she laid her mannikin very gently in the wine, and washed it in the wine all over. Then she went to a cupboard and took a small round cake and laid it on the image's mouth, and then she bore it softly and covered it up. And Sir Simon, who was watching all the time, though he was terribly frightened, saw the lady bend down and stretch out her arms and whisper and sing, and then Sir Simon saw beside her a handsome young man, who kissed her on the lips. And they drank wine out of the golden bowl together, and they ate the cake together. But when the sun rose there was only the little wax doll, and the lady hid it again under the bed in the hollow place. So Sir Simon knew quite well what the lady was, and he waited and he watched, till the time she had said was nearly over, and in a week the year and a day would be done. And one night, when he was watching behind the curtains in her room, he saw her making more wax dolls. And she made five, and hid them away. And the next night she took one out, and held it up, and filled the golden bowl with water, and took the doll by the neck and held it under the water. Then she said——

> Sir Dickon, Sir Dickon, your day is done,
> You shall be drowned in the water wan.

And the next day news came to the castle that Sir Richard had been drowned at the ford. And at night she took another doll and tied a violet cord round its neck and hung it upon a nail. Then she said——

> Sir Rowland, your life has ended its span,
> High on a tree I see you hang.

And the next day news came to the castle that Sir Rowland had been hanged by robbers in the wood. And at night she took another doll, and drove her bodkin right into its heart. Then she said——

> Sir Noll, Sir Noll, so cease your life,
> Your heart piercèd with the knife.

And the next day news came to the castle that Sir Oliver had fought in a tavern, and a stranger had stabbed him in the heart. And at night she took another doll, and held it to a fire of charcoal till it was melted. Then she said——

> Sir John, return, and turn to clay,
> In fire of fever you waste away.

And the next day news came to the castle that Sir John had died in a burning fever. So then Sir Simon went out of the castle and mounted his horse and rode away to the bishop and told him everything. And the bishop sent his men, and they took the Lady Avelin, and everything she had done was found out. So on the day after the year and a day, when she was to have been married, they carried her through the town in her smock, and they tied her to a great stake in the market-place, and burned her alive before the bishop with her wax image hung round her neck. And people said the wax man screamed in the burning of the flames. And I thought of this story again and again as I was lying awake in my bed, and I seemed to see the Lady Avelin in the market-place, with the yellow flames eating up her beautiful white body. And I thought of it so much that I seemed to get into the story myself, and I fancied I was the lady, and that they were coming to take me to be burnt with fire, with all the people in town looking at me. And I wondered whether she cared, after all the strange things she had done, and whether it hurt very much to be burned at the stake. I tried again and again to forget the nurse's stories, and to remember the secret I had seen that afternoon, and what was in the secret wood, but I could only see the dark and a glimmering in the dark, and then it went away, and I only saw myself running, and then a great moon came up white over a dark round hill. Then all the old stories came back again, and the queer rhymes that nurse used to sing to me; and there was one beginning "Halsy cumsy Helen musty," that she used to sing very softly when she wanted me to go to sleep. And I began to sing it to myself inside of my head, and I went to sleep.

The next morning I was very tired and sleepy, and could hardly do my lessons, and I was very glad when they were over and I had had my dinner, as I wanted to go out and be alone. It was a warm day, and I went to a nice turfy hill by the river, and sat down on my mother's old shawl that I had brought with me on purpose. The sky was grey, like the day before, but there was a kind of white gleam behind it, and from where I was sitting I could look down on the town, and it was all still and quiet and white, like a picture. I remembered that it was on that hill that nurse taught me to play an old game called "Troy Town," in which one had to dance, and wind in and out on a pattern in the grass, and then when one had danced and turned long enough the other person asks you questions, and you can't help answering whether you want to or not, and whatever you are told to do you feel you have to do it. Nurse said there used to be a lot of games like that that some people knew of, and there was one by which people could be turned into anything you liked, and an old man her great-grand-mother had seen had known a girl who had been turned into a large snake. And there was another very ancient game of dancing and winding and turning, by which you could take a person out of himself and hide him away as long as you liked, and his body went walking about quite empty, without any sense in it. But I came to that hill because I wanted to think of what had happened the day before, and of the secret of the wood. From the place where I was sitting I could see beyond the town, into the opening I had found, where a little brook had led me into an unknown country. And I pretended I was following the brook over again, and I went all the way in my mind, and at last I found the wood, and crept into it under the bushes, and then in the dusk I saw something that made me feel as if I were filled with fire, as if I wanted to dance and sing and fly up into the air, because I was changed and wonderful. But what I saw was not changed at all, and had not grown old, and I wondered again and again how such things could happen, and whether nurse's stories were really true, because in the daytime in the open air everything seemed quite dif-ferent from what it was at night, when I was frightened, and thought I was to be burned alive. I once told my father one of her little tales, which was about a ghost, and asked him if it was true, and he told me it was not true at all, and that only common, ignorant people believed in such rubbish. He was very angry with nurse for telling me the story, and scolded her, and after that I promised her I would never whisper a word of what she told me, and if I did I should be bitten by the great black snake that lived in the pool in the wood. And all alone on the hill I wondered what was true. I had seen something very amazing and very lovely, and I knew a story, and if I had really seen it, and not made it up out of the dark, and the black bough, and the bright shining that was mounting up to the sky from over the great round hill, but had really seen it in truth, then there were all kinds of wonderful and lovely and terrible things to think of, so I longed and trembled, and I burned and got cold. And I looked down on the town, so quiet and still, like a white picture; and I thought over and over if it could be true. I was a long time before I could make up my mind to anything; there was such a strange fluttering at my heart that seemed to whisper to me all the time that I had not made it up out of my head, and yet it seemed quite impossible, and I knew my father and everybody would say it was dreadful rubbish. I never dreamed of telling him or anybody else a word about it, because I knew it would be of no use, and I should only get laughed at or scolded, so for a long time I was very quiet, and went about thinking and wondering; and at night I used to dream of amazing things, and sometimes I woke up in the early morning and held out my arms with a cry. And I was frightened, too, because there were dangers, and some awful thing would happen to me, unless I took great care, if the story were true. These old tales were always in my head, night and morning, and I went over them and told them to myself over and over again, and went for walks in the places where nurse had told them to me; and when I sat in the nursery by the fire in the evenings I used to fancy nurse was sitting in the other chair, and telling me some wonderful story in a low voice, for fear anybody should be listening. But she used to like best to tell me about things when we were right out in the country, far from the house, because she said she was telling me such secrets, and walls have ears. And if it was something more than ever secret, we had to hide in brakes or woods; and I used to think it was such fun creeping along a hedge, and going very softly, and then we would get behind the bushes or run into the wood all of a sudden, when we were sure that none was watching us; so we knew that we had our secrets quite all to ourselves, and nobody else at all knew anything about them. Now and then, when we had hidden ourselves as I have described, she used to show me all sorts of odd things. One day, I remember, we were in a hazel brake, overlooking the brook, and we were so snug and warm, as though it was April; the sun was quite hot, and the leaves were just coming out. Nurse said she would show me something funny that would make me laugh, and then she showed me, as she had said, how one could turn a whole house upside down, without anybody being able to find out, and the pots and pans would jump about, and the china would be broken, and the chairs would tumble over themselves. I tried it one day in the kitchen, and I found I could do it quite well, and a whole row of plates on the dresser fell off it, and cook's little work-table tilted up and turned right over "before her eyes," as she said, but she was so frightened and turned so white that I didn't do it again, as I liked her. And afterwards, in the hazel copse, when she had shown me how to make things tumble about, she showed me how to make rapping noises, and I learnt how to do that, too. Then she taught me rhymes to say on certain occasions, and peculiar marks to make on other occasions, and other things that her great-grandmother had taught her when she was a little girl herself. And these were all the things I was thinking about in those days after the strange walk when I thought I had seen a great secret, and I wished nurse were there for me to ask her about it, but she had gone away more than two years before, and nobody seemed to know what had become of her, or where she had gone. But I shall always remember those days if I live to be quite old, because all the time I felt so strange, wondering and doubting, and feeling quite sure at one time, and making up my mind, and then I would feel quite sure that such things couldn't happen really, and it began all over again. But I took care not to do certain things that might be very dangerous. So I waited and wondered for a long time, and though I was not sure at all, I never dared to try to find out. But one day I became sure that all that nurse said was quite true, and I was all alone when I found it out. I trembled all over with joy and terror, and as fast as I could I ran into one of the old brakes where we used to go—it was the one by the lane, where nurse made the little clay man—and I ran into it, and I crept into it; and when I came to the place where the elder was, I covered up my face with my hands and lay down flat on the grass, and I stayed there for two hours without moving, whispering to myself delicious, terrible things, and saying some words over and over again. It was all true and wonderful and splendid, and when I remembered the story I knew and thought of what I had really seen, I got hot and I got cold, and the air seemed full of scent, and flowers, and singing. And first I wanted to make a little clay man, like the one nurse had made so long ago, and I had to invent plans and stratagems, and to look about, and to think of things beforehand, because nobody must dream on anything that I was doing or going to do, and I was too old to carry clay about in a tin bucket. At last I thought of a plan, and I brought the wet clay to the brake, and did everything that nurse had done, only I made a much finer image than the one she had made; and when it was finished I did everything that I could imagine and much more than she did, because it was the likeness of something far better. And a few days later, when I had done my lessons early, I went for the second time by the way of the little brook that had led me into a strange country. And I followed the brook, and went through the bushes, and beneath the low branches of trees, and up thorny thickets on the hill, and by dark woods full of creeping thorns, a long, long way. Then I crept through the dark tunnel where the brook had been and the ground was stony, till at last I came to the thicket that climbed up the hill, and though the leaves were coming out upon the trees, everything looked almost as black as it was on the first day that I went there. And the thicket was just the same, and I went up slowly till I came out on the big bare hill, and began to walk among the wonderful rocks. I saw the terrible voor again on everything, for though the sky was brighter, the ring of wild hills all around was still dark, and the hanging woods looked dark and dreadful, and the strange rocks were as grey as ever; and when I looked down on them from the great mound, sitting on the stone, I saw all their amazing circles and rounds within rounds, and I had to sit quite still and watch them as they began to turn about me, and each stone danced in its place, and they seemed to go round and round in a great whirl, as if one were in the middle of all the stars and heard them rushing through the air. So I went down among the rocks to dance with them and to sing extraordinary songs; and I went down through the other thicket, and drank from the bright stream in the close and secret valley, putting my lips down to the bubbling water; and then I went on till I came to the deep, brimming well among the glittering moss, and I sat down. I looked before me into the secret darkness of the valley, and behind me was the great high wall of grass, and all around me there were the hanging woods that made the valley such a secret place. I knew there was nobody here at all besides myself, and that no one could see me. So I took off my boots and stockings, and let my feet down into the water, saying the words that I knew. And it was not cold at all, as I expected, but warm and very pleasant, and when my feet were in it I felt as if they were in silk, or as if the nymph were kissing them. So when I had done, I said the other words and made the signs, and then I dried my feet with a towel I had brought on purpose, and put on my stockings and boots. Then I climbed up the steep wall, and went into the place where there are the hollows, and the two beautiful mounds, and the round ridges of land, and all the strange shapes. I did not go down into the hollow this time, but I turned at the end, and made out the figures quite plainly, as it was lighter, and I had remembered the story I had quite forgotten before, and in the story the two figures are called Adam and Eve, and only those who know the story understand what they mean. So I went on and on till I came to the secret wood which must not be described, and I crept into it by the way I had found. And when I had gone about halfway I stopped, and turned round, and got ready, and I bound the handkerchief tightly round my eyes, and made quite sure that I could not see at all, not a twig, nor the end of a leaf, nor the light of the sky, as it was an old red silk handkerchief with large yellow spots, that went round twice and covered my eyes, so that I could see nothing. Then I began to go on, step by step, very slowly. My heart beat faster and faster, and something rose in my throat that choked me and made me want to cry out, but I shut my lips, and went on. Boughs caught in my hair as I went, and great thorns tore me; but I went on to the end of the path. Then I stopped, and held out my arms and bowed, and I went round the first time, feeling with my hands, and there was nothing. I went round the second time, feeling with my hands and there was nothing. Then I went round the third time, feeling with my hands, and the story was all true, and I wished that the years were gone by, and that I had not so long a time to wait before I was happy for ever and ever.

Nurse must have been a prophet like those we read of in the Bible. Everything that she said began to come true, and since then other things that she told me of have happened. That was how I came to know that her stories were true and that I had not made up the secret myself out of my own head. But there was another thing that happened that day. I went a second time to the secret place. It was at the deep brimming well, and when I was standing on the moss I bent over and looked in, and then I knew who the white lady was that I had seen come out of the water in the wood long ago when I was quite little. And I trembled all over, because that told me other things. Then I remembered how sometime after I had seen the white people in the wood, nurse asked me more about them, and I told her all over again, and she listened, and said nothing for a long, long time, and at last she said, "You will see her again." So I understood what had happened and what was to happen. And I understood about the nymphs; how I might meet them in all kinds of places, and they would always help me, and I must always look for them, and find them in all sorts of strange shapes and appearances. And without the nymphs I could never have found the secret, and without them none of the other things could happen. Nurse had told me all about them long ago, but she called them by another name, and I did not know what she meant, or what her tales of them were about, only that they were very queer. And there were two kinds, the bright and the dark, and both were very lovely and very wonderful, and some people saw only one kind, and some only the other, but some saw them both. But usually the dark appeared first, and the bright ones came afterwards, and there were extraordinary tales about them. It was a day or two after I had come home from the secret place that I first really knew the nymphs. Nurse had shown me how to call them, and I had tried, but I did not know what she meant, and so I thought it was all nonsense. But I made up my mind I would try again, so I went to the wood where the pool was, where I saw the white people, and I tried again. The dark nymph, Alanna, came, and she turned the pool of water into a pool of fire. . . .

EPILOGUE

"That's a very queer story," said Cotgrave, handing back the green book to the recluse, Ambrose. "I see the drift of a good deal, but there are many things that I do not grasp at all. On the last page, for example, what does she mean by 'nymphs'?"

"Well, I think there are references throughout the manuscript to certain 'processes' which have been handed down by tradition from age to age. Some of these processes are just beginning to come within the purview of science, which has arrived at them—or rather at the steps which lead to them—by quite different paths. I have interpreted the reference to 'nymphs' as a reference to one of these processes."

"And you believe that there are such things?"

"Oh, I think so. Yes, I believe I could give you convincing evidence on that point. I am afraid you have neglected the study of alchemy. It is a pity, for the symbolism, at all events, is very beautiful, and moreover if you were acquainted with certain books on the subject, I could recall to your mind phrases which might explain a good deal in the manuscript that you have been reading."

"Yes; but I want to know whether you seriously think that there is any foundation of fact beneath these fancies. Is it not all a department of poetry; a curious dream which man has indulged himself?"

"I can only say that it is no doubt better for the great mass of people to dismiss it all as a dream. But if you ask my veritable belief—that goes quite the other way. No; I should not say belief, but rather knowledge. I may tell you that I have known cases in which men have stumbled quite by accident on certain of these 'processes,' and have been astonished by wholly unexpected results. In the cases I am thinking of there could have been no possibility of 'suggestion' or sub-conscious action of any kind. One might as well suppose a schoolboy 'suggesting' the existence of Aeschylus to himself, while he plods mechanically through the declensions.

"But you have noticed the obscurity," Ambrose went on, "and in this particular case it must have been dictated by instinct, since the writer never thought that her manuscripts would fall into other hands. But the practice is universal, and for most excellent reasons. Powerful and sovereign medicines, which are, of necessity, virulent poisons also, are kept in a locked cabinet. The child may find the key by chance, and drink herself dead; but in most cases the search is educational, and the phials contain precious elixirs for him who has patiently fashioned the key for himself."

"You do not care to go into details?"

"No, frankly, I do not. No, you must remain unconvinced. But you saw how the manuscript illustrates the talk we had last week?"

"Is this girl still alive?"

"No. I was one of those who found her. I knew the father well; he was a lawyer, and had always left her very much to herself. He thought of nothing but deeds and leases, and the news came to him as an awful surprise. She was missing one morning; I suppose it was about a year after she had written what you have read. The servants were called, and they told things, and put the only natural interpretation on them—a perfectly erroneous one.

"They discovered that green book somewhere in her room, and I found her in the place that she described with so much dread, lying on the ground before the image."

"It was an image?"

"Yes; it was hidden by the thorns and the thick undergrowth that had surrounded it. It was a wild, lonely country; but you know what it was like by her description, though of course you will understand that the colours have been heightened. A child's imagination always makes the heights higher and the depths deeper than they really are; and she had, unfortunately for herself, something more than imagination. One might say, perhaps, that the picture in her mind which she succeeded in a measure in putting into words, was the scene as it would have appeared to an imaginative artist. But it is a strange, desolate land."

"And she was dead?"

"Yes. She had poisoned herself—in time. No; there was not a word to be said against her in the ordinary sense. You may recollect a story I told you the other night about a lady who saw her child's fingers crushed by a window?"

"And what was this statue?"

"Well, it was of Roman workmanship, of a stone that with the centuries had not blackened, but had become white and luminous. The thicket had grown up about it and concealed it, and in the Middle Ages the followers of a very old tradition had known how to use it for their own purposes. In fact it had been incorporated into the monstrous mythology of the Sabbath. You will have noted that those to whom a sight of that shining whiteness had been vouchsafed by chance, or rather, perhaps, by apparent chance, were required to blindfold themselves on their second approach. That is very significant."

"And is it there still?"

"I sent for tools, and we hammered it into dust and fragments."

"The persistence of tradition never surprises me," Ambrose went on after a pause. "I could name many an English parish where such traditions as that girl had listened to in her childhood are still existent in occult but unabated vigour. No, for me, it is the 'story' not the 'sequel,' which is strange and awful, for I have always believed that wonder is of the soul."

WILLIAM HOPE HODGSON

The Voice in the Night (1907)

According to H. P. Lovecraft in *Supernatural Horror in Literature*, William Hope Hodgson is "second only to Algernon Blackwood" in the depiction of "the spectral and the abnormal." Spectral horror and abnormality are certainly the essence of "The Voice in the Night," Hodgson's bleakest, most frightening, and most influential story. The terrible force that pursues the hapless castaways in this story is, on the most obvious level (and like other fictional monstrosities from the period, such as those in E. F. Benson's "Caterpillars"), a metaphor for cancer. It is also connected to a larger sense of capricious malignancy and doom in the universe. Pursued by "something worse than death," the young lovers in this story are the archetypal lost souls of the genre; during the terrible eating scene, they feel profound guilt and shame, but the reality is that they are lost because of something utterly beyond their control.

"The Voice in the Night" opens and closes on the sea, Hodgson's favorite setting, which he evokes with a few deft, dark strokes. Hodgson's sea is a singularly inhospitable one, teeming with weedlike and fungoid creatures that give many of his stories a science-fiction flavor, although horror is the dominant emotion. Hodgson has a rather appalling fetish for fungus creatures, but he never explains where this "grey desolation" comes from; it sprouts from nowhere and is as mysterious as the sea itself.

≈ THE VOICE IN THE NIGHT ≈

It was a dark, starless night. We were becalmed in the Northern Pacific. Our exact position I do not know; for the sun had been hidden during the course of a weary, breathless week, by a thin haze which had seemed to float above us, about the height of our mastheads, at whiles descending and shrouding the surrounding sea.

With there being no wind, we had steadied the tiller, and I was the only man on deck. The crew, consisting of two men and a boy, were sleeping forrard in their den; while Will—my friend, and the master of our little craft—was aft in his bunk on the port side of the little cabin.

Suddenly, from out of the surrounding darkness, there came a hail: 'Schooner, ahoy!'

The cry was so unexpected that I gave no immediate answer, because of my surprise.

It came again—a voice curiously throaty and inhuman, calling from somewhere upon the dark sea away on our port broadside:

'Schooner, ahoy!'

'Hullo!' I sung out, having gathered my wits somewhat. 'What are you? What do you want?'

'You need not be afraid,' answered the queer voice, having probably noticed some trace of confusion in my tone. 'I am only an old—man.'

The pause sounded oddly; but it was only afterwards that it came back to me with any significance.

'Why don't you come alongside, then?' I queried somewhat snappishly; for I liked not his hinting at my having been a trifle shaken.

'I—I—can't. It wouldn't be safe. I—' The voice broke off, and there was silence.

'What do you mean?' I asked, growing more and more astonished. 'Why not safe? Where are you?'

I listened for a moment; but there came no answer. And then, a sudden indefinite suspicion, of I knew not what, coming to me, I stepped swiftly to the binnacle, and took out the lighted lamp. At the same time, I knocked on the deck with my heel to waken Will. Then I was back at the side, throwing the yellow funnel of light out into the silent immensity be-

267

yond our rail. As I did so, I heard a slight, muffled cry, and then the sound of a splash, as though someone had dipped oars abruptly. Yet I cannot say that I saw anything with certainty; save, it seemed to me, that with the first flash of the light, there had been something upon the waters, where now there was nothing.

'Hullo, there!' I called. 'What foolery is this!'

But there came only the indistinct sounds of a boat being pulled away into the night.

The I heard Will's voice, from the direction of the after scuttle:

'What's up, George?'

'Come here, Will!' I said.

'What is it?' he asked, coming across the deck.

I told him the queer things which had happened. He put several questions; then, after a moment's silence, he raised his hands to his lips, and hailed:

'Boat, ahoy!'

From a long distance away, there came back to us a faint reply, and my companion repeated his call. Presently, after a short period of silence, there grew on our hearing the muffled sound of oars; at which Will hailed again.

This time there was a reply:

'Put away the light.'

'I'm damned if I will,' I muttered; but Will told me to do as the voice bade, and I shoved it down under the bulwarks.

'Come nearer,' he said, and the oar-strokes continued. Then, when apparently some half-dozen fathoms distant, they again ceased.

'Come alongside,' exclaimed Will. 'There's nothing to be frightened of aboard here!'

'Promise that you will not show the light?'

'What's to do with you,' I burst out, 'that you're so infernally afraid of the light?'

'Because—' began the voice, and stopped short.

'Because what?' I asked, quickly.

Will put his hand on my shoulder.

'Shut up a minute, old man,' he said, in a low voice. 'Let me tackle him.'

He leant more over the rail.

'See here, Mister,' he said, 'this is a pretty queer business, you coming upon us like this, right out in the middle of the blessed Pacific. How are we to know what sort of hanky-panky trick you're up to? You say there's only one of you. How are we to know, unless we get a squint at you—eh? What's your objection to the light anyway?'

As he finished, I heard the noise of the oars again, and then the voice came; but now from a greater distance, and sounding extremely hopeless and pathetic.

'I am sorry—sorry! I would not have troubled you, only I am hungry, and—so is she.'

The voice died away, and the sound of the oars, dipping irregularly, was borne to us.

'Stop!' sung out Will. 'I don't want to drive you away. Come back! We'll keep the light hidden, if you don't like it.'

He turned to me:

'It's a damned queer rig, this; but I think there's nothing to be afraid of?'

There was a question in his tone, and I replied.

'No, I think the poor devil's been wrecked around here, and gone crazy.'

The sound of the oars drew nearer.

'Shove that lamp back in the binnacle,' said Will; then he leaned over the rail, and listened. I replaced the lamp, and came back to his side. The dipping of the oars ceased some dozen yards distant.

'Won't you come alongside now?' asked Will in an even voice. 'I have had the lamp put back in the binnacle.'

'I—I cannot,' replied the voice. 'I dare not come nearer. I dare not even pay you for the—the provisions.'

'That's all right,' said Will, and hesitated. 'You're welcome to as much grub as you can take—' Again he hesitated.

'You are very good,' exclaimed the voice. 'May God, Who understands everything, reward you—' It broke off huskily.

'The—the lady?' said Will, abruptly. 'Is she—'

'I have left her behind upon the island,' came the voice.

'What island?' I cut in.

'I know not its name,' returned the voice. 'I would to God—!' it began, and checked itself as suddenly.

'Could we not send a boat for her?' asked Will at this point.

'No!' said the voice, with extraordinary emphasis. 'My God! No!' There was a moment's pause; then it added, in a tone which seemed a merited reproach:

'It was because of our want I ventured— Because her agony tortured me.'

'I am a forgetful brute,' exclaimed Will. 'Just wait a minute, whoever you are, and I will bring you up something at once.'

In a couple of minutes he was back again, and his arms were full of various edibles. He paused at the rail.

'Can't you come alongside for them?' he asked.

'No—I *dare not*,' replied the voice, and it seemed to me that in its tones I detected a note of stifled craving—as though the owner hushed a mortal desire. It came to me then in a flash, that the poor old creature out there in the darkness, was *suffering* for actual need of that which Will held in his arms; and yet, because of some unintelligible dread, refraining from dashing to the side of our little schooner, and receiving it. And with the lightning-like conviction, there came the knowledge that the Invisible was not mad; but sanely facing some intolerable horror.

'Damn it, Will!' I said, full of many feelings, over which predominated a vast sympathy. 'Get a box. We must float off the stuff to him in it.'

This we did—propelling it away from the vessel, out into the darkness, by means of a boat-hook. In a minute, a slight cry from the Invisible came to us, and we knew that he had secured the box.

A little later, he called out a farewell to us, and so heartful a blessing, that I am sure we were the better for it. Then, without more ado, we heard the ply of oars across the darkness.

'Pretty soon off,' remarked Will, with perhaps just a little sense of injury.

'Wait,' I replied. 'I think somehow he'll come back. He must have been badly needing that food.'

'And the lady,' said Will. For a moment he was silent; then he continued:

'It's the queerest thing ever I've tumbled across, since I've been fishing.'

'Yes,' I said, and fell to pondering.

And so the time slipped away—an hour, another, and still Will stayed with me; for the queer adventure had knocked all desire for sleep out of him.

The third hour was three parts through, when we heard again the sound of oars across the silent ocean.

'Listen!' said Will, a low note of excitement in his voice.

'He's coming, just as I thought,' I muttered.

The dipping of the oars grew nearer, and I noted that the strokes were firmer and longer. The food had been needed.

They came to a stop a little distance off the broadside, and the queer voice came again to us through the darkness:

'Schooner, ahoy!'

'That you?' asked Will.

'Yes,' replied the voice. 'I left you suddenly; but—but there was great need.'

'The lady?' questioned Will.

'The—lady is grateful now on earth. She will be more grateful soon in—in heaven.'

Will began to make some reply, in a puzzled voice; but became confused, and broke off short. I said nothing. I was wondering at the curious pauses, and, apart from my wonder, I was full of a great sympathy.

The voice continued:

'We—she and I, have talked, as we shared the result of God's tenderness and yours—'

Will interposed; but without coherence.

'I beg of you not to—to belittle your deed of Christian charity this night,' said the voice. 'Be sure that it has not escaped His notice.'

It stopped, and there was a full minute's silence. Then it came again:

'We have spoken together upon that which—which has befallen us. We had thought to go out, without telling any, of the terror which has come into our—lives. She is with me in believing that tonight's happenings are under a special ruling, and that it is God's wish that we should tell you all that we have suffered since—since—'

'Yes?' said Will, softly.

'Since the sinking of the *Albatross.*'

'Ah!' I exclaimed, involuntarily. 'She left Newcastle for 'Frisco some six months ago, and hasn't been heard of since.'

'Yes,' answered the voice. 'But some few degrees to the North of the line she was caught in a terrible storm, and dismasted. When the day came, it was found that she was leaking badly, and, presently, it falling to a calm, the sailors took to the boats, leaving—leaving a young lady—my fiancée—and myself upon the wreck.

'We were below, gathering together a few of our belongings, when they left. They were entirely callous, through fear, and when we came up upon

the decks, we saw them only as small shapes afar off upon the horizon. Yet
we did not despair, but set to work and constructed a small raft. Upon this
we put such few matters as it would hold, including a quantity of water
and some ship's biscuit. Then, the vessel being very deep in the water, we
got ourselves on to the raft, and pushed off.

'It was later, when I observed that we seemed to be in the way of some
tide or current, which bore us from the ship at an angle; so that in the
course of three hours, by my watch, her hull became invisible to our
sight, her broken masts remaining in view for a somewhat longer period.
Then, towards evening, it grew misty, and so through the night. The next
day we were still encompassed by the mist, the weather remaining quiet.

'For four days, we drifted through this strange haze, until, on the evening of the fourth day, there grew upon our ears the murmur of breakers at
a distance. Gradually it became plainer, and, somewhat after midnight, it
appeared to sound upon either hand at no very great space. The raft was
raised upon a swell several times, and then we were in smooth water, and
the noise of the breakers was behind.

'When the morning came, we found that we were in a sort of great lagoon; but of this we noticed little at the time; for close before us, through
the enshrouding mist, loomed the hull of a large sailing-vessel. With one
accord, we fell upon our knees and thanked God; for we thought that here
was an end to our perils. We had much to learn.

'The raft drew near to the ship, and we shouted on them, to take us
aboard; but none answered. Presently, the raft touched the side of the
vessel, and, seeing a rope hanging downwards, I seized it and began to
climb. Yet I had much ado to make my way up, because of a kind of grey,
lichenous fungus, which had seized upon the rope, and which blotched
the side of the ship, lividly.

'I reached the rail, and clambered over it, on to the deck. Here, I saw
that the decks were covered, in great patches, with the grey masses, some
of them rising into nodules several feet in height; but at the time, I
thought less of this matter than of the possibility of there being people
aboard the ship. I shouted; but none answered. Then I went to the door
below the poop deck. I opened it, and peered in. There was a great smell of
staleness, so that I knew in a moment that nothing living was within, and
with the knowledge, I shut the door quickly; for I felt suddenly lonely.

'I went back to the side, where I had scrambled up. My—my sweetheart was still sitting quietly upon the raft. Seeing me look down, she

called up to know whether there were any aboard the ship. I replied that the vessel had the appearance of having been long deserted; but that if she would wait a little I would see whether there was anything in the shape of a ladder, by which she could ascend to the deck. Then we would make a search through the vessel together. A little later, on the opposite side of the decks, I found a rope side-ladder. This I carried across, and a minute afterwards, she was beside me.

'Together, we explored the cabins and apartments in the after-part of the ship; but nowhere was there any sign of life. Here and there, within the cabins themselves, we came across odd patches of that queer fungus; but this, as my sweetheart said, could be cleansed away.

'In the end, having assured ourselves that the after portion of the vessel was empty, we picked our ways to the bows, between the ugly grey nodules of that strange growth; and here we made a further search, which told us that there was indeed none aboard but ourselves.

'This being now beyond any doubt, we returned to the stern of the ship, and proceeded to make ourselves as comfortable as possible. Together, we cleared out and cleaned two of the cabins; and after that, I made examination whether there was anything eatable in the ship. This I soon found was so, and thanked God in my heart for His goodness. In addition to this, I discovered the whereabouts of the freshwater pump, and having fixed it, I found the water drinkable, though somewhat unpleasant to the taste.

'For several days, we stayed aboard the ship, without attempting to get to the shore. We were busily engaged in making the place habitable. Yet even thus early, we became aware that our lot was even less to be desired than might have been imagined; for though, as a first step, we scraped away the odd patches of growth that studded the floors and walls of the cabins and saloon, yet they returned almost to their original size within the space of twenty-four hours, which not only discouraged us, but gave us a feeling of vague unease.

'Still, we would not admit ourselves beaten, so set to work afresh, and not only scraped away the fungus, but soaked the places where it had been, with carbolic, a can-full of which I had found in the pantry. Yet, by the end of the week, the growth had returned in full strength, and, in addition, it had spread to other places, as though our touching it had allowed germs from it to travel elsewhere.

'On the seventh morning, my sweetheart woke to find a small patch of it growing on her pillow, close to her face. At that, she came to me, so soon as she could get her garments upon her. I was in the galley at the time, lighting the fire for breakfast.

' "Come here, John," she said, and led me aft. When I saw the thing upon her pillow, I shuddered, and then and there we agreed to go right out of the ship and see whether we could not fare to make ourselves more comfortable ashore.

'Hurriedly, we gathered together our few belongings, and even among these, I found that the fungus had been at work; for one of her shawls had a little lump of it growing near one edge. I threw the whole thing over the side, without saying anything to her.

'The raft was still alongside; but it was too clumsy to guide, and I lowered down a small boat that hung across the stern, and in this we made our way to the shore. Yet, as we drew near to it, I became gradually aware that here the vile fungus, which had driven us from the ship, was growing riot. In places it rose into horrible, fantastic mounds, which seemed almost to quiver, as with a quiet life, when the wind blew across them. Here and there, it took on the forms of vast fingers, and in others it just spread out flat and smooth and treacherous. Odd places, it appeared as grotesque stunted trees, seeming extraordinarily kinked and gnarled—The whole quaking vilely at times.

'At first, it seemed to us that there was no single portion of the surrounding shore which was not hidden beneath the masses of the hideous lichen; yet, in this, I found we were mistaken; for somewhat later, coasting along the shore at a little distance, we descried a smooth white patch of what appeared to be fine sand, and there we landed. It was not sand. What it was, I do not know. All that I have observed, is that upon it, the fungus will not grow; while everywhere else, save where the sand-like earth wanders oddly, pathwise, amid the grey desolation of the lichen, there is nothing but that loathsome greyness.

'It is difficult to make you understand how cheered we were to find one place that was absolutely free from the growth, and here we deposited our belongings. Then we went back to the ship for such things as it seemed to us we should need. Among other matters, I managed to bring ashore with me one of the ship's sails, with which I constructed two small tents, which, though exceedingly rough-shaped, served the purposes for which they were intended. In these, we lived and stored our various necessities, and thus for a matter of some four weeks, all went smoothly and without particular unhappiness. Indeed, I may say with much of happiness—for—for we were together.

'It was on the thumb of her right hand, that the growth first showed. It was only a small circular spot, much like a little grey mole. My God! how the fear leapt to my heart when she showed me the place. We cleaned it, between us, washing it with carbolic and water. In the morning of the following day, she showed her hand to me again. The grey warty thing had returned. For a little while we looked at one another in silence. Then, still wordless, we started again to remove it. In the midst of the operation, she spoke suddenly.

' "What's that on the side of your face, Dear!" Her voice was sharp with anxiety. I put my hand up to feel.

' "There! Under the hair by your ear.—A little to the front a bit." My finger rested upon the place, and then I knew.

' "Let us get your thumb done first," I said. And she submitted, only because she was afraid to touch me until it was cleansed. I finished washing and disinfecting her thumb, and then she turned to my face. After it was finished, we sat together and talked awhile of many things; for there had come into our lives sudden, very terrible thoughts. We were, all at once, afraid of something worse than death. We spoke of loading the boat with provisions and water, and making our way out on to the sea; yet we were helpless, for many causes, and—and the growth had attacked us already. We decided to stay. God would do with us what was His will. We would wait.

'A month, two months, three months passed, and the places grew somewhat, and there had come others. Yet we fought so strenuously with the fear, that its headway was but slow, comparatively speaking.

'Occasionally, we ventured off to the ship for such stores as we needed. There, we found that the fungus grew persistently. One of the nodules on the maindeck became soon as high as my head.

'We had now given up all thought or hope of leaving the island. We had realised that it would be unallowable to go among healthy humans with the thing from which we were suffering.

'With this determination and knowledge in our minds, we knew that we should have to husband our food and water; for we did not know, at that time, but that we should possibly live for many years.

'This reminds me that I have told you that I am an old man. Judged by years this is not so. But—but—'

He broke off; then continued somewhat abruptly:

'As I was saying, we knew that we should have to use care in the matter of food. But we had no idea then how little food there was left, of which to take care. It was a week later, that I made the discovery that all the other bread tanks—which I had supposed full—were empty, and that (beyond odd tins of vegetables and meat, and some other matters) we had nothing on which to depend, but the bread in the tank which I had already opened.

'After learning this, I bestirred myself to do what I could, and set to work at fishing in the lagoon; but with no success. At this, I was somewhat inclined to feel desperate, until the thought came to me to try outside the lagoon, in the open sea.

'Here, at times, I caught odd fish; but, so infrequently, that they proved of but little help in keeping us from the hunger which threatened. It seemed to me that our deaths were likely to come by hunger, and not by the growth of the thing which had seized upon our bodies.

'We were in this state of mind when the fourth month wore out. Then I made a very horrible discovery. One morning, a little before midday, I came off from the ship, with a portion of the biscuits which were left. In the mouth of her tent, I saw my sweetheart sitting, eating something.

' "What is it, my dear?" I called out as I leapt ashore. Yet, on hearing my voice, she seemed confused, and, turning, slyly threw something towards the edge of the little clearing. It fell short, and, a vague suspicion having arisen within me, I walked across and picked it up. It was a piece of the grey fungus.

'As I went to her, with it in my hand, she turned deadly pale; then a rose red.

'I felt strangely dazed and frightened.

' "My dear! My dear!" I said, and could say no more. Yet, at my words, she broke down and cried bitterly. Gradually, as she calmed, I got from her the news that she had tried it the preceding day, and—and liked it. I got her to promise on her knees not to touch it again, however great our hunger. After she had promised, she told me that the desire for it had come suddenly, and that, until the moment of desire, she had experienced nothing towards it, but the most extreme repulsion.

'Later in the day, feeling strangely restless, and much shaken with the thing which I had discovered, I made my way along one of the twisted paths—formed by the white, sand-like substance—which led among the fungoid growth. I had, once before, ventured along there; but not to any great distance. This time, being involved in perplexing thought, I went much further than hitherto.

'Suddenly, I was called to myself, by a queer hoarse sound on my left. Turning quickly, I saw that there was movement among an extraordinarily shaped mass of fungus, close to my elbow. It was swaying uneasily, as though it possessed life of its own. Abruptly, as I stared, the thought came to me that the thing had a grotesque resemblance to the figure of a distorted human creature. Even as the fancy flashed into my brain, there was a slight, sickening noise of tearing, and I saw that one of the branch-like arms was detaching itself from the surrounding grey masses, and coming towards me. The head of the thing—a shapeless grey ball, inclined in my direction. I stood stupidly, and the vile arm brushed across my face. I gave out a frightened cry, and ran back a few paces. There was a sweetish taste upon my lips, where the thing had touched me. I licked them, and was immediately filled with an inhuman desire. I turned and seized a mass of the fungus. Then more, and—more. I was insatiable. In the midst of devouring, the remembrance of the morning's discovery swept into my mazed brain. It was sent by God. I dashed the fragment I held, to the ground. Then, utterly wretched and feeling a dreadful guiltiness, I made my way back to the little encampment.

'I think she knew, by some marvelous intuition which love must have given, so soon as she set eyes on me. Her quiet sympathy made it easier for me, and I told her of my sudden weakness; yet omitted to mention the extraordinary thing which had gone before. I desired to spare her all unnecessary terror.

'But, for myself, I had added an intolerable knowledge, to breed an incessant terror in my brain; for I doubted not but that I had seen the end of one of those men who had come to the island in the ship in the lagoon; and in that monstrous ending, I had seen our own.

'Thereafter, we kept from the abominable food, though the desire for it had entered into our blood. Yet, our drear punishment was upon us; for, day by day, with monstrous rapidity, the fungoid growth took hold of our poor bodies. Nothing we could do would check it materially, and so— and so—we who had been human, became—Well, it matters less each day. Only—only we had been man and maid!

'And day by day, the fight is more dreadful, to withstand the hunger-lust for the terrible lichen.

'A week ago we ate the last of the biscuit, and since that time I have caught three fish. I was out here fishing tonight when your schooner drifted upon me out of the mist. I hailed you. You know the rest, and may God, out of His great heart, bless you for your goodness to a—a couple of poor outcast souls.'

There was the dip of an oar—another. Then the voice came again, and for the last time, sounding through the slight surrounding mist, ghostly and mournful.

'God bless you! Good-bye!'

'Good-bye,' we shouted together, hoarsely, our hearts full of many emotions.

I glanced about me. I became aware that the dawn was upon us.

The sun flung a stray beam across the hidden sea; pierced the mist dully, and lit up the receding boat with a gloomy fire. Indistinctly, I saw something nodding between the oars. I thought of a sponge—a great, grey nodding sponge—The oars continued to ply. They were grey—as was the boat—and my eyes searched a moment vainly for the conjunction of hand and oar. My gaze flashed back to the—head. It nodded forward as the oars went backward for the stroke. Then the oars were dipped, the boat shot out of the patch of light, and the—the thing went nodding into the mist.

T. H. WHITE

The Troll (1935)

Set in the Arctic Circle, the "outskirts of the world," this story by the author of *The Once and Future King* adroitly captures what Edmund Burke called "the sublime." With remarkably little exposition and the sparest of transitional devices, White moves us into a supremely danger-ous world with "no boundaries," a world where "the Old Things accumu-lated, like driftwood round the edges of the sea." The stark horror of the initial apparition scene—surely one of the most gruesome and fearful ap-paritions in literature—combined with the "stark happiness" of the lyrical and impressionistic mountain-climbing sequence create together a rich counterpoint representative of the ghost story at its peak of perfec-tion. Black magic, Christianity, "psychic" science, and agnosticism are all inextricably part of the texture of this story; each has a clear but ul-timately insignificant part to play in White's drama about the incompre-hensibility and unknowableness of the universe.

It is odd that a story as vivid as "The Troll" went virtually unnoticed for so many years, especially given the fame of its author. Only recently, with a revival of interest in White's short fiction as a whole (see bibliog-raphy), is the story beginning to be recognized as the diabolical little masterpiece it is. Especially riveting is the opening dream vision of blood erupting through a hotel door ("with a viscous ripple"), which admirers of Stanley Kubrick may connect with a similar blood sequence in Kubrick's film *The Shining*. The interesting thing is that White's version is more terrifying: "The Troll" shows us that language can be far more gripping—and more "cinematic"—than cinema itself.

$\sim$ THE TROLL $\sim$

"My father," said Mr. Marx, "used to say that an experience like the one I am about to relate was apt to shake one's interest in mundane matters. Naturally he did not expect to be believed, and he did not mind whether he was or not. He did not himself believe in the supernatural, but the thing happened, and he proposed to tell it as simply as possible. It was stupid of him to say that it shook his faith in mundane affairs, for it was just as mundane as anything else. Indeed the really frightening part about it was the horribly tangible atmosphere in which it took place. None of the outlines wavered in the least. The creature would have been less remarkable if it had been less natural. It seemed to overcome the usual laws without being immune to them.

"My father was a keen fisherman, and used to go to all sorts of places for his fish. On one occasion he made Abisko his Lapland base, a comfortable railway hotel, one hundred and fifty miles within the Arctic circle. He travelled the prodigious length of Sweden (I believe it is as far from the South of Sweden to the North, as it is from the South of Sweden to the South of Italy) in the electric railway, and arrived tired out. He went to bed early, sleeping almost immediately, although it was bright daylight outside; as it is in those parts throughout the night at that time of the year. Not the least shaking part of his experience was that it should all have happened under the sun.

"He went to bed early, and slept, and dreamt. I may as well make it clear at once, as clear as the outlines of that creature in the northern sun, that his story did not turn out to be a dream in the last paragraph. The division between sleeping and waking was abrupt, although the feeling of both was the same. They were both in the same sphere of horrible absurdity, though in the former he was asleep and in the latter almost terribly awake. He tried to be asleep several times.

"My father always used to tell one of his dreams, because it somehow seemed of a piece with what was to follow. He believed that it was a consequence of the thing's presence in the next room. My father dreamed of blood.

"It was the vividness of the dreams that was impressive, their minute detail and horrible reality. The blood came through the keyhole of a locked door which communicated with the next room. I suppose the two rooms had originally been designed *en suite*. It ran down the door panel with a viscous ripple, like the artificial one created in the conduit of Trumpingdon Street. But it was heavy, and smelt. The slow welling of it sopped the carpet and reached the bed. It was warm and sticky. My father woke up with the impression that it was all over his hands. He was rubbing his first two fingers together, trying to rid them of the greasy adhesion where the fingers joined.

"My father knew what he had got to do. Let me make it clear that he was now perfectly wide awake, but he knew what he had got to do. He got out of bed, under this irresistible knowledge, and looked through the keyhole into the next room.

"I suppose the best way to tell the story is simply to narrate it, without an effort to carry belief. The thing did not require belief. It was not a feeling of horror in one's bones, or a misty outline, or anything that needed to be given actuality by an act of faith. It was as solid as a wardrobe. You don't have to believe in wardrobes. They are there, with corners.

What my father saw through the keyhole in the next room was a Troll. It was eminently solid, about eight feet high, and dressed in brightly ornamented skins. It had a blue face, with yellow eyes, and on its head there was a woolly sort of nightcap with a red bobble on top. The features were Mongolian. Its body was long and sturdy, like the trunk of a tree. Its legs were short and thick, like the elephant's feet that used to be cut off for umbrella stands, and its arms were wasted: little rudimentary members like the forelegs of a kangaroo. Its head and neck were very thick and massive. On the whole, it looked like a grotesque doll.

"That was the horror of it. Imagine a perfectly normal golliwog (but without the association of a Christie minstrel) standing in the corner of a room, eight feet high. The creature was as ordinary as that, as tangible, as stuffed, and as ungainly at the joints: but it could move itself about.

"The Troll was eating a lady. Poor girl, she was tightly clutched to its breast by those rudimentary arms, with her head on a level with its mouth. She was dressed in a nightdress which had crumpled up under her armpits, so that she was a pitiful naked offering, like a classical picture of Andromeda. Mercifully, she appeared to have fainted.

"Just as my father applied his eye to the keyhole, the Troll opened its mouth and bit off her head. Then, holding the neck between the bright blue lips, he sucked the bare meat dry. She shrivelled, like a squeezed orange, and her heels kicked. The creature had a look of thoughtful ecstasy. When the girl seemed to have lost succulence as an orange she was lifted into the air. She vanished in two bites. The Troll remained leaning against the wall, munching patiently and casting its eyes about it with a vague benevolence. Then it leant forward from the low hips, like a jack-knife folding in half, and opened its mouth to lick the blood up from the carpet. The mouth was incandescent inside, like a gas fire, and the blood evaporated before its tongue, like dust before a vacuum cleaner. It straightened itself, the arms dangling before it in patient uselessness, and fixed its eyes upon the keyhole.

"My father crawled back to bed, like a hunted fox after fifteen miles. At first it was because he was afraid that the creature had seen him through the hole, but afterwards it was because of his reason. A man can attribute many night-time appearances to the imagination, and can ultimately persuade himself that creatures of the dark did not exist. But this was an appearance in a sunlit room, with all the solidity of a wardrobe and unfortunately almost none of its possibility. He spend the first ten minutes making sure that he was awake, and the rest of the night trying to hope that he was asleep. It was either that, or else he was mad.

"It is not pleasant to doubt one's sanity. There are no satisfactory tests. One can pinch oneself to see if one is asleep, but there are no means of determining the other problem. He spent some time opening and shutting his eyes, but the room seemed normal and remained unaltered. He also soused his head in a basin of cold water, without result. Then he lay on his back, for hours, watching the mosquitoes on the ceiling.

"He was tired when he was called. A bright Scandinavian maid admitted the full sunlight for him and told him that it was a fine day. He spoke to her several times, and watched her carefully, but she seemed to have no doubts about his behaviour. Evidently, then, he was not badly mad: and by now he had been thinking about the matter for so many hours that it had begun to get obscure. The outlines were blurring again, and he determined that the whole thing must have been a dream or a temporary delusion, something temporary, anyway, and finished with; so that there was no good in thinking about it longer. He got up, dressed himself fairly cheerfully, and went down to breakfast.

"These hotels used to be run extraordinary well. There was a hostess always handy in a little office off the hall, who was delighted to answer any questions, spoke every conceivable language, and generally made it her business to make the guests feel at home. The particular hostess at

Abisko was a lovely creature into the bargain. My father used to speak to her a good deal. He had an idea that when you had a bath in Sweden one of the maids was sent to wash you. As a matter of fact this sometimes used to be the case, but it was always an old maid and highly trusted. You had to keep yourself under water and this was supposed to confer a cloak of invisibility. If you popped your knee out she was shocked. My father had a dim sort of hope that the hostess would be sent to bathe him one day: and I dare say he would have shocked her a good deal. However, this is beside the point. As he passed through the hall something prompted him to ask about the room next to his. Had anybody, he enquired, taken number 23?

" 'But, yes,' said the lady manager with a bright smile, '23 is taken by a doctor professor from Upsala and his wife, such a charming couple!'

"My father wondered what the charming couple had been doing, whilst the Troll was eating the lady in the nightdress. However, he decided to think no more about it. He pulled himself together, and went in to breakfast. The Professor was sitting in an opposite corner (the manageress had kindly pointed him out), looking mild and shortsighted, by himself. My father thought he would go out for a long climb on the mountains, since exercise was evidently what his constitution needed.

"He had a lovely day. Lake Torne blazed a deep blue below him, for all its thirty miles, and the melting snow made a lacework of filigree round the tops of the surrounding mountain basin. He got away from the stunted birch trees, and the mossy bogs with the reindeer in them, and the mosquitoes, too. He forded something that might have been a temporary tributary of the Abiskojokk, having to take off his trousers to do so and tucking his shirt up round his neck. He wanted to shout, bracing himself against the glorious tug of the snow water, with his legs crossing each other involuntarily as they passed, and the boulders turning under his feet. His body made a bow wave in the water, which climbed and feathered on his stomach, on the upstream side. When he was under the opposite bank a stone turned in earnest, and he went in. He came up, shouting with laughter, and made out loud a remark which has since become a classic in my family, 'Thank God,' he said, 'I rolled up my sleeves.' He wrung out everything as best he could, and dressed again in the wet clothes, and set off up the shoulder of Niakatjavelk. He was dry and warm again in half a mile. Less than a thousand feet took him over the snow line, and there, crawling on hands and knees, he came face to face with what seemed to be the summit of ambition. He met an ermine. They were both on all fours, so that there was a sort of equality about the encounter, especially as the ermine was higher up than he was. They looked at each other for a fifth of a second, without saying anything, and then the ermine vanished. He searched for it everywhere in vain, for the snow was only patchy. My father sat down on a dry rock, to eat his well-soaked luncheon of chocolate and rye bread.

"Life is such unutterable hell, solely because it is sometimes beautiful. If we could only be miserable all the time, if there could be no such things as love or beauty or faith or hope, if I could be absolutely certain that my love would never be returned: how much more simple life would be. One could plod through the Siberian salt mines of existence without being bothered about happiness. Unfortunately the happiness is there. There is always the chance (about eight hundred and fifty to one) that another heart will come to mine. I can't help hoping, and keeping faith, and loving beauty. Quite frequently I am not so miserable as it would be wise to be. And there, for my poor father sitting on his boulder above the snow, was stark happiness beating at the gates.

"The boulder on which he was sitting had probably never been sat upon before. It was a hundred and fifty miles within the Arctic circle, on a mountain five thousand feet high, looking down on a blue lake. The lake was so long that he could have sworn it sloped away at the ends, proving to the naked eye that the sweet earth was round. The railway line and the half-dozen houses of Abisko were hidden in the trees. The sun was warm on the boulder, blue on the snow, and his body tingled smooth from the spate water. His mouth watered for the chocolate, just behind the tip of his tongue.

"And yet, when he had eaten the chocolate—perhaps it was heavy on his stomach—there was the memory of the Troll. My father fell suddenly into a black mood, and began to think about the supernatural. Lapland was beautiful in the summer, with the sun sweeping round the horizon day and night, and the small tree leaves twinkling. It was not the sort of place for wicked things. But what about the winter? A picture of the Arctic night came before him, with the silence and the snow. Then the legendary wolves and bears snuffled at the far encampments, and the nameless winter spirits moved on their darkling courses. Lapland had always been associated with sorcery, even by Shakespeare. It was at the outskirts of the world that the Old Things accumulated, like driftwood round the edges of the sea. If one wanted to find a wise woman, one went to the rims of the Hebrides; on the coast of Brittany one sought the mass of St. Secaire. And what an outskirt Lapland was! It was an outskirt not only of Europe, but of civilisation. It had no boundaries. The Lapps went with the reindeer, and where the reindeer were was Lapland. Curiously indefinite region, suitable to the indefinite things. The Lapps were not Christians. What a fund of power they must have had behind them, to resist the march of mind. All through the missionary centuries they had held to something: something had stood behind them, a power against Christ. My father realised with a shock that he was living in the age of the reindeer, a period contiguous to the mammoth and the fossil.

"Well, this was not what he had come out to do. He dismissed the nightmares with an effort, got up from his boulder, and began the scramble back to his hotel. It was impossible that a professor from Abisko could become a troll.

"As my father was going in to dinner that evening the manageress stopped him in the hall.

" 'We have had a day so sad,' she said. 'The poor Dr. Professor has disappeared his wife. She has been missing since last night. The Dr. Professor is inconsolable.'

"My father then knew for certain that he had lost his reason.

"He went blindly to dinner, without making any answer, and began to eat a thick sour-cream soup that was taken cold with pepper and sugar. The Professor was still sitting in his corner, a sandy-headed man with thick spectacles and a desolate expression. He was looking at my father, and my father, with the soup spoon half-way to his mouth, looked at him. You know that eye-to-eye recognition, when two people look deeply into each other's pupils, and burrow to the soul? It usually comes before love. I mean the clear, deep, milk-eyed recognition expressed by the poet Donne. Their eyebeams twisted and did thread their eyes upon a double string. My father recognised that the Professor was a Troll, and the Professor recognised my father's recognition. Both of them knew that the Professor had eaten his wife.

"My father put down his soup spoon, and the Professor began to grow. The top of his head lifted and expanded, like a great loaf rising in an oven; his face went red and purple, and finally blue; the whole ungainly upperworks began to sway and topple towards the ceiling. My father looked about him. The other diners were eating unconcernedly. Nobody else could see it, and he was definitely mad at last. When he looked at the Troll again, the creature bowed. The enormous superstructure inclined itself towards him from the hips, and grinned seductively.

"My father got up from his table experimentally, and advanced towards the Troll, arranging his feet on the carpet with excessive care. He did not find it easy to walk, or to approach the monster, but it was a question of his reason. If he was mad, he was mad; and it was essential that he should come to grips with the thing, in order to make certain.

"He stood before it like a small boy, and held out his hand, saying, 'Good-evening.'

" 'Ho! Ho!' said the Troll, 'little mannikin. And what shall I have for my supper to-night?'

"Then it held out its wizened furry paw and took my father by the hand.

"My father went straight out of the dining-room, walking on air. He found the manageress in the passage and held out his hand to her.

" 'I am afraid I have burnt my hand,' he said. 'Do you think you could tie it up?'

"The manageress said, 'But it is a very bad burn. There are blisters all over the back. Of course, I will bind it up at once.'

"He explained that he had burnt it on one of the spirit lamps at the sideboard. He could scarcely conceal his delight. One cannot burn oneself by being insane.

" 'I saw you talking to the Dr. Professor,' said the manageress, as she was putting on the bandage. 'He is a sympathetic gentleman, is he not?'

"The relief about his sanity soon gave place to other troubles. The Troll had eaten its wife and given him a blister, but it had also made an unpleasant remark about its supper that evening. It proposed to eat my father. Now very few people can have been in a position to decide what to do when a troll earmarks them for its next meal. To begin with, although it was a tangible Troll in two ways, it had been invisible to the other diners. This put my father in a difficult position. He could not, for instance, ask for protection. He could scarcely go to the manageress and say, 'Professor Skål is an odd kind of werewolf, ate his wife last night, and proposes to eat me this evening.' He would have found himself in a looney-bin at once. Besides, he was too proud to do this, and still too confused. Whatever the proofs and blisters, he did not find it easy to believe in professors that turned into Trolls. He had lived in the normal world all his life, and, at his age, it was difficult to start learning afresh. It would have been quite easy for a baby, who was still co-ordinating the world, to cope with the Troll situation: for my father, not. He kept trying to fit it in somewhere, without disturbing the universe. He kept telling himself that it was nonsense: one did not get eaten by professors. It was like having a fever, and telling oneself that it was all right, really, only a delirium, only something that would pass.

"There was that feeling on the one side, the desperate assertion of all the truths that he had learned so far, the tussle to keep the world from drifting, the brave but intimidated refusal to give in or to make a fool of himself.

"On the other side there was stark terror. However much one struggled to be merely deluded, or hitched up momentarily in an odd pocket of space-time, there was panic. There was the urge to go away as quickly as possible, to flee the dreadful Troll. Unfortunately the last train had left Abisko, and there was nowhere else to go.

"My father was not able to distinguish these trends of thought. For him they were at the time intricately muddled together. He was in a whirl. A proud man, and an agnostic, he stuck to his muddled guns alone. He was terribly afraid of the Troll, but he could not afford to admit its existence. All his mental processes remained hung up, whilst he talked on the terrace, in a state of suspended animation, with an American tourist who had come to Abisko to photograph the midnight sun.

"The American told my father that the Abisko railway was the northernmost electric railway in the world, that twelve trains passed through it every day travelling between Upsala and Narvik, that the population of Abo was 12,000 in 1862, and that Gustavus Adolphus ascended the throne of Sweden in 1611. He also gave some facts about Greta Garbo.

"My father told the American that a dead baby was required for the mass of St. Secaire, that an elemental was a kind of mouth in space that sucked at you and tried to gulp you down, that homeopathic magic was practised by the aborigines of Australia, and that a Lapland woman was careful at her confinement to have no knots or loops about her person, lest these should make the delivery difficult.

"The American, who had been looking at my father in a strange way for some time, took offense at this and walked away; so that there was nothing for it but to go to bed.

"My father walked upstairs on will power alone. His faculties seemed to have shrunk and confused themselves. He had to help himself with the banister. He seemed to be navigating himself by wireless, from a spot about a foot above his forehead. The issues that were involved had ceased to have any meaning, but he went on doggedly up the stairs, moved forward by pride and contrariety. It was physical fear that alienated him from his body, the same fear that he had felt as a boy, walking down long corridors to be beaten. He walked firmly up the stairs.

"Oddly enough, he went to sleep at once. He had climbed all day and been awake all night and suffered emotional extremes. Like a condemned man, who was to be hanged in the morning, my father gave the whole business up and went to sleep.

"He was woken at midnight exactly. He heard the American on the terrace below his window, explaining excitedly that there had been a cloud on the last two nights at 11:58, thus making it impossible to photograph the midnight sun. He heard the camera click.

"There seemed to be a sudden storm of hail and wind. It roared at his window-sill, and the window curtains lifted themselves taut, pointing horizontally into the room. The shriek and rattle of the tempest framed the window in a crescendo of growing sound, an increasing blizzard directed towards himself. A blue paw came over the sill.

"My father turned over and hid his head in the pillow. He could feel the domed head dawning at the window and the eyes fixing themselves upon the small of his back. He could feel the places physically, about four inches apart. They itched. Or else the rest of his body itched, except those places. He could feel the creature growing into the room, glowing like ice, and giving off a storm. His mosquito curtains rose in its afflatus, uncovering him, leaving him defenceless. He was in such an ecstasy of terror that he almost enjoyed it. He was like a bather plunging for the first time into freezing water and unable to articulate. He was trying to yell, but all he could do was to throw a series of hooting noises from his paralysed lungs. He became a part of the blizzard. The bedclothes were gone. He felt the Troll put out its hands.

"My father was an agnostic, but, like most idle men, he was not above having a bee in his bonnet. His favourite bee was the psychology of the Catholic Church. He was ready to talk for hours about psycho-analysis and the confession. His greatest discovery had been the rosary.

"The rosary, my father used to say, was intended solely as a factual occupation which calmed the lower centres of the mind. The automatic telling of the beads liberated the higher centres to meditate upon the mysteries. They were a sedative, like knitting or counting sheep. There was no better cure for insomnia than a rosary. For several years he had given up deep breathing or regular counting. When he was sleepless he lay on his back and told his beads, and there was a small rosary in the pocket of his pyjama coat.

"The Troll put out its hands, to take him round the waist. He became completely paralysed, as if he had been winded. The Troll put its hand upon the beads.

"They met, the occult forces, in a clash above my father's heart. There was an explosion, he said, a quick creation of power. Positive and negative. A flash, a beam. Something like the splutter with which the antenna of a tram meets its overhead wires again, when it is being changed about.

"The Troll made a high squealing noise, like a crab being boiled, and began rapidly to dwindle in size. It dropped my father and turned about, and ran wailing, as if it had been terribly burnt, for the window. Its colour waned as its size decreased. It was one of those air-toys now, that expire with a piercing whistle. It scrambled over the window-sill, scarcely larger than a little child, and sagging visibly.

"My father leaped out of bed and followed it to the window. He saw it drop on the terrace like a toad, gather itself together, stumble off, staggering and whistling like a bat, down the valley of the Abiskojokk.

"My father fainted.

"In the morning the manageress said, 'There has been such a terrible tragedy. The poor Dr. Professor was found this morning in the lake. The worry about his wife had certainly unhinged his mind.'

"A subscription for a wreath was started by the American, to which my father subscribed five shillings; and the body was shipped off next morning, on one of the twelve trains that travel between Upsala and Narvik every day."

R. MURRAY GILCHRIST

The Return (1894)

The forgotten tales of Robert Murray Gilchrist are good examples of the ghost stories of the Decadence. Rather hazy and unconvincing in their plots, they have rich atmosphere and wildly metaphoric language. Gilchrist, who was primarily a novelist, wrote only one collection of weird stories, *The Stone Dragon*, but it is a masterpiece—dazzling, eccentric, original, and unfortunately rare.

"The Return," a romantic tale involving two lovers meeting after a twenty-year separation, is a typically ornate story from the collection. The reader should not look for modern clarity or verisimilitude; the attraction of this story lies in the magic of its language. Exotic, otherworldly, and brilliantly artificial, Gilchrist's style evokes a highly perfumed dreamscape that fairly reeks of the 1890s. Beneath the surface glitter, however, lurks a subtle, deeply felt sense of mystery and terror. Gilchrist's descriptive powers are formidable: his ghoulish moons, vibrating trees, "snake-like ivy," and diabolical landscapes breathe a vivid life that overwhelms and compensates for the dated, effusive dialogue.

Despite their stagy language, the characters are nevertheless compelling and poignant, especially the women. The "strange horror" and "air of weary grief" surrounding the heroine's stepmother are almost palpable. As for the heroine herself, she chillingly embodies the story's central struggle between the seductive lures of love and death.

There is a powerful tension in this story, one typical of its period, between a passion for life and a fascination with corruption. This tension is felt in the structure of the narrative, which has nothing to do with the gradual build-up typical of the modern ghostly tale: the narrative ripens quickly, then just as suddenly droops and decays. "The Return" is in the tradition of Wilde and Machen, but Gilchrist's music, which is unrelenting and has no rests, is unmistakably his own.

290

≈ THE RETURN ≈

Five minutes ago I drew the window curtain aside and let the mellow sunset light contend with the glare from the girandoles. Below lay the orchard of Vernon Garth, rich in heavily flowered fruit-trees—yonder a medlar, here a pear, next a quince. As my eyes, unaccustomed to the day, blinked rapidly, the recollection came of a scene forty-five years past, and once more beneath the oldest tree stood the girl I loved, mischievously plucking yarrow, and, despite its evil omen, twining the snowy clusters in her black hair. Again her coquettish words rang in my ears: 'Make me thy lady! Make me the richest woman in England, and I promise thee, Brian, we shall be the happiest of God's creatures.' And I remembered how the mad thirst for gold filled me: how I trusted in her fidelity, and without reasoning or even telling her that I would conquer fortune for her sake, I kissed her sadly and passed into the world. Then followed a complete silence until the *Star of Europe*, the greatest diamond discovered in modern times, lay in my hand—a rough unpolished stone not unlike the lumps of spar I had often seen lying on the sandy lanes of my native county. This should be Rose's own, and all the others that clanked so melodiously in their leather bulse should go towards fulfilling her ambition. Rich and happy I should be soon, and should I not marry an untitled gentlewoman, sweet in her prime? The twenty years' interval of work and sleep was like a fading dream, for I was going home. The knowledge thrilled me so that my nerves were strung tight as iron ropes and I laughed like a young boy. And it was all because my home was to be in Rose Pascal's arms.

I crossed the sea and posted straight for Halkton village. The old hostelry was crowded. Jane Hopgarth, whom I remembered a ruddy-faced child, stood on the box-edged terrace, courtesying in matronly fashion to the departing mail-coach. A change in the sign-board drew my eye; the white lilies had been painted over with a mitre, and the name changed from the Pascal Arms to the Lord Bishop. Angrily aghast at this disloyalty, I cross-questioned the ostlers, who hurried to and fro, but failing to obtain any coherent reply I was fain to content myself with a mental denunciation of the times.

At last I saw Bow-Legged Jeffries, now bent double with age, sunning himself at his favourite place, the side of the horse-trough. As of old he was chewing a straw. No sign of recognition came over his face as he gazed at me, and I was shocked, because I wished to impart some of my gladness to a fellow-creature. I went to him, and after trying in vain to make him speak, held forth a gold coin. He rose instantly, grasped it with palsied fingers, and, muttering that the hounds were starting, hurried from my presence. Feeling half sad I crossed to the churchyard and gazed through the grated window of the Pascal burial chapel at the recumbent and undisturbed effigies of Geoffrey Pascal, gentleman, of Bretton Hall; and Margot Maltrevor his wife, with their quaint epitaph about a perfect marriage enduring for ever. Then, after noting the rankness of the docks and nettles, I crossed the worn stile and with footsteps surprising fleet passed towards the stretch of moorland at whose further end stands Bretton Hall.

Twilight had fallen ere I reached the cottage at the entrance of the park. This was in a ruinous condition: here and there sheaves in the thatched roof had parted and formed crevices through which smoke filtered. Some of the tiny windows had been walled up, and even where the glass remained snake-like ivy hindered any light from falling into their thick recesses.

The door stood open, although the evening was chill. As I approached, the heavy autumnal dew shook down from the firs and fell upon my shoulders. A bat, swooping in an undulation, struck between my eyes and fell to the grass, moaning querulously. I entered. A withered woman sat beside the peat fire. She held a pair of steel knitting-needles which she moved without cessation. There was no thread upon them, and when they clicked her lips twitched as if she had counted. Some time passed before I recognised Rose's foster-mother, Elizabeth Carless. The russet colour of her cheeks had faded and left a sickly grey; those sunken, dimmed eyes were utterly unlike the bright black orbs that had danced so mirthfully. Her stature, too, had shrunk. I was struck with wonder. Elizabeth could not be more than fifty-six years old. I had been away twenty years; Rose was fifteen when I left her, and I had heard Elizabeth say that she was only twenty-one at the time of her darling's weaning. But what a change! She had such an air of weary grief that my heart grew sick.

Advancing to her side I touched her arm. She turned, but neither spoke nor seemed aware of my presence. Soon, however, she rose, and helping herself along by grasping the scanty furniture, tottered to a window and peered out. Her right hand crept to her throat; she untied the string of her gown and took from her bosom a pomander set in a battered silver case. I cried out; Rose had loved that toy in her childhood; thousands of times we played ball with it. . . . Elizabeth held it to her mouth and mumbled it, as if it were a baby's hand. Maddened with impatience, I caught her shoulder and roughly bade her say where I should find Rose. But something awoke in her eyes, and she shrank away to the other side of the house-place: I followed; she cowered on the floor, looking at me with a strange horror. Her lips began to move, but they made no sound. Only when I crossed to the threshold did she rise; and then her head moved wildly from side to side, and her hands pressed close to her breast, as if the pain there were too great to endure.

I ran from the place, not daring to look back. In a few minutes I reached the balustraded wall of the Hall garden. The vegetation there was wonderfully luxuriant. As of old, the great blue and white Canterbury bells grew thickly, and those curious flowers to which tradition has given the name of 'Marie's Heart' still spread their creamy tendrils and blood-coloured bloom on every hand. But 'Pascal's Dribble,' the tiny spring whose water pulsed so fiercely as it emerged from the earth, has long since burst its bounds, and converted the winter garden into a swamp, where a miniature forest of queen-of-the-meadow filled the air with melancholy sweetness. The house looked as if no careful hand had touched it for years. The elements had played havoc with its oriels, and many of the latticed frames hung on single hinges. The curtain of the blue parlour hung outside, draggled and faded, and half hidden by a thick growth of bindweed.

With an almost savage force I raised my arm high above my head and brought my fist down upon the central panel of the door. There was no need for such violence, for the decayed fastenings made no resistance, and some of the rotten boards fell to the ground. As I entered the hall and saw the ancient furniture, once so fondly kept, now mildewed and crumbling to dust, quick sobs burst from my throat. Rose's spinet stood beside the door of the withdrawing-room. How many carols had we sung to its music! As I passed my foot struck one of the legs and the rickety structure groaned as if it were coming to pieces. I thrust out my hand to steady it, but at my touch the velvet covering of the lid came off and the tiny gilt ornaments rattled downwards. The moon was just rising and only half her disc was visible over the distant edge of the Hell Garden. The light in the room was very uncertain, yet I could see the keys of the instrument were stained brown, and bound together with thick cobwebs.

Whilst I stood beside it I felt an overpowering desire to play a country ballad with an over-word of 'Willow browbound.' The words in strict accordance with the melody are merry and sad by turns: at one time filled with light happiness, at another bitter as the voice of one bereaved for ever of joy. So I cleared off the spiders and began to strike the keys with my forefinger. Many were dumb, and when I struck them gave forth no sound save a peculiar sigh; but still the melody rhythmed as distinctly as if a low voice crooned it out of the darkness. Wearied with the bitterness, I turned away.

By now the full moonlight pierced the window and quivered on the floor. As I gazed on the tremulous pattern it changed into quaint devices of hearts, daggers, rings, and a thousand tokens more. All suddenly another object glided amongst them so quickly that I wondered whether my eyes had been at fault—a tiny satin shoe, stained crimson across the lappets. A revulsion of feeling came to my soul and drove away all my fear. I had seen that selfsame shoe white and unsoiled twenty years before, when vain, vain Rose danced amongst her reapers at the harvest-home. And my voice cried out in ecstasy, 'Rose, heart of mine! Delight of all the world's delights!'

She stood before me, wondering, amazed. Alas, so changed! The red-and-yellow silk shawl still covered her shoulders; her hair still hung in those eldritch curls. But the beautiful face had grown wan and tired, and across the forehead lines were drawn like silver threads. She threw her arms round my neck and, pressing her bosom heavily on mine, sobbed so piteously that I grew afraid for her, and drew back the long masses of hair which had fallen forward, and kissed again and again those lips that were too lovely for simile. Never came a word of chiding from them. 'Love,' she said, when she had regained her breath, 'the past struggle was sharp and torturing—the future struggle will be crueller still. What a great love yours was, to wait and trust for so long! Would that mine had been as powerful! Poor, weak heart that could not endure!'

The tones of a wild fear throbbed through all her speech, strongly, yet with insufficient power to prevent her feeling the tenderness of those moments. Often, timorously raising her head from my shoulder, she looked about and then turned with a soft, inarticulate, and glad murmur to hide her face on my bosom. I spoke fervently; told of the years spent away from her; how, when working in the diamond-fields she had ever been present in my fancy; how at night her name had fallen from my lips in my only prayer; how I had dreamed of her amongst the greatest in the land—the richest, and, I dare swear, the loveliest woman in the world. I grew warmer still: all the gladness which had been constrained for so long now burst wildly from my lips: a myriad of rich ideas resolved into words, which, being spoken, wove one long and delicious fit of passion. As we stood together, the moon brightened and filled the chamber with a light like the day's. The ridges of the surrounding moorland stood out in sharp relief.

Rose drank in my declarations thirstily, but soon interrupted me with a heavy sigh. 'Come away,' she said softly. 'I no longer live in this house. You must stay with me to-night. This place is so wretched now; for time, that in you and me has only strengthened love, has wrought much ruin here.'

Half leaning on me, she led me from the precincts of Bretton Hall. We walked in silence over the waste that crowns the valley of the Whitelands and, being near the verge of the rocks, saw the great pinewood sloping downwards, lighted near us by the moon, but soon lost in density. Along the mysterious line where the light changed into gloom, intricate shadows of withered summer bracken struck and receded in a mimic battle. Before us lay the Priests' Cliff. The moon was veiled by a grove of elms, whose ever-swaying branches alternately increased and lessened her brightness. This was a place of notoriety—a veritable Golgotha—a haunt fit only for demons. Murder and theft had been punished here; and to this day fireside stories are told of evil women dancing round that Druids' circle, carrying hearts plucked from gibbeted bodies.

'Rose,' I whispered, 'why have you brought me here?'

She made no reply, but pressed her head more closely to my shoulder. Scarce had my lips closed ere a sound like the hiss of a half-strangled snake vibrated amongst the trees. It grew louder and louder. A monstrous shadow hovered above.

Rose from my bosom murmured. 'Love is strong as Death! Love is strong as Death!'

I locked her in my arms, so tightly that she grew breathless. 'Hold me,' she panted. 'You are strong.'

A cold hand touched our foreheads so that, benumbed, we sank together to the ground, to fall instantly into a dreamless slumber.

When I awoke the clear grey light of the early morning had spread over the country. Beyond the Hell Garden the sun was just bursting through the clouds, and had already spread a long golden haze along the horizon. The babbling of the streamlet that runs down to Halkton was so distinct that it seemed almost at my side. How sweetly the wild thyme smelt! Filled with tender recollections of the night, without turning, I called Rose Pascal from her sleep.

'Sweetheart, sweetheart, waken! waken! waken! See how glad the world looks—see the omens of a happy future.'

No answer came. I sat up, and looking round me saw that I was alone. A square stone lay near. When the sun was high I crept to read the inscription carved thereon:—'*Here, at four cross-paths, lieth, with a stake through the bosom, the body of Rose Pascal, who in her sixteenth year wilfully cast away the life God gave.*'

ALGERNON BLACKWOOD

A Haunted Island (1906)

This gripping story is one of the many Algernon Blackwood master-pieces that has been relegated to almost total obscurity. Unlike the expansive narrative in Blackwood's more familiar works such as "The Willows" and "The Wendigo," "A Haunted Island" has an unusual tautness and momentum. Also unusual is the diversity of shuddery effects Blackwood compresses into a single story. Although Blackwood is best known for his outdoor tales, he is similar to E. F. Benson in that he could also turn out haunted-house tales ("The Listener," "The Occupant of the Room") as claustrophobic as those of Poe. In "A Haunted Island" he combines both types of story, moving in and out between the magnificent desolation of a remote Canadian island and the cramped nightmarishness of a supernaturally besieged cottage. This is one of Blackwood's most cinematic and sensual tales; in addition to truly bold spectral imagery, Blackwood delivers a sonorous range of natural and "psychical" sounds, from overtly Gothic thunder to "ominous and over-whelming silence."

The plot involves intertwining dimensions and planes of existence, a motif also popular in science fiction. The notion of death as another dimension that occasionally collides with or penetrates our own is also found in Wells's "Plattner Story," although Wells's tidy narrative is worlds apart from Blackwood's primitivistic atmosphere. Blackwood is far more radical and immediate than the supremely civilized Wells: in "The Plattner Story," "the world of the dead" is a foreign country; here it is brought dismayingly close to home.

A HAUNTED ISLAND

The following events occurred on a small island of isolated position in a large Canadian lake, to whose cool waters the inhabitants of Montreal and Toronto flee for rest and recreation in the hot months. It is only to be regretted that events of such peculiar interest to the genuine student of the psychical should be entirely uncorroborated. Such unfortunately, however, is the case.

Our own party of nearly twenty had returned to Montreal that very day, and I was left in solitary possession for a week or two longer, in order to accomplish some important 'reading' for the law which I had foolishly neglected during the summer.

It was late in September, and the big trout and maskinonge were stirring themselves in the depths of the lake, and beginning slowly to move up to the surface waters as the north winds and early frosts lowered their temperature. Already the maples were crimson and gold, and the wild laughter of the loons echoed in sheltered bays that never knew their strange cry in the summer.

With a whole island to oneself, a two-storey cottage, a canoe, and only the chipmunks, and the farmer's weekly visit with eggs and bread, to disturb one, the opportunities for hard reading might be very great. It all depends!

The rest of the party had gone off with many warnings to beware of Indians, and not to stay late enough to be the victim of a frost that thinks nothing of forty below zero. After they had gone, the loneliness of the situation made itself unpleasantly felt. There were no other islands within six or seven miles, and though the mainland forests lay a couple of miles behind me, they stretched for a very great distance unbroken by any signs of human habitation. But, though the island was completely deserted and silent, the rocks and trees that had echoed human laughter and voices almost every hour of the day for two months could not fail to retain some memories of it all; and I was not surprised to fancy I heard a shout or a cry as I passed from rock to rock, and more than once to imagine that I heard my own name called aloud.

In the cottage there were six tiny little bedrooms divided from one another by plain unvarnished partitions of pine. A wooden bedstead, a mattress, and a chair, stood in each room, but I only found two mirrors, and one of these was broken.

The boards creaked a good deal as I moved about, and the signs of occupation were so recent that I could hardly believe I was alone. I half expected to find someone left behind, still trying to crowd into a box more than it would hold. The door of one room was stiff, and refused for a moment to open, and it required very little persuasion to imagine someone was holding the handle on the inside, and that when it opened I should meet a pair of human eyes.

A thorough search of the floor led me to select as my own sleeping quarters a little room with a diminutive balcony over the verandah roof. The room was very small, but the bed was large, and had the best mattress of them all. It was situated directly over the sitting-room where I should live and do my 'reading', and the miniature window looked out to the rising sun. With the exception of a narrow path which led from the front door and verandah through the trees to the boat-landing, the island was densely covered with maples, hemlocks, and cedars. The trees gathered in round the cottage so closely that the slightest wind made the branches scrape the roof and tap the wooden walls. A few moments after sunset the darkness became impenetrable, and ten yards beyond the glare of the lamps that shone through the sitting-room windows—of which there were four—you could not see an inch before your nose, nor move a step without running up against a tree.

The rest of that day I spent moving my belongings from my tent to the sitting-room, taking stock of the contents of the larder, and chopping enough wood for the stove to last me for a week. After that, just before sunset, I went round the island a couple of times in my canoe for precaution's sake. I had never dreamed of doing this before, but when a man is alone he does things that never occur to him when he is one of a large party.

How lonely the island seemed when I landed again! The sun was down, and twilight is unknown in these northern regions. The darkness comes up at once. The canoe safely pulled up and turned over on her face, I groped my way up the little narrow pathway to the verandah. The six lamps were soon burning merrily in the front room; but in the kitchen, where I 'dined', the shadows were so gloomy, and the lamplight so inadequate, that the stars could be seen peeping through the cracks between the rafters.

I turned in early that night. Though it was calm and there was no wind, the creaking of my bedstead and the musical gurgle of the water over the rocks below were not the only sounds that reached my ears. As I lay awake, the appalling emptiness of the house grew upon me. The corridors and vacant rooms seemed to echo innumerable footsteps, shufflings, the rustle of skirts, and a constant undertone of whispering. When sleep at length overtook me, the breathings and noises, however, passed gently to mingle with the voices of my dreams.

A week passed by, and the 'reading' progressed favourably. On the tenth day of my solitude, a strange thing happened. I awoke after a good night's sleep to find myself possessed with a marked repugnance for my room. The air seemed to stifle me. The more I tried to define the cause of this dislike, the more unreasonable it appeared. There was something about the room that made me afraid. Absurd as it seems, this feeling clung to me obstinately while dressing, and more than once I caught myself shivering, and conscious of an inclination to get out of the room as quickly as possible. The more I tried to laugh it away, the more real it became; and when at last I was dressed, and went out into the passage, and downstairs into the kitchen, it was with feelings of relief, such as I might imagine would accompany one's escape from the presence of a dangerous contagious disease.

While cooking my breakfast, I carefully recalled every night spent in the room, in the hope that I might in some way connect the dislike I now felt with some disagreeable incident that had occurred in it. But the only thing I could recall was one stormy night when I suddenly awoke and heard the boards creaking so loudly in the corridor that I was convinced there were people in the house. So certain was I of this, that I had descended the stairs, gun in hand, only to find the doors and windows securely fastened, and the mice and black-beetles in sole possession of the floor. This was certainly not sufficient to account for the strength of my feelings.

The morning hours I spent in steady reading; and when I broke off in the middle of the day for a swim and luncheon, I was very much surprised, if not a little alarmed, to find that my dislike for the room had, if anything, grown stronger. Going upstairs to get a book, I experienced the most marked aversion to entering the room, and while within I was conscious all the time of an uncomfortable feeling that was half uneasiness and half apprehension. The result of it was that, instead of reading, I spent the afternoon on the water paddling and fishing, and when I got home about sundown, brought with me half a dozen delicious black bass for the supper-table and the larder.

As sleep was an important matter to me at this time, I had decided that if my aversion to the room was so strongly marked on my return as it had been before, I would move my bed down into the sitting-room, and sleep there. This was, I argued, in no sense a concession to an absurd and fanciful fear, but simply a precaution to ensure a good night's sleep. A bad night involved the loss of the next day's reading,—a loss I was not prepared to incur.

I accordingly moved my bed downstairs into a corner of the sitting-room facing the door, and was moreover uncommonly glad when the operation was completed, and the door of the bedroom closed finally upon the shadows, the silence, and the strange *fear* that shared the room with them.

The croaking stroke of the kitchen clock sounded the hour of eight as I finished washing up my few dishes, and closing the kitchen door behind me, passed into the front room. All the lamps were lit, and their reflectors, which I had polished up during the day, threw a blaze of light into the room.

Outside the night was still and warm. Not a breath of air was stirring; the waves were silent, the trees motionless, and heavy clouds hung like an oppressive curtain over the heavens. The darkness seemed to have rolled up with unusual swiftness, and not the faintest glow of colour remained to show where the sun had set. There was present in the atmosphere that ominous and overwhelming silence which so often precedes the most violent storms.

I sat down to my books with my brain unusually clear, and in my heart the pleasant satisfaction of knowing that five black bass were lying in the ice-house, and that tomorrow morning the old farmer would arrive with fresh bread and eggs. I was soon absorbed in my books.

As the night wore on the silence deepened. Even the chipmunks were still; and the boards of the floors and walls ceased creaking. I read on steadily till, from the gloomy shadows of the kitchen, came the hoarse sound of the clock striking nine. How loud the strokes sounded! They were like blows of a big hammer. I closed one book and opened another, feeling that I was just warming up to my work.

This, however, did not last long. I presently found that I was reading the same paragraphs over twice, simple paragraphs that did not require such effort. Then I noticed that my mind began to wander to other things, and the effort to recall my thoughts became harder with each digression. Concentration was growing momentarily more difficult. Presently I discovered that I had turned over two pages instead of one, and had not noticed my mistake until I was well down the page. This was becoming serious. What was the disturbing influence? It could not be physical fatigue. On the contrary, my mind was unusually alert, and in a more receptive condition than usual. I made a new and determined effort to read, and for a short time succeeded in giving my whole attention to my subject. But in a very few moments again I found myself leaning back in my chair, staring vacantly into space.

Something was evidently at work in my subconsciousness. There was something I had neglected to do. Perhaps the kitchen door and windows were not fastened. I accordingly went to see, and found that they were! The fire perhaps needed attention. I went to see, and found that it was all right! I looked at the lamps, went upstairs into every bedroom in turn, and then went round the house, and even into the ice-house. Nothing was wrong; everything was in its place. Yet something *was* wrong! The conviction grew stronger and stronger within me.

When I at length settled down to my books again and tried to read, I became aware, for the first time, that the room seemed growing cold. Yet the day had been oppressively warm, and evening had brought no relief. The six big lamps, moreover, gave out heat enough to warm the room pleasantly. But a chilliness, that perhaps crept up from the lake, made itself felt in the room, and caused me to get up to close the glass door opening on to the verandah.

For a brief moment I stood looking out at the shaft of light that fell from the windows and shone some little distance down the pathway, and out for a few feet into the lake.

As I looked, I saw a canoe glide into the pathway of light, and immediately crossing it, pass out of sight again into the darkness. It was perhaps a hundred feet from the shore, and it moved swiftly.

I was surprised that a canoe should pass the island at that time of night, for all the summer visitors from the other side of the lake had gone home weeks before, and the island was a long way out of any line of water traffic.

My reading from this moment did not make very good progress, for somehow the picture of that canoe, gliding so dimly and swiftly across the narrow track of light on the black waters, silhouetted itself against the background of my mind with singular vividness. It kept coming between

my eyes and the printed page. The more I thought about it the more surprised I became. It was of larger build than any I had seen during the past
summer months, and was more like the old Indian war canoes with the
high curving bows and stern and wide beam. The more I tried to read, the
less success attended my efforts; and finally I closed my books and went
out on the verandah to walk up and down a bit, and shake the chilliness
out of my bones.

The night was perfectly still, and as dark as imaginable. I stumbled
down the path to the little landing wharf, where the water made the very
faintest of gurgling under the timbers. The sound of a big tree falling in
the mainland forest, far across the lake, stirred echoes in the heavy air,
like the first guns of a distant night attack. No other sound disturbed the
stillness that reigned supreme.

As I stood upon the wharf in the broad splash of light that followed me
from the sitting-room windows, I saw another canoe cross the pathway of
uncertain light upon the water, and disappear at once into the impenetrable gloom that lay beyond. This time I saw more distinctly than before.
It was like the former canoe, a big birch-bark, with high-crested bows and
stern and broad beam. It was paddled by two Indians, of whom the one in
the stern—the steerer—appeared to be a very large man. I could see this
very plainly; and though the second canoe was much nearer the island
than the first, I judged that they were both on their way home to the
Government Reservation, which was situated some fifteen miles away
upon the mainland.

I was wondering in my mind what could possibly bring any Indians
down to this part of the lake at such an hour of the night, when a third
canoe, of precisely similar build, and also occupied by two Indians, passed
silently round the end of the wharf. This time the canoe was very much
nearer shore, and it suddenly flashed into my mind that the three canoes
were in reality one and the same, and that only one canoe was circling the
island!

This was by no means a pleasant reflection, because, if it were the correct solution of the unusual appearance of the three canoes in this lonely
part of the lake at so late an hour, the purpose of the two men could only
reasonably be considered to be in some way connected with myself. I had
never known of the Indians attempting any violence upon the settlers
who shared the wild, inhospitable country with them; at the same time, it
was not beyond the region of possibility to suppose . . . But then I did
not care even to think of such hideous possibilities, and my imagination

immediately sought relief in all manner of other solutions to the problem, which indeed came readily enough to my mind, but did not succeed in recommending themselves to my reason.

Meanwhile, by a sort of instinct, I stepped back out of the bright light in which I had hitherto been standing, and waited in the deep shadow of a rock to see if the canoe would again make its appearance. Here I could see, without being seen, and the precaution seemed a wise one.

After less than five minutes the canoe, as I had anticipated, made its fourth appearance. This time it was not twenty yards from the wharf, and I saw that the Indians meant to land. I recognized the two men as those who had passed before, and the steerer was certainly an immense fellow. It was unquestionably the same canoe. There could be no longer any doubt that for some purpose of their own the men had been going round and round the island for some time, waiting for an opportunity to land. I strained my eyes to follow them in the darkness, but the night had completely swallowed them up, and not even the faintest swish of the paddles reached my ears as the Indians plied their long and powerful strokes. The canoe would be round again in a few moments, and this time it was possible that the men might land. It was well to be prepared. I knew nothing of their intentions, and two to one (when the two are big Indians!) late at night on a lonely island was not exactly my idea of pleasant intercourse.

In a corner of the sitting-room, leaning up against the back wall, stood my Marlin rifle, with ten cartridges in the magazine and one lying snugly in the greased breech. There was just time to get up to the house and take up a position of defence in that corner. Without an instant's hesitation I ran up to the verandah, carefully picking my way among the trees, so as to avoid being seen in the light. Entering the room, I shut the door leading to the verandah, and as quickly as possible turned out every one of the six lamps. To be in a room so brilliantly lighted, where my every movement could be observed from outside, while I could see nothing but impenetrable darkness at every window, was by all laws of warfare an unnecessary concession to the enemy. And this enemy, if enemy it was to be, was far too wily and dangerous to be granted any such advantages.

I stood in the corner of the room with my back against the wall, and my hand on the cold rifle-barrel. The table, covered with my books, lay between me and the door, but for the first few minutes after the lights were out the darkness was so intense that nothing could be discerned at all. Then, very gradually, the outline of the room became visible, and the framework of the windows began to shape itself dimly before my eyes.

After a few minutes the door (its upper half of glass), and the two windows that looked out upon the front verandah, became specially distinct; and I was glad that this was so, because if the Indians came up to the house I should be able to see their approach, and gather something of their plans. Nor was I mistaken, for there presently came to my ears the peculiar hollow sound of a canoe landing and being carefully dragged up over the rocks. The paddles I distinctly heard being placed underneath, and the silence that ensued thereupon I rightly interpreted to mean that the Indians were stealthily approaching the house. . . .

While it would be absurd to claim that I was not alarmed—even frightened—at the gravity of the situation and its possible outcome, I speak the whole truth when I say that I was not overwhelmingly afraid for myself. I was conscious that even at this stage of the night I was passing into a psychical condition in which my sensations seemed no longer normal. Physical fear at no time entered into the nature of my feelings; and though I kept my hand upon my rifle the greater part of the night, I was all the time conscious that its assistance could be of little avail against the terrors that I had to face. More than once I seemed to feel most curiously that I was in no real sense a part of the proceedings, nor actually involved in them, but that I was playing the part of a spectator—a spectator, moreover, on a psychic rather than on a material plane. Many of my sensations that night were too vague for definite description and analysis, but the main feeling that will stay with me to the end of my days is the awful horror of it all, and the miserable sensation that if the strain had lasted a little longer than was actually the case my mind must inevitably have given way.

Meanwhile I stood still in my corner, and waited patiently for what was to come. The house was as still as the grave, but the inarticulate voices of the night sang in my ears, and I seemed to hear the blood running in my veins and dancing in my pulses.

If the Indians came to the back of the house, they would find the kitchen door and window securely fastened. They could not get in there without making considerable noise, which I was bound to hear. The only mode of getting in was by means of the door that faced me, and I kept my eyes glued on that door without taking them off for the smallest fraction of a second.

My sight adapted itself every minute better to the darkness. I saw the table that nearly filled the room, and left only a narrow passage on each side. I could also make out the straight backs of the wooden chairs pressed up against it, and could even distinguish my papers and inkstand lying on the white oilcloth covering. I thought of the gay faces that had gathered round that table during the summer, and I longed for the sunlight as I had never longed for it before.

Less than three feet to my left the passage-way led to the kitchen, and the stairs leading to the bedrooms above commenced in this passage-way, but almost in the sitting-room itself. Through the windows I could see the dim motionless outlines of the trees: not a leaf stirred, not a branch moved.

A few moments of this awful silence, and then I was aware of a soft tread on the boards of the verandah, so stealthy that it seemed an impression directly on my brain rather than upon the nerves of hearing. Immediately afterwards a black figure darkened the glass door, and I perceived that a face was pressed against the upper panes. A shiver ran down my back, and my hair was conscious of a tendency to rise and stand at right angles to my head.

It was the figure of an Indian, broad-shouldered and immense; indeed, the largest figure of a man I have ever seen outside of a circus hall. By some power of light that seemed to generate itself in the brain, I saw the strong dark face with the aquiline nose and high cheek-bones flattened against the glass. The direction of the gaze I could not determine; but faint gleams of light as the big eyes rolled round and showed their whites, told me plainly that no corner of the room escaped their searching.

For what seemed fully five minutes the dark figure stood there, with the huge shoulders bent forward so as to bring the head down to the level of the glass; while behind him, though not nearly so large, the shadowy form of the other Indian swayed to and fro like a bent tree. While I waited in an agony of suspense and agitation for their next movement little currents of icy sensation ran up and down my spine and my heart seemed alternately to stop beating and then start off again with terrifying rapidity. They must have heard its thumping and the singing of the blood in my head! Moreover, I was conscious, as I felt a cold stream of perspiration trickle down my face, of a desire to scream, to shout, to bang the walls like a child, to make a noise, or do anything that would relieve the suspense and bring things to a speedy climax.

It was probably this inclination that led me to another discovery, for when I tried to bring my rifle from behind my back to raise it and have it pointed at the door ready to fire, I found that I was powerless to move.

The muscles, paralysed by this strange fear, refused to obey the will. Here indeed was a terrifying complication!

*

There was a faint sound of rattling at the brass knob, and the door was pushed open a couple of inches. A pause of a few seconds, and it was pushed open still further. Without a sound of footsteps that was appreciable to my ears, the two figures glided into the room, and the man behind gently closed the door after him.

They were alone with me between the four walls. Could they see me standing there, so still and straight in my corner? Had they, perhaps, already seen me? My blood surged and sang like the roll of drums in an orchestra; and though I did my best to suppress my breathing, it sounded like the rushing of wind through a pneumatic tube.

My suspense as to the next move was soon at an end—only, however, to give place to a new and keener alarm. The men had hitherto exchanged no words and no signs, but there were general indications of a movement across the room, and whichever way they went they would have to pass round the table. If they came my way they would have to pass within six inches of my person. While I was considering this very disagreeable possibility, I perceived that the smaller Indian (smaller by comparison) suddenly raised his arm and pointed to the ceiling. The other fellow raised his head and followed the direction of his companion's arm. I began to understand at last. They were going upstairs, and the room directly overhead to which they pointed had been until this night my bedroom. It was the room in which I had experienced that very morning so strange a sensation of fear, and but for which I should then have been lying asleep in the narrow bed against the window.

The Indians then began to move silently around the room; they were going upstairs, and they were coming round my side of the table. So stealthy were their movements that, but for the abnormally sensitive state of the nerves, I should never have heard them. As it was, their cat-like tread was distinctly audible. Like two monstrous black cats they came round the table toward me, and for the first time I perceived that the smaller of the two dragged something along the floor behind him. As it trailed along over the floor with a soft, sweeping sound, I somehow got the impression that it was a large dead thing with outstretched wings, or a large, spreading cedar branch. Whatever it was, I was unable to see it even in outline, and I was too terrified, even had I possessed the power over my muscles, to move my neck forward in the effort to determine its nature.

Nearer and nearer they came. The leader rested a giant hand upon the table as he moved. My lips were glued together, and the air seemed to burn in my nostrils. I tried to close my eyes, so that I might not see as they passed me; but my eyelids had stiffened, and refused to obey. Would they never get by me? Sensation seemed also to have left my legs, and it was as if I were standing on mere supports of wood or stone. Worse still, I was conscious that I was losing the power of balance, the power to stand upright, or even to lean backwards against the wall. Some force was drawing me forward, and a dizzy terror seized me that I should lose my balance, and topple forward against the Indians just as they were in the act of passing me.

Even moments drawn out into hours must come to an end some time, and almost before I knew it the figures had passed me and had their feet upon the lower step of the stairs leading to the upper bedrooms. There could not have been six inches between us, and yet I was conscious only of a current of cold air that followed them. They had not touched me, and I was convinced that they had not seen me. Even the trailing thing on the floor behind them had not touched my feet, as I had dreaded it would, and on such an occasion as this I was grateful even for the smallest mercies.

The absence of the Indians from my immediate neighbourhood brought little sense of relief. I stood shivering and shuddering in my corner, and, beyond being able to breathe more freely, I felt no whit less uncomfortable. Also, I was aware that a certain light, which, without apparent source or rays, had enabled me to follow their every gesture and movement, had gone out of the room with their departure. An unnatural darkness now filled the room, and pervaded its every corner so that I could barely make out the positions of the windows and the glass doors.

As I said before, my condition was evidently an abnormal one. The capacity for feeling surprise seemed, as in dreams, to be wholly absent. My senses recorded with unusual accuracy every smallest occurrence, but I was able to draw only the simplest deductions.

The Indians soon reached the top of the stairs, and there they halted for a moment. I had not the faintest clue as to their next movement. They appeared to hesitate. They were listening attentively. Then I heard one of them, who by the weight of his soft tread must have been the giant, cross the narrow corridor and enter the room directly overhead—my own little bedroom. But for the insistence of that unaccountable dread I had experienced there in the morning, I should at that very moment have been lying in the bed with the big Indian in the room standing beside me.

For the space of a hundred seconds there was silence, such as might have existed before the birth of sound. It was followed by a long quivering shriek of terror, which rang out into the night, and ended in a short gulp before it had run its full course. At the same moment the other Indian left his place at the head of the stairs, and joined his companion in the bedroom. I heard the 'thing' trailing behind him along the floor. A thud followed, as of something heavy falling, and then all became as still and silent as before.

It was at this point that the atmosphere, surcharged all day with the electricity of a fierce storm, found relief in a dancing flash of brilliant lightning simultaneously with a crash of loudest thunder. For five seconds every article in the room was visible to me with amazing distinctness, and through the windows I saw the tree trunks standing in solemn rows. The thunder pealed and echoed across the lake and among the distant islands, and the flood-gates of heaven then opened and let out their rain in streaming torrents.

The drops fell with a swift rushing sound upon the still waters of the lake, which leaped up to meet them, and pattered with the rattle of shot on the leaves of the maples and the roof of the cottage. A moment later, and another flash, even more brilliant and of longer duration than the first, lit up the sky from zenith to horizon, and bathed the room momentarily in dazzling whiteness. I could see the rain glistening on the leaves and branches outside. The wind rose suddenly, and in less than a minute the storm that had been gathering all day burst forth in its full fury.

Above all the noisy voices of the elements, the slightest sounds in the room overhead made themselves heard, and in the few seconds of deep silence that followed the shriek of terror and pain, I was aware that the movements had commenced again. The men were leaving the room and approaching the top of the stairs. A short pause, and they began to descend. Behind them, tumbling from step to step, I could hear that trailing 'thing' being dragged along. It had become ponderous!

I awaited their approach with a degree of calmness, almost of apathy, which was only explicable on the ground that after a certain point Nature applies her own anaesthetic, and a merciful condition of numbness supervenes. On they came, step by step, nearer and nearer, with the shuffling sound of the burden behind growing louder as they approached.

They were already half-way down the stairs when I was galvanized afresh into a condition of terror by the consideration of a new and horrible possibility. It was the reflection that if another vivid flash of lightning were to come when the shadowy procession was in the room, perhaps when it was actually passing in front of me, I should see everything in detail, and worse, be seen myself! I could only hold my breath and wait—wait while the minutes lengthened into hours, and the procession made its slow progress round the room.

The Indians had reached the foot of the staircase. The form of the huge leader loomed in the doorway of the passage, and the burden with an ominous thud had dropped from the last step to the floor. There was a moment's pause while I saw the Indian turn and stoop to assist his companion. Then the procession moved forward again, entered the room close on my left, and began to move slowly round my side of the table. The leader was already beyond me, and his companion, dragging on the floor behind him the burden, whose confused outline I could dimly make out, was exactly in front of me, when the cavalcade came to a dead halt. At the same moment, with the strange suddenness of thunderstorms, the splash of the rain ceased altogether, and the wind died away into utter silence.

For the space of five seconds my heart seemed to stop beating, and then the worst came. A double flash of lightning lit up the room and its contents with merciless vividness.

The huge Indian leader stood a few feet past me on my right. One leg was stretched forward in the act of taking a step. His immense shoulders were turned towards his companion, and in all their magnificent fierceness I saw the outline of his features. His gaze was directed upon the burden his companion was dragging along the floor; but his profile, with the big aquiline nose, high cheek-bone, straight black hair, and bold chin, burnt itself in that brief instant into my brain, never again to fade.

Dwarfish, compared with this gigantic figure, appeared the proportions of the other Indian, who, within twelve inches of my face, was stooping over the thing he was dragging in a position that lent to his person the additional horror of deformity. And the burden, lying upon a sweeping cedar branch which he held and dragged by a long stem, was the body of a white man. The scalp had been neatly lifted, and blood lay in a broad smear upon the cheeks and forehead.

Then, for the first time that night, the terror that had paralysed my muscles and my will lifted its unholy spell from my soul. With a loud cry I stretched out my arms to seize the big Indian by the throat, and, grasping only air, tumbled forward unconscious upon the ground.

I had recognized the body, and *the face was my own!* . . .

It was bright daylight when a man's voice recalled me to consciousness. I was lying where I had fallen, and the farmer was standing in the room with the loaves of bread in his hands. The horror of the night was still in my heart, and as the bluff settler helped me to my feet and picked up the rifle which had fallen with me, with many questions and expressions of condolence, I imagined my brief replies were neither self-explanatory nor even intelligible.

That day, after a thorough and fruitless search of the house, I left the island, and went over to spend my last ten days with the farmer; and when time came for me to leave, the necessary reading had been accomplished, and my nerves had completely recovered their balance.

On the day of my departure the farmer started early in his big boat with my belongings to row to the point, twelve miles distant, where a little steamer ran twice a week for the accommodation of hunters. Late in the afternoon I went off in another direction in my canoe, wishing to see the island once again, where I had been the victim of so strange an experience.

In due course I arrived there, and made a tour of the island. I also made a search of the little house, and it was not without a curious sensation in my heart that I entered the little upstairs bedroom. There seemed nothing unusual.

Just after I re-embarked, I saw a canoe gliding ahead of me around the curve of the island. A canoe was an unusual sight at this time of the year, and this one seemed to have sprung from nowhere. Altering my course a little, I watched it disappear around the next projecting point of rock. It had high curving bows, and there were two Indians in it. I lingered with some excitement, to see if it would appear again round the other side of the island; and in less than five minutes it came into view. There were less than two hundred yards between us, and the Indians, sitting on their haunches, were paddling swiftly in my direction.

I never paddled faster in my life than I did in those next few minutes. When I turned to look again, the Indians had altered their course, and were again circling the island.

The sun was sinking behind the forests on the mainland, and the crimson-coloured clouds of sunset were reflected in the waters of the lake, when I looked round for the last time, and saw the big bark canoe and its two dusky occupants still going round the island. Then the shadows deepened rapidly; the lake grew black, and the night wind blew its first breath in my face as I turned a corner, and a projecting bluff of rock hid from my view both island and canoe.

R. H. BENSON

The Watcher (1903)

A priest and a private chamberlain to Pope Pius X, Robert Hugh Benson wrote ghost stories that are infused with allegorical elements and theological allusions. Occasionally these detract from the ghostly atmosphere, but for the most part Benson keeps them under admirable control. At his best, Benson was capable of creating highly original variations on traditional Gothic themes. "My Own Tale," for example, is a haunted-house story about a house haunted by nothingness, by "an extraordinary emptiness . . . like a Catholic cathedral in Protestant hands."

Benson's ghost stories are collected in two volumes, *The Light Invisible* (1903) and *The Mirror of Shalott* (1907). His most inventive storytelling device consists of having tales recounted by haunted Catholic priests who have undergone terrifying experiences. One of the most unusual and powerful of these is "The Watcher," an obscure tale first introduced to American readers by Hugh Lamb. Terse, compact, and atmospheric, "The Watcher" is characteristic of Benson's best work in that its rather ordinary allegory is upstaged by a chilling and memorable apparition scene. The moral is clear, but the vision itself is wonderfully inexplicable.

≈ THE WATCHER ≈

*'Il faut d'abord rendre l'organe de
la vision analogue et semblable a
l'objet qu'il doit contempler.'*

Maeterlinck

One morning, the priest and I went out soon after breakfast and walked up and down a grass path between two yew hedges; the dew was not yet off the grass that lay in shadow; and thin patches of gossamer still hung like torn cambric on the yew shoots on either side. As we passed for the second time up the path, the old man suddenly stooped and, pushing aside a dock-leaf at the foot of the hedge, lifted a dead mouse, and looked at it as it lay stiffly on the palm of his hand. I saw that his eyes filled slowly with the ready tears of old age.

'He has chosen his own resting-place,' he said. 'Let him lie there. Why did I disturb him?'—and he laid him gently down again; and then gathering a fragment of wet earth he sprinkled it over the mouse. 'Earth to earth, ashes to ashes,' he said, 'in sure and certain hope'—and then he stopped; and straightening himself with difficulty walked on, and I followed him.

'You once expressed an interest,' he said, 'in my tales of the visions of Nature I have seen. Shall I tell you how once I saw a very different sight?

'I was eighteen years old at the time, that terrible age when the soul seems to have dwindled to a spark overlaid by a mountain of ashes—when blood and fire and death and loud noises seem the only things of interest, and all tender things shrink back and hide from the dreadful noonday of manhood. Someone gave me one of those shot-pistols that you may have seen, and I loved the sense of power that it gave me, for I had never had a gun. For a week or two in the summer holidays I was content with shooting at a mark, or at the level surface of water, and delighted to see the cardboard shattered, or the quiet pool torn to shreds along its mirror where the sky and the green lay sleeping. Then that ceased to interest me, and I longed to see a living thing suddenly stop living at my will. Now,' and he held up a deprecating hand, 'I think sport is necessary for some natures. After all, the killing of creatures is necessary for man's food, and sport as you will tell me is a survival of man's delight in obtaining food,

314

and it requires certain noble qualities of endurance and skill. I know all that, and I know further that for some natures it is a relief—an escape for humours that will otherwise find an evil outlet. But I do know this—that for me it was not necessary.

'However, there was every excuse, and I went out in good faith one summer evening, intending to shoot some rabbits as they ran to cover from the open field. I walked along the inside of a fence with a wood above me and on my left, and the green meadow on my right. Well, owing probably to my own lack of skill, though I could hear the patter and rush of the rabbits all round me, and could see them in the distance sitting up listening with cocked ears, as I stole along the fence, I could not get close enough to fire at them with any hope of what I fancied was success; and by the time that I had arrived at the end of the wood I was in an impatient mood.

'I stood for a moment or two leaning on the fence looking out of that pleasant coolness into the open meadow beyond; the sun had at that moment dipped behind the hill before me and all was in shadow except where there hung a glory about the topmost leaves of a beech that still caught the sun. The birds were beginning to come in from the fields, and were settling one by one in the wood behind me, staying here and there to sing one last line of melody. I could hear the quiet rush and then the sudden clap of a pigeon's wings as he came home, and as I listened I heard pealing out above all other sounds the long liquid song of a thrush somewhere above me. I looked up idly and tried to see the bird, and after a moment or two caught sight of him as the leaves of the beech parted in the breeze, his head lifted and his whole body vibrating with the joy of life and music. As someone has said, his body was one beating heart. The last radiance of the sun over the hill reached him and bathed him in golden warmth. Then the leaves closed again as the breeze dropped, but still his song rang out.

'Then there came on me a blinding desire to kill him. All the other creatures had mocked me and run home. Here at least was a victim, and I would pour out the sullen anger that had been gathering during my walk, and at least demand this one life as a substitute. Side by side with this I remembered clearly that I had come out to kill for food: that was my one justification. Side by side I saw both these things, and I had no excuse— no excuse.

'I turned my head every way and moved a step or two back to catch sight of him again, and, although this may sound fantastic and over-wrought, in my whole being was a struggle between light and darkness.

Every fibre of my life told me that the thrush had a right to live. Ah! he had earned it, if labour were wanting, by this very song that was guiding death towards him, but black sullen anger had thrown my conscience, and was now struggling to hold it down till the shot had been fired. Still I waited for the breeze, and then it came, cool and sweet-smelling like the breath of a garden, and the leaves parted. There he sang in the sunshine, and in a moment I lifted the pistol and drew the trigger.

'With the crack of the cap came silence overhead, and after what seemed an interminable moment came the soft rush of something falling and the faint thud among last year's leaves. Then I stood half terrified, and stared among the dead leaves. All seemed dim and misty. My eyes were still a little dazzled by the bright background of sunlit air and rosy clouds on which I had looked with such intensity, and the space beneath the branches was a world of shadows. Still I looked a few yards away, trying to make out the body of the thrush, and fearing to hear a struggle of beating wings among the dry leaves.

'And then I lifted my eyes a little, vaguely. A yard or two beyond where the thrush lay was a rhododendron bush. The blossoms had fallen and the outline of dark, heavy leaves was unrelieved by the slightest touch of colour. As I looked at it, I saw a face looking down from the higher branches.

'It was a perfectly hairless head and face, the thin lips were parted in a wide smile of laughter, there were innumerable lines about the corners of the mouth, and the eyes were surrounded by creases of merriment. What was perhaps most terrible about it all was that the eyes were not looking at me, but down among the leaves; the heavy eyelids lay drooping, and the long, narrow, shining slits showed how the eyes laughed beneath them. The forehead sloped quickly back, like a cat's head. The face was the colour of earth, and the outlines of the head faded below the ears and chin into the gloom of the dark bush. There was no throat, or body or limbs so far as I could see. The face just hung there like a down-turned Eastern mask in an old curiosity shop. And it smiled with sheer delight, not at me, but at the thrush's body. There was no change of expression so long as I watched it, just a silent smile of pleasure petrified on the face. I could not move my eyes from it.

'After what I suppose was a minute or so, the face had gone. I did not see it go, but I became aware that I was looking only at leaves.

'No; there was no outline of leaf, or play of shadows that could possibly have taken the form of a face. You can guess how I tried to force myself to believe that that was all; how I turned my head this way and that to catch it again; but there was no hint of a face.

'Now, I cannot tell you how I did it; but although I was half beside myself with fright, I went forward towards the bush and searched furiously among the leaves for the body of the thrush; and at last I found it, and lifted it. It was still limp and warm to the touch. Its breast was a little ruffled, and one tiny drop of blood lay at the root of the beak below the eyes, like a tear of dismay and sorrow at such an unmerited, unexpected death.

'I carried it to the fence and climbed over, and then began to run in great steps, looking now and then awfully at the gathering gloom of the wood behind, where the laughing face had mocked the dead. I think, looking back as I do now, that my chief instinct was that I could not leave the thrush there to be laughed at, and that I must get it out into the clean, airy meadow. When I reached the middle of the meadow I came to a pond which never ran quite dry even in the hottest summer. On the bank I laid the thrush down, and then deliberately but with all my force dashed the pistol into the water; then emptied my pockets of the cartridges and threw them in too.

'Then I turned again to the piteous little body, feeling that at least I had tried to make amends. There was an old rabbit hole near, the grass growing down in its mouth, and a tangle of web and dead leaves behind. I scooped a little space out among the leaves, and then laid the thrush there: gathered a little of the sandy soil and poured it over the body, saying, I remember, half unconsciously, 'Earth to earth, ashes to ashes, in sure and certain hope'—and then I stopped, feeling I had been a little profane, though I do not think so now. And then I went home.

'As I dressed for dinner, looking out over the darkening meadow where the thrush lay, I remember feeling happy that no evil thing could mock the defenceless dead out there in the clean meadow where the wind blew and the stars shone down.'

ALFRED NOYES

Midnight Express (1935)

The Doppelgänger, or double, is one of the most enduring devices in
ancient folk tales as well as in Gothic fiction. As a symbol, it has gradually
accrued numerous permutations of meaning: it is sometimes a representative of retribution, sometimes a harbinger of death, and sometimes
an emblem of multiplicity and complexity in the human personality. It
can be angelic or demonic and has been exploited in a variety of imaginative ways by Hoffman, Poe, Conrad, Cynthia Asquith, and many others.

In this lyrical story by the poet Alfred Noyes, the Doppelgänger is decidedly demonic, an omen not only of death but of the strange circularity
of life *and* death. The intricate winding and unwinding of vicious circles
in "Midnight Express" is reminiscent of Le Fanu, but the latter had none
of Noyes's mythlike purity and fairy-tale simplicity. A story with no beginning or end, "Midnight Express" is a beautifully sustained shiver. It
has the texture of a dark ritual, one that invokes what Freud calls "the
uncanny"—"that class of the terrifying which leads back to something
long known to us, once very familiar."

It is unfortunate that Noyes wrote only a handful of weird tales, for he
was clearly a master of the form. This is his most famous offering, and
even it is known only to devotees of the genre. I must say that including
it here made me a bit uncomfortable; it is basically a story about what
happens to people who read too many ghost stories.

318

≈ MIDNIGHT EXPRESS ≈

It was a battered old book, bound in red buckram. He found it, when he was twelve years old, on an upper shelf in his father's library; and, against all the rules, he took it to his bedroom to read by candlelight, when the rest of the rambling old Elizabethan house was flooded with darkness. That was how young Mortimer always thought of it. His own room was a little isolated cell, in which, with stolen candle ends, he could keep the surrounding darkness at bay, while everyone else had surrendered to sleep and allowed the outer night to come flooding in . By contrast with those unconscious ones, his elders, it made him feel intensely alive in every nerve and fibre of his young brain. The ticking of the grandfather clock in the hall below; the beating of his own heart; the long-drawn rhythmical "ah" of the sea on the distant coast, all filled him with a sense of overwhelming mystery; and, as he read, the soft thud of a blinded moth, striking the wall above the candle, would make him start and listen like a creature of the woods at the sound of a cracking twig.

The battered old book had the strangest fascination for him, though he never quite grasped the thread of the story. It was called *The Midnight Express*, and there was one illustration, on the fiftieth page, at which he could never bear to look. It frightened him.

Young Mortimer never understood the effect of that picture on him. He was an imaginative, but not a neurotic youngster; and he avoided that fiftieth page as he might have hurried past a dark corner on the stairs when he was six years old, or as the grown man on the lonely road, in the *Ancient Mariner*, who, having once looked round, walks on, and turns no more his head. There was nothing in the picture—apparently—to account for this haunting dread. Darkness, indeed, was almost its chief characteristic. It showed an empty railway platform—at night—lit by a single dreary lamp; an empty railway platform that suggested a deserted and lonely junction in some remote part of the country. There was only one figure on the platform: the dark figure of a man, standing almost directly under the lamp, with his face turned away toward the black mouth of a tunnel, which—for some strange reason—plunged the imagination of the child into a pit of horror. The man seemed to be listening.

His attitude was tense, expectant, as though he were awaiting some fearful tragedy. There was nothing in the text, so far as the child read, and could understand, to account for this waking nightmare. He could neither resist the fascination of the book, nor face that picture in the stillness and loneliness of the night. He pinned it down to the page facing it, with two long pins, so that he should not come upon it by accident. Then he determined to read the whole story through. But, always, before he came to page fifty, he fell asleep; and the outlines of what he had read were blurred; and the next night he had to begin again; and again, before he came to the fiftieth page, he fell asleep.

He grew up, and forgot all about the book and the picture. But half way through his life, at that strange and critical time when Dante entered the dark wood, leaving the direct path behind him, he found himself, a little before midnight, waiting for a train at a lonely junction; and, as the station clock began to strike twelve, he remembered; remembered like a man awaking from a long dream—

There, under the single dreary lamp, on the long glimmering platform, was the dark and solitary figure that he knew. Its face was turned away from him toward the black mouth of the tunnel. It seemed to be listening, tense, expectant, just as it had been thirty-eight years ago.

But he was not frightened now, as he had been in childhood. He would go up to that solitary figure, confront it, and see the face that had so long been hidden, so long averted from him. He would walk up quietly, and make some excuse for speaking to it: he would ask it, for instance, if the train was going to be late. It should be easy for a grown man to do this; but his hands were clenched, when he took the first step, as if he, too, were tense and expectant. Quietly, but with the old vague instincts awaking, he went toward the dark figure under the lamp, passed it, swung round abruptly to speak to it; and saw—without speaking, without being able to speak—

It was himself—staring back at himself—as in some mocking mirror, his own eyes alive in his own white face, looking into his own eyes, alive—

The nerves of his heart tingled as though their own electric currents would paralyze it. A wave of panic went through him. He turned, gasped, stumbled, broke into a blind run, out through the deserted and echoing ticket office, on to the long moonlit road behind the station. The whole countryside seemed to be utterly deserted. The moonbeams flooded it with the loneliness of their own deserted satellite.

He paused for a moment, and heard, like the echo of his own footsteps, the stumbling run of something that followed over the wooden floor within the ticket office. Then he abandoned himself shamelessly to his fear; and ran, sweating like a terrified beast, down the long white road between the two endless lines of ghostly poplars each answering another, into what seemed an infinite distance. On one side of the road there was a long straight canal, in which one of the lines of poplars was again endlessly reflected. He heard the footsteps echoing behind him. They seemed to be slowly, but steadily, gaining upon him. A quarter of a mile away, he saw a small white cottage by the roadside, a white cottage with two dark windows and a door that somehow suggested a human face. He thought to himself that, if he could reach it in time, he might find shelter and security—escape.

The thin implacable footsteps, echoing his own, were still some way off when he lurched, gasping, into the little porch; rattled the latch, thrust at the door, and found it locked against him. There was no bell or knocker. He pounded on the wood with his fists until his knuckles bled. The response was horribly slow. At last, he heard heavier footsteps within the cottage. Slowly they descended the creaking stair. Slowly the door was unlocked. A tall shadowy figure stood before him, holding a lighted candle, in such a way that he could see little either of the holder's face or form; but to his dumb horror there seemed to be a cerecloth wrapped round the face.

No words passed between them. The figure beckoned him in; and, as he obeyed, it locked the door behind him. Then, beckoning him again, without a word, the figure went before him up the crooked stair, with the ghostly candle casting huge and grotesque shadows on the white-washed walls and ceiling.

They entered an upper room, in which there was a bright fire burning, with an armchair on either side of it, and a small oak table, on which there lay a battered old book, bound in dark red buckram. It seemed as though the guest had been long expected and all things were prepared.

The figure pointed to one of the armchairs, placed the candlestick on the table by the book (for there was no other light but that of the fire) and withdrew without a word, locking the door behind him.

Mortimer looked at the candlestick. It seemed familiar. The smell of the guttering wax brought back the little room in the old Elizabethan house. He picked up the book with trembling fingers. He recognized it at once, though he had long forgotten everything about the story. He re-

membered the inkstain on the title page; and then, with a shock of recollection, he came on the fiftieth page, which he had pinned down in childhood. The pins were still there. He touched them again—the very pins
which his trembling childish fingers had used so long ago.

He turned back to the beginning. He was determined to read it to the
end now, and discover what it all was about. He felt that it must all be set
down there, in print; and, though in childhood he could not understand
it, he would be able to fathom it now.

It was called *The Midnight Express*; and, as he read the first paragraph,
it began to dawn upon him slowly, fearfully, inevitably—

*It was the story of a man who, in childhood, long ago, had chanced upon a
book, in which there was a picture that frightened him. He had grown up and
forgotten it, and one night, upon a lonely railway platform, he had found
himself in the remembered scene of the picture; he had confronted the solitary
figure under the lamp; recognized it, and fled in panic. He had taken shelter
in a wayside cottage; had been led to an upper room, found the book awaiting
him and had begun to read it right through, to the very end, at last.—And
this book, too, was called* The Midnight Express. *And it was the story of a
man who, in childhood—It would go on thus, forever and forever, and forever. There was no escape.*

But when the story came to the wayside cottage, for the third time, a
deeper suspicion began to dawn upon him, slowly, fearfully, inevitably—
Although there was no escape, he could at least try to grasp more clearly
the details of the strange circle, the fearful wheel, in which he was
moving.

There was nothing new about the details. They had been there all the
time; but he had not grasped their significance. That was all. *The strange
and dreadful being that had led him up the crooked stair—who and what was
That?*

The story mentioned something that had escaped him. The strange
host, who had given him shelter, was about his own height. Could it be
that he also—And was this why the face was hidden?

At the very moment when he asked himself that question, he heard the
click of the key in the locked door.

The strange host was entering—moving toward him from behind—
casting a grotesque shadow, larger than human, on the white walls in the
guttering candlelight.

It was there, seated on the other side of the fire, facing him. With a
horrible nonchalance, as a woman might prepare to remove a veil, it

raised its hands to unwind the cerecloth from its face. He knew to whom it would belong. But would it be dead or living?

There was no way out but one. As Mortimer plunged forward and seized the tormentor by the throat, his own throat was gripped with the same brutal force. The echoes of their strangled cry were indistinguishable; and when the last confused sounds died out together, the stillness of the room was so deep that you might have heard—the ticking of the old grandfather clock, and the long-drawn rhythmical "ah" of the sea, on a distant coast, thirty-eight years ago.

But Mortimer had escaped at last. Perhaps, after all, he had caught the midnight express.

It was a battered old book, bound in red buckram . . .

L. T. C. ROLT

The Mine (1948)

The most charmingly old-fashioned ghost story in this collection, "The Mine" has all the traditional ingredients of the classic spook tale: a howling wind, an amiable fireside, and an old sage with a pipe telling a supernatural story to an excited circle of listeners. It even has the story within a story told in dialect, a risky strategy considering the large number of dull and irritatingly unintelligible dialect tales produced by authors (even normally reliable ones like Quiller-Couch, Stevenson, and M. R. James) obsessed with authenticity. Here it all works: L. T. C. Rolt combines folkloric spontaneity with artful sophistication to produce a near-perfect little gem.

Appearances to the contrary, "The Mine" is indeed highly sophisticated. The delightful music of the dialect is sustained throughout, but not the ramblings and affectations that usually go with it; the storyteller, who has a "natural sense of drama," keeps his narrative crisp and terse, carefully editing and selecting details that make the ghost at the end a truly fearful apparition. Rolt's sense of place in depicting the haunted mine is so exacting that the reader feels a strange immediacy, despite the distance created by having the ghost emerge, not from one, but from two layers of stories within stories. As M. R. James pointed out, most ghost stories need a certain amount of narrative distance; paradoxically, the supernatural assailant can only become immediate to the reader if it begins its attack from reasonably far away, both in time and space.

What the apparition emerges from here is the "angry" darkness of the mines, a darkness captured by Rolt with considerable lyricism and punch. An engineer by profession, Rolt created a very special spectral environment in his bewitched mines and canals, demonstrating once again that ghosts are perfectly comfortable in dwellings decidedly less elegant than Gothic houses.

≈ THE MINE ≋

There was a high west wind over the Shropshire March—a boisterous, buffeting wind that swept down the slopes of the Long Mynd and over the Vale of Severn to send November leaves whirling through the darkness from the mane of Wenlock Edge. It cried about the walls of the Miner's Arms at Cliedden, hurling sudden scuds of rain to rattle like flung gravel against the windowpanes. It was a night to make men glad of the warmth and cheer of the fireside.

"Why is it called Hell's Mouth? Ah, now that's a long story, that is."

With a natural sense of drama, the old man paused to allow the interest of his audience to quicken. He took a deep and noisy draught from the mug which was mulling on the hob, filled a yellowing clay with fine black shag from a battered tin and lit it with an untidy spill of newspaper which he thrust between the bars of the grate. Then at last, settling himself more comfortably in the chimney-corner, he began his tale.

"If you got here afore dark, maybe you noticed the old mines on the hill yonder. Well, they were lead-mines, and were working up to—let me see—fifteen years ago; all but the one right on top of the hill, that is, and that's been closed these fifty years. Now, this be the mine you've been on about, though in the old days it were called Long Barrow Mine because there's a great mound up there which they do say was some old burial-place when Adam was a boy-chap. I never heard tell of anyone who could say rightly who were buried there, although folks who know about such things have set to a-digging there many a time, but never got much for-rarder. Not that any of them stayed at it very long. It seemed to get on their nerves like, for it be a queer lonely place up there even in day-time, and, though rabbits do swarm on these hills, you'll never see a one there, nor any other natural creature neither. Knowing what I know, I don't blame them for packing up.

"Now, in the old days when my father were a young man there was a horse-tram road—Ginny Rails we call 'em—between the mines and Cliedden Wharf down here in the valley. This wharf was the end of an old arm that used to run to the Shroppie Cut by Fens Moss, but it has been dry now these many years, and you wouldn't see no sign of it today save you knew where to look. About the time I was born the railway came, and soon after that they made a steam tramway up to the mines. They kept the same narrow gauge, only the track were different—better laid, and went a deal farther round, to ease the grade. They still used horses then to draw the trams up the branch roads from the mines ready for the engine to pick up, and this were my first job as a nipper, walking one of these horses up from Half-way Mine to the main road. Then, when I was twenty or thereabouts, I got the job of firing on one of the engines, and proud as Punch I was. She'd seem pretty queer to you folks nowadays, but she was a grand little engine in them days, and I used to keep her brass Bristol fashion, and the copper band round her funnel shone like my mother's kettle.

"It was about this time—one Michaelmas—that the trouble started in Long Barrow Mine. I can remember it as plain as if it were yesterday. We had our shed up there then, and we'd just come up with our last load of empties, unhooked, and were running the engine into shed, when the chaps came up off shift. Now, the path from the mine down the hill led past the door of our shed, and I dropped my fire and was having a last look round just to see as everything was right for the night as they come walking by. Usually they would be a-chattering, joking and calling to each other, for they were a merry lot, but this night they were quiet like or talking hushed to each other, and this was the first thing that struck me as being a bit queer. So when one of them that was a cousin of mine—Joe Beecher his name was—come walking by, I called out to him to know what they was all acting so glum about. He turned back into the shed and told me what the trouble was. It was fast falling dark by this time, but I can see his face now in the light of my fire, which was still a-glowing between the rails by the door.

"They had struck a new vein just about that time and it seems that Joe and his mate had been working on this new level. Mind you, it wasn't like the mines you know of today, for there was only about fifteen men at the most below ground. Well, at midday they knocked off for a bite of "Tommy," and started walking back to the road to join their mates. When they got half of the way, he said, his mate Bill remembered he'd left his tea-can behind, and set off back to fetch it while Joe went on and joined the others. They had a laugh about Bill when he was so long finding his can, but when snapping time was nearly up and still no sign of him, Joe said he got a bit worried, and set off down the level to see what had happened to him. He got to the end, and then he said he came over horrid queer because Bill wasn't there at all, so that he felt scared of the dark and the hush there, and hollered out for the others to come down. So they came and looked, too, and sure enough there was nothing to be seen of Joe's mate. There'd been no fall to bury him, and of course there was no other way out of the level. They just stood there for a moment very quiet like, and then set off back to the road again as fast as they could. Joe said something seemed to be telling him that the sooner he cleared out the better for him, and he reckoned the others must have felt that way, too. He finished up by saying something that sounded a bit crazed to me at the time, about the darkness being angry. Anyway, none of them durst set foot in that level for a long while after that."

The old man paused, drained his beer-mug, and, sucking the drooping fringe of his moustache, seemed to ruminate sadly over its emptiness.

His mug replenished and his reeking pipe re-lit, he settled himself once more and resumed his tale.

"Nothing else happened for a twelve-month or more, except that they had to give up the new level because no one would work there. But there come a time when they'd worked out the veins on the old levels, and it was a matter of opening up the new level again, seeing as it was very rich, or shutting down altogether. Things had quieted down a bit by this, mind, but for all that they had to give the chaps more pay afore they'd agree to go back.

"It must have been a fortnight or more after they'd started on the new level again, that we were up there waiting for a return load of trams, and had gone into the winding-house to have a word with Harry Brymer, who was engine-man there in them days. Died ten year ago up at his daughter's at Coppice Holt, he did. It was an old beam winder as was there then, gone for scrap a long time back, though you can still see the engine-house plain as can be on top of the hill, while the old chimney be a landmark ten mile away on a clear day.

"Well, Harry was telling us how they'd had nothing but trouble ever since they'd started on the new level—nothing much, mind, but just enough to make the men nervy and talk of an ill luck on the place, although Harry said he reckoned nothing to it for his part.

"It was while we were talking to Harry, leaning over the guard rails round the drum and having a smoke, that the bell wire started to play the monkey. There was no such new-fangled notion as electricity in those days, of course, and the signal for winding was a bell as was hung on the wall and rung from the shaft bottom by a wire cable working through

pulleys and guides. Well, it was this cable that started a jangling to and fro
in the guides just enough to set the bell moving, but not enough to ring it
proper. The three of us stopped our clacking and stood dumbstruck
watching this bell moving and the cable jerking. And somehow it felt
queer standing there in the half-light watching it and waiting for it to
make up its mind, like, whether to ring or not. Then all of a sudden it
starts ringing like mad, and kept on, too; so Harry started winding while
we went to the doorway to look for the cage, for by that time we had a
notion as summat was up. When her came there was only one man on her
and that was Joe Beecher; I just caught a sight of his face as he come up
and I'll never forget the way he looked. He never said nor shouted
nothing, nor even saw us, but almost afore the cage stopped he was off and
away across the yard, and we could see him running for dear life over the
waste mound and along the hill-side. And as he ran he kept looking back
over his shoulder and then running the harder, for all the world as though
Old Nick hisself were after him. Then he got to Dyke Wood, and we lost
sight of him because it was that dark under the trees.

"Now this gave Harry and me a pretty turn, I can tell you, but that was
nothing to my mate. When we were watching Joe a-running he lets out a
yell like a screech owl and then cries out loud, 'Run, run, for Christ's
sake!' When we couldn't see Joe no more we turned to look at him and
he'd gone down all of a heap on the floor. We reckoned then he must have
seen summat as we missed, but it was some hours afore he came round,
and a week or more afore he could talk plain. Even then it very near set
him off again in the telling. I can tell you that if I'd known then what it
was he saw, I'd never have gone down that mine as I did with several
others as had been working above ground. Even as it was, it was a bit
strange, to say the least, going down in that cage and wondering what we
were going to see when we got to the bottom.

"I know that none of us expected what we did find when we had stepped
out of the cage and walked off down the new level—just the quiet and
the dark—not a sign of a mortal soul. I understood then what poor Joe
had meant about the darkness being angry. I'm not an educated man; if I
were maybe I could find a better word for the feeling there was down in
that mine. It just told me pretty plain that we weren't wanted down there,
and the sooner we cleared out the better for us. I reckon the others must
have felt the same thing, for we soon set off back to the cage, walking
pretty smart for a start and finishing at a run, so that we fell a-jostling

back into the cage like so many sheep into a pen, and mighty glad we were to see daylight, I can tell you."

The old man paused, rubbing his hands nervously one over the other and drawing his chair nearer to the fire as though suddenly chilled.

"We found Joe Beecher in Dyke Wood," he went on, "at the bottom of the old quarry as there is there. We covered up his face quick with a coat. I didn't fear God nor man in them days, but it were too much for me, and it didn't seem right that a mortal face should take that shape.

"Meanwhile, of course, my mate was took pretty bad. He'd just lie on his bed come day go day and not a word to anyone, but in the night he'd start shaking all over and crying out something terrible, same as he'd done the first time in the engine-house. He nearly drove his old woman crazy, too, but after a time he quieted down until one day he was man enough to tell us what it was he saw.

"Then he said that when the cage came up there was something crouched a-top of it, holding on to the cables. He couldn't see it very plain, he said, not half as clear as he could see Joe even in the half-light, but it had a human shape, he thought, even if it did seem terrible tall and thin, and it seemed to be a kind of dirty white all over, like summat that's grown up in the dark and never had no light. When the cage stopped it come down and made after Joe as quick and quiet as a cat after a sparrow. He could hear Joe's running plain enough across the yard, he said, but this thing made never a sound, though it went fast enough and was catching up on him, so that when he got to the edge of the wood it looked as if it was reaching out for him with its arms.

"Well, I can't tell you no more. No one never went down that mine again, and we cut the cage ropes and the guides and covered over the mouth of the shaft with girt great old timbers all bolted fast. A bit foolish, maybe you'll think, but when we heard my mate's tale we fancied, like, that something might come acrawling up. Any road, that's how it come to be named Hell's Mouth instead of Long Barrow. For myself I reckon hell be too good a name for it. Bible says hell be fire and brimstone, but at any rate fire is something I can understand and I could abide it better than the dark and the quiet down there."

V. THE CONTEMPORARY GHOST STORY

ELIZABETH BOWEN

Hand in Glove (1952)

With the possible exception of Henry James, perhaps no one but Elizabeth Bowen has so deftly depicted the hostilities and despairs that lie beneath the glittering facades of wealth and gentility. Despite their impeccable taste and manners, Bowen's wealthier characters, with their blocked ambitions and short-circuited relationships, are frequently (in this story, literally) at one another's throats.

Yet the surfaces of her short stories are as polished as her characters. Nowhere is her prose more silken and meticulous, more rich in ominous nuances, than in her numerous ghost stories, spread through four volumes, which combine psychological and supernatural shudders to depict obsessions in human relationships. "Hand in Glove," a particularly obsessive piece, is one of the most overtly supernatural of these stories. Although set in a splendidly evoked bygone era, it is nevertheless strangely modern. If it doesn't have a modern ghost, it does depict, as Bowen puts it, "the modern way of seeing one." Bowen's eloquent essay on the condition of the modern ghost (in the introduction to Lady Cynthia Asquith's *Second Ghost Book*, where "Hand in Glove" first appeared) can serve as an introduction not only to her own work but also to the contributions of other contemporary English writers who labor to make their ghosts credible.

> Ghosts have grown up. Far behind lie their clanking and moaning days; they have laid aside their original bag of tricks—bleeding hands, luminous skulls and so on. Their manifestations are, like their personalities, oblique, subtle, perfectly calculated to get the modern person under the skin. . . . Ghosts exploit the horror latent behind reality: for this reason, they prefer prosaic scenes—today's haunted room has a rosy wallpaper. Half-tones of daylight, the livid hush before thunderstorms, glass-clear dusk or hallucinatory sunsets suit them better than out-and-out pitch-dark night. Worst of all, contemporary ghosts are credible.
>
> (From the Beagle edition, pp. vii–viii.)

"Hand in Glove" illustrates this modernity admirably. The "half-tones of daylight" emerge here as an "apricot afterglow"; the "livid hush" is so

332

unnerving that it pierces up through the very floor of the house; the ghost is horribly "credible" indeed; and the purpose of the story is manifestly to show the "horror latent behind reality."

The reader should be warned that "Hand in Glove," like a great deal of Bowen's work, is a rather cold story. It is cold not only in the subtle brutality of its plot but in its aloof narrative voice. Bowen draws her characters with precision but with little warmth; she does not seem to particularly like these people. Also problematic to some readers will be the pace—"Hand in Glove" takes its time getting under way. Nevertheless, it is this very leisureliness, as well as the iciness, which makes the climax so desolating and dramatic.

～ HAND IN GLOVE ～

Jasmine Lodge was favourably set on a residential, prettily-wooded hill-side in the south of Ireland, overlooking a river and, still better, the roofs of a lively garrison town. Around 1904, which was the flowering period of the Miss Trevors, girls could not have had a more auspicious home—the neighbourhood spun merrily round the military. Ethel and Elsie, a spirited pair, garnered the full advantage—no ball, hop, picnic, lawn tennis, croquet or boating party was complete without them; in winter, though they could not afford to hunt, they trimly bicycled to all meets, and on frosty evenings, with their guitars, set off to *soirées*, snug inside their cab in their fur-tipped capes.

They possessed an aunt, a Mrs Varley de Grey, *née* Elysia Trevor, a formerly notable local belle, who, drawn back again in her widowhood to what had been the scene of her early triumphs, occupied a back bedroom in Jasmine Lodge. Mrs Varley de Grey had had no luck: her splashing match, in its time the talk of two kingdoms, had ended up in disaster—the well-born captain in a cavalry regiment having gone so far as to blow out his brains in India, leaving behind him nothing but her and debts. Mrs Varley de Grey had returned from India with nothing but seven large trunks crammed with recent finery; and she also had been impaired by shock. This had taken place while Ethel and Elsie, whose father had married late, were still unborn—so it was that, for as long as the girls recalled, their aunt had been the sole drawback to Jasmine Lodge. Their parents had orphaned them, somewhat thoughtlessly, by simultaneously dying of scarlet fever when Ethel was just out and Elsie soon to be—they were therefore left lacking a chaperone and, with their gift for putting everything to use, propped the aunt up in order that she might play that role. Only when her peculiarities became too marked did they feel it necessary to withdraw her: by that time however, all the surrounding ladies could be said to compete for the honour of taking into society the sought-after Miss Trevors. From then on, no more was seen or heard of Mrs Varley de Gray. ("Oh, just a trifle unwell, but nothing much!") She remained upstairs, at the back; when the girls were giving one of their

334

little parties, or a couple of officers came to call, the key of her room would be turned in the outer lock.

The girls hung Chinese lanterns from the creepered verandah, and would sit lightly strumming on their guitars. Not less fascinating was their badinage, accompanied by a daring flash of the eyes. They were known as the clever Miss Trevors, not because of any taint of dogmatism or book-learning—no, when a gentleman cried "Those girls have brains!" he meant it wholly in admiration—but because of their accomplishments, ingenuity, and agility. They took leading parts in theatricals, lent spirit to numbers of drawing-room games, were naughty mimics, and sang duets. Nor did their fingers lag behind their wits—they constructed lampshades, crêpe paper flowers and picturesque hats; and, above all, varied their dresses marvellously—no one could beat them for ideas, snipping, slashing or fitting. Once more allowing nothing to go to waste, they had remodelled the trousseau out of their aunt's trunks, causing sad old tulles and tarlatans, satins and *moiré* taffetas to appear to have come from Paris only today. They re-stitched spangles, pressed ruffles crisp, and revived many a corsage of squashed silk roses. They went somewhat softly about that task, for the trunks were all stored in the attic immediately over the back room.

They wore their clothes well. "A pin on either of those two would look smart!" declared other girls. All that they were short of was evening gloves—they had two pairs each, which they had been compelled to buy. *What* could have become of Mrs Varley de Grey's presumably sumptuous numbers of this item, they were unable to fathom, and it was too bad. Had gloves been overlooked in her rush from India?—or, were they here, in that *one* trunk the Trevors could not get at? All other locks had yielded to pulls or pickings, or the sisters found keys to fit them, or they had used the toolbox; but this last stronghold defied them. In that sad little soiled silk sack, always on her person, Mrs Varley de Grey, they became convinced, hoarded the operative keys, along with some frippery rings and brooches—all true emeralds, pearls and diamonds having been long ago, as they knew, sold. Such contrariety on their aunt's part irked them— meanwhile, gaieties bore hard on their existing gloves. Last thing at nights when they came in, last thing in the evenings before they went out, they would manfully dab away at the fingertips. So, it must be admitted that a long whiff of benzine pursued them as they whirled round the ball-room floor.

They were tall and handsome—nothing so soft as pretty, but in those

days it was a vocation to be a handsome girl; many of the best marriages
had been made by such. They carried themselves imposingly, had good
busts and shoulders, waists firm under the whalebone, and straight backs.
Their features were striking, their colouring high; low on their foreheads
bounced dark mops of curls. Ethel was, perhaps, the dominant one, but
both girls were pronounced to be full of character.

Whom, and still more when, did they mean to marry? They had already
seen regiments out and in; for quite a number of years, it began to seem,
bets in the neighborhood had been running high. Sympathetic spy-glasses
were trained on the conspicuous gateway to Jasmine Lodge; each new
cavalier was noted. The only trouble might be, their promoters claimed,
that the clever Trevors were always so surrounded that they had not a
moment in which to turn or choose. Or otherwise, could it possibly be
that the admiration aroused by Ethel and Elsie, and their now institu-
tional place in the local scene, scared out more tender feeling from the
masculine breast? It came to be felt, and perhaps by the girls themselves,
that, having lingered so long and so puzzlingly, it was up to them to bring
off (like their aunt) a *coup*. Society around this garrison town had long
plumed itself upon its romantic record; summer and winter, Cupid shot
his darts. Lush scenery, the oblivion of all things else bred by the steamy
climate, and perpetual gallivanting—all were conducive. Ethel's and
Elsie's names, it could be presumed, were by now murmured wherever
the Union Jack flew. Nevertheless, it was time they should decide.

Ethel's decision took place late one spring. She set her cap, in a manner
worthy of her, at the second son of an English marquess. Lord Fred had
come on a visit, for the fishing, to a mansion some miles down the river
from Jasmine Lodge. He first made his appearance, with the rest of the
house-party, at one of the more resplendent military balls, and was understood to be a man-about-town. The civilian glint of his *pince-nez*, at
once serene and superb, instantaneously wrought, with his great name,
on Ethel's heart. She beheld him, and the assembled audience, with ap-
probation, looked on at the moment so big with fate. The truth, it
appeared in a flash, was that Ethel, though so condescending with her
charms, had not from the first been destined to love a soldier; and that
here, after long attrition, her answer was. Lord Fred was, by all, at once
signed over to her. For his part, he responded to her attentions quite
gladly, though in a somewhat dazed way. If he did not so often dance with
her—indeed, how could he, for she was much besought?—he could at
least be perceived to gaze. At a swiftly-organised river picnic, the next

evening, he by consent fell to Ethel's lot—she had spent the foregoing morning snipping and tacking at a remaining muslin of Mrs Varley de Grey's, a very fresh forget-me-not-dotted pattern. The muslin did not survive the evening out, for when the moon should have risen, rain poured into the boats. Ethel's good-humoured drollery carried all before it, and Lord Fred wrapped his blazer around her form.

Next day, more rain; and all felt flat. At Jasmine Lodge the expectant deck chairs had to be hurried in from the garden, and the small close rooms, with their greeneried windows and plentiful bric-à-brac, gave out a stuffy, resentful, indoor smell. The maid was out; Elsie was lying down with a migraine; so it devolved on Ethel to carry up Mrs Varley de Grey's tea—the invalid set very great store by tea, and her manifestations by door-rattlings, sobs and mutters were apt to become disturbing if it did not appear. Ethel, with the not particularly dainty tray, accordingly entered the back room, this afternoon rendered dark by its outlook into a dripping uphill wood. The aunt, her visage draped in a cobweb shawl, was as usual sitting up in bed. "Aha!" she at once cried, screwing one eye up and glittering round at Ethel with the other, "so what's all this in the wind today?"

Ethel, as she lodged the meal on the bed, shrugged her shoulders, saying, "I'm in a hurry."

"No doubt you are. The question is, will you get him?"

"Oh, drink your tea!" snapped Ethel, her colour rising.

The old wretch responded by popping a lump of sugar into her cheek and sucking at it while she fixed her wink on her niece. She then observed: "*I* could tell you a thing or two!"

"We've had enough of *your* fabrications, Auntie."

"Fabrications!" croaked Mrs Varley de Gray. "And who's been the fabricator, I'd like to ask? Who's so nifty with the scissors and needle? Who's been going a-hunting in my clothes?"

"Oh, what a fib!" exclaimed Ethel, turning her eyes up. "Those old musty miserable bundles of things of yours—would Elsie or I consider laying a finger on them?"

Mrs Varley de Grey replied, as she sometimes did, by heaving up and throwing the tray at Ethel. Nought, therefore, but cast-off kitchen china nowadays was ever exposed to risk; and the young woman, not trying to gather the debris up, statuesquely, thoughtfully stood with her arms folded, watching tea-steam rise from the carpet. Today, the effort seemed to have been too much for Aunt Elysia, who collapsed on her pillows,

faintly blue in the face. "Rats in the attic," she murmured. "*I've* heard
them, rats in the attic! Now where's my tea?"

"You've had it," said Ethel, turning to leave the room. However, she
paused to study a photograph in a tarnished, elaborate silver frame.
"Really quite an Adonis, poor Uncle Harry. From the first glance, you
say, he never looked back?"

"My lovely tea," said the widow, beginning to sob.

As Ethel slowly put down the photograph her eyes could be seen to cal-
culate, her mouth hardened and a reflective cast came over her brow.
Step by step, once more she approached the bed, and, as she did so, altered
her tune. She suggested, in a beguiling tone, "You said you could tell me a
thing or two . . . ?"

Time went on; Lord Fred, though for ever promising, still failed to
come within Ethel's grasp. Ground gained one hour seemed to be lost the
next—it seemed, for example, that things went better for Ethel in the
afternoons, in the open air, than at the dressier evening functions. It was
when she swept down on him in full plumage that Lord Fred seemed to
contract. Could it be that he feared his passions?—she hardly thought
so. Or did her complexion not light up well? When there was a question of
dancing, he came so late that her programme already was black with other
names, whereupon he would heave a gallant sigh. When they did take the
floor together, he held her so far at arm's length, and with his face turned
so far away, that when she wished to address him she had to shout—she
told herself this must be the London style, but it piqued her, naturally.
Next morning, all was as it was before, with nobody so completely assid-
uous as Lord Fred—but, through it all, he still never came to the point.
And worse, the days of his visit were running out; he would soon be back
in the heart of the London season. "Will you ever get him, Ethel, now, do
you think?" Elsie asked, with trying solicitude, and no doubt the neighbourhood wondered also.

She conjured up all her fascinations. But was something further
needed, to do the trick?

It was now that she began to frequent her aunt.

In that dank little back room looking into the hill, proud Ethel
humbled herself, to prise out the secret. Sessions were close and long.
Elsie, in mystification outside the door, heard the dotty voice of their
relative rising, falling, with, now and then, blood-curdling little knowing
laughs. Mrs Varley de Grey was back in the golden days. Always, though,

of a sudden it would break off, drop back into pleas, whimpers and jagged breathing. No doctor, though she constantly asked for one, had for years been allowed to visit Mrs Varley de Grey—the girls saw no reason for that expense, or for the interference which might follow. Aunt's affliction, they swore, was confined to the head; all she required was quiet, and that she got. Knowing, however, how gossip spreads, they would let no servant near her for more than a minute or two, and then with one of themselves on watch at the door. They had much to bear from the foetid state of her room.

"You don't think you'll kill her, Ethel?" the out-of-it Elsie asked. "Forever sitting on top of her, as you now do. Can it be healthy, egging her on to talk? What's this attraction, all of a sudden?—whatever's this which has sprung up between you two? She and you are becoming quite hand-in-glove."

Elsie merely remarked this, and soon forgot: she had her own fish to fry. It was Ethel who had cause to recall the words—for, the afternoon of the very day that they were spoken, Aunt Elysia whizzed off on another track, screamed for what was impossible and, upon being thwarted, went into a seizure unknown before. The worst of it was, at the outset her mind cleared—she pushed her shawl back, reared up her unkempt grey head and looked at Ethel, unblinkingly studied Ethel, with a lucid accumulation of years of hate. "You fool of a gawk," she said, and with such contempt! "Coming running to me to know how to trap a man. Could *you* learn, if it was from Venus herself? Wait till I show you beauty. Bring down those trunks!"

"Oh, Auntie."

"Bring them down, I say. I'm about to dress myself up."

"Oh, but I cannot: they're heavy; I'm single-handed."

"Heavy?—they came here heavy. But there've been rats in the attic. *I* saw you, swishing downstairs in my *eau-de-nil*."

"Oh, you dreamed that!"

"Through the crack of the door.—Let me up, then. Let us go where they are, and look—we shall soon see!" Aunt Elysia threw back the bed-clothes and began to get up. "Let's take a look," she said, "at the rats' work." She set out to totter towards the door.

"Oh, but you're not fit!" Ethel protested.

"And when did a doctor say so?" There was a swaying; Ethel caught her in time and, not gently, lugged her back to the bed—and Ethel's mind the whole of this time was whirling, for tonight was the night upon which all hung. Lord Fred's last local appearance was to be, like his first, at a ball: tomorrow he left for London. So it must be tonight, at this ball, or never! How was it that Ethel felt so strangely, wildly confident of the outcome? It was time to begin on her coiffure, lay out her dress. Oh, tonight she would shine as never before! She flung back the bedclothes over the helpless form, heard a clock strike, and hastily turned to go.

"I will be quits with you," said the voice behind her.

Ethel, in a kimono, hair half down, was in her own room, in front of the open glove-drawer, when Elsie came in—home from a tennis party. Elsie acted oddly—she went at once to the drawer and buried her nose in it. "Oh my goodness," she cried, "it's all too true, and it's awful!"

"What is?" Ethel carelessly asked.

"Ethel dear, would you ever face it out if I were to tell you a certain rumour I heard today at the party as to Lord Fred?"

Ethel turned from her sister, took up the heated tongs and applied more crimps to her natural curliness. She said: "Certainly; spit it out."

"Since childhood, he's recoiled from the breath of benzine. He wilts away when it enters the very room!"

"Who says that's so?"

"He confided it to his hostess, who is now spitefully putting it around the country."

Ethel bit her lip and put down the tongs, while Elsie sorrowfully concluded, "And your gloves stink, Ethel, as I'm sure do mine." Elsie then thought it wiser to slip away.

In a minute more, however, she was back, and this time, with still more peculiar air, she demanded: "In what state did you leave Auntie? She was sounding so very quiet that I peeped in, and *I* don't care for the looks of her now at all!" Ethel swore, but consented to take a look. She stayed in there in the back room, with Elsie biting her thumb-nail outside the door, for what seemed an ominous length of time; when she did emerge, she looked greenish, but held her head high. The sisters' eyes met. Ethel said, stonily, "Dozing."

"You're certain she's *not* . . . ? She *couldn't* ever be—you know?"

"Dozing, I tell you." Ethel stared Elsie out.

"If she *was* gone," quavered the frailer sister, "just think of it—why, we'd never get to the ball! And a ball that everything hangs on," she ended, with a scared but conspiratorial glance at Ethel.

"Reassure yourself. Didn't you hear me say?"

As she spoke Ethel, chiefly from habit, locked her late Aunt's door on the outside. The act caused a sort of secret jingle to be heard from inside her fist, and Elsie asked: "What's that you've got hold of, now?" "Just a few little keys and trinkets she made me keep," replied Ethel, disclosing the small bag she had found where she'd looked for it, under the dead one's pillow. "Scurry on now, Elsie, or you'll never be dressed. Care to make use of my tongs, while they're so splendidly hot?"

Alone at last, Ethel drew in a breath, and, with a gesture of resolution, re-tied her kimono-sash tightly over her corset. She took the key from the bag and regarded it, murmuring, "Providential!" then gave a glance upward, towards where the attics were. The late spring sun had set, but an apricot afterglow, not unlike the light cast by a Chinese lantern, crept through the upper storey of Jasmine Lodge. The cessation of all those rustlings, tappings, whimpers and moans from inside Mrs Varley de Grey's room had set up an unfamiliar, somewhat unnerving hush. Not till a whiff of singeing hair announced that Elsie was well employed did Ethel set out on the quest which held all her hopes. Success was imperative—she *must* have gloves. Gloves, gloves . . .

Soundlessly, she set foot on the attic stairs.

Under the skylight she had to suppress a shriek, for a rat—yes, of all things!—leaped at her out of an empty hatbox: and the rodent gave her a wink before it darted away. Now Ethel and Elsie knew for a certain fact that there never *had* been rats in Jasmine Lodge. However, she continued to steel her nerves, and to push her way to the one inviolate trunk.

All Mrs Varley de Grey's other Indian luggage gaped and yawned at Ethel, void, showing its linings, on end or toppling, forming a barricade around the object of her search. She pushed, pitched and pulled, scowling as the dust flew into her hair. But the last trunk, when it came into view and reach, still had something select and bridal about it: on top, the initials E. V. de G. stared out, quite luminous in a frightening way—for indeed how dusky the attic was! Shadows not only multiplied in the corners but seemed to finger their way up the sloping roof. Silence pierced up through the floor from that room below—and, worst, Ethel had the sensation of being watched by that pair of fixed eyes she had not stayed to close. She glanced this way, that way, backward over her shoulder. But, Lord Fred was at stake!—she knelt down and got to work with the key.

This trunk had two neat brass locks, one left, one right, along the front of the lid. Ethel, after fumbling, opened the first—then, so great was her hurry to know what might be within that she could not wait but slipped

her hand in under the lifted corner. She pulled out one pricelessly lacy tip
of what must be a bride-veil, and gave a quick laugh—must not this be an
omen? She pulled again, but the stuff resisted, almost as though it were
being grasped from inside the trunk—she let go, and either her eyes deceived her or the lace began to be drawn back slowly, in again, inch by
inch. What was odder was that the spotless finger tip of a white kid glove
appeared for a moment, as though exploring its way out, then withdrew.

Ethel's heart stood still—but she turned to the other lock. Was a giddy
attack overcoming her?—for, as she gazed, the entire lid of the trunk
seemed to bulge upward, heave and strain so that the E. V. de G. upon it
rippled.

Untouched by the key in her trembling hand, the second lock tore
itself open.

She recoiled, while the lid slowly rose—of its own accord.

She should have fled. But oh, how she craved what lay there exposed!
—layer upon layer, wrapped in transparent paper, of elbow-length mag-
nolia-pure white gloves, bedded on the inert folds of the veil. "Lord
Fred," thought Ethel, "now you're within my grasp!"

That was her last thought, nor was the grasp to be hers. Down on her
knees again, breathless with lust and joy, Ethel flung herself forward on
to that sea of kid, scrabbling and seizing. The glove she had seen before
was now, however, readier for its purpose. At first it merely pounced
after Ethel's fingers, as though making mock of their greedy course; but
the hand within it was all the time filling out . . . With one snowy flash
through the dusk, the glove clutched Ethel's front hair, tangled itself in
her black curls and dragged her head down. She began to choke among the
sachets and tissue—then the glove let go, hurled her back, and made its
leap at her throat.

It was a marvel that anything so dainty should be so strong. So great, so
convulsive was the swell of the force that, during the strangling of Ethel,
the seams of the glove split.

In any case, the glove would have been too small for her.

The shrieks of Elsie, upon the attic threshold, began only when all
other sounds had died down . . . The ultimate spark of the once-famous
cleverness of the Miss Trevors appeared in Elsie's extrication of herself
from this awkward mess—for, who was to credit how Ethel came by her
end? The sisters' reputation for warmth of heart was to stand the survivor
in good stead—for, could those affections nursed in Jasmine Lodge, extending so freely even to the unwell aunt, have culminated in Elsie's

setting on Ethel? No. In the end, the matter was hushed up—which is to say, is still talked about even now. Ethel Trevor and Mrs Varley de Grey were interred in the same grave, as everyone understood that they would have wished. What conversation took place under the earth one does not know.

GERALD KERSH

Men Without Bones (1954)

This nasty little chiller by Gerald Kersh, the author of such wonderfully titled rareties as "The Queen of Pig Island" and "The Extraordinarily Horrible Dummy," is a good example of the horror story that lurks on the borderline of science fiction. Although the mere mention of Mars, space ships, or outer space—all three of which are mentioned in this tale —is enough to make editors and book dealers think "science fiction," there is nonetheless a large horror subgenre that exploits the machinery of science fiction as a means of generating cosmic fear. The Blackwood, Wells, and Hodgson items in this book make selective use of science-fiction motifs, as do American works by writers like Hawthorne ("Rapaccini's Daughter") and Bierce ("The Damned Thing"). Some critics, such as L. Sprague de Camp, even contend that Lovecraft's Cthulhu Mythos tales are in a quasi-science-fiction mode.

In any case, the "little fat men without bones" in this grotesque story are the stuff of nightmares, not of facts and theorems. They induce a "lost, blank look" in the storyteller and stir the hairs on the back of the narrator's neck virtually the moment the tale within a tale commences. They may well do the same for the reader; from the first deadpan spider-killing image to the final surprise revelation, "Men Without Bones" communicates a consistently sticky, crawling species of horror that makes it the most "American" story in this British collection. (Kersh in fact became an American citizen in 1959.)

Indeed, one could argue that the story's "pestilential" mood is so consummately established that the italicized revelation is superfluous. On the other hand, the eccentricity of what is propounded at the end is characteristic of Kersh's oddball imagination (*On an Odd Note* is the title of one of his collections), and the story would surely be less without it.

≈ MEN WITHOUT BONES ≈

We were loading bananas into the *Claire Dodge* at Puerto Pobre, when a
feverish little fellow came aboard. Everyone stepped aside to let him pass
—even the soldiers who guard the port with nickel-plated Remington
rifles, and who go barefoot but wear polished leather leggings. They stood
back from him because they believed that he was afflicted-of-God, mad;
harmless but dangerous; best left alone.

All the time the naphtha flares were hissing, and from the hold came
the reverberation of the roaring voice of the foreman of the gang down
below crying: "Fruta! Fruta! *FRUTA!*" The leader of the dock gang bellowed the same cry, throwing down stem after stem of brilliant green
bananas. The occasion would be memorable for this, if for nothing else—
the magnificence of the night, the bronze of the Negro foreman shining
under the flares, the jade green of that fruit, and the mixed odors of the
waterfront. Out of one stem of bananas ran a hairy grey spider, which
frightened the crew and broke the banana-chain, until a Nicaraguan boy,
with a laugh, killed it with his foot. It was harmless, he said.

It was about then that the madman came aboard, unhindered, and
asked me: "Bound for where?"

He spoke quietly and in a carefully modulated voice; but there was a
certain blank, lost look in his eyes that suggested to me that I keep within
ducking distance of his restless hands which, now that I think of them,
put me in mind of that gray, hairy, bird-eating spider.

"Mobile, Alabama," I said.

"Take me along?" he asked.

"None of my affair. Sorry. Passenger myself," I said. "The skipper's
ashore. Better wait for him on the wharf. He's the boss."

"Would you happen, by any chance, to have a drink about you?"

Giving him some rum, I asked: "How come they let you aboard?"

"I'm not crazy," he said. "Not actually . . . a little fever, nothing
more. Malaria, dengue fever, jungle fever, rat-bite fever. Feverish
country, this, and others of the same nature. Allow me to introduce myself. My name is Goodbody, Doctor of Science of Osbaldeston University.
Does it convey nothing to you? No? Well then; I was assistant to Professor Yeoward. Does *that* convey anything to you?"

I said: "Yeoward, Professor Yeoward? Oh yes. He was lost, wasn't he, somewhere in the upland jungle beyond the source of the Amer River?"

"Correct!" cried the little man who called himself Goodbody. "I saw him get lost."

Fruta!—Fruta!—Fruta!—Fruta! came the voices of the men in the hold. There was rivalry between their leader and the big black stevedor ashore. The flares spluttered. The green bananas came down. And a kind of sickly sigh came out of the jungle, off the rotting river—not a wind, not a breeze—something like the foul breath of high fever.

Trembling with eagerness and, at the same time, shaking with fever chills, so that he had to use two hands to raise his glass to his lips—even so, he spilled most of the rum—Doctor Goodbody said: "For God's sake, get me out of this country—take me to Mobile—hide me in your cabin!"

"I have no authority," I said, "but you are an American citizen; you can identify yourself; the Consul will send you home."

"No doubt. But that would take time. The Consul thinks I am crazy too. And if I don't get away, I fear that I really will go out of my mind. Can't you help me? I'm afraid."

"Come on, now," I said. "No one shall hurt you while I'm around. What are you afraid of?"

"Men without bones," he said, and there was something in his voice that stirred the hairs on the back of my neck. "Little fat men without bones!"

I wrapped him in a blanket, gave him some quinine, and let him sweat and shiver for a while, before I asked, humoring him: "What men without bones?"

He talked in fits and starts in his fever, his reason staggering just this side of delirium:

". . . What men without bones? . . . They are nothing to be afraid of, actually. It is they who are afraid of you. You can kill them with your boot, or with a stick. . . . They are something like jelly. No, it is not really fear—it is the nausea, the disgust they inspire. It overwhelms. It paralyses! I have seen a jaguar, I tell you—a full-grown jaguar—stand frozen, while they clung to him, in hundreds, and ate him up alive! Believe me, I saw it. Perhaps it is some oil they secrete, some odor they give out . . . I don't know . . ."

Then, weeping, Doctor Goodbody said: "Oh, nightmare—nightmare—nightmare! To think of the depths to which a noble creature can be degraded by hunger! Horrible, horrible!"

"Some debased form of life that you found in the jungle above the source of the Amer?" I suggested. "Some degenerate kind of anthropoid?"

"No, no, no. *Men!* Now surely you remember Professor Yeoward's ethnological expedition?"

"It was lost," I said.

"All but me," he said. ". . . We had bad luck. At the Anaña Rapids we lost two canoes, half our supplies and most of our instruments. And also Doctor Terry, and Jack Lambert, and eight of our carriers. . . .

"Then we were in Ahu territory where the Indians use poison darts, but we made friends with them and bribed them to carry our stuff westward through the jungle . . . because, you see, all science starts with a guess, a rumor, an old wives' tale; and the object of Professor Yeoward's expedition was to investigate a series of Indian folk tales that tallied. Legends of a race of gods that came down from the sky in a great flame when the world was very young. . . .

"Line by criss-cross line, and circle by concentric circle, Yeoward localized the place in which these tales had their root—an unexplored place that has no name because the Indians refuse to give it a name, it being what they call a 'bad place'."

His chills subsiding and his fever abating, Doctor Goodbody spoke calmly and rationally now. He said, with a short laugh: "I don't know why, whenever I get a touch of fever, the memory of those boneless men comes back in a nightmare to give me the horrors. . . .

"So, we went to look for the place where the gods came down in flame out of the night. The little tattooed Indians took us to the edge of the Ahu territory and then put down their packs and asked for their pay, and no consideration would induce them to go further. We were going, they said, to a very bad place. Their chief, who had been a great man in his day, signwriting with a twig, told us that he had stayed there once, and drew a picture of something with an oval body and four limbs, at which he spat before rubbing it out with his foot in the dirt. Spiders? we asked. Crabs? What?

"So we were forced to leave what we could not carry with the old chief against our return, and go on unaccompanied, Yeoward and I, through thirty miles of the rottenest jungle in the world. We made about a quarter of a mile in a day . . . a pestilential place! When that stinking wind blows out of the jungle, I smell nothing but death, and panic. . . .

"But, at last, we cut our way to the plateau and climbed the slope, and there we saw something marvelous. It was something that had been a gigantic machine. Originally it must have been a pear-shaped thing, at least a thousand feet long and, in its widest part, six hundred feet in diameter. I don't know of what metal it had been made, because there was only a dusty outline of a hull and certain ghostly remains of unbelievably intricate mechanisms to prove that it had ever been. We could not guess from where it had come; but the impact of its landing had made a great valley in the middle of the plateau.

"It was the discovery of the age! It proved that countless years ago, this planet had been visited by people from the stars! Wild with excitement, Yeoward and I plunged into this fabulous ruin. But whatever we touched fell away to fine powder.

"At last, on the third day, Yeoward found a semi-circular plate of some extraordinarily hard metal, which was covered with the most maddeningly familiar diagrams. We cleaned it, and for twenty-four hours, scarcely pausing to eat and drink, Yeoward studied it. And, then, before the dawn of the fifth day he awoke me, with a great cry, and said: 'It's a map, a map of the heavens, and a chart of a course from Mars to Earth!'"

"And he showed me how those ancient explorers of space had proceeded from Mars to Earth, via the Moon. . . . To crash on this naked plateau in this green hell of a jungle? I wondered. 'Ah, but was it a jungle then?' said Yeoward. 'This may have happened five million years ago!'"

"I said: 'Oh, but surely! it took only a few hundred years to bury Rome. How could this thing have stayed above ground for five thousand years, let alone five million?' Yeoward said: 'It didn't. The earth swallows things and regurgitates them. This is a volcanic region. One little upheaval can swallow a city, and one tiny peristalsis in the bowels of the earth can bring its remains to light again a million years later. So it must have been with the machine from Mars . . .'

" 'I wonder who was inside it,' I said. Yeoward replied: 'Very likely some utterly alien creatures that couldn't tolerate the Earth, and died, or else were killed in the crash. No skeleton could survive such a space of time.'

"So, we built up the fire, and Yeoward went to sleep. Having slept, I watched. Watched for what? I didn't know. Jaguars, peccaries, snakes? None of these beasts climbed up to the plateau; there was nothing for them up there. Still, unaccountably, I was afraid.

"There was the weight of ages on the place. *Respect old age*, one is told. . . . The greater the age, the deeper the respect, you might say. But it is not respect; it is dread, it is fear of time and death, sir! . . . I must have dozed, because the fire was burning low—I had been most careful to keep it alive and bright—when I caught my first glimpse of the boneless men.

"Starting up, I saw, at the rim of the plateau, a pair of eyes that picked up luminosity from the fading light of the fire. *A jaguar*, I thought, and took up my rifle. But it could not have been a jaguar because, when I looked left and right I saw that the plateau was ringed with pairs of shining eyes . . . as it might be, a collar of opals; and there came to my nostrils an odor of God knows what.

"Fear has its smell as any animal-trainer will tell you. Sickness has its smell—ask any nurse. These smells compel healthy animals to fight or to run away. This was a combination of the two, plus a stink of vegetation gone bad. I fired at the pair of eyes I had first seen. Then, all the eyes disappeared while, from the jungle, there came a chattering and a twittering of monkeys and birds, as the echoes of the shot went flapping away.

"And then, thank God, the dawn came. I should not have liked to see by artificial light the thing I had shot between the eyes.

"It was grey and, in texture, tough and gelatinous. Yet, in form, externally, it was not unlike a human being. It had eyes, and there were either vestiges—or rudiments—of head, and neck, and a kind of limbs.

"Yeoward told me that I must pull myself together; overcome my 'childish revulsion', as he called it; and look into the nature of the beast. I may say that he kept a long way away from it when I opened it. It was my job as zoologist of the expedition, and I had to do it. Microscopes and other delicate instruments had been lost with the canoes. I worked with a knife and forceps. And found? Nothing: a kind of digestive system enclosed in very tough jelly, a rudimentary nervous system, and a brain about the size of a walnut. The entire creature, stretched out, measured four feet.

"In a laboratory I could tell you, perhaps, something about it . . . with an assistant or two, to keep me company. As it was, I did what I could with a hunting-knife and forceps, without dyes or microscope, swallowing my nausea—it was a nauseating thing!—memorizing what I found. But, as the sun rose higher, the thing liquefied, melted, until by nine o'clock there was nothing but a glutinous gray puddle, with two green eyes swimming in it. . . . And these eyes—I can see them now—burst with a thick *pop*, making a detestable sticky ripple in that puddle of corruption. . . .

"After that, I went away for a while. When I came back, the sun had burned it all away, and there was nothing but something like what you see after a dead jellyfish has evaporated on a hot beach. Slime. Yeoward had a white face when he asked me: 'What the devil is it?' I told him that I didn't know, that it was something outside my experience, and that although I pretended to be a man of science with a detached mind, nothing would induce me ever to touch one of the things again.

"Yeoward said: 'You're getting hysterical, Goodbody. Adopt the proper attitude. God knows, we are not here for the good of our health. Science, man, science! Not a day passes but some doctor pokes his fingers into fouler things than that!' I said: 'Don't you believe it. Professor Yeoward, I have handled and dissected some pretty queer things in my time, but this is something repulsive. I have nerves? I dare say. Maybe we should have brought a psychiatrist . . . I notice, by the way, that you aren't too anxious to come close to me after I've tampered with that thing. I'll shoot one with pleasure, but if you want to investigate it, try it yourself and see!'

"Yeoward said that he was deeply occupied with his metal plate. There was no doubt, he told me, that this machine that had been had come from Mars. But, evidently, he preferred to keep the fire between himself and me, after I had touched that abomination of hard jelly.

"Yeoward kept himself to himself, rummaging in the ruin. I went about my business, which was to investigate forms of animal life. I do not know what I might have found, if I had had—I don't say the courage, because I didn't lack that—if I had had some company. Alone, my nerve broke.

"It happened one morning. I went into the jungle that surrounded us, trying to swallow the fear that choked me, and drive away the sense of revulsion that not only made me want to turn and run, but made me afraid to turn my back even to get away. You may or may not know that, of all the beasts that live in that jungle, the most impregnable is the sloth. He finds a stout limb, climbs out on it, and hangs from it by his twelve steely claws; a tardigrade that lives on leaves. Your tardigrade is so tenacious that even in death, shot through the heart, it will hang on to its branch. It has an immensely tough hide covered by an impenetrable coat of coarse, matted hair. A panther or a jaguar is helpless against the passive resistance of such a creature. It finds itself a tree, which it does not leave until it has eaten every leaf, and chooses for a sleeping place a branch exactly strong enough to bear its weight.

"In this detestable jungle, on one of my brief expeditions—brief, because I was alone and afraid—I stopped to watch a giant sloth hanging motionless from the largest bough of a half-denuded tree, asleep, impervious, indifferent. Then, out of that stinking green twilight came a horde of those jellyfish things. They *poured up* the tree, and writhed along the branch.

"Even the sloth, which generally knows no fear, was afraid. It tried to run away, hooked itself on to a thinner part of the branch, which broke. It fell, and at once was covered with a shuddering mass of jelly. Those boneless men do not bite: they suck. And, as they suck, their color changes from grey to pink and then to brown.

"But they are afraid of us. There is race-memory involved here. We repel them, and they repel us. When they became aware of my presence, they—I was going to say, ran away—they slid away, dissolved into the shadows that kept dancing and dancing and dancing under the trees. And the horror came upon me, so that I ran away, and arrived back at our camp, bloody about the face with thorns, and utterly exhausted.

"Yeoward was lancing a place in his ankle. A tourniquet was tied under his knee. Near-by lay a dead snake. He had broken its back with that same metal plate, but it had bitten him first. He said: 'What kind of snake do you call this? I'm afraid it is venomous. I feel a numbness in my cheeks and around my heart, and I cannot feel my hands.'

"I said: 'Oh, my God! You've been bitten by a jarajaca!'"

" 'And we have lost our medical supplies,' he said, with regret. 'And there is so much work left to do. Oh, dear me, dear me! . . . Whatever happens, my dear fellow, take *this* and get back.'

"And he gave me that semi-circle of unknown metal as a sacred trust. Two hours later, he died. That night the circle of glowing eyes grew narrower. I emptied my rifle at it, time and again. At dawn, the boneless men disappeared.

"I heaped rocks on the body of Yeoward. I made a pylon, so that the men without bones could not get at him. Then—oh, so dreadfully lonely and afraid!—I shouldered my pack, and took my rifle and my machete, and ran away, down the trail we had covered. But I lost my way.

"Can by can of food, I shed weight. Then my rifle went, and my ammunition. After that, I threw away even my machete. A long time later, that semi-circular plate became too heavy for me, so I tied it to a tree with liana-vine, and went on.

"So I reached the Ahu territory, where the tattooed men nursed me and were kind to me. The women chewed my food for me, before they fed me, until I was strong again. Of the stores we had left there, I took only as much as I might need, leaving the rest as payment for guides and men to man the canoe down the river. And so I got back out of the jungle. . . .

"Please give me a little more rum." His hand was steady, now, as he drank, and his eyes were clear.

I said to him: "Assuming that what you say is true: these 'boneless men'—they were, I presume, the Martians? Yet it sounds unlikely, surely? Do invertebrates smelt hard metals and——"

"Who said anything about Martians?" cried Doctor Goodbody. "No, no, no! The Martians came here, adapted themselves to new conditions of life. Poor fellows, they changed, sank low; went through a whole new process—a painful process of evolution. What I'm trying to tell you, you fool, is that Yeoward and I did *not* discover Martians. Idiot, don't you see? *Those boneless things are men. We are Martians!*"

ROSEMARY TIMPERLEY

Harry (1955)

A prolific practitioner of the traditional ghost story in contemporary settings, Rosemary Timperley has a special fondness for tales involving children. These are not the fearful "evil" children of Henry James and Arthur Machen but simply children who see things differently. As Freud noted in "The Uncanny," the tale of terror frequently attempts to recapture a child's vision of reality, one in which the natural and the supernatural blend together in a common bedazzlement.

"Harry" moves from the child's world, which contains wonders such as Christine's "imaginary playmate," to the "mad" world of the old woman, whose perspective is much like Christine's. This is the romantic vision of Yeats and Machen, in which the very young and the very old see things—"the dead who aren't dead and the living who aren't alive"—never apprehended by normal adults like Christine's mother (touchingly portrayed as she is) or her fatuous doctor.

"They say the place is haunted," says the old woman. "But what's the fuss about? Life and death. They're very close." This "closeness" of life and death, of seers and their ghosts, is a secret shared by overly "imaginative" children and "mad" old ladies. As this marvelously symmetrical story ends exactly as it begins, youth collapses into age, childhood into death; the tiny gap is closed, and life and death are one.

≈ HARRY ≈

Such ordinary things make me afraid. Sunshine. Sharp shadows on grass. White roses. Children with red hair. And the name—Harry. Such an ordinary name.

Yet the first time Christine mentioned the name, I felt a premonition of fear.

She was five years old, due to start school in three months' time. It was a hot, beautiful day and she was playing alone in the garden, as she often did. I saw her lying on her stomach in the grass, picking daisies and making daisy-chains with laborious pleasure. The sun burned on her pale red hair and made her skin look very white. Her big blue eyes were wide with concentration.

Suddenly she looked towards the bush of white roses, which cast its shadow over the grass, and smiled.

"Yes, I'm Christine," she said. She rose and walked slowly towards the bush, her little plump legs defenceless and endearing beneath the too short blue cotton skirt. She was growing fast.

"With my mummy and daddy," she said clearly. Then, after a pause, "Oh, but *they* are my mummy and daddy."

She was in the shadow of the bush now. It was as if she'd walked out of the world of light into darkness. Uneasy, without quite knowing why, I called her:

"Chris, what are you doing?"

"Nothing." The voice sounded too far away.

"Come indoors now. It's too hot for you out there."

"Not too hot."

"Come indoors, Chris."

She said: "I must go in now. Good-bye," then walked slowly towards the house.

"Chris, who were you talking to?"

"Harry," she said.

"Who's Harry?"

"Harry."

354

I couldn't get anything else out of her, so I just gave her some cake and milk and read to her until bedtime. As she listened, she stared out at the garden. Once she smiled and waved. It was a relief finally to tuck her up in bed and feel she was safe.

When Jim, my husband, came home I told him about the mysterious 'Harry'. He laughed.

"Oh, she's started that lark, has she?"

"What do you mean, Jim?"

"It's not so very rare for only children to have an imaginary companion. Some kids talk to their dolls. Chris has never been keen on her dolls. She hasn't any brothers or sisters. She hasn't any friends her own age. So she imagines someone."

"But why has she picked that particular name?"

He shrugged. "You know how kids pick things up. I don't know what you're worrying about, honestly I don't."

"Nor do I really. It's just that I feel extra responsible for her. More so than if I were her real mother."

"I know, but she's all right. Chris is fine. She's a pretty healthy, intelligent little girl. A credit to you."

"And to you."

"In fact, we're thoroughly nice parents!"

"And so modest."

We laughed together and he kissed me. I felt consoled.

Until next morning.

Again the sun shone brilliantly on the small, bright lawn and white roses. Christine was sitting on the grass, cross-legged, staring towards the rose bush, smiling.

"Hello," she said. "I hoped you'd come. . . . Because I like you. How old are you? . . . I'm only five and a piece. . . . I'm *not* a baby! I'm going to school soon and I shall have a new dress. A green one. Do you go to school? . . . What do you do then?" She was silent for a while, nodding, listening, absorbed.

I felt myself going cold as I stood there in the kitchen. "Don't be silly. Lots of children have an imaginary companion," I told myself desperately. "Just carry on as if nothing were happening. Don't listen. Don't be a fool."

But I called Chris in earlier than usual for her mid-morning milk.

"Your milk's ready, Chris. Come along."

"In a minute." This was a strange reply. Usually she rushed in eagerly for her milk and the special sandwich cream biscuits, over which she was a little gourmande.

"Come now, darling," I said.

"Can Harry come too?"

"No!" The cry burst from me harshly, surprising me.

"Goodbye, Harry. I'm sorry you can't come in but I've got to have my milk," Chris said, then ran towards the house.

"Why can't Harry have some milk too?" she challenged me.

"Who *is* Harry, darling?"

"Harry's my brother."

"But Chris, you haven't got a brother. Daddy and mummy have only got one child, one little girl, that's you. Harry can't be your brother."

"Harry's my brother. He says so." She bent over the glass of milk and emerged with a smeary top lip. Then she grabbed at the biscuits. At least 'Harry' hadn't spoilt her appetite!

After she'd had her milk, I said, "We'll go shopping now, Chris. You'd like to come to the shops with me, wouldn't you?"

"I want to stay with Harry."

"Well you can't. You're coming with me."

"Can Harry come too?"

"No."

My hands were trembling as I put on my hat and gloves. It was chilly in the house nowadays, as if there were a cold shadow over it in spite of the sun outside. Chris came with me meekly enough, but as we walked down the street, she turned and waved.

I didn't mention any of this to Jim that night. I knew he'd only scoff as he'd done before. But when Christine's 'Harry' fantasy went on day after day, it got more and more on my nerves. I came to hate and dread those long summer days. I longed for grey skies and rain. I longed for the white roses to wither and die. I trembled when I heard Christine's voice prattling away in the garden. She talked quite unrestrainedly to 'Harry' now.

One Sunday, when Jim heard her at it, he said:

"I'll say one thing for imaginary companions, they help a child on with her talking. Chris is talking much more freely than she used to."

"With an accent," I blurted out.

"An accent?"

"A slight cockney accent."

"My dearest, every London child gets a slight cockney accent. It'll be much worse when she goes to school and meets lots of other kids."

"We don't talk cockney. Where does she get it from? Who can she be getting it from except Ha---" I couldn't say the name.

"The baker, the milkman, the dustman, the coalman, the window cleaner—want any more?"

"I suppose not." I laughed ruefully. Jim made me feel foolish.

"Anyway," said Jim, "*I* haven't noticed any cockney in her voice."

"There isn't when she talks to us. It's only when she's talking to—to him."

"To Harry. You know, I'm getting quite attached to young Harry. Wouldn't it be fun if one day we looked out and saw him?"

"Don't," I cried. "Don't say that! It's my nightmare. My waking nightmare. Oh, Jim, I can't bear it much longer."

He looked astonished. "This Harry business is really getting you down, isn't it?"

"Of course it is! Day in, day out, I hear nothing but 'Harry this,' 'Harry that,' 'Harry says,' 'Harry thinks,' 'Can Harry have some?' 'Can Harry come too?'—it's all right for you out at the office all day, but I have to live with it: I'm—I'm afraid of it, Jim. It's so queer."

"Do you know what I think you should do to put your mind at rest?"

"What?"

"Take Chris along to see old Dr Webster tomorrow. Let him have a little talk with her."

"Do you think she's ill—in her mind?"

"Good heavens, no! But when we come across something that's beyond us, it's as well to take professional advice."

Next day I took Chris to see Dr Webster. I left her in the waiting-room while I told him briefly about Harry. He nodded sympathetically, then said:

"It's a fairly unusual case, Mrs James, but by no means unique. I've had several cases of children's imaginary companions becoming so real to them that the parents got the jitters. I expect she's rather a lonely little girl, isn't she?"

"She doesn't know any other children. We're new to the neighbourhood, you see. But that will be put right when she starts school."

"And I think you'll find that when she goes to school and meets other children, these fantasies will disappear. You see, every child needs company of her own age, and if she doesn't get it, she invents it. Older people who are lonely talk to themselves. That doesn't mean that they're crazy, just that they need to talk to someone. A child is more practical. Seems silly to talk to oneself, she thinks, so she invents someone to talk to. I honestly don't think you've anything to worry about."

"That's what my husband says."

"I'm sure he does. Still, I'll have a chat with Christine as you've brought her. Leave us alone together."

I went to the waiting-room to fetch Chris. She was at the window. She said: "Harry's waiting."

"Where, Chris?" I said quietly, wanting suddenly to see him with her eyes.

"There. By the rose bush."

The doctor had a bush of white roses in his garden.

"There's no-one there," I said. Chris gave me a glance of unchildlike scorn. "Dr Webster wants to see you now, darling," I said shakily. "You remember him, don't you? He gave you sweets when you were getting better from chicken pox."

"Yes," she said and went willingly enough to the doctor's surgery. I waited restlessly. Faintly I heard their voices through the wall, heard the doctor's chuckle, Christine's high peal of laughter. She was talking away to the doctor in a way she didn't talk to me.

When they came out, he said: "Nothing wrong with her whatever. She's just an imaginative little monkey. A word of advice, Mrs James. Let her talk about Harry. Let her become accustomed to confiding in you. I gather you've shown some disapproval of this 'brother' of hers so she doesn't talk much to you about him. He makes wooden toys, doesn't he, Chris?"

"Yes, Harry makes wooden toys."

"And he can read and write, can't he?"

"And swim and climb trees and paint pictures. Harry can do everything. He's a wonderful brother." Her little face flushed with adoration.

The doctor patted me on the shoulder and said: "Harry sounds a very nice brother for her. He's even got red hair like you, Chris, hasn't he?"

"Harry's got red hair," said Chris proudly, "redder than my hair. And he's nearly as tall as daddy, only thinner. He's as tall as you, mummy. He's fourteen. He says he's tall for his age. What *is* tall for his age?"

"Mummy will tell you about that as you walk home," said Dr Webster. "Now, goodbye, Mrs James. Don't worry. Just let her prattle. Goodbye, Chris. Give my love to Harry."

"He's there," said Chris, pointing to the doctor's garden. "He's been waiting for me."

Dr. Webster laughed. "They're incorrigible, aren't they?" he said. "I know one poor mother whose children invented a whole tribe of imaginary natives whose rituals and taboos ruled the household. Perhaps you're lucky, Mrs James!"

I tried to feel comforted by all this, but I wasn't. I hoped sincerely that when Chris started school this wretched Harry business would finish.

Chris ran ahead of me. She looked up as if at someone beside her. For a brief, dreadful second, I saw a shadow on the pavement alongside her own—a long, thin shadow—like a boy's shadow. Then it was gone. I ran to catch her up and held her hand tightly all the way home. Even in the comparative security of the house—the house so strangely cold in this hot weather—I never let her out of my sight. On the face of it she behaved no differently towards me, but in reality she was drifting away. The child in my house was becoming a stranger.

For the first time since Jim and I had adopted Chris, I wondered seriously: Who is she? Where does she come from? Who were her real parents? Who is this little loved stranger I've taken as a daughter? Who *is* Christine?

Another week passed. It was Harry, Harry all the time. The day before she was to start school, Chris said:

"Not going to school."

"You're going to school tomorrow, Chris. You're looking forward to it. You know you are. There'll be lots of other little girls and boys."

"Harry says he can't come too."

"You won't want Harry at school. He'll—" I tried hard to follow the doctor's advice and appear to believe in Harry—"He'll be too old. He'd feel silly among little boys and girls, a great lad of fourteen."

"I won't go to school without Harry. I want to be with Harry." She began to weep, loudly, painfully.

"Chris, stop this nonsense! Stop it!" I struck her sharply on the arm. Her crying ceased immediately. She stared at me, her blue eyes wide open and frighteningly cold. She gave me an adult stare that made me tremble. Then she said:

"You don't love me. Harry loves me. Harry wants me. He says I can go with him."

"I will not hear any more of this!" I shouted, hating the anger in my voice, hating myself for being angry at all with a little girl—*my* little girl —mine——

I went down on one knee and held out my arms.

"Chris, darling, come here."

She came, slowly. "I love you," I said. "I love you, Chris, and I'm real. School is real. Go to school to please me."

"Harry will go away if I do."

"You'll have other friends."

"I want Harry." Again the tears, wet against my shoulder now. I held her closely.

"You're tired, baby. Come to bed."

She slept with the tear stains still on her face.

It was still daylight. I went to the window to draw her curtains. Golden shadows and long strips of sunshine in the garden. Then, again, like a dream, the long thin clear-cut shadow of a boy near the white roses. Like a mad woman I opened the window and shouted:

"Harry! Harry!"

I thought I saw a glimmer of red among the roses, like close red curls on a boy's head. Then there was nothing.

When I told Jim about Christine's emotional outburst he said: "Poor little kid. It's always a nervy business, starting school. She'll be all right once she gets there. You'll be hearing less about Harry too, as time goes on."

"Harry doesn't want her to go to school."

"Hey! You sound as if you believe in Harry yourself!"

"Sometimes I do."

"Believing in evil spirits in your old age?" he teased me. But his eyes were concerned. He thought I was going 'round the bend' and small blame to him!

"I don't think Harry's evil," I said. "He's just a boy. A boy who doesn't exist, except for Christine. And who *is* Christine?"

"None of that!" said Jim sharply. "When we adopted Chris we decided she was to be our own child. No probing into the past. No wondering and worrying. No mysteries. Chris is as much ours as if she'd been born of our flesh. Who is Christine indeed! She's our daughter—and just you remember that!"

"Yes, Jim, you're right. Of course you're right."

He'd been so fierce about it that I didn't tell him what I planned to do the next day while Chris was at school.

Next morning Chris was silent and sulky. Jim joked with her and tried to cheer her, but all she would do was look out of the window and say: "Harry's gone."

"You won't need Harry now. You're going to school," said Jim.

Chris gave him that look of grown-up contempt she'd given me sometimes.

She and I didn't speak as I took her to school. I was almost in tears. Although I was glad for her to start school, I felt a sense of loss at parting with her. I suppose every mother feels that when she takes her ewe-lamb to school for the first time. It's the end of babyhood for the child, the beginning of life in reality, life with its cruelty, its strangeness, its barbarity. I kissed her goodbye at the gate and said:

"You'll be having dinner at school with the other children, Chris, and I'll call for you when school is over, at three o'clock."

"Yes, Mummy." She held my hand tightly. Other nervous little children were arriving with equally nervous parents. A pleasant young teacher with fair hair and a white linen dress appeared at the gate. She gathered the new children towards her and led them away. She gave me a sympathetic smile as she passed and said: "We'll take good care of her."

I felt quite light-hearted as I walked away, knowing that Chris was safe and I didn't have to worry.

Now I started on my secret mission. I took a bus to town and went to the big, gaunt building I hadn't visited for over five years. Then, Jim and I had gone together. The top floor of the building belonged to the Greythorne Adoption Society. I climbed the four flights and knocked on the familiar door with its scratched paint. A secretary whose face I didn't know let me in.

"May I see Miss Cleaver? My name is Mrs James."

"Have you an appointment?"

"No, but it's very important."

"I'll see." The girl went out and returned a second later. "Miss Cleaver will see you, Mrs James."

Miss Cleaver, a tall, thin, grey-haired woman with a charming smile, a plain, kindly face and a very wrinkled brow, rose to meet me. "Mrs James. How nice to see you again. How's Christine?"

"She's very well. Miss Cleaver, I'd better get straight to the point. I know you don't normally divulge the origin of a child to its adopters and vice versa, but I must know who Christine is."

"Sorry, Mrs. James," she began, "our rules . . ."

"Please let me tell you the whole story, then you'll see I'm not just suffering from vulgar curiosity."

I told her about Harry.

When I finished, she said: "It's very queer. Very queer indeed. Mrs

James, I'm going to break my rule for once. I'm going to tell you in strict confidence where Christine came from.

"She was born in a very poor part of London. There were four in the family, father, mother, son and Christine herself."

"Son?"

"Yes. He was fourteen when—when it happened."

"When what happened?"

"Let me start at the beginning. The parents hadn't really wanted Christine. The family lived in one room at the top of an old house which should have been condemned by the Sanitary Inspector in my opinion. It was difficult enough when there were only three of them, but with a baby as well life became a nightmare. The mother was a neurotic creature, slatternly, unhappy, too fat. After she'd had the baby she took no interest in it. The brother, however, adored the little girl from the start. He got into trouble for cutting school so he could look after her.

"The father had a steady job in a warehouse, not much money, but enough to keep them alive. Then he was sick for several weeks and lost his job. He was laid up in that messy room, ill, worrying, nagged by his wife, irked by the baby's crying and his son's eternal fussing over the child—I got all these details from neighbours afterwards, by the way. I was also told that he'd had a particularly bad time in the war and had been in a nerve hospital for several months before he was fit to come home at all after his demob. Suddenly it all proved too much for him.

"One morning, in the small hours, a woman in the ground floor room saw something fall past her window and heard a thud on the ground. She went out to look. The son of the family was there on the ground. Christine was in his arms. The boy's neck was broken. He was dead. Christine was blue in the face but still breathing faintly.

"The woman woke the household, sent for the police and the doctor, then they went to the top room. They had to break down the door, which was locked and sealed inside. An overpowering smell of gas greeted them, in spite of the open window.

"They found husband and wife dead in bed and a note from the husband saying:

> 'I can't go on. I am going to kill them all.
> It's the only way.'

"The police concluded that he'd sealed up door and windows and turned on the gas when his family were asleep, then lain beside his wife until he drifted into unconsciousness, and death. But the son must have wakened. Perhaps he struggled with the door but couldn't open it. He'd be too weak to shout. All he could do was pluck away the seals from the window, open it, and fling himself out, holding his adored little sister tightly in his arms.

"Why Christine herself wasn't gassed is rather a mystery. Perhaps her head was right under the bedclothes, pressed against her brother's chest—they always slept together. Anyway, the child was taken to hospital, then to the home where you and Mr James first saw her . . . and a lucky day that was for little Christine!"

"So her brother saved her life and died himself?" I said.

"Yes. He was a very brave man."

"Perhaps he thought not so much of saving her as of keeping her with him. Oh dear! That sounds ungenerous. I didn't mean to be. Miss Cleaver, what was his name?"

"I'll have to look that up for you." She referred to one of her many files and said at last: "The family's name was Jones and the fourteen-year-old brother was called 'Harold'."

"And did he have red hair?" I murmured.

"That I don't know, Mrs James."

"But it's Harry. The boy was Harry. What does it mean? I can't understand it."

"It's not easy, but I think perhaps deep in her unconscious mind Christine has always remembered Harry, the companion of her babyhood. We don't think of children as having much memory, but there must be images of the past tucked away somewhere in the little heads. Christine doesn't *invent* this Harry. She *remembers* him. So clearly that she's almost brought him to life again. I know it sounds far-fetched, but the whole story is so odd that I can't think of any other explanation."

"May I have the address of the house where they lived?"

She was reluctant to give this information, but I persuaded her and set out at last to find No. 13 Canver Row, where the man Jones had tried to kill himself and his whole family and almost succeeded.

The house seemed deserted. It was filthy and derelict. But one thing made me stare and stare. There was a tiny garden. A scatter of bright uneven grass splashed the bald brown patches of earth. But the little garden had one strange glory that none of the other houses in the poor sad street possessed—a bush of white roses. They bloomed gloriously. Their scent was over-powering.

I stood by the bush and stared up at the top window.

A voice startled me: "What are you doing here?"

It was an old woman, peering from the ground floor window.

"I thought the house was empty," I said.

"Should be. Been condemned. But they can't get me out. Nowhere else to go. Won't go. The others went quickly enough after it happened. No-one else wants to come. They say the place is haunted. So it is. But what's the fuss about? Life and death. They're very close. You get to know that when you're old. Alive or dead. What's the difference?"

She looked at me with yellowish, bloodshot eyes and said: "I saw him fall past my window. That's where he fell. Among the roses. He still comes back. I see him. He won't go away until he gets her."

"Who—who are you talking about?"

"Harry Jones. Nice boy he was. Red hair. Very thin. Too determined though. Always got his own way. Loved Christine too much, I thought. Died among the roses. Used to sit down here with her for hours, by the roses. Then died there. Or do people die? The church ought to give us an answer, but it doesn't. Not one you can believe. Go away, will you? This place isn't for you. It's for the dead who aren't dead, and the living who aren't alive. Am I alive or dead? You tell me. I don't know."

The crazy eyes staring at me beneath the matted white fringe of hair frightened me. Mad people are terrifying. One can pity them, but one is still afraid. I murmured:

"I'll go now. Goodbye," and tried to hurry across the hard hot pavements although my legs felt heavy and half-paralysed, as in a nightmare.

The sun blazed down on my head, but I was hardly aware of it. I lost all sense of time or place as I stumbled on.

Then I heard something that chilled my blood.

A clock struck three.

At three o'clock I was supposed to be at the school gates, waiting for Christine.

Where was I now? How near the school? What bus should I take?

I made frantic enquiries of passers-by, who looked at me fearfully, as I had looked at the old woman. They must have thought I was crazy.

At last I caught the right bus and, sick with dust, petrol fumes and fear, reached the school. I ran across the hot, empty playground. In a classroom, the young teacher in white was gathering her books together.

"I've come for Christine James. I'm her mother. I'm so sorry I'm late. Where is she?" I gasped.

"Christine James?" The girl frowned, then said brightly: "Oh, yes, I remember, the pretty little red-haired girl. That's all right, Mrs James. Her brother called for her. How alike they are, aren't they? And so devoted. It's rather sweet to see a boy of that age so fond of his baby sister. Has your husband got red hair, like the two children?"

"What did—her brother—say?" I asked faintly.

"He didn't say anything. When I spoke to him, he just smiled. They'll be home by now, I should think. I say, do you feel all right?"

"Yes, thank you. I must go home."

I ran all the way home through the burning streets.

"Chris! Christine, where are you! Chris! Chris!" Sometimes even now I hear my own voice of the past screaming through the cold house. "Christine! Chris! Where are you? Answer me! Chrrriiiiiss!" Then: "Harry! Don't take her away! Come back! Harry! Harry!"

Demented, I rushed out into the garden. The sun struck me like a hot blade. The roses glared whitely. The air was so still I seemed to stand in timelessness, placelessness. For a moment, I seemed very near to Christine, although I couldn't see her. Then the roses danced before my eyes and turned red. The world turned red. Blood red. Wet red. I fell through redness to blackness to nothingness—to almost death.

For weeks I was in bed with sunstroke which turned to brain fever. During that time Jim and the police searched for Christine in vain. The futile search continued for months. The papers were full of the strange disappearance of the red-haired child. The teacher described the 'brother' who had called for her. There were newspaper stories of kidnapping, baby-snatching, child-murders.

Then the sensation died down. Just another unsolved mystery in police files.

And only two people knew what had happened. An old crazed woman living in a derelict house, and myself.

Years have passed. But I walk in fear.

Such ordinary things make me afraid. Sunshine. Sharp shadows on grass. White roses. Children with red hair. And the name—Harry. Such an ordinary name!

WALTER DE LA MARE

Bad Company (1955)

This somber and poignant de la Mare tale, which appeared in his final collection, represents the author of "A: B: O." at the height of his powers. Nearly sixty years separates the publication of these two stories, and the contrast between the two is fascinating: in "A: B: O." we find an improvisatory fluidity and intensity, a search for a voice; here we find a mature compression and an austerity that waste not a word or an effect. From the first remarkable paragraph, a concise essay on what constitutes an evil face, we are pulled irresistibly into de la Mare's uniquely spectral world. The story moves from a subterranean railway station to a dingy series of alleys to a "malignant room" in a "vile, jaded, forsaken" house, a seemingly infinite underground. Even when we are allowed a brief look at the sky, we find it black and starless.

Yet despite this greater stylistic control, we find ourselves in fundamentally the same world as that of "A: B: O." Again we confront a preoccupation with isolation and loneliness (which becomes outright reclusiveness in late de la Mare) and experience a corresponding aura of deathly stillness; again we are allowed a glimpse of seemingly motiveless depravity. The allegorical questions posed at the end are an attempt to soften this severe vision of evil, as is the narrator's benevolent action in regard to what he refers to, in a welcome moment of deadpan humor, as "the vilest letter that has ever come my way. Even in print." Nevertheless, we receive not the "feeblest flicker" or "remotest signal" of whether the ghost in this story, who is "bad company" indeed, is made to sleep any happier.

≈ BAD COMPANY ≈

It is very seldom that one encounters what would appear to be sheer unadulterated evil in a human face; an evil, I mean, active, deliberate, deadly, dangerous. Folly, heedlessness, vanity, pride, craft, meanness, stupidity—yes. But even Iagos in this world are few, and devilry is as rare as witchcraft.

One winter's evening some little time ago, bound on a visit to a friend in London, I found myself on the platform of one of its many subterranean railway stations. It is an ordeal that one may undergo as seldom as one can. The glare and glitter, the noise, the very air one breathes affect nerves and spirits. One expects vaguely strange meetings in such surroundings. On this occasion, the expectation was justified. The mind is at times more attentive than the eye. Already tired, and troubled with personal cares and problems, which a little wisdom and enterprise should have refused to entertain, I had seated myself on one of the low, wooden benches to the left of the entrance to the platform, when, for no conscious reason, I was prompted to turn my head in the direction of a fellow traveller, seated across the gangway on the fellow to my bench some few yards away.

What was wrong with him? He was enveloped in a loose cape or cloak, sombre and motionless. He appeared to be wholly unaware of my abrupt scrutiny. And yet, I doubt it; for the next moment, although the door of the nearest coach gaped immediately opposite him, he had shuffled into the compartment I had entered myself, and now in its corner, confronted me, all but knee to knee. I could have touched him with my hand. We had, too, come at once into an even more intimate contact than that of touch. Our eyes—his own fixed in a dwelling and lethargic stare—had instantly met, and no less rapidly mine had uncharitably recoiled, not only in misgiving, but in something little short of disgust. The effect resembled that of an acid on milk, and for the time being cast my thoughts into confusion. Yet that one glance had taken him in.

He was old—over seventy. A wide-brimmed rusty and dusty black hat concealed his head—a head fringed with wisps of hair, lank and paper-grey. His loose, jaded cheeks were of the colour of putty; the thin lips

above the wide unshaven and dimpled chin showing scarcely a trace of
red. The cloak suspended from his shoulders mantled him to his shins.
One knuckled, cadaverous, mittened hand clasped a thick ash stick, its
handle black and polished with long usage. The only sign of life in his
countenance was secreted in his eyes—fixed on mine—hazed and dully
glistening, as a snail in winter is fixed to a wall. There was a dull deliberate
challenge in them, and as I fancied, something more than that. They
suggested that he had been in wait for me; that for him it was almost "well
met"!

For minutes together I endeavoured to accept their challenge, to make
sure. Yet I realised, fascinated the while, that he was well aware of the
futility of this attempt, as a snake is of the restless, fated bird in the
branches above its head.

Such a statement, I am aware, must appear wildly exaggerated, but I
can only record my impression. It was already latish—much later than I
had intended. The passengers came and went, and, whether intentionally
or not, none consented to occupy the seat vacant beside him. I fixed my
eyes on an advertisement—that of a Friendly Society I remember!—
immediately above his head, with the intention of watching him in the
field of an eye that I could not persuade to meet his own in full focus
again.

He had instantly detected this ingenious device. By a fraction of an
inch he had shifted his grasp upon his stick. So intolerable, at length,
became the physical—and psychical—effect of his presence on me that I
determined to leave the train at the next station, and there to await the
next. And at this precise moment, I was conscious that he had not only
withdrawn his eyes, but closed them.

I was not so easily to free myself of his company. A glance over my
shoulder as, after leaving the train, I turned towards the lift, showed him
hastily groping his way out of the carriage. The metal gate clanged. The
lift slid upwards and, such is the contrariness of human nature, a faint
disappointment followed. One may, for example, be appalled and yet en-
grossed in reading, an account of some act of infamous cruelty.

Concealing myself as best I could at the book-stall, I awaited the next
lift-load. Its few passengers having dispersed, he himself followed. In
spite of age and infirmity, he *had*, then, ascended alone the spiral staircase. Glancing, it appeared, neither to right nor left, he passed rapidly
through the barrier. And yet—*had* he not seen me?

The ticket collector raised his head, opened his mouth, watched his

retreating figure, but made no attempt to retrieve *his*. It was dark now—
the dark of London. In my absence underground, minute frozen pellets of
snow had fallen, whitening the streets and lulling the sound of the traffic.
On emerging into the street, he turned in the direction of the next
station—my own. Yet again—had he, or had he not, been aware that he
was being watched? However that might be, my journey lay his way, and
that way my feet directed me; although I was already later than I had
intended. I followed him, led on, no doubt, in part—merely by the effect
he had had on me. Some twenty or thirty yards ahead, his dark shapeless-
ness showed—distinct against the whitening pavement.

The waters of the Thames, I was aware, lay on my left. A muffled blast
from the siren of a tug announced its presence. Keeping my distance, I
followed him on. One lamp-post—two—three. At that, he seemed to
pause for a moment, as if to listen, momentarily glanced back (as I
fancied) and vanished.

When I came up with it, I found that this third lamp-post vaguely illuminated the mouth of a narrow, lightless alley between highish walls. It
led me, after a while, into another alley, yet dingier. The wall on the left
of this was evidently that of a large garden; on the right came a row of
nondescript houses, looming up in their neglect against a starless sky.

The first of these houses *appeared* to be occupied. The next two were
vacant. Dingy curtains, soot-grey against their snowy window-sills, hung
over the next. A litter of paper and refuse—abandoned by the last long
gust of wind that must have come whistling round the nearer angle of the
house—lay under the broken flight of steps up to a mid-Victorian porch.
The small snow clinging to the bricks and to the worn and weathered
cement of the wall only added to its gaunt lifelessness.

In the faint hope of other company coming my way, and vowing that I
would follow no further than to the outlet of yet another pitch-black and
uninviting alley or court—which might indeed prove a dead end—I
turned into it. It was then that I observed, in the rays of the lamp over
my head, that in spite of the fineness of the snow and the brief time that
had elapsed, there seemed to be no trace on its surface of recent footsteps.

A faintly thudding echo accompanied me on my way. I have found it
very useful—in the country—always to carry a small electric torch in my
greatcoat pocket; but for the time being I refrained from using it. This
alley proved not to be blind. Beyond a patch of waste ground, a nebulous,
leaden-grey vacancy marked a loop here of the Thames—I decided to go
no further; and then perceived a garden gate in the wall to my right. It was

ajar, but could not long have been so because no more than an instant's flash of my torch showed marks in the snow of its recent shifting. And yet there was little wind. On the other hand, here was the open river, just a breath of a breeze across its surface might account for this. The cracked and blistered paint was shimmering with a thin coat of rime—of hoar-frost, and as if a finger had but just now scrawled in there, a clumsy arrow showed, its 'V' pointing inward. A tramp, an errand-boy, mere accident might have accounted for this. It may indeed have been a mark made some time before on the paint.

I paused in an absurd debate with myself, chiefly I think because I felt some little alarm at the thought of what might follow; yet led on also by the conviction that I had been intended, decoyed to follow. I pushed the gate a little wider open, peered in, and made my way up a woody path beneath ragged unpruned and leafless fruit trees towards the house. The snow's own light revealed a ramshackle flight of steps up to a poor, frenchified sort of canopy above french windows, one-half of their glazed doors ajar. I ascended, and peered into the intense gloom beyond it. And thus and then prepared to retrace my steps as quickly as possible, I called (in tones as near those of a London policeman as I could manage): "Hello there! Is anything wrong? Is anyone wanted?" After all, I could at least explain to my fellow-passenger if he appeared that I found both his gate and his window open; and the house was hardly pleasantly situated.

No answer was returned to me. In doubt and disquietude, but with a conviction that all was not well, I flashed my torch over the walls and furniture of the room and its heavily framed pictures. How could any-thing be "well"—with unseen company such as this besieging one's senses! Ease and pleasant companionship, the room may once have been capable of giving; in its dirt, cold, and neglect, it showed nothing of that now. I crossed it, paused again in the passage beyond it, and listened. I then entered the room beyond that. Venetian blinds, many of the slats of which had outworn their webbing, and heavy, crimson chenille side-curtains concealed its windows.

The ashes of a fire showed beyond rusty bars of the grate under a black marble mantlepiece. An oil lamp on the table, with a green shade, exuded a stink of paraffin; beyond was a table littered with books and papers, and an overturned chair. There I could see the bent-up old legs, per-ceptibly lean beneath the trousers, of the occupant of the room. In no doubt of whose remains these were, I drew near, and with bared teeth and icy, trembling fingers, drew back the fold of the cloak that lay over the face. Death has a strange sorcery. A shuddering revulsion of feeling took possession of me. This cold, once genteel, hideous, malignant room—and this!

The skin of the blue loose cheek was drawn tight over the bone; the mouth lay a little open, showing the dislodged false teeth beneath; and the dull unspeculative eyes stared out from beneath lowered lids towards the black mouth of the chimney above the fireplace. Vileness and iniquity had left their marks on the lifeless features, and yet it was rather with compassion than with horror and disgust that I stood regarding them. What desolate solitude, what misery must this old man, abandoned to himself, have experienced during the last years of his life; encountering nothing but enmity and the apprehension of his fellow creatures. I am not intending to excuse or even commiserate what I cannot understand, but the almost complete absence of any goodness in the human spirit cannot but condemn the heart to an appalling isolation. Had he been murdered, or had he come to a violent but natural end? In either case, horror and terror must have supervened.

That I had been enticed, deliberately led on, to this discovery I hadn't the least doubt, extravagant though this, too, may seem. Why? What for?

I could not bring myself to attempt to light the lamp. Besides, in that last vigil, it must have burnt itself out. My torch revealed a stub of candle on the mantlepiece. I lit that. He seemed to have been engaged in writing when the enemy of us all had approached him in silence and had struck him down.

A long and unsealed envelope lay on the table. I drew out the contents —a letter and a Will, which had been witnessed some few weeks before, apparently by a tradesman's boy and, possibly, by some derelict char-woman, Eliza Hinks. I knew enough about such things to be sure that the Will was valid and complete. This old man had been evidently more than fairly rich in this world's goods, and reluctant to surrender them. The letter was addressed to his two sisters: "To my two Sisters, Amelia and Maude." Standing there in the cold and the silence, and utterly alone— for, if any occupant of the other world had decoyed me there, there was not the faintest hint in consciousness that he or his influence was any longer present with me—I read the vilest letter that has ever come my way. Even in print. It stated that he knew the circumstances of these two remaining relatives—that he was well aware of their poverty and physical conditions. One of them, it seemed, was afflicted with cancer. He then proceeded to explain that, although they should by the intention of their mother have had a due share in her property and in the money she had left, it rejoiced him to think that his withholding of this knowledge must continually have added to their wretchedness. Why he so hated them was only vaguely suggested.

The Will he had enclosed with the letter left all that he died possessed of to—of all human establishments that need it least—the authorities of Scotland Yard. It was to be devoted, it ran, to the detection of such evil doers as are ignorant or imbecile enough to leave their misdemeanours and crimes detectable.

It is said that confession is good for the soul. Well then, as publicly as possible, I take this opportunity of announcing that, there and then, I made a little heap of envelope, letter and Will on the hearth and put a match to them. When every vestige of the paper had been consumed, I stamped the ashes down. I had touched nothing else. I would leave the vile, jaded, forsaken house to reveal its own secret; and I might ensure that that would not be long delayed.

What continues to perplex me is that so far as I can see no other agency but that of this evil old recluse himself had led me to my discovery. Why? Can it have been with this very intention? I stooped down and peeped and peered narrowly in under the lowered lids in the light of my torch, but not the feeblest flicker, remotest signal—or faintest syllabling echo of any message rewarded me. Dead fish are less unseemly.

And yet. Well—we are all of us, I suppose, at any extreme *capable* of remorse and not utterly shut against repentance. Is it possible that this priceless blessing is not denied us even when all that's earthly else appears to have come to an end?

ROBERT AICKMAN

The Same Dog (1975)

Robert Aickman, who died in 1980, was one of the most accomplished contemporary avatars of the English ghost story tradition. He was fond of saying that the ghost story at its best is "akin to poetry." No more persuasive exponent of this theory exists than Aickman's own fiction. With its exquisitely shaded ambiguities, precisely tuned diction, and bell-like musicality, Aickman's work is consummately "poetic," a triumphant rejoinder to the notion that the ghost story as an art is dead.

Aickman's fiction is similar to poetry also in that it often needs to be reread. Its shuddery secrets can be apprehended only through rigorous care and concentration. Aickman liked to quote Sacheverall Sitwell's statement that "in the end it is the mystery that lasts and not the explanation," and Aickman's stories, like those of de la Mare and Campbell, are sometimes aggressively enigmatic.

"The Same Dog," which combines fairyland and haunted-house motifs, is mysterious in an altogether satisfying way. Since much of the tale is told from a child's point of view (in startling contrast to Rosemary Timperley's "Harry," in which the adult point of view makes the experience less immediate but more stark), there is nothing arbitrary about the mystery: children have the quite accurate sense, keenly depicted here, that adults really do keep secrets from them, and the young hero's excruciating problem of being kept in the dark by adults—all the more painful in that he is an outsider even in his own family—dovetails with the supernatural secrets that cast an increasingly ominous shadow over the story. In addition to the otherworldly puzzle, we have its equally compelling context—the sense of how children experience the real world itself to be ghostly and inexplicable. The final shivery episode ensures that as an adult the hero will never, for better or worse, completely lose that sense.

"The Same Dog" features an unusual sensitivity not only to the special qualities of a child's world but also to children as individual people. Hilary and Mary are altogether charming, lifelike characters, and the strange tragedy that befalls them has a memorable poignance pre-cisely because they are so lifelike. Although Aickman has all the spectral atmosphere one could ask (note especially the careful descriptions of a "droopy and distorted" southern-Surrey countryside and of an imposing haunted house), he is fundamentally interested in character. The brief but intense relationship between Hilary and Mary is the center of the story, and it is so touchingly drawn that the last line, which should be silly, is instead, as Aickman would say, poetry.

≋ THE SAME DOG ≋

Though there were three boys, there were also twelve long years between Hilary Brigstock and his immediately elder brother, Gilbert. On the other hand, there was only one year and one month between Gilbert and the future head of the family, Roger.

Hilary could not remember when first the suggestion entered his ears that his existence was the consequence of a "mistake". Possibly he had in any case hit upon the idea already, within his own head. Nor did his Christian name help very much: people always supposed it to be the name of a girl, even though his father asserted loudly on all possible occasions that the idea was a complete mistake, a product of etymological and historical ignorance, and of typical modern sloppiness.

And his mother was dead. He was quite unable to remember her, however hard he tried; as he from time to time did. Because his father never remarried, having as clear and definite views about women as he had about many other things, Hilary grew up against an almost entirely male background. In practice, this background seemed to consist fundamentally of Roger and Gilbert forever slugging and bashing at one another, with an occasional sideswipe at their kid brother. So Hilary, though no milksop, tended to keep his own counsel and his own secrets. In particular, there are few questions asked by a young boy when there is no woman to reply to them; or, at least, few questions about anything that matters.

The family lived in the remoter part of Surrey. There was a very respectable, rather expensive, semi-infant school, Briarside, to which most of the young children were directed from the earliest age practicable. Hilary was duly sent there, as had been his brothers ahead of him, in order to learn some simple reading and figuring, and how to catch a ball, before being passed on to the fashionable preparatory school, Gorselands, on his way to Cheltenham or Wellington. Some of the family went to the one place, some to the other. It was an unusual arrangement, and outsiders could never see the sense in it.

Almost unavoidably, Briarside was a mixed establishment (though it would have been absurd to describe it as co-educational), and there Hilary formed a close and remarkable friendship with a girl, two years older than himself, named Mary Rossiter. The little girls at the school were almost the first Hilary had ever met. Even his young cousins were all boys, as happens in some families.

Mary had dark, frizzy hair, which stuck out round her head; and a rather flat face, with, however, an already fine pair of large, dark eyes, which not only sparkled, but seemed to move from side to side in surprising jerks as she spoke, which, if permitted, she did almost continuously. Generally she wore a shirt or sweater and shorts, as little girls were beginning to do at that time, and emanated extroversion; but occasionally, when there was a school celebration, more perhaps for the parents than for the tots, she would appear in a really beautiful silk dress, eclipsing everyone, and all the more in that the dress seemed not precisely right for her, but more like a stage costume. Mary Rossiter showed promise of natural leadership (some of the mums already called her "bossy"), but her fine eyes were for Hilary alone; and not only her eyes, but hands and lips and tender words as well.

From within the first few days of his arrival, Hilary was sitting next to Mary at the classes (if such they could be called) and partnering her inseparably in the playrooms and the garden. The establishment liked the boys to play with boys, the girls with the girls, and normally no admonition whatever was needed in those directions; but when it came to Hilary and Mary, the truth was that already Mary was difficult to resist when she was set upon a thing. She charmed, she smiled, and she persisted. Moreover, her father was very rich; and it was obvious from everything about her that her parents doted on her.

There were large regions of the week which the school did not claim to fill. Most of the parents awaited the release of their boys and girls and bore them home in small motor cars of the wifely kind. But Mary was left, perhaps dangerously, with her freedom; simply because she wanted it to be like that. At least, she wanted it to be like that after she had met Hilary. It is less certain where she had stood previously. As for Hilary, no one greatly cared—within a wide span of hours—whether he was home or not. There was a woman named Mrs Parker who came in each day and did all that needed to be done and did it as well as could be expected (Hilary's father would not even have considered such a person "living in"); but she had no authority to exercise discipline over Hilary, and, being thoroughly modern in her ideas, no temperamental inclination either. If

Hilary turned up for his tea, it would be provided. If he did not, trouble was saved.

Hilary and Mary went for long, long walks; for much of the distance, hand in hand. In the midst of the rather droopy and distorted southern-Surrey countryside (or one-time countryside), they would find small, worked-out sandpits, or, in case of rain, disused collapsing huts, and there they would sit close together, or one at the other's feet, talking without end, and gently embracing. He would force his small fingers through her wiry mop and make jokes about electricity coming out at the ends. She would touch the back of his neck, inside his faded red shirt, with her lips, and nuzzle into the soft, fair thicket on top of his head. They learned the southern-Surrey byways and bridlepaths remarkably thoroughly, for six or eight miles to the south-east, and six or eight miles to the south-west; and, in fact, collaborated in drawing a secret map of them. That was one of the happiest things they ever did. They were always at work revising the secret map, by the use of erasers, and adding to it, and colouring it with crayons borrowed from Briarside. They never tired of walking, because no one had ever said they should.

One day they were badly frightened.

They were walking down a sandy track, which they did not exactly know, when they came upon a large property with a wall round it. The wall was high and apparently thick. It had been covered throughout its length with plaster, but much of the plaster had either flaked, or fallen completely away, revealing the yellow bricks within, themselves tending to crumble. The wall was surmounted by a hipped roofing, which projected, in order to throw clear as much as possible of any rain that might descend; and this roofing also was much battered and gapped. One might have thought the wall to be in a late state of disease. It was blotched and mottled in every direction. None the less, it continued to be very far from surmountable, even by a fully grown person.

Hilary took a run at it, clutching at a plant which protruded from a gap in the exposed pointing, and simultaneously setting his foot upon the plaster at the bottom of a large space where the rest of the plaster had fallen away. The consequence was instant disaster. The plant leapt from its rooting, and at the same time the plaster on which Hilary's small weight rested fell off the wall in an entire large slab, and shattered into smaller pieces among the rank grass and weeds below, where Hilary lay also.

"Hilary!" It was an authentic scream, and of authentic agony.

"It's all right, Mary." Hilary resolutely raised himself, resolutely refused to weep. "I'm all right. Really I am."

She had run to him and was holding him tightly.

"Mary, please. I'll choke."

Her arms fell away from him, but uncertainly.

"We'd better go home," she said.

"No, of course not. I'm perfectly all right, I tell you. It was nothing." But this last he did not really believe.

"It was *terrible*," said Mary, with solemnity. She was wearing a skirt that day, a small-scale imitation of an adult woman's tweed skirt, and he could see her knees actually knocking together.

He put his arm round her shoulder, but, as he did so, became aware that he was shaking himself. "Silly," he said affectionately. "It wasn't anything much. Let's go on."

But she merely stood there, quivering beneath his extended arm.

There was a perceptible pause. Then she said: "I don't like this place."

It was most unlike her to say such a thing. He had never before known her to do so.

But always he took her seriously. "What's the matter?" he asked. "I *am* all right, you know. I truly am. You can feel me if you like."

And then the dog started barking—if, indeed, one could call it a bark. It was more like a steady growling roar, with a clatter mixed up in it, almost certainly of gnashing teeth: altogether something more than barking, but unmistakably canine, all the same—horribly so. Detectably it came from within the domain behind the high wall.

"Hilary," said Mary, "let's run."

But her unusual attitude had put Hilary on his mettle.

"I don't know," he said. "Not yet."

"What d'you mean?" she asked.

"I see it like this," said Hilary, rubbing a place on his knee. "Either the dog is chained up, or shut in behind that wall, and we're all right. Or else he isn't, and it's no good our running."

It was somewhat the way that Mary's own influence had taught him to think, and she responded to it.

"Perhaps we should look for some big stones," she suggested.

"Yes," he said. "Though I shouldn't think it'll be necessary. I think he must be safely shut up in some way. He'd have been out by now otherwise."

"*I'm* going to look," said Mary.

There are plenty of stones in the worn earth of southern Surrey, and many old bricks and other constructional detritus also. Within two or three minutes, Mary had assembled a pile of such things.

In the meantime, Hilary had gone on a little along the track. He stood there, listening to the clamorous dog almost calmly.

Mary joined him, holding up the front part of her skirt, which contained four of the largest stones, more than she could carry in her hands.

"We won't need them," said Hilary, with confidence. "And if we do, they're everywhere."

Mary leaned forward and let the stones fall to the ground, taking care that they missed her toes. Possibly the quite loud thuds made the dog bark more furiously than ever.

"Perhaps he's standing guard over buried treasure?" suggested Mary.

"Or over some fairy kingdom that mortals may not enter," said Hilary.

They talked about such things for much of the time when they were together. Once they had worked together upon an actual map of Fairyland, and with Giantland adjoining.

"He might have lots of heads," said Mary.

"Come on, let's look," said Hilary.

"Quietly," said Mary, making no other demur.

He took her hand.

"There *must* be a gate," she remarked, after they had gone a little further, with the roaring, growling bark as obstreperous as ever.

"Let's hope it's locked then," he replied. At once he added: "Of course it's locked. He'd have been out by now otherwise."

"You said that before," said Mary. "But perhaps the answer is that there is no gate. There can't always be a gate, you know."

But there was a gate; a pair of gates, high, wrought iron, scrolled, rusted, and heavily padlocked. Through them, Hilary and Mary could see a large, palpably empty house, with many of the windows glassless, and the paint on the outside walls surviving only in streaks and smears, pink, green, and blue, as the always vaguely polluted atmosphere added its corruption to that inflicted by the weather. The house was copiously mockbattlemented and abundantly ogeed: a structure, without doubt, in the Gothic Revival taste, though of a period uncertain over at least a hundred years. Some of the heavy chimney-stacks had broken off and fallen. The front door, straight before them, was a recessed shadow. It was difficult to see whether it was open or shut. The paving stones leading to it were lost in mossy dampness.

"Haunted house," said Mary.

"What's that?" enquired Hilary.

"Don't exactly know," said Mary. "But Daddy says they're *every-where*, though people don't realize it."

"But how can you tell?" asked Hilary, looking at her seriously and a little anxiously.

"Just by the look," replied Mary with authority. "You can tell at once when you know. It's a mistake to look for too long, though."

"Ought we to put it on the map?"

"I suppose so. I'm not sure."

"Is that dog going to bark all day, d'you think?"

"He'll stop when we go away. Let's go, Hilary."

"Look!" cried Hilary, clutching at her. "Here he is. He must have managed to break away. We must show no sign of fear. That's the important thing."

Curiously enough, Mary seemed in no need of this vital guidance. She was already standing rigidly, with her big eyes apparently fixed on the animal, almost as if hypnotized.

Of course, the tall, padlocked bars stood between them and the dog; and another curious thing was that the dog seemed to realize the fact, and to make allowance for it, in a most undoglike manner. Instead of leaping up at the bars in an endeavour to reach the two of them, and so to caress or bite them, it stood well back and simply stared at them, as if calculating hard. It barked no longer, but instead emitted an almost continuous sound halfway between a growl and a whine, and quite low.

It was a big, shapeless, yellow animal, with long, untidy legs, which shimmered oddly, perhaps as it sought a firm grip on the buried and slippery stones. The dog's yellow skin seemed almost hairless. Blotchy and draggled, it resembled the wall outside. Even the dog's eyes were a flat, dull yellow. Hilary felt strange and uneasy when he observed them; and next he felt upset as he realized that Mary and the dog were gazing at one another as if under a spell.

"Mary!" he cried out. "Mary, don't look like that. Please don't look like that."

He no longer dared to touch her, so alien had she become.

"Mary, let's go. You said we were to go." Now he had begun to cry, while all the time the dog kept up its muffled internal commotion, almost like soft singing.

In the end, but not before Hilary had become very wrought up, the tension fell away from Mary, and she was speaking normally.

"Silly," she said, caressing Hilary. "It's quite safe. You said so your-self."

He had no answer to that. The careful calculations by which earlier he had driven off the thought of danger had now proved terrifyingly irrele-vant. All he could do was subside to the ground and lose himself in tears, his head between his knees.

Mary knelt beside him. "What are you crying about, Hilary? There's no danger. He's a friendly dog, really."

"He's not, he's not."

She tried to draw his hands away from his face. "Why are you crying, Hilary?" One might have felt that she quite urgently needed to know.

"I'm frightened."

"What are you frightened of? It can't be the dog. He's gone."

At that, Hilary slowly uncurled, and forgetting, on the instant, to con-tinue weeping, directed his gaze at the rusty iron gates. There was no dog visible.

"Where's he gone, Mary? Did you see him go?"

"No, I didn't actually *see* him," she replied. "But he's gone. And that's what you care about, isn't it?"

"But *why* did he go? We're still here."

"I expect he had business elsewhere." He knew that she had acquired that explanation too from her father, because she had once told him so.

"Has he found a way out?"

"Of course he hasn't."

"How can you tell?"

"He's simply realized that we don't mean any harm."

"I don't believe you. You're just saying that. Why are you saying that, Mary? You were more scared than I was when we came here. What's hap-pened to you, Mary?"

"What's happened to me is that I've got back a little sense." From whom, he wondered, had she learned to say *that*? It was so obviously in-sincere, that it first hurt, and then once more frightened him.

"I want to go home," he said.

She nodded, and they set off, but not hand in hand.

There was one more incident before they had left the area behind them.

As they returned up the gently sloping, sandy track, Hilary kept his eyes on the ground, carefully not looking at the yellow wall on his left, or looking at it as little as possible, and certainly not looking backwards over his shoulder. At the place where the wall bore away leftwards at a right angle, the track began to ascend rather more steeply for perhaps a hundred yards, to a scrubby tableland above. They were walking in silence, and Hilary's ears, always sharper than the average, were continuously strained for any unusual sound, probably from behind the wall, but possibly, and even more alarmingly, not. When some way up the steeper slope, he seemed to hear something, and could not stop himself from looking back.

There was indeed something to see, though Hilary saw it for only an instant.

At the corner of the wall, there was no special feature, as one might have half-expected, such as a turret or an obelisk. There was merely the turn in the hipped roofing. But now Hilary saw, at least for half a second, that a man was looking over, installed at the very extremity of the internal angle. There was about half of him visible, and he seemed tall and slender and bald. Hilary failed to notice how he was dressed: if, indeed, he was dressed at all.

Hilary jerked back his head. He did not feel able to mention what he had seen to Mary, least of all now.

He did not feel able, in fact, to mention the sight to anyone. Twenty years later, he was once about to mention it, but even then decided against doing so. In the meantime, and for years after these events, the thought and memory of them lay at the back of his mind; partly because of what had already happened, partly because of what happened soon afterwards.

The outing must have upset Hilary more than he knew, because the same evening he felt ill, and was found by Mrs Parker to have a temperature. That was the beginning of it, and the end of it was not for a period of weeks; during which there had been two doctors, and, on some of the days and nights, an impersonal nurse, or perhaps two of them also. There had also been much bluff jollying along from Hilary's father; Hilary's brothers being both at Wellington. Even Mrs Parker had to be reinforced by a blowsy teenager named Eileen.

In the end, and quite suddenly, Hilary felt as good as new: either owing to the miracles of modern medicine, or, more probably, owing to the customary course of nature.

"You may feel right, old son," said Doctor Morgan-Vaughan; "but you're *not* right, not yet."

"When can I go back to school?"

"Do you want to go back, son?"

"Yes," said Hilary.

"Well, well," said Doctor Morgan-Vaughan. "Small boys felt differently in my day."

"When can I?" asked Hilary.

"One fine day," said Doctor Morgan-Vaughan. "There's no hurry about it. You've been ill, son, really ill, and you don't want to do things in a rush."

So a matter of two months had passed before Hilary had any inkling of the fact that something had happened to Mary also. He would have liked to see her, but had not cared, rather than dared, to suggest it. At no time had he even mentioned her at home. There was no possibility of his hearing anything about her until his belated return to school.

Even then, the blowsy teenager was sent with him on the first day, lest, presumably, he faint at the roadside or vanish upwards to Heaven. His heart was heavy and confused, as he walked; and Eileen found difficulty in conversing with a kid of his kind anyway. He was slightly relieved by the fact that when they arrived at the school, she had no other idea than to hasten off with alacrity.

The headmistress (if so one might term her), who was also part-proprietor of the establishment, a neat lady of 36, was waiting specially for Hilary's arrival after his illness; and greeted him with kindness and a certain understanding. The children also felt a new interest in him, though with most of them it was only faint. But there was a little girl with two tight plaits and a gingham dress patterned with asters and sunflowers, who seemed more sincerely concerned about what had been happening to him. Her name was Valerie Watkinson.

"Where's Mary?" asked Hilary.

"Mary's dead," said Valerie Watkinson solemnly.

Hilary's first response was merely hostile. "I don't believe you," he said.

Valerie Watkinson nodded three or four times, even more solemnly.

Hilary clutched hold of both her arms above the elbows. "I don't believe you," he said again.

Valerie Watkinson began to cry. "You're hurting me."

Hilary took away his hands. Valerie did not move or make any further complaint. They stood facing one another in silence for a perceptible pause, with Valerie quietly weeping.

"Is it true?" said Hilary in the end.

Valerie nodded again behind her tiny handkerchief with a pinky-blue Swiss milkmaid on one corner. "You're very pale," she gasped out, her mouth muffled.

She stretched out a small damp hand. "Poor Hilary. Mary was your friend. I'm sorry for you, Hilary."

"Did she go to bed with a temperature?" asked Hilary. He was less unaccustomed than most children to the idea of death because he was perfectly well aware that of late he himself was said to have escaped death but narrowly.

This time Valerie shook her head, though with equal solemnity. "No," she said. "At least, I don't think so. It's all a mystery. We haven't been *told* she's dead. We thought she was ill, like you. Then Sandy saw something in the paper." Sandy Stainer was a podgy sprawling boy with, as one might suppose, vaguely reddish hair.

"What did he see?"

"Something nasty," said Valerie with confidence. "I don't know what it was. We're not supposed to know."

"Sandy knows."

"Yes," said Valerie.

"Hasn't he told?"

"He's been told not to. Miss Milland had him in her room."

"But don't you want to know yourself?"

"No, I don't," said Valerie, with extreme firmness. "My mummy says it's enough for us to know that poor Mary's dead. She says that's what really matters."

It was certainly what really mattered to Hilary. He passed his first day back at school looking very pallid and speaking no further word except when directly addressed by Miss Milland or Mrs Everson; both of whom agreed, after school hours, that Hilary Brigstock had been sent back before he should have been. It was something to which they were entirely accustomed: the children often seemed to divide into those perpetually truant and those perpetually in seeming need of more care and attention than they were receiving at home. That it should be so was odd in such a professional and directorial area; though Mrs Cartier, who looked in every now and then to teach elementary French, and was a Maoist, said it was just what one always found.

Hilary had never spoken to Sandy Stainer, nor ever wanted to. The present matter was not one which he would care to enquire about in such a quarter. Moreover, he knew perfectly well that he would be told nothing, but merely tormented. Sandy Stainer's lips had somehow been sealed in some remarkably effective way; and he would be likely to find, in such a situation, clear conscience and positive social sanction for quiet arm-twisting and general vexing of enquirers, especially of enquirers known to be as vulnerable as Hilary. And Mary had been so much to Hilary that he had no other close friend in the school—probably no other friend there at all. Perhaps Hilary was one of those men who are designed for one woman only.

Certainly he had no little friends outside the school; nor had ever been offered any. Nor, as usual, was the death of Mary a matter that could be laid before his father. In any case, what could his father permit himself to tell him; when all was so obscure, and so properly so?

Within a day or two, Hilary was back in bed once more, and again missing from school.

Doctor Morgan-Vaughan could not but suspect this time that the trouble contained a marked element of "the psychological"; but it was an aspect of medicine that had always struck him as almost entirely unreal, and certainly as a therapeutic dead end, except for those resolved to mine it financially. He preferred to treat visibly physiological disturbances with acceptably physiological nostra. In the present case, he seriously thought of again calling in Doctor Oughtred, who had undoubtedly made a very real contribution in the earlier manifestation of the child's illness.

"Do you read the local paper, Mrs Parker?" asked Hilary, whiter than the sheets between which he lay.

"I don't get round to it," replied Mrs Parker, in her carefully uncommitted way. "We take it in. Mr Parker feels we should."

"Why does he feel that?"

"Well, you want to know what's going on around you, don't you?"

"Yes," said Hilary.

"Not that Mr Parker reads anything very much. Why should he, when he's got the wireless? The *Advertiser* just piles up in heaps till the waste people come for it from the hospital."

"What do they do with it at the hospital?"

"Pulp it, I believe. You've got to do what you can for charity, haven't you?"

"Bring me all the local papers in the heap, Mrs Parker. I'm ill too. It's just like the hospital."

"You couldn't read them," said Mrs Parker, as before; carefully not conceding.

"I *could*," said Hilary.

"How's that? You can't read."

"I can," said Hilary. "I can read anything. Well, almost anything. Bring me the papers, Mrs Parker."

She expressed no surprise that he should want to read something so boring even to her; nor did it seem to strike her that there might be anything significant in his demand. In fact, she could think of nothing to say; and as, in any case, she was always wary about what she let fall in the ambience of her employment, she left Hilary's room without one word more.

But, as much as three days later, Eileen had something to say when she brought him his midday meal (not a very imaginative one) and an assembly of pills.

"You *are* old-fashioned," remarked Eileen. "At least that's what Mrs Parker thinks."

"What d'you mean?" asked Hilary in a sulky tone, because he disliked Eileen.

"Asking for the *Advertiser*, when you can't even read it."

"I *can* read it," said Hilary.

"I know more than Mrs Parker knows," said Eileen. "It's that little girl, isn't it? Mary Rossiter, your little sweetheart."

Hilary said nothing.

"I've seen you together. I know. Not that I've told Mrs Parker."

"You *haven't?*"

"Not likely. Why should I tell *her?*"

Hilary considered that.

"She's a silly cow," said Eileen casually.

Hilary was clutching with both hands at the sheet. "Do you know what happened to Mary?" he asked, looking as far away from Eileen as he could look.

"Not exactly. She was interfered with, and mauled about. Bitten all over, they say, poor little thing. But it's been hushed up proper, and you'd better hurry and forget all about her. That's all you *can* do, isn't it?"

In the end, having passed at Briarside and at Gorselands through the more difficult years of the Second World War, Hilary went to Wellington also. His father thought it a tidier arrangement: better adapted to more restricted times. By then, of course, Hilary's brothers, Roger and Gilbert, had left the school, though in neither case for the university. There seemed no point, they both decided; and their father had had no difficulty in agreeing. He had been to a university himself, and it had seemed to him more of a joke than anything else, and a not particularly useful one.

Despite the intermittent connection with Wellington, theirs had not been a particularly army family, and it was with surprise that Mr Brigstock learned of his youngest son's decision to make the army his career, especially as the war was not so long concluded. Hilary, as we have said, was no milksop, and no doubt the Wellington ethos had its influence; but, in any case, it is a mistake to think that an officers' mess is manned solely by good-class rowdies. There are as many (and, naturally, as few) sensitive people in the army as in most other places; and some of them find their way there precisely because they are so.

A further complexity is that the sensitive are sometimes most at their ease with the less sensitive. Among Hilary's friends at the depot, was a youth named Callcutt, undisguisedly extrovert, very dependable. On one occasion, Hilary Brigstock took Callcutt home for a few days of their common leave.

It was not a thing he did often, even now. The atmosphere of his home still brought out many reserves in him. It would hardly be too much to say that he himself went there as little as possible. But by now both Roger and Gilbert were married, and had homes of their own, as they frequently mentioned; so that Hilary was beginning to expect qualms within him on the subject of his father's isolation, and surely, loneliness. Late middle-aged people living by themselves were always nowadays said to be lonely. Unlike most sons, Hilary at times positively wished that his father would marry again, as people in his situation were expected to do; that his father's views on the subject of women had somehow become less definite.

And really the place was dull. Stranded there with Callcutt, Hilary perceived luminously, as in a minutely detailed picture, how entirely dull, in every single aspect, his home was.

More secrets are improperly disclosed from boredom than from any other motive; and more intimacies imparted, with relief resulting, or otherwise.

"I love it here," said Callcutt, one day after lunch, when Mr Brigstock had gone upstairs for the afternoon, as he normally did.

"That's fine," replied Hilary. "What do you love in particular about it?"

"The quiet," said Callcutt immediately. "I think one's home should be a place where one can go for some quiet. You're a lucky chap."

"Yes," agreed Hilary. "Quiet it certainly is. Nowadays, at least. When my two elder brothers were here, it wasn't quiet at all."

"Remind me where they are now?"

"Married. Both of them. With homes of their own."

"Nice girls?"

"So-so."

"Kids?"

"Two each."

"Boys?"

"All boys. We only breed boys."

"*Only?*"

"There hasn't been a girl in the Brigstock family within living memory."

"Saves a lot of trouble," said Callcutt.

"Loses a lot of fun," said Hilary.

"Not at that age."

"*Particularly*, perhaps, at that age."

"How's that? You're not one of these Lolita types, like old what-not?"

"When I was a child I knew a girl who meant more to me than any girl has meant to me since. More, indeed, than anyone at all. Remember that I never knew my mother."

"Lucky chap again," said Callcutt. "Well, in some ways. No, I shouldn't have said that. I apologize. Forget it."

"That's all right."

"Tell me about your girl friend. I'm quite serious. As a matter of fact, I know perfectly well what you meant about her."

Hilary hesitated. Almost certainly, if it had not been for the absence of other topics, other possible activities, other interests, he would never have mentioned Mary Rossiter at all. He had never spoken of her to a soul for the twenty years since she had vanished, and for at least half that time he had thought of her but infrequently.

"Well, if you like, I *will* tell you. For what it's worth, which isn't much, especially to a third party. But we've nothing else to do."

"Thank the Lord!" commented Callcutt.

"I feel the Brigstocks should do more to provide entertainment."

"Good God!" rejoined Callcutt.

So, for the first time, Hilary imparted much of the story to another. He told how sweet Mary Rossiter had been, how they used to go for surprisingly long walks together, how they found the crumbling wall, and heard, and later saw, the shapeless, slithery dog, which seemed the colour of the wall, and saw also the collapsing mansion or near-mansion, which Mary, just like a kid, had immediately said must be a haunted house. Hilary even told Callcutt about the maps that the two children had drawn together, and that they had been maps not only of Surrey, but of Fairyland, and Giantland, and the Land of Shades also.

"Good preparation for the army," observed Callcutt.

But Hilary did not tell Callcutt about the lean, possibly naked, man he had so positively seen at the extremest angle of the wall. He had been about to tell him, simply without thinking, at the point where the incident came in the narrative; but he passed over the matter.

"Bloody savage dogs!" said Callcutt. "I'm against them. Especially in towns. Straining at the leash, and defecating all over the pavements. Something wrong with the owner's virility, I always think."

"This was the worst dog you ever saw," Hilary responded. "I'm quite confident of that."

"I hate them all," said Callcutt sweepingly. "They carry disease."

"That was the least in the case of the dog I was talking about," observed Hilary. And he told Callcutt of what had happened next—as far as he could tell it.

"Oh, God!" exclaimed Callcutt.

"I suppose it was what people used to call a mad dog."

"But that was well before your time, even if you *were* a kid. There aren't so many mad dogs these days. Anyway, what happened to the dog? Shot, I take it?"

"I have no idea."

"But surely it must have been shot? Things couldn't just have been left at that."

"Well, probably it was shot. I just don't know. I wasn't supposed to know anything at all about what had happened."

"Good God, it *should* have been shot. After doing a thing like that."

"I daresay it *was*."

There was a pause while Callcutt wrestled with his thoughts and Hilary with his memories; memories of which he had remembered little for some longish time past.

"It was the most frightful thing," Callcutt summed up at last. "I say: could we pay a visit to the scene of the crime? Or would that be too much?"

"Not too much if I can find the place." This was indeed how one thing led to another. "I haven't been there since."

"I suppose not," said Callcutt, who hadn't thought of that. Then had added: "What, never?"

"Never," said Hilary. "After all, I'm not here very often."

"Whose car shall we take?"

"As far as I can recall the lie of the land, we had better walk. I daresay it's all caravans and bungalows by now."

And so, substantially, it proved. It would no doubt be wrong to suggest that the municipal authority or statutory body or honorary trustees responsible for the conservation of an open space had in any major degree permitted the public heritage to diminish in area or beauty, but whereas formerly the conserved terrain had merged off into pastures and semi-wild woodland, now it seemed to be encircled almost up to the last inch with houses. They were big, expensive houses, but they had converted the wilderness of Hilary's childhood into something more like a public park, very beaten down, and with the usual close network of amateur footpaths, going nowhere in particular, because serving no function. Round the edge of this slightly sad area Hilary and Callcutt prowled and prospected.

"It was somewhere about here," said Hilary. "Certainly on this side."

"I should have said it had all changed so much that we were unlikely to get far without comparative maps. None of these houses can be more than ten or twelve years old."

They varied greatly in style: from Cotswold to Moroccan, from Ernest George to Frank Lloyd Wright. Some seemed still to value seclusion, but more went in for neighbourliness and open plan. Despite all the desperation of discrepancy, there was a uniformity of tone which was even more depressing.

"I agree that my place has disappeared," said Hilary. "Been built over. Of course it was pretty far gone even then."

The houses were served by a rough road, almost certainly "unadopted". It assured them a precarious degree of freedom from casual motor traffic.

One of the biggest houses was in the Hollywood style: a garish structure with brightly coloured faience roof, much Spanish ironwork, mass-produced but costly, and a flight of outside steps in bright red tiles. The property was surrounded by a scumbled white wall. Hilary and Callcutt stared in through the elaborate, garden-of-remembrance gates.

"It's like a caricature of the old place," said Hilary. "Much smaller, and much louder—but still . . ."

The windows were all shut and there was no one in sight. Even the other houses seemed all to lie silent, and on the rough road nothing and no one passed. The two men continued to peer through the bars of the gate, ornate but trivial.

From round the back of the house to their left emerged, in like silence, a large, moulting, yellow dog. They could hardly even hear the patter of its large feet on the composition flagstones.

Hilary said nothing until the dog, which originally they saw head on, had turned and, with apparent indifference to them, displayed the full length of its right flank. Then he spoke: "Bogey," he said, "that's the same dog." Callcutt was known to his intimates as Bogey, following some early incident in his military life.

Callcutt thought before speaking. Then he said: "Rubbish, Hilary. Dogs don't live twenty years." But he wasn't quite sure of that.

"That one has."

But now the dog began to bark, growling and baying most frighteningly, though, as on the previous occasion, not coming right up to the gate, or attempting to charge at them. If the fact that, a moment before, it seemed not to have seen them, might have been attributed to extreme senility, there was nothing remotely senile about its furious, almost rabid aggression now; and even less, perhaps, about the calculating way it placed itself, whatever might have been the reason. It stood a shapeless, sulphurous mass on its precisely chosen ground, almost like a Chinese demon.

"That is just what it did before," Hilary shouted above the uproar. "Stood like that and came no nearer."

"If you can call it standing," Callcutt shouted back.

He was appalled by the dog, and did not fail to notice that Hilary had turned white, and was clinging to the decorative gate-bars. But in the end Callcutt looked upwards for a second. He spoke again, or rather shouted. "There's a wench at one of the upstairs windows. We'd better clear out."

Before Hilary had managed any reply, which the barking of the dog in any case made difficult, there was a further development. The glass-panelled front door of the house opened, and a woman walked out.

Perhaps she had emerged to quiet the dog and apologize, perhaps, on the contrary, to reinforce the dog's antagonism to strangers: to Hilary it was a matter of indifference. The woman was of about his own age, but he knew perfectly well who she was. She was the grown-up Mary Rossiter, who twenty years before had been killed by a dog, probably a mad dog, possibly a dog that had been shot, certainly a most unusual dog, this very present dog, in fact.

Whatever he felt like, Hilary did not pass out. "Do you mind if we go?"

He withdrew his gaze and, without really waiting for Callcutt, began to walk away sharply. Again, it was somewhat as on the previous occasion: veritably, he was behaving exactly as a small boy might behave.

He did not pace out along the rough road, past the houses. Instead, he walked straight into the dilapidated public forest. Callcutt had almost to run after him, in a rather absurd way.

Hilary could not be unaware that while he retreated, the dog had stopped its noise. Perhaps he had even gone far enough to have passed beyond earshot, though it seemed unlikely. None the less, it was quite a chase for Callcutt, and with the most uncomfortable overtones.

Hilary pulled himself together quite quickly, however—once more, as before; and was even able to tell Callcutt exactly what he had apprehended—or, as he put it to Callcutt, fancied.

"I'd have taken to my heels myself, I promise you that," said Callcutt.

"I know it was Mary," said Hilary. "I know it."

They remained silent for some time as they walked over the patchy, tired ground.

Then Callcutt spoke. There was something he could not keep to himself, and Hilary seemed all right now.

"You know how we were laughing about the names of those houses? Samandjane, and Pasadena, and Happy Hours, and all that; the executive style. Do you know what the doggy house is called?"

Hilary shook his head. "I forgot to look."

"You wouldn't believe it. The name above our heads was Maryland."

RAMSEY CAMPBELL

The Scar (1969)

The Invocation (1982)

The most sophisticated stylist in current supernatural fiction, Ramsey Campbell has succeeded more brilliantly than any other writer in bringing the supernatural tale up to date without sacrificing the literary standards that Le Fanu, James, and other early masters made an indelible part of the tradition. Campbell's style is unique and unmistakable: his images, which dwell on the disorderliness of everyday middle- and lower-class life, have a jagged, contemporary edge; his chronologies are subtly distorted so that memories appear and dissolve like apparitions, revealing themselves as memories only by their sudden absence; his dreams disperse themselves into reality so that his stories always flirt with surrealism; his sentences have a tangy, dissonant musicality.

Campbell's characters and settings represent a radical departure from both the upper-class elegance of M. R. James and the natural splendor of Blackwood. The horrors in his stories inhabit shabby tenement houses, anonymous offices, haunted highways, and sinister telephone booths; the victims are alienated college students, harrassed secretaries, struggling middle-class families, and down-and-out street people. We live in a tough, menacing world, these stories imply, one in which supernatural conspiracies seem oddly credible and appropriate.

Since the publication of *Demons by Daylight* (1973), Campbell's first collection in his own voice (his earlier stories consisting largely of Lovecraftian pastiches), he has become increasingly concerned with the psychology of the supernatural encounter. His ghosts and demons are among the most hellish in the literature, but like Le Fanu's they often spring as much from the psyches of his doomed heroes as from a hostile cosmos.

"The Scar" is early Campbell, but it demonstrates a radical break with the Lovecraftian mannerisms of *The Inhabitant of the Lake* (1964), Campbell's first collection of stories. Conceptually and stylistically, "The Scar" seems remarkably mature, especially for a writer in his early twenties. It exhibits sharp insight into human relationships and family tensions as well as a seamless unity of setting, plot, and characterization. The reader should be cautioned that it is also, like the work of Aickman (whom Campbell admires above all other contemporary spectral writers) rather subtle and oblique; indeed, it is one of those wonderful stories that is at least twice as terrifying on the second reading.

From the first family argument to the final shuddery confrontation in a bombed-out cellar, "The Scar" is intensely grim and disturbing. With hallucinatory vividness, the story captures the "anonymity" and "inertia" of Liverpool, Campbell's favorite setting. The hero, "tottering on the edge of revelation" as the ominous events unfold, is a victim of his own passivity as well as of the invading force; the heroine is "trapped" by her loyalty to her husband and refuses to acknowledge the sinister changes in his personality. Lindsay Rice's terrible insight is also the story's theme: he is genuinely shocked to find that sudden catastrophic and inexplicable events can happen to "normal" middle-class families as well as to alienated loners like himself. This couldn't possibly be happening to the Rossiters, he thinks; "their lives were solid, not ephemeral like his own." In Campbell's endlessly collapsing world, however, nothing is ever "solid"; stability is an utter illusion.

The later "Invocation," which receives in this book its first anthology publication, is also radically unsettling, not only in the terrible creature it calls down from the clouds but in the way it tangles up fantasies with actual events. Campbell has said that this tale is based on the frightening notion from his Catholic upbringing that thoughts are as important as, if not inseparable from, reality. The key to this story lies in its title: this "invocation" is one of the most subtle and inadvertent in supernatural fiction, and the reader who fails to pay close attention to the clouds that accompany Ted's cursing of the noisy old lady upstairs will miss it altogether.

The fragmented texture of "The Invocation" neatly dovetails with its constant references to cinema. Campbell's characters are continually remembering films, which are more "real" to them than an increasingly unreal world and which serve as an explicit parallel to Campbell's own technique. An avid moviegoer and film scholar, Campbell writes in an aggressively cinematic style: his restless "camera" constantly cuts from scene to scene, chopping off large chunks of transitional material and leaving us with fragments connected by nightmares. (Ironically, film-makers have expropriated many techniques—montage, flashback, sur-realism—from earlier modern writers like Conrad and Joyce; Campbell's fiction thus brings us full circle.)

An editor and connoisseur of supernatural horror as well as a writer, Campbell is surely aware of the antecedents in these stories; there is a bit of Jack Finney's *Invasion of the Body Snatchers* in "The Scar," as well as another appearance by the irrepressible Doppelgänger; and the nasty ending of "The Invocation" bears a slight resemblance to M. R. James's "Ash-Tree." Yet nothing in the earlier literature quite prepares us for Campbell's nightmarishness. It is not merely ghosts that terrify us in these taut, exciting stories; it is the modern world.

∾ THE SCAR ∾

"It was most odd on the bus today," Lindsay Rice said.

Jack Rossiter threw his cigarette into the fire and lit another. His wife Harriet glanced at him uneasily; she could see he was in no mood for her brother's circumlocutions.

"Most odd," said Lindsay. "Rather upsetting, in fact. It reminded me, the Germans—now was it the Germans? Yes I think it was the Germans—used to have this thing about *doppelgangers*, the idea being that if you saw your double it meant you were going to die. But of course you didn't see him. That's right, of course, I should explain."

Jack moved in his armchair. "I'm sorry, Lindsay," he interrupted, "I just don't see where you're tending. I'm sorry."

"It's all right, Lindsay," Harriet said. "Jack's been a bit tired lately. Go on."

But at that moment the children tumbled into the room like pierrots, their striped pajamas bold against the pastel lines of wallpaper. "Douglas tried to throw me into the bath, and he hasn't brushed his teeth!" Elaine shouted triumphantly.

"There'll be spankings for two in a minute," Jack threatened, but he smiled. "Good night, darling. Good night, darling. No, you've had a hard day, darling, I'll put them to bed."

"Not so hard as you," Harriet said, standing up. "You stay and talk to Lindsay."

Jack grimaced inwardly; he had wanted Harriet to rest, but somehow it now appeared as if he'd been trying to escape Lindsay. "Sorry, Lindsay, you were saying?" he prompted as the thumping on the staircase ceased.

"Oh, yes, on the bus. Well, it was this morning, I saw someone who looked like you. I was going to speak to him until I realized." Rice glanced around the room; although his weekly invitation was of some years' standing, he could never remember exactly where everything was. Not that it mattered: the whole was solid. Armchairs, television, bookcase full of Penguins and book-club editions and Shorrock's *Valuer's Manual* —there it was, on top of the bookcase, the wedding photograph which Jack had carefully framed for Harriet. "Yes, he was as thin as you've been

396

getting, but he had a scar from here to here." Rice encompassed his left temple and jawbone with finger and thumb like dividers.

"So he wasn't really my double. My time hasn't run out after all."

"Well, I hope not!" Rice laughed a little too long; Jack felt his mouth stretching as he forced it to be sociable. "We've been slackening off at the office," Rice said. "How are things at the jeweller's? Nothing stolen yet, I hope?"

"No, everything's under control," Jack replied. Feet ran across the floor above. "Hang on, Lindsay," he said, "sounds like Harriet's having trouble."

Harriet had quelled the rebellion when he arrived; she closed the door of the children's room and regarded him. "Christ, the man's tact!" he exploded.

"Shh, Jack, he'll hear you." She put her arms around him. "Don't be cruel to Lindsay," she pleaded. "You know I always had the best of everything and Lindsay never did—unhappy at school, always being put down by my father, never daring to open his mouth—darling, you know he finds it difficult to talk to people. Now I've got you. Surely we can spare him kindness at least."

"Of course we can." He stroked her hair. "It's just that—damn it, not only does he say I'm losing weight as though I'm being underfed or something, but he asks me if the shop's been broken into yet!"

"Poor darling, don't worry. I'm sure the police will catch them before they raid the shop. And if not, there's always insurance."

"Yes, there's insurance, but it won't rebuild my display! Can't you understand I take as much pride in my shop as you take in the house? Probably some jumped-up little skinheads who throw the loot away once their tarty little teenyboppers have played with it!"

"That doesn't sound like you at all, Jack," Harriet said.

"I'm sorry, love. You know I'm really here. Come on, I'd better fix up tomorrow night with Lindsay."

"If you feel like a rest we could have him round here."

"No, he opens out a bit when he's in a pub. Besides, I like the walk to Lower Brichester."

"Just so long as you come back in one piece, my love."

Rice heard them on the stairs. He hurried back to his chair from the bookcase where he had been inspecting the titles. One of these days he must offer to lend them some books—anything to make them like him more. He knew he'd driven Jack upstairs. Why couldn't he be direct instead of circling the point like a wobbling whirligig? But every time he tried to grasp an intention or a statement it slid out of reach. Even if he hung a sign on his bedroom wall—he'd once thought of one: "I shall act directly"—he would forget it before he left the flat. Even as he forgot his musings when Jack and Harriet entered the room.

"I'd better be off," he said. "You never can tell with the last bus round here."

"I'll see you tomorrow night, then," Jack told him, patting his shoulder. "I'll call round and pick you up."

But he never had the courage to invite them to his flat, Lindsay thought; he knew it wasn't good enough for them. Not that they would show it—rather would they do everything to hide their feelings out of kindness, which would be worse. Tomorrow night as usual he would be downstairs early to wait for Jack in the doorway. He waved to them as they stood linked in their bright frame, then struck off down the empty road. The fields were grey and silent, and above the semi-detached roofs the moon was set in a plush ring of cold November mist. At the bus-stop he thought: I wish I could do something for them so they'd be grateful to me.

Harriet was bending over the cooker; she heard no footsteps—she had no chance to turn before the newspaper was over her face.

"I see the old Jack's back with us," she said, fighting off the *Brichester Herald*.

"You haven't seen it?" He guided her hand to the headline: *Youths Arrested—Admit to Jewel Thefts.* He was beaming; he read the report again with Harriet, the three boys who'd hoped to stockpile jewellery but had been unable to market it without attracting the police. "Maybe now we can all get some sleep," he said. "Maybe I can give up smoking."

"Don't give it up for me, Jack, I know you need it. But if you *did* give it up I'd be very happy."

Douglas and Elaine appeared, pummelling toward their tea. "Now just you sit down and wait," Jack said, "or we'll eat it for you."

After tea he lit a cigarette, then glanced at Harriet. "Don't worry, darling," she advised. "Take things easy for a while. Come on, monsters, you can help clear up." She knew the signs—spilled sugar, dropped knife; Jack would turn hypertense with relief if he didn't rest.

But ten minutes later he was in the kitchen. "Must go," he said. "Give myself time for a stroll before I meet Lindsay. Anyway, the news ought to give the conversation a lift."

"Come back whole, darling," Harriet said, not knowing.

Yes, he liked to walk through Lower Brichester. He'd made the walk, with variations, for almost two years; ever since his night out drinking with Rice had settled into habit. It had been his suggestion, primarily to please Harriet, for he knew she liked to think he and Lindsay were friends; but by now he met Lindsay out of a sense of duty, which was rarely proof against annoyance as the evening wore on. Never mind, there was the walk. If he felt insecure, as he often did when walking—the night, Harriet elsewhere—he gained a paradoxical sense of security from Lower Brichester; the bleared fish-and-chip shop windows, the crowds outside pubs, a drunk punching someone's face with a soft moist sound—it re-assured him to think that here was a level to which he could never be reduced.

Headlights blazed down a side-street, billowing with mist and motor-cycle fumes. They spotlighted a broken wall across the street from Ros-siter; a group of girls huddled on the shattered bricks, laughing forth fog as the motorcycle gang fondled them roughly with words. Rossiter gazed at them; no doubt the jewel thieves had been of the same mould. He felt a little guilty as he watched the girls, embracing themselves to keep out the cold; but he had his answer ready—nothing would change them, they were fixed; if he had money, it was because he could use it properly. He turned onward; he would have to use the alley on the right if he were not to keep Rice waiting.

Suddenly the shrieks of laughter behind the roaring engines were cut off. A headlight was feeling its way along the walls, finding one house pro-truding part of a ruined frontage like a piece of jigsaw, the next dismally curtained, its neighbor shuttered with corrugated tin, its makeshift door torn down like an infuriating lid. For a moment the beam followed a fig-ure: a man in a long black coat swaying along the pavement, a grey woolen sock pulled down over his face. The girls huddled closer, silently. Jack shuddered; the exploratory progress of the figure seemed unformed, un-directed. Then the light was gone; the girls giggled in the darkness, and beyond a streetlamp the figure fumbled into the tin-shuttered house. Jack turned up his coat collar and hurried into the alley. The engines roared louder.

He was halfway up the alley when he heard the footsteps. The walls were narrow; there was barely room for the other, who seemed in a hurry, to pass. Jack pressed against the wall; it was cold and rough beneath his hand. Behind him the footsteps stopped.

He looked back. The entrance to the alley whirled with fumes, against which a figure moved toward him, vaguely outlined. It held something in its hand. Jack felt automatically for his lighter. Then the figure spoke.

"You're Jack Rossiter." The voice was soft and anonymous yet somehow penetrated the crescendi of the motorcycles. "I'll be visiting your shop soon."

For a moment Jack thought he must know the man, though his face was merely a black egg in the shadows; but something in the figure's slow approach warned him. Suddenly he knew what the remark implied. Cold rushed into his stomach, and metal glinted in the figure's hand. Jack retreated along the wall, his fingers searching frantically for a door. His foot tangled with an abandoned tin; he kicked it toward the figure and ran.

The fog boiled round him; metal clattered; a foot hooked his ankle and tripped him. The engines were screaming; as Jack raised his head a car's beam thrust into his eyes. He scrabbled at potato peelings and sardine tins, and struggled to his knees. A foot between his shoulders ground him down. The car's light dimmed and vanished. He struggled onto his back, cold peel sticking to his cheek, and the foot pressed on his heart. The metal closed in the figure's palm. Above him hands displayed the tin which he had kicked. The insidious voice said something. When the words reached him, Rossiter began to tear at the leg in horror and fury. The black egg bent nearer. The foot pressed harder, and the rusty lid of the tin came down toward Jack's face.

Though the bandage was off he could still feel the cut, blazing now and then from his temple to his jawbone. He forced himself to forget; he stuffed fuel into the living-room fire and opened his book. But it failed to soothe him. Don't brood, he told himself savagely, worse is probably happening in Lower Brichester at this moment. If only Harriet hadn't seen him unbandaged at the hospital! He could feel her pain more keenly than his own since he'd come home. He kept thinking of her letting the kettle scream so that he wouldn't hear her sobbing in the kitchen. Then she'd brought him coffee, her face still wet beneath her hair from water to wash away the tears. Why had he told her at the hospital "It's not what he did to me, it's what he said he'd do to Douglas and Elaine"? He cursed himself for spreading more suffering than he himself had had to stand. Even Rice had seemed to feel himself obscurely to blame, although Jack had insisted that it was his own fault for walking through that area.

"Go and say goodnight to Daddy," Harriet called.

The children paddled in. "Daddy's face is getting better," Elaine said.

He saw the black egg bearing down on them. God, he swore, if he should lay one finger—! "Daddy's surviving his accident," he told them. "Good night, children."

Presently he heard Harriet slowly descending the stairs, each step a thought. Suddenly she rushed into the room and hid her face on his chest. "Oh, please, please, darling, what did he say about the children?" she cried.

"I won't have you disturbed, my love," he said, holding her as she trembled. "I can worry enough for both of us. And as long as you take them there and back to school, it doesn't matter what the sod said."

"And what about your shop?" she asked through her tears.

"Never mind the shop!" He tried not to think of his dream of the smashed window, of the foul disorder he might find one morning. "The police will find him, don't you worry."

"But you couldn't even describe—" The doorbell rang. "Oh God, it's Lindsay," she said. "Could you go, darling? I can't let him see me like this."

"Oh, that's good—I mean I'm glad you've got the bandage off," said Lindsay. Behind him the fog swallowed the bedraggled trees and blotted out the fields. He stared at Jack, then muttered "Sorry, better let you close the door."

"Come in and get some fire," Jack said. "Harriet will have the coffee ready in a minute."

Rice plodded round the room, then sat down opposite Jack. He stared at the wedding photograph. He rubbed his hands and gazed at them. He looked up at the ceiling. At last he turned to Jack: "What—" he glanced around wildly—"what's that you're reading?"

"*The Heart of the Matter.* Second time, in fact. You should try it sometime."

Harriet looked in, dabbing at one eye. "Think I rubbed in some soap," she explained. "Hello, Lindsay. If we're talking about books, Jack, you said you'd read *The Lord of the Rings.*"

"Well, I can't now, darling, since I'm working tomorrow. Back to work at last, Lindsay. Heaven knows what sort of a state the shop will be in with Phillips in charge."

"You always said you could rely on him in an emergency," Harriet protested.

"Well, this is the test. Yes, white as usual for me, please, darling."

Harriet withdrew to the kitchen. "I read a book this week," Rice caught at the conversation, "about a man—what's his name, no, I forget—whose friend is in danger from someone, he finds out—and he finally pulls this someone off a cliff and gets killed himself." He was about to add "At least he did something with himself. I don't like books about people failing," but Jack took the cue:

"A little unrealistic for me," he said, "after what happened."

"Oh, I never asked," Rice's hands gripped each other, "where did it?"

"Just off the street parallel to yours, the next but two. In the alley."

"But that's where—" he lost something again—"where there's all sorts of violence."

"You shouldn't live so near it, Lindsay," Harriet said above a tray. "Make the effort. Move soon."

"Depressing night," Jack remarked as he helped Rice don his coat. "Drop that book in sometime, Lindsay. I'd like to read it."

Of course he wouldn't, Rice thought as he breathed in the curling fog and met the trees forming from the murk; he'd been trying to be kind. Rice had failed again. Why had he been unable to speak, to tell Jack that he had seen his double leave the bus and enter an abandoned house opposite that alley? The night of the mutilation Rice had waited in his doorway, feeling forsaken, sure that Jack had decided not to come; ashamed now, he blamed himself—Jack would be whole now if Rice hadn't made him feel it was his duty to meet him. Something was going to happen; he sensed it looming. If he could only warn them, prevent it—but prevent what? He saw the figures falling from the cliff-top against the azure sky, the seagulls screaming around him—but the mist hung about him miserably, stifling his intentions. He began to hurry to the bus-stop.

The week unfolded wearily. It was as formless in Rice's mind as the obscured fields when he walked up the Rossiters' street again, his book collecting droplets in his hand. He rang the bell and waited, shivering; the windows were blurred by mist.

"Oh, Lindsay," said Harriet. She had run to the door; it was clear she had been crying. "I don't know whether—"

Jack appeared in the hall, one hand possessively gripping the living-room doorframe, the cigarette upon his lip flaking down his shirt. "Is it your night already?" he demanded of Rice. "I thought it'd be early to bed for us. Come in for God's sake, don't freeze us to death."

Harriet threw Lindsay a pleading look which he could not interpret. "Sorry," he said. "I didn't know you were tired."

"Who said tired? Come on, man, start thinking! God, I give up." Jack threw up his hands and whirled into the living-room.

"Lindsay, Jack's been having a terrible time. The shop was broken into last night."

"What's all that whispering?" a voice shouted. "Aren't I one of the family any more?"

"Jack, don't be illogical. Surely Lindsay and I can talk." But she motioned Lindsay into the living-room.

"Treating me like a stranger in my own house!"

Lindsay dropped the book. Suddenly he realized what he'd seen: Jack's face was paler, thinner than last week; the scar looked older than seemed possible. He bent for the book. No, what he was thinking was absurd; Harriet would have noticed. Jack was simply worried. It must be worry.

"Brought me a book, have you? Let's see it, then. Oh, for God's sake, Lindsay, I can't waste my time with this sort of thing!"

"Jack!" cried Harriet. "Lindsay brought it specially."

"Don't pity Lindsay, he won't thank you for it. You think we're patronizing you, don't you Lindsay? Inviting you up the posh end of town?"

This couldn't be, Rice thought; not in this pastel living-room, not with the wedding photograph fixed forever; their lives were solid, not ephemeral like his own. "I—don't know what you mean," he faltered.

"Jack, I won't have you speaking to Lindsay like that," Harriet said. "Lindsay, would you please help me make the coffee?"

"Siding with your brother now," Jack accused. "I don't need him at a time like this. I need you. You've forgotten the shop already, but I haven't. I suppose I needn't expect any comfort tonight."

"Oh, Jack, try and get a grip on yourself," but now her voice was softer. Don't! Lindsay warned her frantically. That's exactly what he wants!

"Take your book, Lindsay," Jack said through his fingers, "and make sure you're invited in future." Harriet glanced at him in anguish and hurried Lindsay out.

"I'm sorry you've been hurt, Lindsay," she said. "Of course you're always welcome here. You know we love you. Jack didn't mean it. I knew something would happen when I heard about the shop. Jack just ran out of it and didn't come back for hours. But I didn't know it would be like this—" Her voice broke. "Maybe you'd better not come again until Jack's more stable. I'll tell you when it's over. You do understand, don't you?"

"Of course, it doesn't matter," Lindsay said, trembling with formless thoughts. On the hall table a newspaper had been crumpled furiously; he saw the headline—*Jeweller's Raided—Displays Destroyed.* "Can I have the paper?" he asked.

"Take it, please. I'll get in touch with you, I promise. Don't lose heart."

As the door closed Rice heard Jack call "Harriet!" in what sounded like despair. Above, the children were silhouetted on their bedroom window; as Rice trudged away the fog engulfed them. At the bus-stop he read the report; a window broken, destruction everywhere. He gazed ahead blindly. Shafts of bilious yellow pierced the fog, then the grey returned. "Start thinking," was it? Oh yes, he could think—think how easy it would be to fake a raid, knowing the insurance would rebuild what had been destroyed—but he didn't want the implications; the idea was insane, anyway. Who would destroy simply in order to have an excuse for appearing emaciated, unstable? But his thoughts returned to Harriet; he avoided thinking what might be happening in that house. You're jealous! he tried to tell himself. He's her husband! He has the right! Rice became aware that he was holding the book which he had brought for Jack. He stared at the tangled figures falling through blue drops of condensation, then thrust the book into the litter-bin between empty tins and a sherry bottle. He stood waiting in the fog.

The fog trickled through Rice's kitchen window. He leaned his weight on the sash, but again it refused to shut. He shrugged helplessly and tipped the beans into the saucepan. The tap dripped once; he gripped it and screwed it down. Below the window someone came out coughing and shattered something in the dustbin. The tap dripped. He moved toward it, and the bell rang.

It was Harriet in a headscarf. "Oh, don't come in," he said. "It's not fit, I mean—"

"Don't be silly, Lindsay," she told him edgily. "Let me in." Her eyes gathered details: the twig-like crack in one corner of the ceiling, the alarm clock whose hand had been amputated, the cobweb supporting the lamp-flex from the ceiling like a bracket. "But this is so depressing," she said. "Don't stay here, Lindsay. You must move."

"It's just the bed's not made," he tried to explain, but he could see her despairing. He had to turn the subject. "Jack all right?" he asked, then remembered, but too late.

She pulled off her headscarf. "Lindsay, he hasn't been himself since they wrecked the shop," she said with determined calm. "Rows all the time, breaking things—he broke our photograph. He goes out and gets drunk half the evenings. I've never seen him so irrational." Her voice faded. "And there are other things—that I can't tell you about—"

"That's awful. That's terrible." He couldn't bear to see Harriet like this; she was the only one he had ever loved. "Couldn't you get him to see someone, I mean—"

"We've already had a row about that. That was when he broke our photograph."

"How about the children? How's he been to them?" Instantly two pieces fitted together; he waited, chill with horror, for her answer.

"He tells them off for playing, but I can protect them."

How could she be so blind? "Suppose he should do something to them," he said. "You'll have to get out."

"That's one thing I won't do. He's my husband, Lindsay. It's up to me to look after him."

She can't believe that! Lindsay cried. He tottered on the edge of revelation, and fought with his tongue. "Don't you think he's acting as if he was a different person?" He could not be more explicit.

"After what happened that's not so surprising." She drew her headscarf through her fingers and pulled it back, drew and pulled, drew and pulled; Lindsay looked away. "He's left all the displays in Phillips' hands. He's breaking down, Lindsay. I've got to nurse him back. He'll survive, I know I will."

Survive! Lindsay thought with bitterness and horror. And suddenly he remembered that Harriet had been upstairs when he'd described his encounter on the bus; she would never realize, and his tongue would never allow him to tell her. Behind her compassion he sensed a terrible devotion to Jack which he could not break. She was as trapped as he was in this flat. Yet if he could not speak, he must act. The plan against him was clear: he'd been banished from the Rossiters' home, he was unable to protest, Harriet would be alone. There was only one false assumption in the plan, and it concerned himself. It must be false. He could help. He gazed at Harriet; she would never understand, but perhaps she needn't suspect.

The beans sputtered and smouldered in the pan. "Oh, Lindsay, I'm awfully sorry," Harriet said. "You must have your tea. I've got to get back before he comes home. I only called to tell you not to come round for a while. Please don't. I'll be all right."

"I'll stay away until you tell me," Lindsay lied. As she reached the hall he called out; he felt bound to make what would happen as easy as he could for her. "If anything should happen—" he fumbled—"you know, while Jack's—disturbed—I can always help to look after the children."

Rice could hear the children screaming from the end of the street. He began to walk toward the cries. He hadn't meant to go near the house; if his plan were to succeed, Harriet must not see him. Harriet—why wasn't she protecting the children? It couldn't be the Rossiters' house, he argued desperately; sounds like that couldn't reach the length of the street. But the cries continued, piercing with terror and pain; they dragged his footsteps nearer. He reached the house and could no longer doubt. The bedrooms were curtained, the house was impossibly impassive, reflecting no part of the horror within; the fog clung greyly to the grass like scum on reeds. He could hear Elaine sobbing something and then screaming. Rice wanted to break in, to stop the sounds, to discover what was holding Harriet back; but if he went in his plan would be destroyed. His palms prickled; he wavered miserably, and the silver pavement slithered beneath him.

The front door of the next house opened and a man—portly, red-faced, bespectacled, grey hair, black overcoat, valise clenched in his hand like a weapon—strode down the path, grinning at the screams. He passed Rice and turned at his aghast expression: "What's the matter, friend," he asked with amusement in his voice, "never have your behind tanned when you were a kid?"

"But listen to them!" Rice said unevenly. "They're *screaming!*"

"And I should damn well think so, too," the other retorted. "You know Jack Rossiter? Decent chap. About as much of a sadist as I am, and his kids ran in just now when we were having breakfast with some nonsense about their father doing something dreadful to them. I grabbed them by the scruff of their necks and dragged them back. One thing

wrong with Rossiter—he was too soft with those kids, and I'm glad he
seems to have learned some sense. Listen, you know who taught kids to
tell tales on their parents? The bloody Nazis, that's who. There'll be no
kids turning into bloody Nazis in this country if *I* can help it!"

He moved away, glancing back at Rice as if suspicious of him. The cries
had faded; perhaps a door had closed. Stunned, Rice realized that he had
been seen near the house; his plan was in danger. "Well, I mustn't waste
any more time," he called, trying to sound casual, and hurried after the
man. "I've got to catch my bus."

At the bus-stop, next to the man who was scanning the headlines and
swearing, Rice watched the street for the figure he awaited, shivering
with cold and indecision, his nostrils smarting with the faint stench of
wet smoke. A bus arrived; his companion boarded. Rice stamped his feet
and stared into the distance as if awaiting another; an inner critic told him
he was overacting. When the bus had darkened and merged with the fog,
he retraced his steps. At the corner of the street he saw the fog solidify
into a striding shape. The mist pulled back like web from the scarred face.

"Oh, Jack, can you spare a few minutes?" he said.

"Why, it's the prodigal brother-in-law!" came in a mist steaming from
the mouth beside the scar. "I thought Harriet had warned you off? I'm in
a hurry."

Again Rice was caught by a compulsion to rush into the house, to discover what had happened to Harriet. But there were the children to protect; he must make sure they would never scream again. "I thought I saw
you—I mean, I did see you in Lower Brichester a few weeks ago," he said,
feeling the fog obscuring security. "You were going into a ruined house."

"Who, me? It must have been my—" But the voice stopped; breath
hung before the face.

Rice let his hatred drive out the words. "Your double? But then where
did he go? Come on, I'll show you the house."

For a moment Rice doubted; perhaps the figure would laugh and stride
into the mist. Ice sliced through his toes; he tottered and then plunged.
"How did you make sure there was nobody about?" he forced through
swollen lips. "When you got rid of him?"

The eyes flickered; the scar shifted. "Who, Phillips? God, man, I never
did know what you meant half the time. He'll be wondering where I am—
I'll have to think up a story to satisfy him."

"I think you'll be able to do that." Cold with fear as he was, Rice was

still warmed by fulfillment as he sensed that he had the upper hand, that
he was able to taunt as had the man on the cliff-top before the plunge. He
plunged into the fog, knowing that now he would be followed.

The grey fields were abruptly blocked by a more solid anonymity, the
streets of Lower Brichester, suffocating individuality, erasing it through
generations. Whenever he'd walked through these streets with Jack on
the short route to the pub each glance of Jack's had reminded him that
he was part of this anonymity, this inertia. But no longer, he told himself.
Signs of life were sparse; a postman cycled creaking by; beyond a window
a radio announcer laughed; a cat curled among milk-bottles. The door was
rolled down on a pinball arcade, and a girl in a cheap fur coat was leaping
about in the doorway of a boutique to keep herself warm until the keys
arrived. Rice felt eyes finger the girl, then revert to him; they had
watched him since the beginning of the journey, although the figure
seemed to face always forward. Rice glanced at the other; he was gazing
in the direction of his stride, and the scar wrinkled with a faint sneer.
Soon now, Rice thought, and a block of ice grew in his stomach while the
glazing of the pavement cracked beneath his feet.

They passed a square foundation enshrining a rusty pram; here a bomb
had blown a house asunder. The next street, Rice realized, and dug his
nails into the rubber of the torch in his pocket. The blitz had almost by-
passed Brichester; here and there one passed from curtained windows to
a gaping house, eventually rebuilt if in the town, neglected in Lower Brichester. Was this the key? Had someone been driven underground by
blitz conditions, or had something been released by bombing? In either
case, what form of camouflage would they have had to adopt to live? Rice
thought he knew, but he didn't want to think it through; he wanted to put
an end to it. And round a corner the abandoned house focused into
view.

A car purred somewhere; the pavement was faintly numbered for hop-
scotch. Rice gazed about covertly; there must be nobody in sight. And at
his side the figure did the same. Terrified, Rice yet had to repress a nervous giggle. "There's the house," he said. "I suppose you'll want to go
in."

"If you've got something to show me." The scar wrinkled again.

Bricks were heaped in what had been the garden; ice glistened in their
pores. Rice could see nothing through the windows, which were
shuttered with tin. A grey corrugated sheet had been peeled back from the
doorway; it scraped at Rice's ankle as he entered.

The light was dim; he gripped his torch. Above him a shattered skylight illuminated a staircase full of holes through which moist dust fell. To his right a door, one panel gouged out, still hung from a hinge. He hurried into the room, kicking a stray brick.

The fireplace gaped, half curtained by a hanging strip of wallpaper. Otherwise the room was bare, deserted probably for years. Of course the people of the neighborhood didn't have to know exactly what was here to avoid it. In the hall tin rasped.

Rice ran into the kitchen, ahead on the left. Fog had penetrated a broken window; it filled his mouth as he panted. Opposite the cloven sink he saw a door. He wrenched it open, and in the other room the brick clattered.

Rice's hands were gloved in frozen iron; his nails were shards of ice thrust into the fingertips, melting into his blood. One hand clutched towards the back door. He tottered forward and heard the children scream, thought once of Harriet, saw the figures on the cliff. I'm not a hero! he mouthed. How in God's name did I get here? And the answer came: because he'd never really believed what he'd suspected. But the torch was shining, and he swung it down the steps beyond the open door.

They led into a cellar; bricks were scattered on the floor, bent knives and forks, soiled plates leading the torch-beam to tattered blankets huddled against the walls, hints of others in the shadows. And in one corner lay a man, surrounded by tins and a strip of corrugated metal.

The body glistened. Trembling, his mouth gaping at the stench which thickened the air, Rice descended, and the torch's circle shrank. The man in the corner was dressed in red. Rice moved nearer. With a shock he realized that the man was naked, shining with red paint which also marked the tins and strip of metal. Suddenly he wrenched away and retched.

For a moment he was engulfed by nausea; then he heard footsteps in the kitchen. His fingers burned like wax and blushed at their clumsiness, but he caught up a brick. "You've found what you expected, have you?" the voice called.

Rice reached the steps, and a figure loomed above him, blotting out the light. With studied calm it felt about in the kitchen and produced a strip of corrugated tin. "Fancy," it said, "I thought I'd have to bring you here to see Harriet. Now it'll have to be the other way round." Rice had no time to think; focusing his horror, fear and disgust with his lifetime of inaction, he threw the brick.

Rice was shaking by the time he had finished. He picked up the torch from the bottom step and as if compelled turned its beam on the two corpses. Yes, they were of the same stature—they would have been identical, except that the face of the first was an abstract crimson oval. Rice shuddered away from his fascination. He must see Harriet—it didn't matter what excuse he gave, illness or anything, so long as he saw her. He shone the beam toward the steps to light his way, and the torch was wrested from his hand.

He didn't think; he threw himself up the steps and into the kitchen. The bolts and lock on the back door had been rusted shut for years. Footsteps padded up the steps. He fell into the other room. Outside an ambulance howled its way to hospital. Almost tripping on the brick, he reached the hall. The ambulance's blue light flashed in the doorway and passed, and a figure with a grey sock covering its face blocked the doorway.

Rice backed away. No, he thought in despair, he couldn't fail now; the fall from the cliff had ended the menace. But already he knew. He backed into something soft, and a hand closed over his mouth. The figure plodded toward him; the grey wool sucked in and out. The figure was his height, his build. He heard himself saying, "I can always help to look after the children." And as the figure grasped a brick he knew what face waited beneath the wool.

≈ THE INVOCATION ≈

He opened the gate stealthily; perhaps she wouldn't see him. But he had hardly touched the path when she unbent from the garden. "There you are, Ted," she said, waving a fistful of weeds at him in vague reproof. "A young man was asking for you."

That would have been Ken, about their holiday. "Thank you, Mrs Dame," he said, and made to hurry up the path.

"Call me Cecily." She'd taken to saying that every time she saw him. "I've asked Mr Mellor if I can plant some flowers. I like to see a bit of colour. If you want something done there's no use waiting for someone else to do it," she said, kicking the calf-high grass.

"Oh, right." He had no chance now of hurrying away; the cats from the ground-floor flat were drawing themselves about his legs, like eager fur stoles.

She added the weeds to a heap and mopped her forehead. "Isn't it hot. You'd think they could give us a breeze. Still, it won't be long before we're complaining about the cold. We're never satisfied, are we?"

I would be, Ted thought, if you'd shut up for just a few minutes. I must be going, he opened his mouth to say as cats surged around his feet.

"Well, I'd better let you go. You'll be wanting to get on with your studies." But her gaze halted him. "I've said it before and I'll say it again," she said, "you remind me of my son."

Oh no, he thought. God, not this anecdote again. Her wiry body had straightened, her hands were clasped behind her back as if she was a child reciting to an audience. "He was always in his books, never ready for his dinner," she said. "Him and his father, sitting all over the place with their feet up, in their books. It was always: just let me finish this chapter. And after his father died he got worse."

Cats streamed softly over Ted's feet, birds rose clapping from trees along the dual carriageway as she went on. "He was sitting there reading that *Finian's Wake* and I happened to know it hadn't any chapters. I don't know how anyone can waste their time with such stuff. Just let me finish this chapter, he said, while his dinner went cold. I was so furious I picked up a cream puff and threw it at him. I didn't mean it to go on his book, but he said I did and used that as an excuse to leave me."

411

Last time the cream puff had been a plate of baked beans on toast. "Yeah, well," Ted muttered, shaking a kitten from his ankle. "I'm keeping you from your work."

As he stamped upstairs, the wood amplified his peevishness. Right, sure, she was lonely, she wanted someone to talk to. But he had work to do. And really, there was no wonder she was lonely. Few people would be prepared to suffer her for long.

In his flat his essay was waiting, but he didn't feel like writing now. He cursed: on the way home he had made himself ready to sit down and write. He tried to phone Ken, but the party line was occupied by two women, busy surpassing each other's ailments.

He opened the window. The flowers in the decanter on the sill had withered, and he threw them toward the pile of weeds two storeys below. Mrs Dame was nowhere in sight. After a while he heard her climbing the stairs, wheezing a little. For a moment he feared she might knock, for a chat. But the wheezing faded upward, and soon he heard her footsteps overhead.

His essay lay on the table, surrounded by texts. *Butcher's Films: a Structural History. Les Films "Z+" de BUTCHER's et ses amis. The Conventions of the British B-feature and the Signature of Montgomery Tully: a Problem in Decipherment.* When he'd chosen cinema as a subject he had expected to enjoy himself. Well, at least there was Hitchcock to look forward to next term.

The last line he'd written waited patiently. "The local-rep conventions of the British B-feature—" How on earth had he meant to continue? He liked the phrase too much to delete it. He stared emptily at the page. At last he stood up. Perhaps when he'd found out what Ken wanted he would be able to write.

As soon as he picked up the phone he heard Mrs Dame's voice. "He said I distracted him from his reading. He sat there with his feet up and said that."

God, no! He would never get through now. She saved up her phone calls for the evenings, when they were cheaper; then she would chatter for hours. Before he could utter the sound he was tempted to make, he slammed the receiver into its cradle. Her voice—muttering through the ceiling, drifting down into the open window—faltered for a moment, then went on. The occasional word or phrase came clear, plucking at his attention, tempting his ears to strain.

He couldn't write unless he carried everything to the library, and that was a mile away. Surely he could read. He gazed at *Les Films* "Z+", translating mentally from the point at which he'd stopped reading. "Within the most severe restrictions of the budget, these gleams of imagination are like triumphant buds. One feels the delight of the naturalist who discovers a lone flower among apparently barren rocks." But the room was growing darker as the sky filled with cloud. As he peered more closely at the text, Mrs Dame's voice insinuated words into his translation. "Consider too the moment (one of the most beautiful in the entire British cinema) in *Master Spy* where June Thorburn discovers that her suspicions of Stephen Murray are, after all, unfounded. The direction and acting are simply the invisible frame of the script. Such simplicity and directness are a cream puff."

"God!" He shoved his chair back violently; it clawed the floorboards. Her muttering seeped into the room, her words formed and dissolved. The heat made him feel limp and cumbersome, the heavy dimness strained his eyes. He went to the window to breathe, to find calm.

As he reached the window her voice ceased. Perhaps her listener had interrupted. Silence touched him softly through the window, like a breeze. The thickening sky changed slowly, almost indiscernibly. The traffic had gone home to dinner. The trees along the carriageway held their poses, hardly trembling. The hole which had been advancing along the roadway was empty and silent now, surrounded by dormant warning lights. Ted leaned his elbows on the sill.

But the silence wasn't soothing. It was unnatural, the product of too many coincidences; it couldn't last for long. His nerves were edgily alert for its breaking. Overhead a ragged black mass was descending, blotting out half the sky. It seemed to compress the silence. No doubt because he was unwillingly alert. Ted felt as though he was being watched too. Surely the silence, in its brittleness and tension, must be like the silence of a forest when a predator was near.

He started. Mrs Dame's voice had recommenced, an insistent bumbling. It nagged violently at him. Even if he shut the window, trapping himself with the heat, there was nowhere in his flat he could escape her voice. He began to curse loudly: "Jesus God almighty . . ." He combined everything sexual, religious, or scatological he could think of, and found that he knew a good many words.

When at last he was silent he heard Mrs Dame's voice, wandering unchecked. His chest felt tight, perhaps holding back a scream of rage. His surroundings seemed to have altered subtly, for the worse. Beyond the

trees that divided the carriageway the houses brooded, gloomily luminous, beneath the slumped dark sky. Dull red blobs hung around the hole
in the road; the sullenly glowing foliage looked paralyzed. The ominous
mumbling of the city, faint yet huge, surrounded him. He felt more
strongly as though he was being watched. He blamed everything he felt on
her voice. "I wish something would shut you up for a while," he said as
loudly as he could, and began to turn away.

Something halted him. The silence was closer, more oppressive; it
seemed actually to have muffled Mrs Dame's voice. Everything shone
luridly. A dark hugeness stooped toward him. The mass of black cloud had
altered; it was an enormous slowly smouldering head. Its eyes, sooty unequal blotches, shifted lethargically; jagged teeth lengthened and dissolved in the tattered smile. As the mass spread almost imperceptibly
across the grey, its smile widening, it seemed to lean toward him. It
pressed darkness into the room.

He flinched back, and saw that the decanter was toppling from the sill.
He must have knocked it over. It was odd he hadn't felt the impact. He
caught the decanter and replaced it on the sill. No wonder he hadn't felt
it, no wonder his imagination was getting in his way: Mrs Dame's
muttering had won.

When he switched on the light it looked dim, cloaked by smoke. Darkness still made its presence felt in the room; so did the sense of watching.
He'd had enough. There was no point in trying to work. Another evening
wasted. He clumped downstairs angrily, tensely determined to relax.
Overhead the clouds were moving on, still keeping their rain to themselves.

Ken wasn't in any of the pubs: not the Philharmonic, nor O'Connor's,
nor the Grapes, nor the Augustus John. Ted became increasingly frus-
trated and depressed. He must make sure of this holiday. He was going
away with Ken for a long weekend in three days, if they were going at all.
Just a few days' break from Mrs Dame would let him work, he was sure.
He managed to chat and to play bar billiards. More and more students
crowded in, the ceiling of smoke thickened and sank. His tankards huddled together on the table.

When at last he rambled home from an impromptu party Mrs Dame's
light was out. The sight heartened him. Perhaps now he could write. And
perhaps not, he thought, laughing at his beery clumsiness as he fumbled
with his sandals.

The decanter caught his attention. A small dark object was visible inside it, at the bottom. He raised the sash in the hope of a breeze, then he examined the decanter. The facets of cut glass distorted the object; so did the beer. He couldn't make it out. A lump of soot, a shifting pool of muddy fluid, a dead insect? No doubt it would be clearer in the morning. His sandals flopped underfoot on the floorboards, like loose tongues. He extricated his feet at last, and slid into bed.

Pounding woke him. He rose carefully and took two aspirins. After a while some of the pounding went away; the rest stayed outside, in the road. He gazed from the window, palms over his ears. A pneumatic drill was inching the hole along the roadway toward him.

He squinted painfully at the decanter. Something had lodged in it, but what? The cut glass confused his view. As he turned the decanter in his hands the object seemed to swell, to move of its own accord; there was a suggestion of long feelers or legs. Yet when he peered down the glass throat the decanter looked empty, and when he shook it upside down nothing rattled or fell out. Perhaps when he'd knocked over the decanter it had cracked, perhaps he was seeing a flaw. He hoped not; he'd found the decanter black with grime in a junk shop nearby, he had been proud of his find once he'd cleaned it. Maybe one day, he thought, I'll have something to decant. That woman upstairs will make me into a wino.

He hurried to class and blinked at the film. Monochrome figures posed, reading their lines. He might just as well have his eyes closed. He listened to the heroine's description of the plot so far. She'd missed out a scene— no, his mind had; he'd blacked out for a moment. He blinked at a talking tableau, then his eyes sank closed again; just let him rest them a moment longer. Music woke him: THE END. Afterwards, fellow students applauded his honest response.

At least he managed to contact Ken, who had retrieved his tent and sleeping-bags from a borrower. He would call for Ted in his van. Ted relaxed. Now nothing could disturb him in his flat, not even Mrs Dame.

When he heard her as he neared the house he smiled wryly. She didn't bother him so much now. She had a friend to tea; he heard spoons rattling demurely in china. The evening grew cold, and he closed the window. Voices penetrated the ceiling; occasionally he heard Mrs Dame's friend, chattering shrilly in an attempt to outdistance Mrs Dame, who headed her off easily and began another anecdote. Rather her than me, Ted thought, laughing. He turned to his essay and quickly wrote several pages.

Later he became less tolerant. He couldn't be expected to endure her waking him up. When he went to bed the night seemed oppressively tense, as though clouds were hanging low and electric, although the sky was clear. He felt restless and irritable, but eventually slept—only to be woken by Mrs Dame. He could tell by the cadence of her voice that she was talking, almost shouting, in her sleep. Perhaps the tension of the night was affecting her. Can't she even shut up when she's asleep? he thought, glaring at the dark.

As he lay on his side he could see a faint distorted ghost of the decanter, projected by the streetlamps onto the fitted wardrobe. It was moving. No, a darker shadow was squeezing out of the watery outline of the neck. He turned his head sharply. Some kind of insect, or a spider, was emerging; he saw long legs twitching on the glass lip. He hoped it would go out through the gap he'd left beneath the sash. If only it were a genie emerging from the bottle it could go and silence Mrs Dame. He closed his eyes, reaching for slumber before he woke entirely, and tried to lull the crick in his neck to sleep.

A cry woke him. Was it one of the ground-floor cats? He lay in his own warmth and tried not to care, but his heart kept him awake. A bell tolled two o'clock. The next cry was louder. His heart leapt, racing, though he realized now that it was Mrs Dame, crying out in her sleep. Couldn't she even have a nightmare quietly? He might just as well be in bed with her, God forbid. She was moaning now; muffled as it was, it sounded rather like a singer's doodling. After a while it soothed him to sleep.

Good God, what now? He kept his eyes determinedly shut. It must be dawn, for light was filtering through his eyelids. Soon he heard the sound again: a faint squeaking of claws on glass. It would be one of the cats— they often appeared on the sill, furry ghosts mopping at the window. He sighed. All we need now is a brass band, to play me a lullaby. He dragged more of the blanket over his ear.

The decanter was rocking. Something was struggling to squeeze back into the glass mouth. The legs scrabbled, squeaking on the glass, trying to force the swollen body down. But the body was larger than the mouth of the decanter. The decanter tipped over, fell, smashed. Ted woke gasping and leapt out of bed.

The decanter lay in fragments. His head felt as if it had been cracked open too. He sat on the bed and made himself calm down. The glimpse of the insect, the sound of the cat's claws, the fall of the decanter: these were the sources of his dream, which must have lasted only the second before he woke. Yesterday he must have replaced the decanter unstably. His head throbbed jaggedly, his heart jerked. Glaring upward made him feel a little better. It was all that woman's fault.

The day's lectures examined the theme of misunderstanding in Butcher's films. Ted's eyes burned. The lecturer swam forward, hot and bright, droning. Misunderstanding. Here again we see the theme. Once more the theme of misunderstanding. When Ted walked home at last his mind was dull, featureless. Tonight he'd have an early night.

If that woman let him sleep. Well, tonight he'd wake her if he had to. She had no right to keep other people awake with her restlessness. He couldn't hear her as he approached the house; that was encouraging. An old woman was hobbling up the front path, stopping to rest her shopping-bag. "I'll carry that for you," he said, and she turned. It was Mrs Dame.

He managed to disguise his gasp as a cough. Once before he'd seen her ill, white-faced, when she had tripped on the stairs. But now, for the first time, she looked old. She was stooped, her skin hung slumped on her; she massaged her ankles, which were clearly painful. "Thank you," she said when he picked up the shopping-bag. She seemed hardly to recognize him.

"Can I get you anything?" he said, dismayed.

She smiled weakly at him. Her face looked like wax, a little melted. "No thank you. I'm all right now."

He could hardly believe that he wished she were more talkative. "Have you been to the doctor?"

"I don't need him," she said with a hint of her old vitality. "He's got enough old crocks to see to without me wasting his time. I'll be all right when my legs have had a bit of a rest."

He left the bag outside her door. He felt vaguely guilty: now he'd have some peace—but good God, it wasn't he who'd made her ill, was it? Nevertheless he felt embarrassed when, going down, he met her on his landing. "Thank you," she said as she began to clamber up the last flight of stairs. He smiled nervously, blushing for no reason he understood, and fled into his flat.

Later he brought home his dinner. As he ate the curry from its plastic container, he felt uneasy. The city wound down quietly into evening; a few boys shouted around a football, occasional cars swished past, but they weren't what he was straining to hear. He was waiting irritably, anxiously, for Mrs Dame's voice.

She would be all right. She had been when she'd fallen on the stairs. Or perhaps she wouldn't be; after all, she was getting old. In any case, there was nothing he could do. He washed up his fork, and turned to his essay. His eyes felt as though they were smouldering.

The interchangeable personalities of many British B-feature performers, he wrote. The white page glared; his eyes twitched. Around him the room wavered in sympathy, and something scuttled across the wardrobe. When he glanced round, there was only the noise of a car emerging from the side street opposite. It must have been that: the car's headlights hurrying the shadow of branches over the wardrobe, like a bunch of long rapid legs.

He finished his sentence somehow. Some performances actually imitate the performances of stars, he went on, which sometimes has the effect   The silence distracted him, as if someone was watching, mutely reproving; his eyes felt hot and huge. What effect? Reproving him for what? He sighed, and capped his pen. At least he was going away tomorrow. There was no point in forcing himself to write now, when he was so aware of waiting to hear Mrs Dame's voice.

Later he heard her, when he went upstairs to the toilet; there was none on his floor. Beneath the unshaded bulb the bare dusty stairs looked old and cheerless. As he climbed them he heard a sound like the song of a wind in a cranny. Not until he reached the top landing did he realize that the sound was composed of words—that it was her voice.

"Leave my legs," she was pleading feebly. "Leave them now." Her voice sounded slurred, as if she was drunk. She was only talking in her sleep, that was why she sounded so odd. He heard a violent snore, then silence. After a while her voice recommenced. What was she saying now? He tiptoed across the landing and stooped carefully toward her door.

As his ear touched the panel he heard a sound beyond. Had she fallen out of bed? Certainly something large and soft had fallen, and it seemed to be surrounded by a pattering on the carpet. The time-switch clicked out, blinding him with darkness.

In a moment he heard her voice. "Leave them now," she moaned, "leave them." She was all right, she must have pushed something off the bed: probably the bedspread. If he knocked he would only wake her. He fumbled in the dark for the time-switch. Behind him her voice slurred, moaning.

When he returned to his flat he found that now he'd heard her voice, he could still hear it: an almost inaudible blurred sound, rising and falling. It reminded him unpleasantly of the sound a fly's wings make, struggling as a spider feasts. The night seemed very cold. He closed the window and filled a hot water bottle. Her voice buzzed, trapped.

It must have been that unpleasant resemblance that led, when sleep overtook him at least, to the dream. Something was tapping on the window, softly, insistently. He turned his head reluctantly. Dawn coated everything like smoke, but he could see a large dark shape dangling beyond the pane, spinning slowly, swaying lightly toward the glass, bumping against it. It was a package with a withered face: Mrs Dame's face, which had grown a thick grey beard. No, the beard was web, filling her slack mouth as though it was a yawning crevice. Her face bobbed up in the window-frame; she was being reeled in from above. He tried to wake, but sleep dragged him down, grey and vague as the dawn.

Eventually the pneumatic drill woke him. He lay sweating, tangled in the blankets. Sunlight filled the room, which was very hot. Gradually, too gradually, the dream faded. He lay welcoming the light. At last he fished out the hot water bottle, which flopped under the bed. He was enormously glad to get up—and about time; he had overslept. Ken would be here soon.

He opened the windows and ate breakfast hastily. The flat overhead was silent, so far as he could hear over the chattering of the drill. Should he go up and knock? But then he mightn't be able to escape her conversation, when he ought to be getting ready for the weekend. Her friends would look after her if she needed help. He might go up, if he had time before Ken arrived.

He hurried about, checking that plugs were unplugged, sockets switched off. The space between the fitted wardrobe and the ceiling distracted him. The gap was dim, but at the back, against the wall, he could see a large dark mass. He must clean up the flat. A horn was shouting a tune below, in the road. It was Ken's van.

He closed the window and grabbed his bulging rucksack. The road repairers were directly outside now; as he slammed the door of the flat and shoved it to make sure, it sounded as though the drill was in his room. The sound like scuttling on the floorboards must be a vibration from the drill.

Ken drove through the Saturday morning traffic. The van plunged into the Mersey Tunnel, and out to North Wales. Neither Ken nor Ted had any lectures until Tuesday. They walked and climbed in the sharp air; they drank, and drove singing back to their tent. Above them mountains and stars glittered, distant and cold.

When they returned to Liverpool on Monday night they were famished. They ate at the Kebab House. O'Connor's was just down the block; friends cheered as they entered. Several hours later the barman got rid of them at last. "If you're driving I'm walking," Ted told Ken, trying to hold a shop-front still.

He walked home, from side to side of the back streets. Moonlight glinted on the smooth red sandstone of the Anglican cathedral, at the top of its tremendous steps; nearby he heard a smash of glass, shouts, screams. Fragments of streets led down toward the river. Along Princes Road, trees and lamp-standards stood unmoving; Ted tried to compete with them, but couldn't manage it. His leaning pushed him forward, almost at a run, to the house. He couldn't remember when he'd been so drunk; he ought to have had more than one meal today. Mrs Dame's window was dark and silent. She must be asleep.

His flat was full of a block of silence. The silence seemed lifeless, his flat unwelcoming—bare floorboards, the previous tenant's paint on the walls. Surely he wasn't yearning to hear that woman's voice. Something rustled as he entered the main room: a page among the books on the table. Some performances actually imitate the performances of stars, it said, which sometimes has the effect   What effect? Never mind. He'd finish that tomorrow.

He gazed at the tousled bed. What a mess to come home to. But the way he felt at the moment, he could sleep on anything. The tangled tunnel of blankets looked warmer than the chill flat. Some performances actually imitate   The sentence nagged him like a tune whose conclusion he couldn't remember. Forget it. Brush teeth, wash face, fall into bed.

He pushed the kitchen door further open, and heard something move away from it, rustling faintly. They were still rustling when he found the light-switch: a couple of moths, several large flies, all withered. Well, it was the spider season, but he wished the spiders would clear up after themselves.

He stooped to pick up the dustpan, and frowned. Beneath the window lay a scattering of small bones, of a mouse or a bird. Of course, he'd forgotten to close the kitchen window before leaving. One of the cats from downstairs must have slipped in; it was probably responsible for the insects too.

Water clanked and squeaked in the pipes. The tap choked on knots as he splashed icy water on his face, gasping. As he dabbed water from his eyes, a shadow scuttled over the fitted wardrobe. The wardrobe door rattled, and then the floorboards in the main room. Only headlights through branches, only vibrations from the road. Some performances actually

He padded across the cold boards and switched off the light, then he slid into the tangle of blankets. God, they weren't so warm; his toes squirmed. And he'd forgotten to take out last week's hot water bottle, damn it. He could feel it dragging at the bedclothes; it was hanging down beyond the mattress, in a sack of loose blanket. He tried to hook it with his toes, but couldn't reach it. At least it wouldn't chill his feet.

The bed drifted gently on a sea of beer. Some performances have the Oh come on, he thought angrily. He glared at the room, to tire his eyes. It glowed faintly with moonlight, as though steeped in luminous paint. He glared at the glimmering wardrobe, at the dark gap above. What was that, at the back? It must be the accumulation of dust which he had to clean out, but it was pale as the moonlight, of which its appearance must be an effect. It looked like a tiny body, its head in the shadows, its limbs drawn up into a withered tangle. God, it looked like a colourless baby; he could even see one of its hands, could count the shrivelled fingers. What on earth was it? But the wardrobe was sailing sideways on his beer. He closed his eyes and drifted down, down into sleep.

A figure lay on a bed. Its face was dim, as was the dark shape crouched at the foot of the bed. Limbs—many of them, it seemed—reached for the sleeper, inching it down the bed. The figure writhed helplessly, its hands fluttered feebly as the wings of an ensnared fly. It moaned.

Ted woke. His eyes opened, fleeing the dream; the room sprang up around him, glowing dimly. He lay on his back, while his heart thudded like a huge soft drum. The luminous room looked hardly more reassuring than the dream. God, he would almost have preferred Mrs Dame's muttering to this.

And now he wouldn't be able to sleep, because he was painfully cold. He couldn't feel his legs, they were so numb. He reached down to massage them. His hands seemed retarded and clumsy; they touched his legs and found them stiff, but his legs couldn't feel his fingers at all. Had he been lying awry, or was it the cold? He rubbed his thighs and cursed his awkwardness.

He couldn't move his feet. Though he strained, the dim hump in the blankets at the far end of the bed stood absolutely still. Panic was gathering. He lifted the blankets and pushed them back. His blood felt slow and thick; so did he.

Before he uncovered his legs the hump in the blankets collapsed, although he hadn't felt his feet move. Something dragged at the bedclothes, and he heard it thump the floor softly, in the sack of blankets beyond the mattress. Only the hot water bottle. At once he remembered that he had fished the bottle out of the bed last week.

He managed to sit up, and threw the blankets away violently. Panic filled him, overwhelming but vague. He was swaying; he had to punch the mattress in order to prop himself up. His shadow dimmed the bed, he could hardly see his legs. They looked short, perhaps because of the dimness, and oddly featureless, like smooth glistening sticks. He couldn't move them at all.

As he stared down, struggling feebly and frantically to clear his mind, the dim hump came groping hungrily out of the tangle of blankets.

VI. A SELECTED BIBLIOGRAPHY OF ENGLISH GHOST STORIES

(Note: To make the reader's search easier, I have emphasized recent over obscure editions. For a bibliography that includes major spook novels, see the annotated bibliographies by Gary Crawford and myself in *Horror Literature: A Core Collection and Reference Guide*, ed. Marshall B. Tymn [New York: Bowker, 1981].)

Aickman, Robert. *Cold Hand in Mine: Strange Stories.* New York: Scribner's, 1975; Berkeley, 1979.

———. *Dark Entries.* London: Collins, 1964.

———. *Intrusions.* London, Gollancz, 1981.

———. *Painted Devils: Strange Stories.* New York: Scribner's, 1979.

———. *Powers of Darkness.* London: Collins, 1966.

———. *Sub Rosa: Strange Tales.* London: Gollancz, 1968.

———. *Tales of Love and Death.* Gollancz, 1977.

Asquith, Cynthia. *This Mortal Coil.* Sauk City, Wis.: Arkham House, 1947.

Benson, A. C. *Basil Netherby.* London: Hutchinson, 1927.

———. *Paul, the Minstrel, and Other Stories.* 1911; rpt. New York: Arno, 1977.

Benson, E. F. *"And the Dead Spake" and The Horror Horn.* London: Doran, 1923.

———. *More Spook Stories.* London: Hutchinson, 1934.

———. *The Room in the Tower and Other Stories.* London: Mills and Boon, 1912.

———. *Spook Stories.* 1928: rpt. New York: Arno, 1976.

———. *Visible and Invisible.* London: Hutchinson, 1923.

Benson, R. H. *The Light Invisible.* London: Isbister, 1903.

———. *The Mirror of Shalott.* London: Pitman, 1907.

Blackwood, Algernon. *Ancient Sorceries and Other Tales.* London: Collins, 1927.

———. *Best Ghost Stories of Algernon Blackwood.* Ed. E. F. Bleiler. New York: Dover, 1973.

————. *The Dance of Death and Other Tales.* New York: Dial Press, 1928.

————. *Day and Night Stories.* London: Cassell, 1917.

————. *The Doll and One Other.* Sauk City, Wis.: Arkham House, 1946.

————. *The Empty House and Other Ghost Stories.* London: Eveleigh Nash, 1906.

————. *Incredible Adventures.* New York: Macmillan, 1914.

————. *John Silence, Physician Extraordinary.* London: Eveleigh Nash, 1908.

————. *The Listener and Other Stories.* 1907; rpt. New York: Arno, 1977.

————. *The Lost Valley and Other Stories.* 1914; rpt. New York: Arno, 1977.

————. *Pan's Garden: A Volume of Nature Stories.* New York: Macmillan, 1912.

————. *Shocks.* London: Grayson & Grayson, 1935.

————. *Strange Stories.* 1929; rpt. New York: Arno, 1977.

————. *The Tales of Algernon Blackwood.* London: Martin Secker, 1939.

————. *Ten Minute Stories.* 1914; rpt. New York: Arno, 1977.

————. *Tongues of Fire and Other Sketches.* London: Jenkins, 1924.

————. *The Willows and Other Queer Tales.* London: Collins, 1934.

Bowen, Elizabeth. *The Cat Jumps and Other Stories.* London: Jonathan Cape, 1934.

————. *The Demon Lover and Other Stories.* London: Jonathan Cape, 1945.

————. *Encounters.* London: Sidgwick & Jackson, 1923.

————. *Joining Charles and Other Stories.* London: Constable, 1929.

Bowen, Marjorie. *Kecksies and Other Twilight Tales.* Sauk City, Wis.: Arkham House, 1976.

Burrage A. M. *Between the Minute and the Hour.* London: Jenkins, 1967.

————. *Some Ghost Stories.* London: Cecil Palmer, 1927.

————. *Someone in the Room.* London: Jarrolds, 1931.

Caldecott, Andrew. *Fires Burn Blue.* London: Arnold, 1948.

————. *Not Exactly Ghosts.* London: Arnold, 1947.

Campbell, Ramsey. *Demons by Daylight.* Sauk City, Wis.: Arkham House, 1973; Jove, 1979.

————. *The Height of the Scream.* Sauk City, Wis.: Arkham House, 1976.

————. *Dark Companions.* New York: Macmillan, 1982.

Conrad, Joseph. *Heart of Darkness.* 1902; rpt. New York: Norton, 1963.

————. *A Set of Six.* London: Methuen, 1908.

————. *The Shadow Line.* London: Dent, 1917.

————. *Tales of Unrest*. 1908; rpt. New York: Penguin, 1977.

Cowles, Frederick. *The Horror of Abbot's Grange*. London: Muller, 1936.

————. *The Night Wind Howls*. London: Muller, 1938.

Cross, John Keir. *The Other Passenger*. 1944; rpt. Ballantine, 1961.

Dare, M. P. *Unholy Relics and Other Uncanny Tales*. London: Arnold, 1947.

De la Mare, Walter. *A Beginning and Other Stories*. London: Faber & Faber, 1955.

————. *The Connoisseur and Other Stories*. London: Collins, 1926.

————. *Eight Tales*. Sauk City, Wis.: Arkham House, 1971.

————. *On the Edge*. London: Faber and Faber, 1930.

————. *The Riddle and Other Stories*. London: Selwyn and Blount, 1923.

————. *The Wind Blows Over*. London: Faber and Faber, 1936.

Doyle, Arthur Conan. *The Supernatural Tales of Arthur Conan Doyle*. Ed. E. F. Bleiler. New York: Dover, 1979.

————. *Tales of Terror and Mystery*. 1922; rpt. New York: Doubleday, 1977.

Du Maurier, Daphne. *Echoes from the Macabre*. New York: Doubleday, 1977; Avon, 1978.

Gilchrist, R. Murray. *The Stone Dragon and Other Tragic Romances*. London: Methuen, 1894. For individual tales from this rare work, see Hugh Lamb's anthologies, *The Thrill of Horror* (1975); *Return from the Grave* (1977); and *Terror by Gaslight* (1975), all published by Taplinger.

Gray, Sir Arthur. *Tedious Brief Tales of Granta and Gramarye*. London: Heffer, 1919.

Hardy, Thomas. *Wessex Tales*. 1896; rpt. New York: St. Martin's, 1978.

Hartley, L. P. *The Killing Bottle*. London and New York: Putnam, 1932.

————. *Night Fears*. London: Putnam, 1924.

————. *The Travelling Grave and Other Stories*. Sauk City, Wis.: Arkham House, 1948. The easiest way to find Hartley's ghost stories is to go to *The Complete Short Stories*. London: Hamish, Hamilton, 1973.

Harvey, W. F. *The Beast With Five Fingers and Other Tales*. 1928; rpt. New York: Dutton, 1947.

————. *Midnight House*. London: Dent, 1910.

————. *Midnight Tales*. London: Dent, 1946.

Hodgson, William Hope. *Carnacki the Ghost Finder*. 1913; rpt. Sauk City, Wis.: Mycroft & Moran, 1947.

————. *The Luck of the Strong*. London: Eveleigh Nash, 1916.

————. *Men of Deep Waters*. 1914; rpt. Sauk City, Wisc.: Arkham House, 1967.

James, Henry. *Stories of the Supernatural*. Ed. Leon Edel. New York: Taplinger, 1970; paperback edition, 1980.

————. *The Turn of the Screw*. 1898; rpt. New York: Norton, 1966.

James, M. R. *The Collected Ghost Stories of M. R. James*. 1931; rpt. New York: St. Martin's, 1974.

————. *Ghost Stories of an Antiquary*. 1904; rpt. New York: Dover, 1971. (The 1974 Penguin volume contains *More Ghost Stories of An Antiquary* in the same edition.)

Kersh, Gerald. *The Horrible Dummy and Other Stories*. London: Heinemann, 1944.

————. *Men Without Bones*. New York: Paperback Library, 1962.

————. *Neither Man Nor Dog*. London: Heinemann, 1946.

————. *Nightshades and Damnations*. New York: Fawcett, 1968.

Kipling, Rudyard. *Actions and Reactions*. London: Macmillan, 1909.

————. *Phantoms and Fantasies*. New York: Doubleday, 1965.

————. *Traffics and Discoveries*. London: Macmillan, 1904.

Landon, Percival. *Raw Edges: Studies and Stories of These Days*. London: Heinemann, 1908.

Lawrence, Margery. *Number Seven, Queen Street*. Sauk City, Wis.: Mycroft & Moran, 1969.

Le Fanu, Sheridan. *Best Ghost Stories*. Ed. E. F. Bleiler. New York: Dover, 1964.

————. *Ghost Stories and Mysteries*. Ed. E. F. Bleiler. New York: Dover, 1975.

————. *Ghost Stories and Tales of Mystery*. 1850; rpt. Arno, 1977.

————. *In a Glass Darkly*. Bentley, 1872.

————. *The Purcell Papers*. 1880; rpt. Sauk City. Wis.: Arkham House, 1975. (The contents of this edition are not entirely the same as those of the original.)

Lee, Vernon. *For Maurice, Five Unlikely Stories*. 1927; rpt. New York: Arno, 1976.

————. *Hauntings, Fantastic Stories*. London: Heinemann, 1890.

————. *Pope Jacynth and Other Fantastic Tales*. London: Grant Richards, 1904.

————. *The Snake Lady and Other Stories*. New York: Grove Press, 1954.

Machen, Arthur. *The Children of the Pool and Other Stories*. 1936; rpt. New York: Arno, 1976.

————. *The Great God Pan and The Inmost Light.* 1894; rpt. New York: Arno, 1977.

————. *The House of Souls.* 1906; rpt. New York: Arno, 1977.

————. *Tales of Horror and the Supernatural.* 1949; rpt. New York: Pinnacle, 1971.

Malden, R. H. *Nine Ghosts.* London: Arnold, 1943.

Metcalfe, John. *The Feasting Dead.* Sauk City, Wis.: Arkham House, 1954.

————. *The Smoking Leg and Other Stories.* London: Jarrolds, 1925.

Munby, A. N. L. *The Alabaster Hand and Other Ghost Stories.* London: Dobson, 1949.

Munroe, H. H. [Saki]. *Beasts and Super-beasts.* 1914; rpt. New York: Core Collection, 1978. (Saki's weird tales are most easily obtainable in the *Complete Works.* New York: Doubleday, 1976.)

Nesbit, E. *Fear.* London: Paul, 1910.

————. *Grim Tales.* London: Innes, 1893.

O'Donnell, Elliott. *Dread of Night: Five Short Ghost Stories.* Dublin: Pillar, 1945.

Oliphant, Margaret. *Stories of the Seen and Unseen.* 1889; rpt. New York: Arno, 1977.

Onions, Oliver. *The Collected Ghost Stories of Oliver Onions.* 1935; rpt. New York: Dover, 1971.

————. *Widdershins.* 1911; rpt. New York: Arno, 1976.

Quiller-Couch, Arthur. *I Saw Three Ships and Other Winter Tales,* 1902; rpt. New York: Arno, 1977.

————. *Noughts and Crosses.* 1891; rpt. New York: Arno, 1977.

————. *Old Fires and Profitable Ghosts.* 1900; rpt. New York: Arno, 1973.

Riddell, Mrs. J. H. *The Collected Ghost Stories of Mrs. J. H. Riddell.* Ed. E. F. Bleiler. New York: Dover, 1977.

Rolt, L. T. C. *Sleep No More.* London: Constable, 1948.

Shiel, M. P. *Here Comes the Lady.* London: Richards Press, 1928.

————. *The Pale Ape and Other Pulses.* London: Laurie, 1911.

————. *Xelucha and Others.* Sauk City, Wis.: Arkham House, 1975.

Smith, Basil A. *The Scallion Stone.* Chapel Hill, N.C.: Whispers Press, 1980.

Stevenson, Robert Louis. *Island Night's Entertainment.* 1893; rpt. New York: Scholarly, 1970.

————. *The Merry Men and Other Tales and Fables.* London: Chatto & Windus, 1887 (includes "Markheim" and "Thrawn Janet").

————. *The Strange Case of Dr. Jekyll and Mr. Hyde.* 1886; rpt. New York: Dutton, 1954 (includes *The Merry Men*).

Stoker, Bram. *The Bram Stoker Bedside Companion.* New York: Taplinger, 1973.

————. *Dracula's Guest.* 1897; rpt. New York: Zebra, 1978.

Swain, E. G. *The Stoneground Ghost Tales.* London: Heffer, 1912.

Wakefield, H. R. *Best Ghost Stories.* Chicago: Academy Chicago, 1982.

————. *The Clock Strikes Twelve.* Sauk City, Wis.: Arkham House, 1946.

————. *Ghost Stories.* 1932; rpt. New York: Arno, 1976.

————. *Strayers from Sheol.* Sauk City, Wis.: Arkham House, 1961.

————. *They Return at Evening.* New York: Appleton, 1928.

Walpole, Hugh. *All Souls' Night.* New York: Doubleday, 1933.

Wells, H. G. *Complete Short Stories.* 1927; rpt. New York: St. Martin's, 1974.

————. *The Country of the Blind and Other Stories.* 1911; rpt. New York: Arno, 1977.

————. *Thirty Strange Stories.* 1897; rpt. New York: Arno, 1977.

————. *Twelve Stories and a Dream.* 1903; rpt. New York: Arno, 1977.

White, T. H. *Gone to Ground.* London: Collins, 1935; New York: Putnam's, 1935.

————. *The Maharajah and Other Stories.* New York: Putnam's, 1981.

Yeats, W. B. *Mythologies.* 1959; rpt. New York: Collier, 1972.

VII. GENERAL BIBLIOGRAPHIC
AND REFERENCE AIDS

Ashley, Mike. *Who's Who in Horror and Fantasy Fiction.* 1977; rpt. New York: Taplinger, 1978. Offers brief but useful coverage of 400 writers.

Barzun, Jacques, and Wendell H. Taylor. *A Catalogue of Crime.* New York: Harper and Row, 1971; second impression corrected, 1974. Deals mainly with the mystery genre but contains an excellent annotated bibliography of ghost stories.

Bleiler, E. F. *The Checklist of Fantastic Literature.* 1948; rpt. Glen Rock, N. J.: Firebell, 1978. A pioneer bibliography covering some 6,000 supernatural and science-fiction works from 1800–1948. The reprint contains numerous corrections and additions.

_____. *The Guide to Supernatural Fiction.* Kent State, Ohio: Kent State University Press, 1983. An annotated bibliography of supernatural fiction from 1800 to 1960. Covers 1,775 books, including several thousand short stories; an invaluable work.

Frank, Frederick S., and Gary W. Crawford. *Annual Bibliography of Gothic Studies.* A thorough, scholarly compilation, available yearly from the Gothic Press, Baton Rouge, La.

Siemon, Fred. *Ghost Story Index.* Munroe, N. Y.: Library Research Associates, 1967. Index by author and title of over 2,200 ghost stories in 190 collections.

Steinbrunner, Chris, and Otto Penzler. *Encyclopedia of Mystery and Detection.* New York: McGraw Hill, 1976. Primarily devoted to the mystery field but contains useful material on supernatural fiction.

Tuck, Donald H. *The Encyclopedia of Science Fiction and Fantasy.* 3 vols.: vol. 1, Chicago: Advent, 1974; vol. 2, Chicago, Advent, 1978; vol. 3, forthcoming. A standard reference work, especially useful for its listings of stories in anthologies. Annotations are brief, focusing mainly on biographical information.

Tymn, Marshall, ed. *Horror Literature: A Core Collection and Reference Guide*. New York: Bowker, 1981. A comprehensive annotated bibliography covering the Gothic period to the present. In addition to fiction, the book covers poetry, periodicals, biography, and criticism. Contributors are Frederick S. Frank, Benjamin Franklin Fisher, Jack Sullivan, Gary W. Crawford, Robert Weinberg, Steve Eng, Mike Ashley, and Peter Haining.

————. *Year's Scholarship in Science Fiction, Fantasy, and Horror Literature*. An annual compilation from Kent State University Press.